LO... ...ES
COLLECTION

*When courageous knights risked all
to win the hand of their lady!*

Don't miss any of this stunning collection!

Medieval
LORDS & LADIES
COLLECTION

The
War of the
Roses

Sarah Westleigh & Joanna Makepeace

*M&B™ and M&B™ with the Rose Device
are trademarks of the publisher.
Harlequin Mills & Boon Limited, Eton House,
18-24 Paradise Road, Richmond, Surrey TW9 1SR*

MEDIEVAL LORDS & LADIES COLLECTION
© Harlequin Books S.A. 2007

The publisher acknowledges the copyright holders of the individual works as follows:

Loyal Hearts © Sarah Westleigh 1991
The Traitor's Daughter © Joanna Makepeace 2001

ISBN: 978 0 263 85883 9

53-0907

*Printed and bound in Spain
by Litografía Rosés S.A., Barcelona*

Loyal Hearts
by
Sarah Westleigh

Sarah Westleigh has enjoyed a varied life. Working as a local government officer in London, she qualified as a chartered quantity surveyor. She assisted her husband in his chartered accountancy practice, at the same time managing an employment agency. Moving to Devon, she finally found time to write, publishing short stories and articles, before discovering historical novels.

Chapter One

1399

Philippa crouched in the narrow embrasure, straining to see through the slit, but the sun glinting on steel so dazzled her eyes that details were obscured as the body of some fifty men, all mounted, approached the castle.

They'd been warned of Bolingbroke's unlawful landing at Ravenspur and of his march through England to intercept King Richard on his return from Ireland, so sight of the contingent of men advancing on Alban Castle came as no surprise. The Earl of Tewkesbury and his heir, Roger d'Alban, were prepared.

The drawbridge was already lowered, the portcullis raised. The Earl and his son, both in full harness and mounted on their armoured destriers, their squires a half-length behind, proudly flourishing their lords' banners, led some half-dozen foot-soldiers carrying halberds or pikes from the safety of the castle walls, where all the manor folk had hurriedly gathered at first sign of the approaching army.

Philippa watched anxiously as the portcullis came down behind them and the drawbridge was raised again. No one knew what would happen, and the party setting off to challenge the advancing column looked pitifully small. Her father, for all his present bellicose manner, was not one to retain a large body of liveried men-at-arms to maintain his local rights.

Philippa hated the chamber at the top of the tower. Draughty, chill even in midsummer, it was the last place she wanted to be, but she had been sent up to safety while her father and brother donned their armour and went out to face Henry Bolingbroke's force.

''Can you see what is happening?'' asked an anxious voice from behind her.

She glanced over her shoulder at her sister-in-law, Mary, whose round, normally cheerful face was drawn into lines of worry under her fussy, frilly veil. Behind her, watched over by their nurse, Mary's two children, Lionel and Maud, sat on the dusty floor, teasing a kitten with a piece of straw.

''Not really.'' Philippa peered out of the slit again. ''Father and the others have gone out, and the drawbridge has been raised behind them. Father and Roger are riding towards the others. Oh, Mary, I do hope Father keeps his temper!''

''So do I! The lord my husband, too. They're as

bad as one another when it comes to remaining calm!''

''They will spark each other off. How I wish I were with them!''

Mary gave a soft, rueful laugh. ''I can't see you doing much to calm them down, Pippa! All you d'Albans are as bad as one another! Admit it; if you were a man, you'd be out there urging them on!''

''Sitting around waiting for something to happen makes me jumpy. I do get angry sometimes, but I don't have Father's temper!'' protested Philippa.

''Perhaps not,'' admitted Mary with a shrug, ''but you are always jumping into something rash.''

Diverted, Philippa eyed her sister-in-law askance. ''What exactly do you mean by that?''

''''Tis only last week that you risked injury to use your crop on a worthless drover—''

''He was flogging his mules unmercifully! One of them was almost dead!''

''Aye, but you nearly caused a riot in Tewkesbury, and now the beast is in our stables eating our fodder! You never think, Pippa!''

''I did. I knew what I was doing: saving that poor animal from a miserable death!'' She turned back to the slit, indicating what was going on outside with an impatient gesture. ''If I were a man I'd want to be doing something, but that doesn't mean I would want to fight Bolingbroke's men! Surely there's no need to come to blows! All Father has to do is refuse, quite politely, to support Henry. Those men will accept

that, and go on their way. I do not think they intend
to use force, and they have not come equipped for a
siege.''

''I hope you are right. We could not withstand
one.''

The two parties had stopped ten paces apart. They
exchanged words. Her father was angry, judging by
his gestures. Then, so abruptly that Philippa almost
missed his action, Hugh d'Alban grasped his battle-
axe, waved it wildly in the air and, with a fearsome
war cry, charged the leader of the opposing party.

Philippa gasped. Mary gave a cry of consternation
without knowing exactly what was happening, and the
two children stopped playing, arrested by the blood-
curdling shout.

''What was that?'' asked Mary in a frightened
voice.

''Twas Grandsire's war cry!'' exclaimed Lionel
excitedly, crowding to the slit. ''Let me see!''

''Go away!'' snapped Philippa, pushing him off.

''Behave yourself!'' ordered his mother hoarsely,
wrenching him away. ''Pippa, what is happening?''
Slowly, Philippa turned from her vantage point. Her
small face wore a stunned expression. ''Pippa?''
Mary's voice rose to a squeak of anxiety. ''Pippa,
what is it?''

''He tipped Father out of his saddle,'' muttered
Philippa, her voice strangled.

''Who did?''

"The knight leading Bolingbroke's men. Mary, I think I recognised his banner."

"And?"

"'Tis Giles. Sir Giles d'Evreux."

Mary swallowed, eyeing her sister-in-law carefully. "Well," she observed bracingly, "you knew he was in Paris with Henry. He naturally returned with him. But what of your father? Is he all right? Are they fighting? What of Roger?" she ended anxiously.

Philippa turned back to have another look. "Father is still on the ground," she relayed slowly, a frown of concentration and puzzlement marring the smooth creaminess of her brow. "There's a lot of milling about, our men are surrounded, but I don't think they are fighting—there's no clash of steel. I can't see Roger."

She jumped from the embrasure and ran to the doorway, her unbound hair a black cloud around her determined face. "I'm going down to see. You'd better stay here with the children."

"But Roger—"

"If anything happens to both my sire and your husband, Lionel will be Earl of Tewkesbury. Look after him!" ordered Philippa, darting a glance at the dark-haired boy, who had barely seen five summers yet.

"How can you remain so calm?" wailed Mary.

"They've picked Grandsire up!" reported Lionel excitedly from the embrasure. "I think they are carrying him back!"

"Calm?" snapped Philippa with a scornful snort.

"Stay here!" she warned again and, gathering up her skirts, fled down the uneven stone stairs, round and round, until she emerged, panting, in the Great Hall.

A babble of voices greeted her. She pushed her way through the throng of women and children sheltering there, ignoring the anxious enquiries thrown at her, and passed behind the screens and out of the door. At the top of the steps leading down to the courtyard she halted.

"Lady Philippa!"

The relieved cry echoed thinly across a bailey thronging with manor men arming themselves as best they could. She located its source as the gatehouse. Picking up her skirts again, she sped down the steps, and met the gate ward's messenger halfway across.

"What is it?"

"They are carrying the Earl back, my lady. Gibbon does not know if he should allow them entry."

At that moment a commanding voice rang out from the other side of the moat. "Open up, I say! We come in peace! Earl Hugh needs attention!"

Philippa's lips compressed into a tight line. She knew that voice. If he had harmed her father..."Tell Gibbon to lower the drawbridge. Raise the portcullis and admit them," she ordered.

What else could she do? Her father was now clearly unable to challenge the intruders further, and the forces at her disposal were too weak for her to consider resistance. She would be inviting slaughter. She stood waiting, erect and defiant, as the drawbridge creaked into place and the portcullis rumbled up.

First to enter the yard was a tall man riding a grey horse so light in colour that at first it appeared pure white, though much of its body was covered by a rich caparison of deepest azure embroidered with gold. Neither man nor beast was armoured for battle, though the man wore a breastplate covered by a brilliant scarlet jupon charged with the d'Evreux devices and a bascinet with dependent chain-mail to protect his throat. His long sword was sheathed, his lance held upright, the pennon at its point fluttering idly in the slight breeze created by his movement.

It was Giles. The lean gawkiness of youth had gone, replaced by a more mature breadth of shoulder and assurance of manner; he had grown a beard and developed some interesting lines on his long, tanned face; but otherwise he looked much the same. His deep-set eyes, more blue than grey, met hers with a suddenly arrested expression in their depths.

"Pippa?" he asked in that nerve-tingling voice she remembered so well, frowning as though he was in some doubt.

"Aye. 'Tis small wonder you scarcely recognise me, sir. 'Tis more than five summers since you last honoured this castle with your presence!" The old, familiar sense of dazzlement almost overwhelmed her, but she fought it down. She tore her eyes from his assessing gaze with a distinct effort, directing them towards the figure being carried in by his own men. "What have you done to my sire?" she demanded angrily.

"Nothing untoward."

His voice followed her as she darted across the cobbles and pushed her way through the gaggle of men surrounding her father. They'd removed his helm, and she could see his face clearly. His eyes were open. They shifted restlessly. An inarticulate noise came from his throat. The right side of his face remained wooden, unmoving.

Philippa's stomach lurched. Her hands clenched at her sides "Take him inside," she whispered. "To the solar."

She whirled round on Giles, who had by now dismounted, and was approaching her. "Nothing, you say?" she stormed. "Nothing? When he cannot move a muscle on one side of his face?"

"I did not cause that," declared Giles firmly. "I unhorsed him, but what else could I do? He came at me with his battle-axe. Was I to sit there and be slain? I have unhorsed men times without number in the lists, and been tipped from the saddle myself, without suffering more than a bruise or two. He had a seizure, Pippa. The day is hot, his gorget too tight, and all that armour too heavy. The effort was too much for him."

"What did you say to make him attack you so?" she demanded fiercely.

He lifted his head in an arrogant gesture, his features suddenly taut. His eyes changed from surprised bluishness to grey ice. "I merely asked him to join me in supporting the Duke of Lancaster's just cause, no more. He seemed to take my request amiss. He yelled that Bolingbroke was a traitor, and I no better, and attacked. You know his temper, Pippa," he added on a more conciliatory note. "He was spoiling for a fight."

Philippa did not deign to reply. She threw him a fulminating glance, closed her mind to his excuses, and followed her father's inert body into the building, leaving Giles d'Evreux to follow or not, as he pleased.

A sigh went around the Great Hall as their lord was carried in. Philippa cried out for everyone to leave. "'Tis safe to return to your homes," she told the women gathered there. "There will be no fighting. Take your children and menfolk with you."

As the crowd began to shuffle out Philippa trod heavily up the stairs to their solar, where her father had been carried and laid on the great bed. "Leave us, all of you," she ordered tightly. "All except Guy and you, of course, Sir Magnus," she added, waving the priest to the bed. "Father looks like to have need of your holy services. Guy, remove his armour."

The Earl's squire set about his task while Philippa anxiously watched her father's face.

"Shall I not remain with you, my lady?"

Philippa turned quickly to smile briefly at the small, round woman who had tended her needs so well over the last years.

"Oh, yes, Ida. But first run up to the tower and ask Lady Mary to come down, will you?"

"Of course, lady."

As Ida left, Giles entered the chamber, striding purposefully to the side of the bed.

"Go away!" snapped Philippa, attempting to push the knight aside. "Can you not see that your presence is making matters worse?" Her father's eyes were fixed on the other man with a belligerence unusual even for him. His attempts to voice his anger brought the quick tears to her eyes. "He is disappointed in you, Giles," she told the tall figure at her side thickly. "He did not expect his prospective son-in-law to turn traitor!"

"I am no traitor!" grated Giles. "'Tis Richard who has turned traitor! Traitor to all the promises he made his uncle, John of Gaunt. He has confiscated all the Lancastrian estates! Henry but demands his right of inheritance restored."

"So he marches with an army? Oh, go away, Giles," ordered Philippa wearily. "I have too much to do to argue with you now."

"I have sent for a physician."

Philippa looked up at him, surprised by the sudden softening of his tone. "Thank you," she murmured, none too graciously, before returning her attention to the man lying like a log on the bed while Guy attempted to remove the latest in heavy plate armour, which had been its wearer's undoing.

God's blood! What a slough! Giles stood with uncharacteristic indecision, watching the scene before him. He was concerned for the man, who had been a friend of his family for years, but the thing that had totally thrown him was seeing Philippa again.

Was it really five years since he had last set eyes on the child to whom he had been betrothed this eight years since? Certainly, he remembered her as a scraggy youngster of some fifteen summers with little to recommend her in the way of looks, although he had always admired her lively ways and free spirit, and enjoyed her company. In a desultory kind of way he had looked forward to one day taming his young bride and turning her into an obedient wife and mother. But, although at fiteen she had been of marriageable age, there had seemed to be little hurry to burden himself with a wife and family. The women at Lancaster's court were charming, and many had been available. He had felt no desire or need to bed a maid without a hint of womanly softness about her body. There was time enough to produce an heir.

For Giles was the second son, with his fortune to make. His father had served John of Gaunt for most of his life, and had been created Earl of Acklane during the declining years of Edward III's reign, when the nation had been virtually ruled by John, the great Duke of Lancaster.

Giles had joined Lancaster's court at an early age, and been schooled in all the ideals of knightly conduct—of courage, compassion, generosity, honour and courtesy—viewing Henry Bolingbroke, Gaunt's heir, five years his senior, as a model of chivalry. When Henry, then Earl of Derby, had sought his allegiance, he had been delighted to join his close band of followers. Since then Henry had been good to him. It had seemed both appropriate and exciting to accompany his lord into exile. There had been jousts aplenty, and he had increased his fortune considerably in the twelve months he had been abroad.

The thoughts buzzed around in his head as he stood in a corner of the solar, arms folded across his chest, watching the scene by the bed.

He wished Hugh d'Alban no harm. Fiery he might be, but he was also kindly and loyal, though Giles felt his loyalty to be misplaced in the present circumstances. For the last ten years, until his untimely death earlier in the year, Lancaster had guided Richard, who had seemed to respect his uncle's advice. Now, with Gaunt's wise, restraining hand gone, Richard seemed bent on pursuing personal policies which could only lead to disaster.

But it was on Hugh's daughter that most of his attention was fixed.

How could any maid change so much? Her body showed signs of delicious curves under the flowing lines of her gown. The leaf-green colour contrasted well with the blackness of her long, curling hair. He was suddenly taken with a longing to see that hair spread on the pillows, where he could bury his face in its silky fragrance. He knew it was fragrant, with a faint perfume of rosemary. He'd caught a whiff as he'd bent over the bed earlier.

"Guy, let me help!"

Her light, musical voice, overlaid by anxiety, penetrated his thoughts, and he watched her quick, capable movements as she helped the squire to divest Hugh of his breastplate and unlatch the heavy gorget he wore around his neck.

Giles took a step forward, about to offer his help in lifting the heavy body, but halted in his tracks. One refusal of his assistance was quite enough. He would not expose himself to her anger and scorn a second time. 'Twas a pity they'd met again under such difficult circumstances. He'd imagined riding peacefully into Alban Castle, enlisting the support of Hugh d'Alban and renewing acquaintance with his betrothed. Even if still reluctant to bed the wench, he knew he could not put off fulfilling his part of the betrothal contract for much longer. At seven and twenty, he must begin to take his responsibilities seriously.

Giles's eyes devoured Philippa's features as she bent over her father. She'd been a plain child. But now her face had taken on an intriguing shape—a broad, high forehead and wide, prominent cheekbones hollowing down to a narrow chin in which the fascinating trace of a cleft caught his attention for a long moment until his eyes shifted back to the dark mole sited near the curving lips of her full, passionate mouth. Her creamy skin held a trace of moist flush as she laboured to make her father comfortable. What colour were her eyes? He tried to remember, and caught an impression of deep, deep black, as fathomless as the night, fringed by equally dark, long lashes which were even now forming lush crescents on the perfect texture of her cheeks.

Her eyes were closed as Sir Magnus said a prayer over her father's still body. As the priest finished the incomprehensible Latin words, she crossed herself and murmured, "Amen."

A stir at the doorway made her turn. Mary bustled in, anxious and out of breath.

"Pippa! Is he recovered? Where is Roger?"

"No, he has not. Though I believe he is breathing more easily. And I do not know what has become of Roger."

Giles's quiet voice intervened. "He disappeared while we were tending the Earl."

"Disappeared?" gasped Mary.

"I fear so, my lady. He was not hurt, of that I can assure you. But he slipped away, and of his present whereabouts I have no knowledge."

Philippa, surprised by his still being in the chamber, sent him a hostile glance. "No doubt he wished to avoid the company of traitors!" she snapped.

Giles's lips tightened. The wench should not be speaking to her future lord in such a manner! But when had Pippa ever minded her words? he mused wryly. In the child such outspokenness had been endearing. But in his wife…She was upset. No doubt she would see reason anon. Meanwhile, a certain sympathy with her plight made him reluctant to add to her troubles.

He bowed. "I will leave you to recover your temper, my lady," he said with sarcastic courtesy and, turning on his heel, left the chamber with a jingle of spurs.

"Really, Pippa! Did you have to antagonise him so?" remonstrated Mary. "He could make life very difficult for us an he willed!"

"Pshaw!" Philippa flounced round to look down anxiously on her father. "He's done that already! With father incapacitated and Roger gone, what are we to do?"

"Manage as best we can until your father recovers and my husband returns!" declared Mary with unexpected spirit.

Philippa stared in surprise, then shrugged. Mary had been châtelaine of Alban Castle since her marriage to Roger almost seven years ago. She was used to being in charge of the household, and found satisfaction in bustling around, seeing to the day-to-day affairs Philippa found tedious.

"Now," Mary began with determined cheerfulness, "we must make the Earl comfortable. Have you discovered what is amiss?"

"He cannot speak, his face is stiff down one side, and I do not think he can move his leg or arm. Giles," said Philippa with a derisive snort, "says it is a seizure."

Mary bent over her father-in-law, taking his hand and judging his response. "I have seen this condition before," she said at last, "in my uncle. 'Tis an apoplexy, I fear."

"Will he recover?" asked Philippa anxiously.

"Probably. I do not think he will die, Pippa. But he may never again be able to use his arm or leg properly."

"Poor father!" Philippa scowled angrily. "It is all Giles's fault!"

"You can't say that, Pippa. If your father hadn't lost his temper—"

"He would not have had cause to if Giles had not come!"

Mary shook her head, but said no more, seemingly too occupied in making Hugh d'Alban comfortable to argue with her tempestuous sister-in-law.

Philippa watched in fretful silence. Mary was so efficient it made her sick. Not that she couldn't do everything that might be required of her as a wife if she had to. Except embroidery. She looked down at her long, tapering fingers in disgust. They would never do what she wanted—the stitches came out uneven, and the cloth ended up a crumpled mess. Otherwise, 'twas just that she preferred wandering the countryside on her palfrey, or practising archery in the butts, or gathering herbs—even snaring conies and other wild animals for meat, or netting fish in the castle stews. Or just sitting in some secluded nook, watching the birds and animals going about their business.

Philippa moved restlessly, feeling superfluous in the sick-room now that Mary had taken charge. ''I'll go and see if the physician is coming,'' she told her sister abruptly, and left the solar.

No doubt Giles had sent to Tewkesbury for medical help. Her chamber was on the upper floor of a recently built two-storey wing, flanking the kitchens and stores. Its glazed window would offer an extensive view of the track from Tewkesbury. To reach it she must leave by the Hall and cross part of the bailey. She stood at the top of the steps, irresolute. The physician could not be expected for a few hours yet.

The yard was no less full than it had been earlier. The manor folk had gone, but the fifty soldiers who had accompanied Giles were busy rubbing their horses down in or near the stables. They would want to bed down in the Great Hall with the d'Alban retainers and servitors. Mary would no doubt see to the provision of extra straw for their pallets. Giles, who was nowhere to be seen, would be offered the guest chamber, she supposed. He could share it with any other knights in his party.

Had Mary ordered extra food for supper? Philippa doubted her sister had had time. She sped down the steps, diverting her way to the vast kitchen. The blast of heat almost knocked her backwards as she entered. Sweating scullions, some almost naked, staggered about carrying steaming cauldrons, or bent over the blazing hearths—which made the risk of fire so great that they had to be isolated in a separate building—turning spits on which joints of meat roasted. Cooks and their assistants, scarcely less hot, laboured over chopping boards, rammed huge pestles into enormous mortars, and stirred the contents of huge bowls with large wooden spoons. Someone was rolling out pastry for pies, someone else kneading dough.

The head cook, a Gascon the Earl had brought back from one of his campaigns in Aquitaine, stopped work and moved over to meet her.

He bowed low. "*Ma Dame*."

"Gaston, have you been told to increase the number of dishes for supper?" asked Philippa.

"Buffey, the steward, suggested more food would be needed, *Ma Dame*."

"Of course!" Philippa felt foolish. She should have realised that Buffey and Mary between them would not forget to give the order. "There appear to be about fifty extra men," she said quickly, attempting to cover the futility of her visit. "Can you manage?"

"We are baking more bread. Supper may be delayed, but we shall provide sufficient victuals to feed everyone."

"Excellent."

Philippa supposed that the marshal of the horses had received orders to issue rations for the extra animals. Should she make sure? In any case, she would like to see that her palfrey was not disturbed by the new arrivals. She left the kitchen with a sense of relief and set off across the bailey towards the stables.

Actually, she just wanted to keep moving, to keep her mind occupied. Her own thoughts were uncomfortable.

She found Blaze, a five-year-old gelding, quietly munching his fodder. He greeted her with a soft whinny, and nuzzled her hand. His glossy chestnut coat shone, even in the dim interior of the stables, and the broad white streak running down his face, which had given him his name, stood out boldly.

Philippa kissed the mark fondly before she left the animal and made for the stall where the rescued mule stood. She ran her hands over the animal, feeling its ribs, the roughness of the hair over previous wounds, the scabs where the sores caused by the rub of a wooden pannier cradle were healing.

Several horse-grooms worked near by, and she turned to the nearest. "Do you think he's better?" she asked eagerly.

"Aye, my lady," he responded cheerfully. "'Tis my belief he'll be sound as a bell once his ribs are covered with flesh. You've got yourself a good pack-animal there."

"I thought he would die."

The churl grinned. "Small chance o' that now."

Philippa smiled at him. "Thanks to your care."

Looking round, she saw Giles's light grey horse gleaming palely a couple of stalls further along. The stallion was called Majesty. She knew that, because

Giles had brought him the last time he had visited Alban Castle. Then Majesty had been a young colt under training, showing every sign of deserving his patrician name. Now he seemed to know how special he was. His head was held arrogantly high, like his master's. His eyes held a softness which would disappear in battle, again just like his master's. Philippa shivered involuntarily as she remembered the ice in Giles's glare earlier. She wanted him to look at her softly, teasingly, as he had done when she was a child and there was no anger between them.

Today his gaze had been either assessing or remote. But why did she long for Giles to behave as the charming, playful young man of her childish dreams when she hated him now?

Would he still want her to marry him? Her stomach muscles tightened on the thought. They'd been betrothed for eight years; such a contract was not easily broken. But if both parties were willing…and Giles had shown little eagerness to make her his bride! He had left her to fret at being left a maid all these years, when most young maidens were married by sixteen. As Mary had been. Why, Mary was scarce two years older than herself, and already had two grown children!

He must be reluctant to wed with her, or he would not have tarried so long. As she was reluctant to wed with him! She would insist the betrothal be broken. Absently, she stroked the muzzle of the great horse, and spoke into his ear.

"I will not marry him, Majesty. He cannot force me!"

"You think not?"

Giles stood behind her, his feet planted firmly apart, his arms folded across his broad chest, his features set in a quizzical expression. He had shed his helmet and the attached mail, revealing sun-bleached golden-brown hair and a closely trimmed beard. She fought down the sudden leaping of her pulses.

"You cannot *want* to wed with me, Giles!" she cried, "else you would have sought my hand long ere this! And now—how can I marry the man responsible for my father's being struck down?"

His expression hardened, his firm chin lifted. "Even were your accusation true, 'twould be easily done." His voice was dry, implacable. "You will honour the contract exchanged between our families. Your father would wish it."

"He would not! He would help me to break it! Did you not see how he glared at you earlier?"

"Aye, I know," admitted Giles, but neither his stance nor his features relaxed one jot of their grimness. "His anger will pass. It has no foundation. We will be wed as soon as possible." He unfolded his arms and reached out for her shoulders. "I should have sought my bride sooner, but I intend to remedy the situation with all possible dispatch. Henry is headed for Bristol. We will be wed there."

Chapter Two

Giles's fingers bit into her tender flesh like steel claws, drawing her closer. Philippa knew with dreadful certainty that he was going to kiss her. She squirmed in his hold and beat against his chest with impotent clenched fists. As his mouth drew threateningly nearer she turned her face away with a low cry of protest.

Her desperate struggles made no impression; he simply moved an arm to clamp her against him while his other hand anchored her head so that his lips could plunder hers.

Philippa gritted her teeth and stiffened. Giles had never kissed her before, except her hand in greeting or farewell. Why did he have to do so now? His heart thudded hard and fast under her clenched fingers, trapped helplessly between their bodies. His lips ground against hers, almost as though he was angry. It hurt. She made a protesting sound in her throat, but it was some moments before his touch gentled.

He lifted his head for long enough to take a calming breath. His heart slowed its beat. When next they touched hers, his lips were caressing instead of demanding. The tip of his tongue ran shiveringly along the line of her tightly buttoned lips. Rigid within his embrace, Philippa clamped her jaw shut, startled by the intimacy, afraid of the queer sensations his touch was inducing deep within her body.

Eventually he lifted his head again. His nostrils flared and he drew breath deep into his lungs, as though they had been starved of air. Her eyes seemed locked to his. It was impossible to disengage from that glittering challenge, clear despite the dim light in the stable. Slowly, he released her head, dropping his hand to slide it seductively down her neck and arm.

"We need privacy for this," he growled.

Philippa became aware of the men moving about the stables. Her face flamed. She tore her eyes from his, and concentrated her gaze on one of the silver acorns which dusted the scarlet of a jupon slashed by a broad azure band, bearing the d'Evreux golden castle and fleur-de-lis.

"How dare you touch me?" she spat. "You are despicable! I refuse to marry you!"

"You have no choice, my dear little spitfire." Giles grinned, his composure largely regained, though at what cost only he could tell. "I look forward to our bridal bed," he murmured deeply, seductively, as he loosened his hold on her body and took her by the arm to lead her from the stable.

"Then you have a disappointment coming!" snapped Philippa. "I shall not submit willingly to your animal demands!"

"I believe you will, my love. Sooner or later." His husky voice soothed. "And I can be very patient."

Philippa fought against the strange effect his touch and voice seemed to be having on her system. It must be because she had never been kissed before. Any new experience was bound to affect one so.

"I am not your love!" she spat defiantly. Her hair drifted round her small, flushed face, the sun bringing out highlights like those on a raven's wings; her large, beautiful eyes sparkled from their nest of lashes like twin jewels of so dark a midnight blue they might almost have been jet. Her mouth trembled invitingly despite her determination to keep her lips clamped tightly shut. Giles saw their lush, swollen promise, and drew a deep breath, wishing he had sought to claim his bride before. Wishing fate had not conspired to set her so obdurately against his suit.

"You will be," he vowed softly, as tenderness and admiration fought exasperation and desire for pride of place in his emotions.

He had released her arm. Philippa took a quick step backwards, then, with a cry of annoyance, twitched her gown aside and lifted her foot. Her soft, pointed shoe had landed in a pile of horse manure, and the odour rose pungently between them.

"See what you've made me do!" she wailed as anger and a complete sense of impotence and ineptitude swept over her, bringing unwanted tears to hover tremulously on her lower lids before running foolishly down her cheeks.

Giles quickly grasped a handful of straw from a passing groom. "Let me clean it off," he offered and, not waiting for her answer, squatted down and took her foot in his hand.

Stranded on one leg, Philippa found she had no option but to steady herself against his broad shoulder as he worked quickly and efficiently to scrape off the worst of the offending ordure. His muscles rippled under her fingers. Regardless of her balance, Philippa removed her hand as though she'd been stung.

"There!" He finished his task, let go of her foot, and smiled up into her glowering face. "The worst is off. Your servants should be able to remove the rest."

Philippa swiped at the tears running down her face, and tossed her head. "I suppose you think I should thank you," she threw at him, "but, since 'twas your fault I trod in the dung in the first place, I do not consider thanks due. I will leave you to your offensive duties."

"Wait!"

His harsh command halted her as she began to stalk away. She turned to view him haughtily, her brows arched in interrogation. "Why?" she demanded.

"Why should you consider my duties offensive? I came here in peace, to seek support for a just cause and to claim my bride. 'Twas your father's attitude which caused the problems, not mine."

"I cannot agree," she rejoined stiffly. "You now control Alban Castle. You will doubtless dispose your men to keep it safe for the traitor Bolingbroke. That is what I find offensive about your duties, my lord."

"Henry Bolingbroke is no traitor!" gritted Giles. "I have said it before, and I will say it again and again until I can force some sense into your addled brain!"

Philippa shrugged, feigning indifference. "We shall never agree on that," she told him, "and I am sure you cannot want a bride who is so at odds with your beliefs. Break the contract, Giles."

Her voice had become unconsciously pleading. Giles stared into her mutinous face and saw the vulnerable maid lurking behind the façade of maturity.

"I'm sorry, Philippa," he said gently, smiling with all the charm at his command—which he knew from experience was not inconsiderable— "but I have told you 'tis impossible. We must leave for Berkeley tomorrow. Please be ready to accompany me there, and from thence to Bristol."

Philippa stood and stared at him, fighting the allure of his smile. Of his entire person. Oh, he could charm the cockroaches from their cracks in the walls, but he couldn't charm her. She was immune. But he did have such an unsettling effect on her! If she didn't go at once she might be tempted to return his smile. And that would just feed his overweening ego.

She made one last stand. "You cannot force me."

Giles suppressed a sigh. It seemed his future bride

was impervious to the charm which had served him so well in the past. "I fear I can," he told her with forced cheerfulness. "Since your brother has seen fit to abscond, this castle must be evacuated tomorrow. Your family and retainers will travel to your dower manor of Fishacre. They will be safe there until we are able to join them."

"But Father cannot travel!"

"'Tis less than a day's ride. He will be safe in a litter. But his departure can be delayed if the leech deems it necessary."

"You are so thoughtful!" exclaimed Philippa bitterly.

This was a body blow. If Roger returned he would find the castle deserted. No doubt all their stores would be commandeered. He would have no victuals, apart from anything he could scrounge in the village. The manor folk would not let him starve, but what if he managed to raise an army? The village could not feed many men. He might ride on to Fishacre or another of their manors. But none could either house or support even a small company of men.

She eyed Giles narrowly. He stood, planted solidly, eyeing her in return. For what seemed an eternity to Philippa, they took each other's measure. Giles was definitely planning to thwart any plans Roger might have. Philippa knew it. Just as she knew that if she remained at Alban Castle overnight she would have no choice but to accompany Giles in the morning. If she wanted to escape bondage to him, she must make her move that night. She could slip away through the postern, for she had long possessed a spare key. No one would know, except Ida, who would have to accompany her. Even Philippa could not envisage riding about the countryside at night quite alone. They should have a guard, ideally, but who could she ask? Eadulf, the groom who looked after Blaze, might be prepared...

Her lips twitched upwards at the corners as she planned her escape. She dipped her head in apparent submission. "The physician cannot arrive soon enough for me," she stated flatly, and when she turned on her heel and stalked away this time Giles did not stop her.

He stood watching the graceful line of her retreating back, the swing of her hips as she lifted her kirtle from the ground. His eyes narrowed. She was planning something. Her apparent submission to his will rang false. He was used to reading other people's minds, a necessary accomplishment at any court.

Philippa retired to her chamber without further delay. The young mongrel hound she had fostered from a puppy followed her. Spot was never willingly far from her side, and bounded along on long legs, tongue lolling, his fringed tail waving joyously. Philippa patted his rough, mainly creamy coat absently, and teased his one brown ear. No one would miss her. She had no wish to run into Giles again before supper, and the household ran more efficiently without her interference.

Ida was mending and pressing some of her mistress's older clothes. She looked up with an enquiring smile as Philippa burst into the room.

"There you are, my lady. I wondered where you had gone."

"To the stables," responded Philippa breathlessly. "I wanted to see that Blaze and the mule had not been disturbed. How was Father when you left?"

"Much the same." Ida brushed off Spot's exuberant greeting. "That dog is covered in mire!" she exclaimed in disgust.

"Not much, and so am I," responded Philippa, unlatching her shoes with a grimace. "'Tis all those extra horses in the yard. Lady Mary did not need your help?"

"Nay, she had plenty of other assistance, so I returned here to be about my duties."

"'Tis as well, for I wished to speak with you, Ida." Philippa eyed the older woman keenly as she put her arms around the neck of her dog, evading his eager tongue with a soft laugh of protest. Ida had been born some ten winters before herself, and was surely still young enough to relish a little adventure. "Ida, I am going to run away."

"But you cannot, my lady!" cried Ida, scandalised.

"I can, and I will! Lord Giles insists that I accompany him to Bristol, where he intends we shall be wed. Ida," she cried urgently, "you must help me! I cannot marry the man responsible for my father's being struck down!''

"Sweeting," began Ida in distress, "you must think of your future, and that of your family. You cannot simply break a legal agreement at will. Consider the consequences—''

The wary compassion in her servant's eyes brought angry spots of colour to Philippa's cheeks. She did not want pity, but help! She interrupted sternly, "I am considering the consequences of *not* breaking it! A lifetime of marriage to a man I hate!''

Ida pursed her lips doubtfully. "You used to like him well enough.''

"I did not know him then! He is an arrogant dictatorial traitor!" And a lecher, she thought, remembering uneasily his impassioned kiss and the strange effect it had had on her. She shuddered slightly. "How can I possibly marry him, Ida? If you will not help me, then I shall manage on my own!''

So saying, Philippa rummaged in a coffer for a huge circular riding cloak, which she spread upon the bed. On top, she threw a necessary change of smock, hose and veil, her best comb, her pouch of jewels, the rosary given her by her dead mother, and anything else small she thought she might need. As an afterthought, and because she thought she could manage to carry it, she included a change of kirtle and a spare pair of shoes.

Ida watched her furious activity for several minutes before she spoke again. "If you are determined, then of course I will come with you, Lady Pippa. But I do not like it. Will you tell Lady Mary?''

''No! It would only upset her, and she has enough to worry about already, with my father's being so ill and her husband's disappearing without a word! Besides, she would try to stop me, and might tell Sir Giles. I do not like leaving my father,'' Philippa added sadly, ''but he is in good hands, and Giles would not let me stay with him in any case.''

''When do you propose to leave, my lady?''

''The moment the castle is quiet. We will slip out of the postern.''

''On foot?'' asked her tiring-woman, aghast.

''No. You must go and find Eadulf. He will saddle Blaze, and a mount for you. If he would come with us, I should be eternally grateful. Will you ask him? And tell him to meet us, with the horses, by the postern, as soon as he can get there without being noticed after the castle has retired for the night. About midnight, I should think.''

''I will tell him to be there. Where are we going, Lady Pippa?''

''To the Priory in Evesham. The nuns know me; I stayed there for a whole year to learn to read and write. They will give me refuge.''

''For a while, no doubt. But I doubt you will wish to stay there for long. I well remember the way you grumbled at being sent there. As I recall, you disliked living at the Priory so intensely that you threatened to abscond on more than one occasion. Are you not

running from a union you wanted above all else to
the kind of life you have always detested?''

"I do not intend to remain there long. Just until I
have made up my mind what exactly to do. And even
the Priory will be preferable to marriage with a man
I hate. Something will turn up," said Philippa opti-
mistically. "Giles will probably change his mind
when he sees how determined I am to break our contract.''

"I wouldn't count on it," muttered Ida, but she
offered no more arguments. Instead, she went to find
Eadulf.

"He will accompany us," she reported on her return. "He says he could not allow us to wander the
countryside without protection. Though he is no more
happy about this escapade than I am.''

Philippa had given up her preparations to leave,
knowing that Ida would pack for them both, and do
it far more efficiently than she would. She sat at her
window, Spot at her feet, gazing abstractedly at the
track to Tewkesbury, hoping their journey in the opposite direction would be accomplished in safety. The
way to Evesham was by no means a main thoroughfare, and the trees and bushes pressed in close for
much of the distance, though beyond the fringe of
thickets the open fields spread far and wide, their fertile strips growing essential crops or providing pasture
for cattle and sheep. Outlaws or footpads could find
scant shelter there, but attacks on travellers were not
unknown.

Suddenly, her attention was caught by a small party toiling up the slope towards the castle, which was set upon a foothill of the Cotswolds. She sprang to her feet. "I believe the physician is coming!" she cried. "I must go to my father!"

It wanted an hour to supper. It was scarcely three hours since her father's collapse. The messenger must have travelled like the wind, and the leech had made good time. Philippa sped across the sunny court and up the steps to the Great Hall, Spot at her heels, quite forgetting her reluctance to meet with Giles again in her anxiety to reach her father. She wanted to be there when the man pronounced his verdict.

Giles was sitting on a bench with a couple of cronies, drinking ale from an earthenware pot, when she erupted into the Hall. He looked up and rose quickly to his feet.

"Your physician is coming," she threw at him in passing, and continued her rush to the solar.

Mary greeted her with a quiet smile, and received the news of the leech's arrival with unfeigned relief.

"Though I don't know what he can do," she admitted, "except bleed him. Mayhap that would prove beneficial."

Philippa laid her small, cool hand on her father's forehead. His eyes were closed now, and he looked peaceful. Only an unnatural lifelessness in the muscles of his face and a certain sunken appearance about his normally full cheeks indicated that aught was amiss.

The leech strode in, his flowing black gown emitting a great waft of mixed odours: horse, herbs and sweat. Giles followed closely behind. Spot greeted the knight exuberantly, and received an affectionate pat or two in return.

Treacherous beast! He did not like strangers, and avoided Roger when he was home, yet he seemed to have taken to Giles. "Down, Spot!" Philippa growled. "Come here!"

Tail wagging in evident pleasure, the dog obeyed her commands, a stupid grin on his long-nosed, patchy face. The tense atmosphere of the sick-room had not, it seemed, penetrated his thick skull.

"Lie down!" she ordered, and the dog flopped to the rushes, long pink tongue lolling from between large, sharp teeth.

Meanwhile, the physician had begun his examination. He woke the Earl, who had been in a heavy doze, and prodded and poked, seeking reactions. Eventually he confirmed Mary's verdict. "An apoplexy," he muttered.

"Will he recover?" asked Philippa anxiously.

"Only God can tell, Lady Philippa. Pray that he may. He is of a sanguine humour, I believe, and he must be made to sweat. Build the fire and cover him with furs. What was the date of his birth?"

Philippa told him, as nearly as she knew. The man retired to a corner of the chamber and, from somewhere among the folds of his gown, extracted parchments on which horoscopes were charted. He studied them in silence for a long time. Meanwhile, Mary had ordered that the fire be lit and the winter furs be brought. The room became stifling, and everyone except the physician showed evidence of being uncomfortably hot.

He moved at last. "The signs are propitious," he announced. "I will bleed him. That should relieve any pressure on his brain."

The company watched in silence as the slit was made and a small cup filled with the red liquid. Spot whined, disturbed by the scent of fresh blood. The wound was bound, and the physician tied a small model of a man, strung on a length of ribbon, round Earl Hugh's thick neck, before stepping back.

"The patient is not strictly ill," he pronounced solemnly, "merely paralysed. The healing powers will descend into the effigy when the planets are favourably placed, and thence into His Grace."

"Would a journey harm him?"

Philippa jumped as Giles's curt voice asked the question. She glanced anxiously at the physician. Please say it will, she prayed silently. But her prayer was ignored.

"How far?" enquired the leech.

"A day's journey east."

The man puckered his thin lips. "No," he decided. "No, such a journey might be beneficial, provided he is kept warm. It may stimulate his responses. I have known it to happen."

Giles's face broke into a smile of relief. "Thank

you, sir. We are most grateful for your prompt visit, and for your skill. Please accept this purse in payment.'' He handed the man a pouch which appeared to hold several coins. The leech pulled it open, viewed the contents with evident satisfaction, and pulled the draw-string to close it again.

''Your servant, noble lord. I was pleased to oblige.''

''You will remain overnight and examine the patient again on the morrow?''

''Gladly. I shall not return to Tewkesbury before I have assured myself of the Earl's fitness to travel.''

''A bed will be found for you,'' put in Mary practically. ''Meanwhile, you will sup with us, sir.''

The physician bowed. Giles ushered him from the room, then turned to address Mary.

''My lady, I shall be grateful if you will arrange for the household to be ready to travel to Fishacre tomorrow. I have already dispatched a messenger to advise the steward of your coming.''

The blood drained from Mary's face. ''You wish us to leave here?'' she asked faintly.

''Aye, lady, I fear it is necessary. You will not suffer from the move, of that I am assured. You will be safe at Fishacre.''

''But my husband—''

''Departed of his own volition,'' interrupted Giles tersely, ''leaving his sire unconscious on the ground. He must seek his own salvation.''

At that moment a trumpet announced that supper

was served. Philippa stood resolutely at her father's side.

"I will remain here. Have my food sent up. You need relief, Mary, if you are to carry out my lord's imperious orders." Her bitter voice echoed round the stone chamber. "I do not come with you. Sir Giles is forcing me to accompany him to Bristol to be wed."

Mary looked from Giles's inscrutable face to Philippa's rebellious features, and sighed. "You will be better wed," she said eventually. "I wish you both happy."

Philippa shot her an anguished look which Mary could do nothing but ignore. She took her young sister-in-law into her arms and kissed her fondly.

"It will work out, you'll see," she whispered.

It certainly would, thought Philippa dourly. But not in the way the others thought.

It was time to go.

A deep hush had fallen over the castle. She picked up her bundle, took hold of Spot's leash, and motioned to Ida to douse the candle and follow her. The heavy door opened without a sound. She stood in the opening, listening. Giles would be in the guest chamber at the end of the long gallery. His door was tightly shut, and no glimmer of light was to be seen anywhere.

With Ida close behind, Philippa crept along to the stairs. The ground floor was given over to wardrobes, store-rooms and other household offices. A churl snored in a far corner of the entry chamber, but they whispered through without waking him.

The deserted bailey held ghostly shadows in the bright moonlight. Philippa was thankful for the light to pick her way, but fearful of being seen, so she led the way around the perimeter, keeping in the shadow of walls and buildings. In fact, the only movement other than their own that she discerned was that of scavenging rats and prowling cats. Spot let out a low growl as they neared the kennels, and Philippa shushed him urgently; it would not do for the hunting pack to be roused.

They passed safely between the keep and the stables to arrive at the postern without incident. A faint jingle of harness in the deep shadow of the curtain wall told her Eadulf was waiting with the horses. She greeted him softly.

"Think you we can move away without being seen?" she asked anxiously. This was something she had been worrying over for some hours. The horses and riders would be plainly visible in the moonlight.

"We must wait for cloud to cover the moon, my lady. Else the watch will surely spot us."

Philippa scanned the heavens, pleased to see a bank of cloud slowly traversing the sky. "It shouldn't be long," she remarked hopefully. "Let us open the postern in readiness."

"I have already removed the bar, my lady. I need but the key."

"I have it here," said Philippa, handing him the

heavy metal object. The lock turned smoothly, with the merest clunk of sound. ''Let us mount,'' she urged eagerly.

''First let me fix your bundles to your saddles,'' suggested Eadulf.

Philippa thrust hers into his hands, impatient at the delay. Eadulf worked quickly and efficiently and, when he had finished, made a cradle for her foot and threw her up into the saddle.

Queen Anne had introduced the side-saddle some years since, and using it had become fashionable among court ladies. Although Philippa had tried the new riding position, and knew it gave a more dignified appearance, she preferred to sit astride her palfrey, for having the horse between her knees gave her more control. She wore wide skirts for riding and, before settling in her saddle, stood in her stirrups to straighten and arrange the purple fabric of the gown she had chosen. Eadulf spread the slate-grey cloak she wore to cover a trim saffron cote-hardie over the jennet's rump, and she was ready. Ida, less used to horseback, took longer to settle. By the time both women were ready the moon had already disappeared behind one edge of the cloud.

''Quickly,'' urged Eadulf. ''I will close the postern, and follow. But go slowly and quietly. We will attract less attention that way.'' So saying, he flung open the gate. Philippa urged Blaze through on to the narrow wooden causeway, only then fully realising that Eadulf had muffled the horses' hoofs. Once safely on solid ground, she longed to dig her heels into her horse's flanks and break into a gallop, but she knew the groom was right.

Blaze would have welcomed a good run. He fought against the bit, jangling his harness, though, as well as muffling his hoofs, Eadulf had thoughtfully used a simple headstall without bells or other noisy decoration. Philippa heard the postern close, followed by Eadulf's almost silent progress behind. Soon they reached the main track to Evesham, and Philippa allowed Blaze to lengthen his stride, while still keeping him to a walk. The faint plop of hoofs on the soft ground would not carry far. But the moon threatened to emerge from its cover at any moment, and the nearest trees were still some distance away. On the main track, though, they might be any travellers braving the darkness to reach their destination.

Keeping a firm grip on both the reins and her nerve, Philippa kept Blaze moving steadily towards cover. The three horses entered the shadow of the trees, and still no sound of alarm came from the castle.

''We have done it!'' she cried exultantly. ''Come, remove the muffles quickly, and let us make haste! We should reach Evesham long before sunrise.''

Once Eadulf had removed the skins from the horses' hoofs she let Blaze have his head, the others thudding along behind. Spot's excited barking kept them company as he bounded along beside her.

Now she was free of the castle elation took hold of Philippa. She lifted her black head, her unruly hair carefully braided and coiled in a silken fret for the journey, and laughed aloud.

''So much for my lord Giles d'Evreux!'' she shouted to the air. ''If he thinks to force me to his will, he may think again!''

Back in his chamber, Giles slept restlessly, aware of the heavy breathing of the others sharing the room. Annoyed with himself, for normally he slept deeply, though he had the soldier's knack of waking instantly alert, he tossed aside his light covering, and wandered to the window. The moon shone brightly, illuminating the bailey and the buildings surrounding it. A shrill whinny from the stables caught his ear, and he was reminded of his horses, probably as restless as their master in strange surroundings.

On an impulse, Giles donned shirt and braies, his padded grey gambeson and azure hose, laced on a pair of cordwain buskins, and crept out of his chamber and down the stairs. He strode confidently across the moonlit bailey, and entered the darkness of the stable. Majesty whickered in greeting, and Giles went to him, fondling and soothing with hand and voice. He stood for some moments before he realised that several of the other stalls were empty, though many of his men's mounts were tethered in the open for lack of space inside.

A rapid investigation brought an oath of anger to his lips. ''Is anyone about?'' he roared.

A head appeared at the top of the ladder leading to

the hayloft, the liripipe of the man's chaperon falling forwards over one bleary eye. "Aye," said a sleepy voice.

Not one of his own men. They must have bedded down in the Hall.

"Come here, churl!" Giles ordered.

The man threw back the liripipe and descended the ladder with what speed he could.

"Tell me," grated Giles, "which castle horses are missing?"

The groom looked round, a vacant expression on his heavy face. Then a kind of light dawned. "Lady Philippa's palfrey has gone, my lord," he said, "and two of the hacks."

"I thought so," hissed Giles to himself. "Who took them?" he demanded imperiously. "When did they disappear?"

"How should I know, Lord? I bin asleep, like all honest men, and I didn't hear nothing, lord. But Lady Philippa, her wouldn't go far without an escort..."

Wouldn't she? wondered Giles grimly. He'd guessed she was up to something. Why the devil hadn't he had her watched? Because, he thought grimly, he had credited the wench with more sense than to wander the countryside at night!

He stormed back to his chamber to rouse his squire and fellow knights, and on the way unceremoniously threw open the door to Philippa's chamber. Naturally, it was empty. Swearing softly to himself, he roused the men and then rapped on Lady Mary's door.

"Where would she go?" he demanded when he had appraised a bewildered Mary of the facts.

"I do not know! She took Ida with her?" asked Mary in distress.

"Aye, it looks so. And probably a groom."

"Eadulf," guessed Mary. "He is getting on in years, but is devoted to Pippa."

She paused a moment, plucking at the fastening of her hastily donned chamber-gown with nervous fingers. Suddenly they stilled. "She might seek refuge at the Priory where she went for schooling," she told the impatient Giles. "I can think of nowhere else."

"Where is this place?" he snapped.

"Evesham. 'Tis not far—"

"Far enough," growled Giles. "An hour's fast ride." He strode back to the chamber, where the others were hurriedly donning their clothes.

"What is amiss, lord?" asked Wat Instow nervously.

"Nothing that cannot be speedily remedied," Giles told his squire. "My jupon, if you please!"

He addressed the youngest and most personable of the three knights as he climbed into the colourful garment and strapped on his sword-belt. "Sir Malcolm, you will see that half our men are ready to move off to Berkeley by Prime."

"Aye, lord."

"Sir William," he went on, turning to a stout young man, whose sweeping sandy moustache and long beard completely covered the bottom half of a round, ruddy face, "choose ten men, and remain behind to empty the castle of stores. Use the pack-animals, and follow us to Berkeley with any spare mounts."

"You wish me to remove everything, Sir Giles?"

"Everything Lady Mary does not wish to take to Fishacre."

He spoke less briskly to the older knight—a short, stocky man whose weathered face housed kindly blue eyes under bushy brows, and sprouted a sparse, greying beard. "Sir Walter, you have known the Earl for many years. I entrust his safe passage to Fishacre to you. Retain ten men as escort for him and his family and servants. Remain there until you hear from me."

"I shall do as you ask, of course. But will you not be coming back here, Sir Giles?" asked Walter Orpede doubtfully.

"I doubt it. 'Twill be dawn before I can possibly begin to escort Lady Philippa to Berkeley. You have my orders. The castle must be emptied, most of the men must rejoin Henry Bolingbroke, and the d'Alban family must be seen safely to Fishacre." He gestured to his squire, "Come, Wat. We have an unexpected and cursedly inconvenient journey before us!"

Chapter Three

In the moonlight the Priory rose from the fields edging the small town with all the appearance of a ghostly edifice. Philippa shivered slightly, partly from excitement but mostly from superstitious fear. The building had a strange, mysterious aura at odds with its solid, tranquil daytime appearance.

During the journey she had concentrated on the ride, travelling on a wave of euphoria at having evaded detection to escape Alban Castle. But now almost arrived at her destination, the doubts began to crowd her mind. What would she do if the Prioress Mary-Luke refused to give her shelter?

As Eadulf rapped on the great doors, demanding entry, she thrust her doubts aside, sat straight in her saddle, and tilted her chin defiantly.

The nun on night duty gasped in surprise when she slid aside the shutter and recognised the face of her visitor, clearly visible in the pale light of the waning moon.

"Lady Philippa! What brings you here at this hour?"

"I seek refuge, Sister Benedict."

"Refuge, my lady? What possible threat could cause you to travel by night with so few attendants?" demanded the elderly nun, her scandalised tones intimating just what she thought of such irresponsible conduct.

Philippa had no wish to spread news of her difficulties throughout the convent. The sisters found little inside its walls to gossip about, and would seize on her misfortune as a source of endless speculation. She replied with brisk authority.

"Let us in, Sister, and I will explain to Prioress Mary-Luke as soon as she is able to speak with me."

With a disapproving expression on her lined face, Sister Benedict opened the gate to allow the party entry. "Reverend Mother has not long retired after Matins and Lauds. I will not disturb her before the next Office," she told Philippa severely. "Your groom may stable the horses and rest in the men's guest dorter, yonder." Her black habit flapped as she motioned with her hand to an isolated building just inside the gate. "You and your attendant must wait in the women's chamber. You know where that is."

"Aye, Sister, and I thank you." Philippa was desperate to see the Prioress and establish her claim to sanctuary. She slid from her saddle, and handed the reins to Eadulf, turning immediately back to scan the plump features of the nun. "How long before the bell tolls for Prime?" she asked anxiously.

"Dawn breaks early at this time of the year. You will not have too long to wait," replied Sister Benedict, glancing to where her hour-glass stood on a ledge inside the gatehouse cell, the sand running down steadily from an almost full globe. "You must wait until after the Office has been said. Meanwhile, try to obtain some rest."

Philippa nodded. There seemed naught she could do to speed her interview with the Prioress. But Giles would be unable to reach her inside the building. "Come, Ida. Eadulf, we shall need our bundles."

"Your hound would be better in the kennels," muttered Sister Benedict doubtfully.

"Nay, he is used to sleeping with me, and would howl if we were parted. Are there many other guests in the dorter?"

"There seem to be few travellers on the road today, perhaps because of the uproar provoked by Henry Bolingbroke's return. He marched through here early this morning."

"Was his army large?" asked Philippa, unable to deny her curiosity.

"He had thousands of men with him! The column took hours to pass the gate. So many great Lords rode by, and all their retainers and levies! I saw Archbishop Arundel himself!" she said, breathless with awe. "And the Percies and the Nevilles and—"

"Doubtless a magnificent sight," broke in Philippa

curtly. "Take the bundles, Ida. God be with you, Eadulf; sleep well, and my thanks for your escort. We
will decide on your best course on the morrow. God's
blessings, Sister Benedict."

Followed closely by Spot, Philippa and her maid
crossed the courtyard and mounted the stairs to the
sleeping chamber set aside for the use of women travellers. Straw-filled pallets lined the dorter, and, although most appeared empty, snores and snuffles
emerging from the darkness told her several of the
beds were occupied. Philippa trod quietly across the
rush-strewn planks, and sank down tiredly on one
near a window, dimly lit by the last glimmers from
the moon. Ida subsided on its neighbour, and Spot
circled round twice, forming a nest in the rushes between them before settling his long nose on his paws,
though his soft brown eyes remained open, fixed on
his mistress.

Philippa had no intention of sleeping; she wanted
to remain alert to attend chapel and catch the Prioress
as soon as the Office was over. A picture of Giles's
irate face swam before her vision—the last thing she
remembered before she woke to the clang of the bell
calling the sisters to worship.

Philippa sprang up, smoothed her gown, told Spot
to remain where he was and, followed by a fuddled
Ida, who had obviously fallen asleep too, made her
way to the chapel, where the last of the sisters were
filing in from the night stairs.

The voices of the nuns, raised in plainsong, sent a

familiar thrill through Philippa. Despite the hour, despite her uncertainty and anxiety, the swell of the melodious chanting rising to fill the chapel to its vaulted ceiling brought with it a sense of uplift, of peace.

Philippa had always enjoyed the time spent in the chapel, where she could lose herself in the music and her own thoughts. It was the rigorous, austere routine of the nuns' lives, governed by their Rule and the constant tolling of the bell, which sent a shiver of dismay through her. She did not fancy the life of a religious. Yet what other choice was open to her, if she refused to wed with Giles?

Here, in the peace of the chapel, she faced the fact that she would become a social outcast if the d'Evreux family refused to dissolve the betrothal. She had been a full fifteen years old when the contract had been sealed. Only by mutual agreement could she escape her commitment with honour. And Giles had shown no inclination yet to accomodate her wishes.

She had hoped that her determination and obvious dislike would move him to change his mind. Perhaps he would in the end. But in the rational, cold light of all the facts that hope seemed to dim. An ambitious man like Giles would not easily be persuaded to relinquish the rich manors she brought with her to the marriage bed.

What would he do when he discovered she had gone? Would he spare the time to chase an errant bride, not knowing where to look? Philippa squeezed her eyes shut tight and prayed not. Prayed he would be fully occupied by Henry's cause for such a long time to come that his sudden desire to wed her would dim and he would allow the betrothal to be broken. If Henry did not succeed, of course, things could go hard with his supporters, and no one would force her to marry a proven traitor.

A shiver ran right through Philippa. However much she hated him, she had no wish to see Giles tried and executed for treason. Because of his rank he would escape the hanging, drawing and quartering suffered by those of lesser degree. He would be beheaded. She gazed bleakly at the altar, and her hands, clasped on the desk of the prie-dieu in an attitude of prayer, twisted together in sudden agitation. She could wish that fate on no one. Least of all on Giles, whom she had once imagined she loved.

It was suddenly more comfortable to believe Giles's assertions as to Henry Bolingbroke's loyal intentions.

Her hopes that Giles would not know where to look, and that he would not, in any case, spare the time to chase his runaway bride even if he did, were shattered the moment she filed from the chapel after the nuns. She heard a familiar male voice in the outer court.

The Prioress Mary-Luke, alerted by Sister Benedict to her unexpected presence, threw Philippa a shrewd glance and indicated with her black and white swathed head that the girl should follow her. Having spoken quietly to a novice, who scuttled off, Reverend Mother moved swiftly and silently to the chamber, just inside the entrance to the main building, where visitors of both sexes could be entertained. She lit several other candles from the one she carried before turning to face Philippa.

"Well, daughter," she said gently, as Philippa dropped to her knees before her and accepted her blessing, "what trouble has brought you to me this night?"

Philippa swallowed deeply. "I wish to break my betrothal contract, Reverend Mother," she confessed, her voice low and agitated. "I can no longer marry Sir Giles d'Evreux. He has caused much anguish to my family, and is supporting Henry Bolingbroke against our anointed King."

The Prioress ignored the last charge. "What anguish has he caused your family, child?" she enquired.

"My father lies helpless. Had Sir Giles not come demanding his support for a traitorous cause, my sire would not have been stricken by an apoplexy."

Before the Prioress could comment on this statement, they were interrupted by the arrival of the accused himself, shepherded by the novice, who made obeisance and departed. Giles greeted the Prioress, and knelt for her blessing before springing to his feet to give Philippa a cursory bow. The skin stretched tightly over his cheekbones. The muscles bunched round his clenched jaw, and his nostrils pinched in as he drew a long, exasperated breath. An explosive sound made her wince as he exhaled through his mouth.

"Well, Lady Philippa! So you are here. Why did you flee from your duty?" he demanded tersely.

Philippa tilted her chin, her lips compressed. When she spoke, it was from between her teeth.

"You would not listen to my pleas," she informed him fiercely. "'Twas the only way to escape your indecent demand that I marry you with all haste!"

"Indecent? What nonsense is this, Pippa?" barked Giles, momentarily surprised out of his studied formality.

Philippa could find no answer to that. She glared back at him. "How did you find me?" she countered angrily.

"Lady Mary has more sense of duty than you, my lady. She guessed you would seek refuge here. There was nowhere else for you to go."

His remote, formal manner hurt. For some reason she felt doubly betrayed. "Trust Mary to behave with the utmost propriety!" she sniffed.

"My children!" The Prioress's quiet voice broke through their argument, her serene face, in its frame of white linen, mildly admonishing. "Harsh words will not help to resolve your difficulties."

Quietly and rationally, she led them to recount the events of the previous day before delivering her verdict. "I can see no cause for you to break your vows, my daughter," she told Philippa gently. "Go with your affianced husband. He does only what he considers his duty. And go also with God.''

Philippa stared at the Prioress in dismay. In a moment of blinding clarity she realised that the betrothal contract had been sealed by the Church, and was as binding in its sight as any wedding ceremony. Something she had failed to remember when she'd made her decision to run away from Giles. ''You cannot mean it, Reverend Mother!'' she gasped. ''I had thought you would understand, that I could find shelter here until the betrothal contract was dissolved!''

''Which it will never be,'' inserted Giles crisply.

''It is your duty to wed, my child. God grants a great deal of satisfaction to those who execute their duty in an obedient and pious spirit.''

''But I want to take holy vows, Reverend Mother! I wish to become a nun!'' cried Philippa desperately.

The Prioress smiled ruefully, shaking her head. ''I cannot believe you, daughter. I know you too well. You must not be tempted to misuse God's holy calling to escape the trials of life. In a very short while you would be more unhappy here than you will be as the wife of the man chosen for you. You did not settle to the religious life while you were a pupil.''

The smile broadened, became a gentle smile full of understanding. Before she spoke again she glanced from Giles's handsome, determined features, the grim set of his chin belied by the softness lurking in the depths of his eyes, to those of Philippa, rebellious yet lovely, showing all too clearly the uncertainty and immaturity of their bearer. "You have always told me you had a fondness for each other," she reminded Philippa quietly. "With time, respect and affection will return."

Philippa sank to her knees, clasping her hands before her in an attitude of supplication. "Do not force me, Reverend Mother," she whispered.

The Prioress touched the dark, bent head before lifting the girl to her feet. "I cannot force you, daughter. I can only advise. But neither can I allow you to remain here. Your unwarranted presence would unsettle the prayers and the work of the sisters. And before long you would become restless, causing more disruption. God has ordained your path, my child. Obey his will with faith."

Philippa knew she was beaten. A sickness settled in the pit of her stomach. She ran her tongue around dry lips, and raised her eyes to Giles's stern face.

"It seems, my lord, that you have won," she choked bitterly. "I fear you will find little joy in your victory."

Giles bowed. The muscles in his jaw bunched anew. "It gives me little joy to win my bride in this way," he told her grimly. "I regret that you made such a confrontation necessary. Be ready to ride as soon as may be. We must make up the lost time. We travel straight to Berkeley."

"We do not return to Alban?"

"Nay, my lady." His voice softened, and he no

longer used her title as though it were a weapon. "I fear that will not be possible."

"But I have so few of my things with me!"

"Enough for several days, I warrant. And Sir William will have your possessions with him when he joins us. Your further needs can be supplied when we reach Bristol."

She sought wildly to delay the inevitable. "I have barely slept—"

"Neither have I. But I doubt we shall fall out of our saddles with fatigue."

"Ida—"

"And Wat. Both are suffering needlessly as a result of your escapade. Eadulf had better accompany you, since he is here. My grooms are quite busy enough without other horses to see to."

So she would have two familiar faces with her. For an instant a feeling of gratitude almost overcame Philippa's resentment. She stiffened her resolve. "Blaze and the other horses will barely be rested. We travelled fast."

"As did we. Stop making excuses, Pippa." He grinned suddenly, showing the slight irregularity in his gleaming white teeth. "We must not keep the lady Prioress from her duties. I will see you in the courtyard as soon as you have recovered your possessions. And, I believe, your hound," he added, then turned to Mary-Luke to execute a courtly bow. "My apologies for disturbing your peace, my lady. And my gratitude for your wise counsel."

The Prioress smiled benignly. "Take time to break your fasts before you depart. I will order food brought here from the frater." She lifted her hands in benediction. "God be with you, my children."

The sun was well above the horizon by the time they left the Priory. Philippa rode between Giles and his squire, knowing they were expecting her to bolt.

She also knew escape was not possible. Giles was not riding Majesty but Panache, a spirited bay stallion led in his train by a groom, and bred to carry him swiftly wherever he wanted to travel. Blaze would never be able to outrun him. And, as Giles had pointed out, where had she to go? Fishacre? A possibility, but she knew in her heart that she would never survive that journey on her own without mishap. So she rode on proudly, back straight, head held high. She would not give him the satisfaction of chasing her and dragging her back.

Thought of escape being futile, she concentrated on reminding herself how much she hated Giles d'Evreux. A sidelong glance told her that he had removed his cap to allow the breeze to cool his scalp. The rays of the fiery orb rising in the east shone through his sun-bleached hair to form a golden halo. He looked like a Greek god, she thought disgustedly, when he should resemble the devil. To think that she had harboured childish romantic dreams about her betrothed for all those years! He was naught but a cold-hearted, arrogant churl without a grain of honour or chivalry in him!

But an unexpected *frisson* of excitement shook her nerves when he turned his head and caught her gaze with his. For it was the old Giles who looked at her from laughing eyes, turning her stomach. "Cheer up, my love! 'Twill not be so bad, you'll see! Prioress Mary-Luke spoke the truth. We were meant for each other."

"Everything you do and say makes me hate you the more!" cried Philippa recklessly, fighting down the treacherous lift of her spirits occasioned by his wicked, infectious smile.

It vanished like the sun behind a storm cloud. Bushy, gold-tipped brows met over suddenly bleak eyes. "If that is the atmosphere in which you wish to conduct our affairs, then so be it, my lady. I would have preferred a more amicable relationship, but I am entirely ready to reciprocate your ill-feelings," he informed her coldly. "Your behaviour since we met again yesternoon has been nothing if not childish and offensive. I have no reason to feel kindly disposed towards you."

Philippa felt a qualm of regret for her hasty declaration. True, she did hate him, but she could have been more circumspect. She was entirely in the man's power, and to lose his goodwill might mean that she would feel his displeasure. And she had the feeling that Giles's displeasure might be rather alarming.

After that, she rode in silence. Giles and Wat conversed over her head. Ida and Eadulf exchanged idle chatter behind. Spot gambolled alongside. Philippa stared fixedly at the track ahead, wondering what she had done that God should treat her so.

As the great shell keep of Berkeley Castle rose above the Gloucestershire countryside ahead of them, the ancient stonework glowing warmly in the late afternoon sun, Philippa marvelled at the vast, uncountable numbers of Henry's supporters encamped outside the castle's defences. Lords' gay silken pavilions jostled with makeshift shelters erected by men-at-arms, archers and camp followers: the servants and tradesmen, not to mention the women ready to accommodate the needs of the men for a fee. The red rose of Lancaster and the Lancastrian version of the Royal Arms fluttered from almost every pole, counterpointing the splendidly charged pennons of the impressive array of magnates whose support Henry had enlisted.

Young Wat Instow had ridden ahead to discover the situation, Giles's personal badge—an acorn—painted on the arms of his leather jerkin making his allegiance plain for all to see. The party from Alban Castle, under Sir Malcolm de Boyes, had already pitched their tents, and it was from Sir Malcolm that Wat had elicited his information.

"The castle is almost full, lord," Wat reported, riding out to meet them as they approached. "Edmund of Langley, the Duke of York, is here!"

"Is he indeed? As Keeper of the Realm, he has

come to meet the King on his return from Ireland, no doubt. How did he greet Henry?''

"Amicably, I gather. They are in conference now. Room can be found for Lady Philippa and her woman in one of the domestic dorters in the eastern bailey, but we shall have to camp here overnight. Sir Malcolm already has your pavilion erected.''

"'Twill be no hardship in this weather. I thank you, Malcolm,'' he added as the knight strode over to greet them. "Did all go well at Alban this morn?''

"Aye, lord, as far as I know. We left before Sir Walter and the Earl and his family were—''

"What was my father's condition?'' cut in Philippa anxiously.

Sir Malcolm bowed in her direction. They had not dismounted, and he lifted his rather nice brown eyes to her face. "Much the same, my lady. Though I believe he had articulated a word or two, and was able to move the fingers of his hand. The physician gave his permission for him to travel.''

"What of Sir William?'' asked Giles. "He has not arrived as yet?''

"Nay, lord. He expected to be a day at least carrying out your orders.''

Giles frowned. "So long? Were the stores so vast?''

"I do not know, lord. I left, as ordered, before he had properly taken inventory.''

"No doubt he'll catch up ere long. Meanwhile, I will escort the Lady Philippa to the castle.'' Giles turned to Philippa with formal courtesy. "Come, my lady. You should rest comfortably again tonight."

Philippa followed obediently as he prodded Panache forward through the embattled entrance and, having ascertained the direction, threaded his way through the throng to cross one bailey to reach the other.

Her thoughts were far from comfortable. Her father seemed to have improved slightly, but, although the journey might not harm him in itself, he would resent having to make it. Her stomach turned and the sickness returned. Frustration at his helplessness might bring on a relapse. Still, she consoled herself, forcing down her panic, Mary would be well able to cope, and was fond enough of her father-in-law to do her best. She herself could have done little apart from offering her presence, but she would have given much to be with him.

Memories of home filled her momentarily with nostalgia. Alban was small compared to this vast edifice. Thrusting her anxiety behind her, Philippa eyed her surroundings with growing interest, noting the frenetic bustle of all the officials and serfs as they carried out their orders, while tired Lancastrian retainers lounged idly by. The farriers' hammers rang around the yard, horses stamped and neighed in impatience or protest. Pigs, chickens and geese scattered at their approach. There seemed hardly room to move within the castle walls.

Ignoring the ancient tower and passing the more

recently built Great Hall, Giles drew rein before the entrance to the newish building containing the living quarters. He called a servant, who showed them the way to a small, bare, closet-like chamber which contained two pallets crowded together to leave a small space for movement near the doorway.

"You are fortunate," remarked Giles drily. "You will have privacy here."

"Except that there is no door to the chamber, which, being designed for the use of servants, leads directly from that used by the ladies of the castle," returned Philippa sharply.

"You have an arras to shield the doorway. I will find you better lodgings in Bristol," promised Giles. "We will meet again shortly in the Hall, at supper. Farewell, Philippa."

Philippa shifted uneasily and voiced an awareness which had been growing on her since entering the castle. "Is this not where the King's great-grandfather was murdered?" she asked, and cleared her throat to free it of a sudden thickness.

"Aye." Giles met her eyes steadily. "Edward II met his end somewhere in this castle." He smiled grimly. "Richard should have learned from his ancestor's mistakes. The second Edward was extravagant, and attempted to rule through favourites, rather than through Parliament. Richard has not only been profligate and taken bad advice from his cronies, but has tried to take all power into his own hands. He thinks he is above the law, a law unto himself. He must be shown that he is wrong.''

''And you and Henry Bolingbroke are appointed by God to show him the error of his ways?'' scorned Philippa, suddenly angry again. It was better than being scared.

''Henry has been wronged. The duty of every true knight is to see all wrongs righted, be it with or without the King's writ. Richard must answer to Parliament. He has no real power without its consent.''

''Richard is King,'' stated Philippa flatly.

Giles bowed. ''On that at least we are agreed, my lady. We meet at supper.''

Ida found a page to send for water, which arrived in pitchers carried by a file of churls. The fact that it was cold did not matter, since the weather was warm.

Sponged down, changed into her spare kirtle, her hair freshly braided and held in the silken frets, Philippa began to feel better. She would see Henry at supper. And the great Duke of York, Henry's uncle. Richard's uncle, too. How must the old man feel, she wondered, caught between his nephews? Yet he owed duty to Richard, who had left the Realm in his uncle's safe-keeping while he himself went to Ireland to put down a rebellion by that troublesome and elusive chieftain, Art MacMurrach.

Philippa had led a sheltered and uneventful life, seldom venturing further from Alban Castle than Tewkesbury or Evesham, though once a year the whole family travelled to one of the Earl's other castles or manors while Alban was sweetened. These expeditions had seemed like a holiday, and Philippa had made the most of them. Once she had travelled to the beautiful manor house of Acklane in Oxfordshire to meet Giles's parents. But she'd only been twelve at the time, and memory of that important occasion had dimmed.

She didn't want to be here at Berkeley, of course, but she could not help a feeling of importance, of excitement, of destiny, almost, at being caught up in great events. How many women would be able to tell their grandchildren that they had actually seen Henry Bolingbroke on his way to confront his cousin?

If she ever had grandchildren. The knowledge that if she did they were likely to be Giles's too brought a flush to her cheeks and a pout of rebellion to her lips.

Philippa felt quite lost in the vast, lavishly decorated Hall, and was betrayed into a feeling of gladness when Giles strode to her side, and escorted her to a seat beside his own—not at the high table, but well above the salt cellar.

Trumpets flourished. Lionel, Duke of York, strode in, followed by a procession of men which included his nephew Henry Bolingbroke, the Henry Percys—father and son, Ralph Neville, Earl of Westmorland, Archbishop Arundel, and others who had been with Henry in Paris. Philippa had the feeling that, had it not been for her presence, Giles would have been among them.

"See young Thomas Fitzalan, Archbishop Arundel's nephew?" he shouted in her ear. She would not have heard him, else.

"The one in red brocade?" speculated Philippa in return.

"Aye. He, too, is out to regain the inheritance taken from him two years ago when his father was executed for treason. Did you hear of that disgraceful episode, and of the even more disgraceful murder of Richard's other uncle, Thomas, Duke of Gloucester, in Calais?"

"I heard something of the scandalous accusations made against the King," muttered Philippa.

"They were not made without just cause. Richard swore by John the Baptist that his uncle's exile would bring good to both of them, and that no harm would come to the Earl of Arundel. Both men are now dead. Do you wonder that others now lack trust in his assurances?"

"Mayhap not," admitted Phillipa reluctantly.

"You may not remember—you were only a child at the time—but some ten years ago the Earl of Arundel dared, with Gloucester and others, including Henry Bolingbroke, to attempt to limit Richard's excesses. And succeeded, for a while. They became known as the Lords Appellant. Despite appearances to the contrary, Richard never forgave any of them."

Philippa digested this in silence. Politics had never previously touched her life.

Despite his advanced age, Lionel was still a handsome man, his easy-going nature evident in his face. Lavishly robed in purple velvet and ermine, a chaplet of gold set with glowing jewels resting on his sweating brow, he had escorted his nephew to the table and, with the utmost courtesy, placed him next to himself. Before Grace was said, he ordered a flourish of trumpets, and rose again, commanding silence by the lifting of his hand.

''Most here support my nephew Henry Bolingbroke against his cousin, our Sovereign Prince, King Richard, in the matter of his inheritance,'' he began. ''Let it be known that I, too, render him my support. I believe the King has been led into error. I will use my utmost endeavours to bring peace between my nephews, and thus to this Realm.''

A great cheer rang around the vast Hall. Men sprang to their feet, lifting their mugs and goblets to drink to the Duke, Giles among them.

''Even he has deserted the King,'' scowled Philippa in disgust.

''Not deserted. You heard him. He hopes to mediate between the cousins. No one can deny the justice of Henry's cause. And remember, Thomas of Gloucester was York's brother. No doubt he feels as insecure as the rest of the great lords under Richard's capricious rule.''

Philippa's head began to whirl. Only yesterday life

had seemed so black and white, right and wrong so clearly distinguished. Suddenly, there were vast areas of grey in between which she did not wish to examine too closely.

She fixed her eyes on the source of all the confusion, admitting to herself that Henry was an agreeable surprise. Another handsome man—but which Plantagenet was not, according to popular acclaim? Not as tall as his uncle, rather stocky in fact, but reputedly an able soldier, strong, agile, an accomplished jouster and swordsman. Red hair curled into his nape from under a golden chaplet, a serpentine moustache and neatly trimmed beard edged his mouth and chin. His chaplet and robes were simpler than those of the Duke, though the high collar of his houppelande was studded with costly jewels. There was definitely something about him…

A charisma. An innate air of command which York lacked. No easy-going face, Henry's, but one full of determination and authority.

He would be no easy man to defeat.

Chapter Four

The calvacade moved off early the next morning. Philippa found herself more towards the front than the rear of the column, still riding between Giles and his squire. Young Wat proudly carried his knight's lance for him, the azure, twin-tailed pennon with its silver acorn streaming from its head.

Progress was slow. The lords and knights rode heavy destriers, who plodded purposefully forward, bearing the enormous weight of both man and armour. Since they were marching on Bristol, all were prepared for battle. Giles wore his haubergeon under his breastplate, with his bascinet and its dependent chain-mail. His arms and legs remained unprotected, the plates designed to armour them still strapped to Wat's horse.

Pikemen and archers, sweating inside their mailed vests and steel helmets, grooms leading strings of spare horses, servants—some driving meat on the hoof—and many of the whores walked, though a few of the latter rode donkeys or mules. Philippa, although aware of the straggling mass of humanity and beasts stretching for miles behind, was more interested in those who preceded them.

York, Bolingbroke and the magnates, with mounted retinues in attendance, snaked ahead in a brilliant panoply of scintillating armour and colourful surcoats overflown by heraldic banners and pennons borne on a forest of bristling lances. Eadulf travelled well behind, among the grooms, but Ida rode in attendance just ahead of Sir Malcolm de Boyes, who followed Giles closely, leading the men under his command. Of Sir William Grafton there was as yet no sign.

Philippa hoped he would catch up before they reached Bristol. Giles spoke confidently of obtaining necessities there, but supposing the city closed its gates against them? Her riding gown had become dusty and stained, her saffron surcoat crumpled. As for the spare kirtle Ida had packed, that seemed plain and dowdy set against the splendid gowns the ladies at Berkeley had worn. It would be nice to dress up and take her place with pride…

At Giles's side—aye, there lay the rub. It was because of him that she was in a position to shine. As an Earl's daughter she was entitled to a place at court, but what with her being betrothed to Giles, and her father's disinclination to have anything to do with court circles, the opportunity had never before arisen. She sighed gustily, earning an enquiring glance from Giles, which she studiously ignored.

After a long and tedious progress, enlivened only by the constant to and fro of heralds and marshals, Bristol appeared before them. Henry, an experienced general, had already made plans to deploy his forces. By the Priory of Saint James, part of the advancing column split off to the west, seeking to seal off Pyttey Gate and the other gates and bridges in that direction, while the second arm of the pincer moved off to the east, to cover the castle's Nether Gate, Temple Gate and the Redcliffe Gate to the south of the city. Henry and the main force continued ahead, making straight for the New Gate and the castle. The front of the column halted at the crossing of the Frome. Those behind caught up. Philippa eased her aching back. A tense hush fell over the ranks.

Suddenly a cheer went up. The townsfolk had flung open the gates of the city! Word flew round and back from mouth to mouth as the columns began to move forward again.

"What will Courtenay do?" wondered Giles aloud.

"Courtenay?" asked Philippa.

The frigid silence of yesterday had been broken long since. Travelling in such company had brought with it a sense of comradeship which had affected even Philippa's prejudiced mind.

"Sir Peter Courtenay, the Constable of Bristol Castle," Giles told her. "'Tis one of the greatest strongholds in the land. I doubt he will surrender it easily, since he holds it for the King. It is his duty to defend it, and 'twould be difficult to reduce."

Philippa bit her lip. "Will Bolingbroke fight?" she asked apprehensively.

"Only if he must," opined Giles with an expressive gesture of his hand. "He does not seek open confrontation, and must tread warily, for Richard holds his heir, young Harry of Monmouth, hostage."

"Hostage?" This was news to Philippa.

"Aye." Giles's face expressed disgust as he shortened his rein the better to control his mount. "Not officially, of course, but the King refused to allow Harry to leave Court when his father was banished, and took the boy to Ireland with him." He lifted his shoulders in a dismissive shrug. "Henry can as well wait for Richard without the castle's walls as within," he concluded.

The narrow streets of houses which had sprung up outside the city walls seethed with bodies as the column swarmed past. They moved forward only a pace at a time, and Philippa was glad of her stalwart protectors, for once or twice it seemed likely that she would be jostled from her horse's back, so great was the press.

She caught a glimpse of the great keep of the castle, framed by buildings at the end of the narrow lane. York and Bolingbroke had crossed the Frome and halted on the far bank, out of arrow range.

With a flourish of trumpets, York and Lancaster heralds rode slowly forward to state their masters' business. Philippa could just hear the distant voices, enough to grasp the gist of their message: allow their lords entry or be besieged until the King returned.

"I wouldn't come here if I were the King," muttered Philippa.

"Nor I. But Henry will have thought of that. He has spies out to discover the King's intentions."

Philippa glanced sharply at Giles, surprised he had caught her words in the noisy confusion of their progress. "He is exceptionally well organised," she commented sourly.

Giles grinned suddenly. "Henry Bolingbroke is no fool, and an outstanding soldier. Have no fear, Pippa. He will achieve what he desires."

Philippa wished she knew with certainty what that might be.

The wait seemed interminable. The bell of the nearby Dominican Priory tolled the hour of Nones, and its notes were echoed by every Church and Monastery in the city—and there semeed to be many. Philippa filled the time of waiting by eyeing enviously the brilliant bolts of cloth and other goods being snatched to safety from the merchants' stalls lining the narrow, noisome road. At the moment Bolingbroke's following was under control, but, if tens of thousands of men rampaged through the town bent on pillage, it was best to have one's merchandise—and one's womenfolk—safely locked away.

Spot, who had gambolled alongside, keeping well away from the horses' hoofs whenever possible, now forged ahead, foraging among the filth collected in the doorways, where he met up with an aggressive town cur. The snarling animals were well joined in battle before Philippa noticed. She gave a cry of angry alarm.

"Spot! Stop it! Come here at once!"

Not that Spot took the slightest notice, and Philippa was helpless to intervene. Fortunately the other dog's owner appeared to part the combatants. Spot, still bristling, his nose bloodied, eventually obeyed Philippa's anxious calls, and edged near, creeping obediently under the dangerous hoofs.

Giles snorted. "Stupid hound! That cur was twice his weight."

"Spot does not lack courage," Philippa defended her pet hotly.

"Nay. Just sense," grinned Giles.

Luckily, at that moment those in the front surged forward. The horses tossed their heads and strained against their bits. Everyone, including Spot, was diverted from his escapade.

"Hear that, d'Evreux? Courtenay has yielded," shouted a young and comely knight, of around Giles's own age, who was riding just ahead under a pennon bearing his portcullis badge. Triumph rang in his voice.

"Just like that!" exclaimed Giles joyously. "I could not believe he would do such a thing! 'Tis against all precedent! What think you, Beaufort? Was it the presence of York that influenced him?"

"Aye, perhaps, but more likely the fact that Ri-

chard took away his office of Chamberlain and gave
it to his own half-brother, John Holland. Courtenay,
like so many others, bears a grudge against Richard.
He has long been Henry's friend, and the castle sits
in the centre of an insurgent city.'' John Beaufort
smiled and urged his mount forward through the
press. Giles followed, taking Philippa with him.

''You wouldn't think he was born a bastard, and
owes his present honours and fortune to the King,''
remarked Philippa acidly.

Giles glanced at her sharply. ''Nay. He is every
inch a Plantagenet, and very like his father, John of
Gaunt. He is half-brother to Bolingbroke, do not forget, who has played the elder brother from the first.
Henry knighted John Beaufort long before Richard
legitimised him and his siblings as a favour to his
uncle of Lancaster. Beaufort's first loyalty is to
Henry, and always has been. He was devastated by
Richard's arbitrary banishment of his brother.'' He
paused and, if possible, straightened his straight back
even more as he gently prodded Majesty forward.
''No man can help his birth,'' he reminded her coldly.

Philippa coloured. For the moment she had forgotten that her future father-in-law had also been base-
born, though now he was an Earl.

''No. I suppose not,'' she agreed ungraciously, her
knee touching Giles's again as Blaze edged closer to
Majesty.

''And Gaunt defied convention to marry his leman,
once free of his political alliance with Constanza of

Castile. He had loved Katherine Swynford, John's mother, since shortly after Henry's mother, Blanche, died. As she loved him. 'Twas more than just an affair, Philippa,'' he told her gravely. ''Katherine was more his wife than ever Constanza was. She bore him four children, all legitimised now. The youngest, Joan, is wife to Ralph Neville. Be careful whom you label bastard.''

Philippa shifted uncomfortably in her saddle, and patted Blaze's neck to cover her disquiet. After just one evening in Court circles she had sensed the danger lurking in any ill-considered word. Old enmities and treachery seethed beneath the surface. All were united behind Henry Bolingbroke for the moment, but for how long could the present comradeship hold?

''Aye, I will,'' she promised grudgingly.

''Katherine was with John right to the end,'' Giles told her quietly. Somehow they seemed to be moving forward in a private enclave within the cheering, milling masses. Wat had been forced to drop behind. ''When he died, God rest his soul—'' he crossed himself quickly ''—she retired to her manor at Kettlethorpe. She did not seek position or riches. Only love.''

''Why is it,'' wondered Philippa bitterly, ''that love seems to exist only outside marriage?''

''Not always, Pippa.'' Giles's voice had softened, and his jewelled gauntlet came out to touch her thigh. '''Tis often so because men, as well as women, are forced into unsuitable alliances to secure a family's wealth and power. But love can grow, even from a marriage such as that. On occasion, lovers evade the demands of family aggrandisement. My parents were such lucky ones.''

Philippa edged Blaze away from the unsettling reach of that hand as soon as she was able. ''Yet they did not scruple to promise us to each other when I was but a child,'' she pointed out bitterly.

''I could have refused, Pippa. As could you. But if you remember, we rather liked each other. Neither one of us was averse to the match. Had you expressed a dislike—''

''I was too young to know!'' protested Philippa hotly.

''Young, but always very opinionated, my love! As for me—I always believed we would deal well together. Such love is rare, and not necessary to a successful marriage. Mutual respect and tolerance are far more important.''

''You think so?'' Philippa stared at him, disappointed. With his background, she had imagined he would have a more romantic attitude to marriage. His lean face was serious, his almost-blue eyes reassuring as they rested on her doubting features. Their horses collided, and her knee touched his for the umpteenth time. Philippa ignored the peculiar sensation the contact seemed to engender. She could not avoid it, so she must endure.

She was saved further response and speculation, for at that moment a new surge carried them through the gateway and into the castle enclave. Never had she seen such confusion. Knights, men-at-arms and Cheshire archers of the garrison, wearing the White Hart badge of the private army Richard had been recruiting and retaining for several years past, were being herded into a corner of a courtyard already crowded with an assortment of buildings, there to throw down their arms. The chaotic invasion of prancing horses and jubilant knights looked likely to crush all before it, so eager were they to remain close to their leaders.

There could never be room for all Henry's supporters, of course—even the inner bailey would hold only so many pavilions and men. Most retainers would have to find lodgings elsewhere in the town, or even, mayhap, camp outside its walls. But Giles was privileged, and, because of him, so was Philippa.

There were few ladies in Henry's train; most men had left their wives and families behind. But there were a few intrepid women who had decided to follow their husbands, and Philippa was to share a bed with two of them.

"I am here to make sure the Earl does not weaken," Helen Cooksey, Countess of Butterwick, told her as they settled into the chamber allotted to them. Lady Helen, a forceful woman of around five and thirty years, attempted a rather brittle smile with her thin lips, as her tiring-woman fixed the wrought-gold, jewel-encrusted bosses into which her lank hair had been coiled to either side of her angular face. "He wavers between a misplaced loyalty to the King and a desire to regain the offices taken from him and given to Richard's cronies. What do you here, wench?''

''I am to be wed,'' replied Philippa grimly, concentrating on smearing salve on Spot's damaged nose.

''Wed? To whom? When?'' asked Isobel Fortescue, wife to one of Lancaster's tenants, eagerly. Younger than Helen Cooksey, and pretty in an insipid way, she had admitted to accompanying her husband for selfish reasons. ''If I am with him,'' she had confessed, a tide of red sweeping up her neck and face, ''he will not be tempted to seek his pleasure elsewhere.''

''Pshaw!'' Helen had exclaimed. ''What matter if he does? All men go a-whoring to slake their lust and find their pleasure; they bed their wives only to get heirs.''

''Not all,'' Isobel had protested with quiet insistence. ''Miles says I give him more pleasure than any of the lewd women he knew before we were wed. And I... I enjoy receiving him in my bed.'' The blush had deepened, and a secret smile had curved her shapely lips. Now Philippa eyed her warily as she let Spot go, and rose from her knees.

''I have been betrothed to Sir Giles d'Evreux this eight years past.'' She flung out a hand in helpless bewilderment. ''He suddenly insists I honour the contract, and is arranging for us to marry within days.

But I do not want to!'' she burst out, unable to hide her rebellion.

"Oh, but Sir Giles!'' Isobel regarded her as though she had been given the pot of gold at the end of the rainbow. "Why would you not wish to wed with such a renowned knight?''

"Renowned?''

"Aye. Did you not know?'' enquired Helen Cooksey curiously.

Philippa shook her head. Her heart began to beat faster than usual. She really knew very little about her future husband.

"He is famous for his prowess in the lists, and is one of the best swordsmen in the world,'' Isobel informed her eagerly, her eyes shining with enthusiasm.

"I knew he jousted,'' muttered Philippa. "'Tis how he makes his fortune.''

"And a goodly one, I'll warrant! I well remember a tournament at Windsor several years past when he was acclaimed the most worthy knight to take the field! All the ladies were at his feet. He could have wed any maiden there, yet you protest yourself unwilling! Why so?''

"Because he—'' Philippa cut herself off short. These women were on Giles's side in this. She had better not call him traitor. Discretion came hard to her, but she was learning. "He has neglected me for nigh on five years,'' she growled instead. "Now he suddenly wants to wed me in haste, without family or friends present, with my father lying sick, and with no time to prepare a gown…''

''I cannot say that I blame him,'' observed Helen with a cynical smile. ''I dare say he got a surprise when he saw you again, my dear. You must have been full young and undergrown when last you met. Perhaps you did not excite his manhood then, but I'll wager my last gold noble you stir it now!''

It was Philippa's turn to blush. She was not used to such crude talk. ''I cannot think why,'' she retorted stiffly.

''Don't be stupid, wench! You have the face of a dark angel and the body of a goddess. What more is needed to excite a man? Of course he desires you. Make the most of it while you may. His passion will soon die.''

''You speak from experience?'' asked Isobel, with a chilly disdain which surprised Philippa. Isobel did not like Helen Cooksey. Neither, actually, did she.

''I shall have to see that it doesn't, shall I not?'' she returned tartly. Not that she meant to do anything of the kind. She did not want Giles's passion. The thought of his touching her sent shivers of fear down her spine. But she would not admit that to anyone, least of all to the worldly Lady Butterwick.

''I will help you,'' offered Isobel shyly. ''You have enough apparel here to make a goodly bride.''

''Thank you,'' murmured Philippa, not ungrateful for the offer, since it was made in good faith. Sir William had arrived with her coffers, and Isobel had delighted in examining their contents. Philippa suspected the knight had stripped Alban Castle of its entire contents, for all her clothes were there. Something else to hold against Giles.

"I'll vouch the bridegroom would not protest an the wench turned up naked," sniggered the Countess, bringing a new surge of colour to Philippa's pale cheeks.

"Will you wear your chaplet this evening, my lady?" enquired Ida loudly, emphasising her mistress's title with great deliberation.

Philippa smiled gratefully, thankful to feel her blush subside. "Aye, Ida. I must dress as befits my rank."

Helen Cooksey lifted an arched brow and grinned crookedly, passing no comment. But Philippa noted that the older woman subsequently curbed her patronising tone.

The following morning Philippa was woken by the sound of banging in the bailey below. In the pale light of dawn, she slid from the edge of the bed she had shared with the other two women, stepped round the pallets of their servants, and gazed down from the window embrasure.

Men were erecting a scaffold. Her stomach muscles tightened. She knew that some of Richard's officials had been inside the castle, waiting anxiously to meet their King on his hasty return from Ireland to confront his cousin. Surrender of the stronghold had delivered them into Henry's hands, and they had been imprisoned in the Great Dungeon tower.

She looked out across the embattled wall which divided the old Norman castle, where she had been lodged, from the massive keep where the men must be awaiting their doom. There had been talk last evening of their treachery to the realm they had plundered in Richard's name. William Scrope, Earl of Wiltshire, the Treasurer, had come in for the most severe vilification, for he had raised the extortionate taxes and imposed the forced loans so hated by nobility and burgesses alike. But his henchmen, John Bussey, Henry Green and Thomas Bagehot, upstarts of the Royal Household, were scarcely less universally hated.

Philippa gripped the edge of the embrasure so tightly that her knuckles showed white. Could hate warrant a summary execution? The others were awake now, and crowded to the window to see.

"I thought so," said Helen Cooksey with satisfaction. "Those men have ravaged the land with their financial chicanery. They deserve the scaffold."

"Without trial?" demanded Philippa bitterly.

"Oh, they will have been tried by their peers," said Helen carelessly.

"But how can they execute them?" whispered Philippa. "Without the King's sanction 'twould be murder."

"Would the King easily condemn his cronies? Or those who have filled his coffers? Nay, lady, 'tis for the magnates of this land to decide their fate. The great lords have too long been denied their rightful powers.''

"It seems they have already decided," observed Philippa indignantly.

For some reason not clear to her, Bagehot was to be spared. The executions of the other three were to take place immediately after dinner. Nauseated by the prospect, Philippa ate little, sitting in silent protest throughout the lengthy meal.

Giles attempted to divert her thoughts. His cheerful announcement that he had obtained a licence from the bishop, and that they would be wed before Vespers and make supper their wedding feast, brought nothing but frigid silence and a look of such loathing from Philippa's dark, eloquent eyes that Giles stopped trying to humour her.

Insensitive fool! raged Philippa inwardly. To fix their wedding to follow so closely upon the executions! Could he not understand her revulsion?

Apparently not. With consummate composure and complete disregard for her feelings, he worked his way steadily through a pottage of venison broth pungent with herbs, a dish of succulent lampreys, thick slices from a roasted ox and a solitee which consisted of mixed berries cooked in honey. The whole was accompanied by soft white bread and fine Bordeaux wine, and he conversed the while with others at their board.

The executions were on everyone's lips. Philippa found herself the only one with doubts as to their legality. The sentences were considered well deserved, and the sooner carried out the better.

After the meal almost everyone trooped to the bailey, where the scaffold had been erected. It would be fine entertainment to see the detested oppressors' heads roll. Philippa could not bear to watch. Her chamber overlooked the block, so she could find no refuge there. Instead, she found her way to the King's orchard, which was across the moat and bordered the river, though the great defensive wall denied her any view of that, except for the tops of the masts of ships moored in the port beyond the bridge.

Insects filled the arbour with the sound of their lazy drone as they searched the blossoms for nectar. Fruit trees provided shade, roses, herbs and pink gillyflowers filled the summer air with fragrance, masking the stink from the polluted river. Although the waterway sounded busy with small boats plying between the ships and the town, ferrying goods and people under the low arches of the bridge, and shrill cries fractured the peace, Philippa found the place restful. She sank down on the hard turf under a small apple tree, and rested back against its trunk, swatting half-heartedly at a worrisome fly.

Bells throughout the town tolled the hour of Sext—the hour appointed for the executions. Philippa buried her head between her knees, attempting to shut out all sound, knowing cheers would greet each death. But she could not shut off her mind. It was midday. She had so few hours of freedom left. By Vespers, she would be married to Giles.

There was still time to escape. She eyed the steps

leading up to the allure. This stretch of curtain wall was unguarded. From the wall-walk she could climb into an embrasure and plead for a ride in one of the passing boats. If she jumped into the river she should escape injury, though the thought of immersing herself in the filthy water made her shudder with distaste. And mayhap there would be too much bank, too many boats lining it...

If she did risk it, and was successful, most probably someone in the town would give her refuge, for a price. But she had nothing with which to buy such services. She had scant money with her, and what little she had was in the chamber overlooking the executions, together with all her most precious jewellery.

Besides, Giles would find her. Even if he did not, what future did she have? With no money or posessions she would have to beg—or worse—to eat. Much as she hated Giles and all he stood for, marriage to him seemed the lesser evil at the moment. Prioress Mary-Luke had virtually denied her any chance of escape, and had commanded obedience to God's will. Tears squeezed from between her shut eyelids. Why was His will so difficult to accept?

Something touched her downbent head. She jerked upright, instantly defensive.

She looked ready to hiss and claw like a startled kitten, thought Giles ruefully, noting with compassion the tears drying on her cheeks. Poor maid! He wished he could have arranged things otherwise, but wed him she must, and to leave her longer under her father's influence would be to pile up worse trouble for the future. Better that she knew what was happening to their land. Eventually she would see that Richard must be bridled. Enlightenment would end the discord between them. His pulses quickened at the thought of Philippa soft and pliant in his arms. The day would come, he vowed. And soon.

He dropped to the turf beside her. She ostenchta-tiously snatched her skirt aside, tucking its volumi-nous folds under her knees. "I thought you would be enjoying the executions," she remarked icily.

"I do not enjoy such spectacles, Pippa. Whatever you may think of me, I am not a vindictive or sadistic man. Justice must be done, but it can be done without my presence. I would rather talk with my bride."

A shudder ran through Philippa's body, which Giles noticed with a dismay he was careful not to show.

"If you call that justice, we have nothing more to say to each other," she responded flatly.

Giles drew in a deep breath. It seemed his task might be more difficult than he had thought. "Phil-ippa, you are ignorant of the world and of politics," he pointed out reasonably. "You cannot judge such things by what you have seen at Alban Castle. Your sire has been a great knight, but no courtier or poli-tician. How can you know what is right and what is wrong when the nation's future is at stake?"

"I know treason is wrong," muttered Philippa.

"Much depends on your definition of that word."

"Those men," she choked, "they are not traitors! They served the King loyally!"

Too loyally, he thought grimly. But if he admitted that they had only been carrying out their Sovereign's orders, criticism of their actions could be construed as treason. He must temporise. "And right badly, too." He shrugged. "Their greed has made him hated throughout the realm."

"I hate you!"

The words seemed torn from her throat, and echoed hollowly in Giles's gut. She would not listen to reason! Had that episode at Alban really killed all hope for their future together? He eyed the girl's mutinous face, the enmity in her eyes, the heave of her tender breasts under the layers of kirtle and cote-hardie, saw the nervousness she tried to hide, and prayed that it should not be so.

He had once declared patience as one of his virtues, but in truth it was wearing thin, and he wondered at his determination to wed the maid in the face of her fierce opposition. Why not allow her to go her own way? To flirt with danger, as her brother seemed determined to do?

His lips tightened. He could not allow this wench to dictate to him! For her own safety she *would* wed with him, and he would teach her to become a loving and obedient wife.

But how? Charm did not work. He could not cajole. There seemed only one way left. He would have to demand, to order.

"Very well—" he met her hostile gaze coolly "—hate me. Make things difficult for yourself, Philippa. But I swear by the Holy Rood you shall wed with me, and this very day, as arranged." He watched the panic flit across her expressive face, and his voice softened by an almost imperceptible fraction. "I suggest you go to ready yourself for the ceremony. Henry Bolingbroke and all my friends and brothers-in-arms will be present. I feel sure you will not wish to discredit your family by appearing either reluctant or badly attired.''

''My family and friends are not here to see me wed,'' she pointed out shakily.

''My people will not be present, either. When this crisis is over we will throw a feast and invite all our relations and friends to celebrate our union. But it is important that we wed immediately, Pippa. I want you under my protection.''

''Why should I need your protection?'' she demanded frostily. ''Your arrogance is overwhelming. It seems to me it is you who are running into danger. When the King hears you supported Bolingbroke—''

''When peace is made between the cousins, Richard will not move against Henry's supporters. They are too powerful.''

''I still cannot see why I need your protection.''

Giles sighed. '''Tis too complicated to explain, Pippa.'' He did not want to tell her that if peace was not made there could only be one winner. Richard would be forced from the throne. With the following Henry had already amassed Richard must compromise or lose his kingdom. Mayhap he had lost it already. But in her present mood he could not burden her with that knowledge. ''Believe me,'' he told her quietly, ''you will be safer married to me.''

''I suppose,'' she observed scornfully, ''you need to find an excuse for your autocratic demand.''

At that moment the first cry of approval—triumph, glee, satisfaction—carried above the edifice of the castle towers from the bailey beyond. Philippa shut her eyes and fingered the beads at her waist, her lips working in agitated prayer. Giles hastily crossed himself. Watching her anguished face, pity such as he had never known before surged through him.

She was still so young, with so much of life's harshness and hardship yet to face. She could not be expected to see the risks her father and brother ran in opposing one as powerful as Henry Bolingbroke, rightful Duke of Lancaster. Especially now that Henry was backed by the King's own Regent, Lionel, Duke of York. How could she be blamed for not seeing things through his own more experienced and somewhat jaundiced eye?

On an impulse, he reached out for her and drew her to him. Her resistance was nominal. With a choked, piteous cry, she buried her face in the fine velvet of his cote-hardie, and wept.

How long she poured out her grief and uncertainty, her ears closed to the echo of repeated cheers by the sound of her own racking sobs, she never afterwards knew. But the feel of strong, gentle arms holding her had never been more welcome. Giles might have been her father, comforting her in some childish hurt.

He held her cradled against him, her head pressed to his breast by one tenderly caressing hand. She nestled in his arms, soft and infinitely sweet, like a frightened kitten. He held her so until the last cries of triumph from the executions had long died away.

Eventually her sobs quietened, her grief spent. She

felt empty, drained. It took her some moments to realise where she was. She gazed up into Giles's intent
face with eyes whose lids were red-rimmed and swollen with tears.

What she saw there brought a strangled sound from
her throat. She tore herself from his protecting arms
and jumped to her feet. "You need not think—" she
began chokingly, only to be interrupted by Giles's
calm voice.

"I would not presume, my lady." He, too, had
risen. He bowed with faultless formality, his gaze
tender behind the cool façade of his face. "We will
meet again, in the chapel."

Philippa did not see the expression in his eyes. She
only knew that she had allowed her need to overcome
her principles, and that Giles's arms were treacherously seductive.

Chapter Five

Isobel had taken charge, insisting Philippa wear her best gown for the occasion; and Ida, entering into the spirit of the thing, had shaken out and pressed the costly samite of which the kirtle was fashioned. The material's shimmering silken threads, interwoven with silver to form an intricate pattern of drifting leaves and flowers, flowed softly over Philippa's slender hips to the narrow band of miniver fur edging the full, slightly trailing hem. The patterned sleeves and bodice of the kirtle emerged from the miniver trim of a short, sleeveless cote-hardie made from a silvery material and fastened down the front with silver buttons. Ida had lovingly sponged and brushed all the fur to a pristine, snowy whiteness.

Philippa made no protest at the choice. Since leaving Giles in the pleasaunce she had stopped pretending that she could avoid the marriage. She just wanted it to be over quickly. The emotional outburst had left her drained. She had become no more than a puppet for others to manipulate.

Feeling abruptly returned to swamp her in a new wave of panic as she smoothed down the tightly buttoned sleeves of the kirtle, which extended beyond her wrists to cover her knuckles. In less than an hour Giles's ring would rest on the finger she had touched, a sign of his loveless possession. She gripped her hands together, thrusting down her dismay with fierce determination.

He knew she was reluctant to be his bride, but he did not have to know how greatly she feared becoming emotionally ensnared by one she could only think of as an enemy. She had told him she hated him, and she did, most fervently, for the grief he had caused, and yet...and yet, hard as she might try, she could not deny his attraction, the masculine magnetism which intimidated as well as seduced her. His embrace held an allure, a promise of security, of something more fundamental to which she could not put a name.

''We picked forget-me-nots and gillyflowers for your chaplet,'' Isobel explained, placing the carefully woven, fragrant pink and blue circlet on the drifting black curls which hung around Philippa's shoulders and down her back as a sign of her maidenhood. ''You look like a moon princess!'' she declared happily. ''Dark, pale and silvery.''

''Sir Giles would prefer something warmer—a

sun goddess, I'll warrant,'' opined Helen with a derisive laugh.

She had taken little interest in the proceedings so far, confining herself to interjecting a trenchant or ribald comment from time to time. Philippa had hoped she would absent herself from the unwelcome ceremony, but the Countess was already dressed in some splendour for the occasion. Her gown of crimson brocade and cloth of gold completely overshadowed that of the bride. One side of her kirtle had been embroidered with the chevrons and crosslets of her father's coat of arms, the other charged with the swans and battle-axe of Butterwick. The foliated golden coronet set above the jewelled and enamelled boxes covering her ears allowed no trace of hair to mar the perfection of a high, smooth brow. Hard, sharp eyes went with a thin, discontented mouth to impair what could otherwise have been a handsome visage.

Isobel's soft pliancy was hidden beneath the folds of a simple kirtle of saffron flurt silk, most of which was concealed by a rather old-fashioned green damask sideless surcoat, though the hem of the latter was caught up to show the buttercup-coloured skirt beneath. Her fair hair was bound in simple cauls topped by a silver circlet, her cheeks were flushed with pleasure and expectancy, her blue eyes alight with goodwill. The contrast between the two women could not have been greater.

Impulsively, Philippa hugged the younger woman.

"Thank you, Lady Fortescue," she murmured huskily.

"Call me Isobel, do."

"My friends call me Pippa."

Isobel smiled. "I will gladly count myself your friend, Pippa. Don't be nervous. All will be for the best, you'll see."

Philippa straightened her spine and firmed her trembling lips. "I cannot imagine how, but I will try to believe you, Isobel. In any case, there is naught I can do to evade my duty."

"So you will meet the challenge with courage," nodded Isobel bracingly. "I would expect nothing else from you, Pippa."

Courage was something Philippa did not normally lack. Physical courage was no problem, and she could express her opinions with a heat and conviction which amused her family. But to be caught in a trap from which there was no escape...that was different. And to Philippa her enforced marriage was just that.

A page came to summon the bride to the chapel. Ida fastened a heavily jewelled necklace around Philippa's bare throat. "There, sweeting," she whispered, giving her mistress a reassuring hug, "you will shame no one this day."

Philippa followed the page wordlessly, escorted by the two ladies and Ida. Spot roused himself to trot at their heels, tail waving uncertainly, as though he sensed something amiss and was not sure of his welcome. Philippa did not have the heart to bid the dog to stay. Her pet's presence would give her comfort, and she needed all of that she could get.

Giles waited for her by the door of the chapel, his face inscrutable until his eyes lighted on the gossamer figure of his bride, so dainty, so ethereal did she appear in her silvery finery. Warmth and, yes, admiration leapt into his heavily lashed eyes as he extended his hand in welcome.

Something in Philippa's breast contracted painfully at sight of him, tall and straight, his knightly jewelled belt and the glittering baselard in its golden scabbard resting on the azure velvet sheathing his lean hips. His lighter-hued hose clung to his thighs, betraying every movement of the muscles beneath. He, too, wore a chaplet, though his was mostly woven of foliage, with a few marigolds to add the illusion of gold.

Two priests, with a following of youthful acolytes, waited with him. The ceremony proceeded immediately. Philippa promised to take Giles to be her wedded husband, to forsake all other, to hold only unto him in sickness and in health, in riches and in poverty, in well and woe, until death parted them, her throat so tight that the, ''Yea, sir,'' demanded of her would hardly come out.

Giles had made his responses in a firm, determined voice. When directed, he placed a wrought-gold ring on her finger. Philippa wondered where he had got it from. Her thumb found and investigated the strange, intrusive object. Too large, it hung heavy as an iron shackle.

They moved to the altar for the nuptial mass. At the end of the service Giles helped his bride to her feet, and leaned forward to kiss her, as was expected of him. Only Philippa knew that his lips, for all they had appeared to linger, barely touched hers. Even so, the effect had been devastating. Revulsion, she told herself, grimly enduring the tremors coursing through her body.

Outside the chapel the guests crowded round. Philippa found herself being embraced by Henry Bolingbroke. He kissed her heartily and beamed with avuncular goodwill.

"We look forward to the bedding, Lady Philippa," he told her, winking broadly.

Her heart thudding painfully at the reminder of a future ordeal, her face aflame, Philippa forced herself to meet his shrewd eyes, and saw strain in their depths. She could feel the tension emanate from the man's body—a tangible thing, matching her own. For all his apparent confidence and ease of manner, Henry Bolingbroke was strung taut as a bow-string. The shock of this discovery made her forget her own screaming nerves for a moment. It must be costing this man dear to confront his cousin to demand his rightful inheritance. One thing was certain: right or wrong, he did not act lightly. His very life was at stake, not to mention the lives of his children and those of many of his friends.

His impact faded as others claimed the privilege of saluting the bride, and she forgot Henry Bolingbroke in the doubtful pleasure of being kissed by divers men—old, young, rough, courteous, clean, malodorous, sober, drunk.

Giles kept an arm possessively round her waist, a restraint she almost welcomed, but even so some of the more boisterous knights made a meal of it, laughing and chaffing Giles on his good fortune in acquiring so delightful a bride. The touch of some was bearable, of others definitely not.

But none of their kisses produced in her anything like the sensation Giles's brief salute had done. It had not been revulsion she'd felt. She knew exactly what *that* felt like now, having suffered so many unwelcome embraces.

When the party trooped in to the Hall for supper, Philippa was given a place of honour at Henry's right, with Giles on her other side. A festive atmosphere pervaded the company. Three executions and a wedding in one day were worthy of hearty celebration.

Philippa had, to some extent, relaxed. The deed was done. For good or ill, she was Giles's wife. No brooding, no rebellious thoughts could alter fact. As for the bedding... She crumpled a tiny piece of fine white bread between clammy fingers and chewed it round to stop her teeth from chattering, washing the resultant stodge down with a gulp of wine. Her empty stomach rumbled.

She replaced the silver-rimmed maple-wood mazer on the table with shaking hands. Giles lifted the vessel and raised it to his own lips before putting it down and reaching for one of her hands. Philippa wriggled her fingers, trying to escape his firm clasp without making it too obvious. He squeezed the harder.

"Eat, wife," he commanded softly. "You refused dinner. I cannot have my bride fainting from hunger before the night is through."

"You—you brute!" she spat, her cheeks scarlet.

"'Brute'?" He lifted the captive hand to his lips in a courtly salute, the only one present able to see the reckless defiance in his bride's dusky eyes. One shapely, golden-tipped brow lifted in tolerant amusement. "You tempt me to teach you what brutish behaviour is, Pippa." His thumb stroked the palm of the hand he still held seductively. Philippa's arm jerked uncontrollably as the sensation leapt up it, and he laughed softly. "Eat, my love," he murmured huskily. "Here, let me…"

His voice trailed off as he used his knife to cut a piece of roast mutton from the thick slice on the trencher they shared, picked the morsel up in his fingers, and carried it to her mouth. Philippa pressed her lips shut, but Giles merely chuckled and began to tease them with the meat.

She wanted to turn her head away, but his blue-grey eyes in their nests of tawny lashes held hers. Why was she incapable of breaking the spell cast by his gaze? Philippa didn't know, nor why her mouth opened and she accepted the piece of flesh, but she chewed greedily once the taste of the succulent morsel began to stimulate her juices. The moment she swallowed, Giles offered another titbit for her consumption.

To those around his actions were those of a charming, attentive and lover-like bridegroom. Only Philippa knew that it was sheer force of an overwhelming personality which kept her accepting the food from his fingers.

"Thank you, Giles," she managed at last in a strangled whisper. "I can feed myself."

"An you have the will," he agreed dubiously.

"I promise."

He smiled, brilliance lighting his handsome features as he gave her fingers a final squeeze before releasing them. "Courage, my wife," he whispered. There it was again. The admonition to have courage. Why the devil did they all believe she lacked it? 'Twas plain, straightforward inclination she was short of.

Mummers and dancing followed the meal, and the sun had disappeared beneath the horizon before anyone made a move to escort the bridal couple to their chamber.

The men led Giles off while Isobel, Lady Butterwick and a number of other women took Philippa to the State Chamber, loaned to them for the night by an expansive Duke of York. The huge state bed, raised on a platform and draped with purple hangings embroidered with white harts—an uncomfortable reminder that this was the King's bed—intimidated Philippa. She could not look. Nor could she bear to gaze at the royal arms and banners glowing colourfully against the stone walls in the light of myriad candles.

The women fluttered about her, though it was Ida who washed her and rubbed in a liquid, made from rosemary, mint, rose and lemon peel distilled in grape spirit, to perfume her skin. With her hair freshly combed, Philippa was led to the expansive bed and ensconced on a swansdown-filled mattress under a heavy silken coverlet.

"You will not need a blanket tonight," remarked one of the ladies, wife to a member of the castle's garrison.

"They will doubtless indulge in enough exercise to keep them warm," chuckled Lady Helen, with a malicious glance at Philippa's white face.

Isobel leaned forward and whispered in Philippa's ear. "Take no notice of the ribaldry, Pippa," she advised. "Greet your bridegroom with modesty and joy. With Sir Giles to husband, your marriage bed will be a wondrous place, an you will allow it."

Philippa tried to smile acknowledgement. Isobel's romantic dreams and her own were very different. Or—were they?

July had been warm and stormy, and that evening was hot and humid. The silk clung to Philippa's clammy body as she alternated between hot and cold sweats engendered by the temperature and apprehension. She drew the cover up under her armpits as she sank deeper into the mattress and leaned back against the pillows to await the arrival of the groom.

Giles was brought in by a group of boisterous knights, many far from sober, led by Henry Boling-broke. Her husband wore a long, fur-trimmed gown, which was torn from his shoulders as he reached the bed.

Philippa knew what a naked man looked like; she had caught forbidden glimpses of her father and brothers—though two of them, Daniel and Hugo, had died of the plague four years since—living as they had in the close confines of Hall and solar until more recent years. She was no innocent about mating, either. Dogs, cats, horses—the farm animals too—she had witnessed them all. As a child, before her mother's death in childbirth, she had heard her parents, seen the heaving bulk of shifting bedclothes... heard her father's grunts and her mother's cries...and wondered whether they were of pain or pleasure until she had heard the woman's soft laugh and the man's whispered endearments.

'Twas natural, normal and nothing to be shamed about. So why did her face grow warm, her hands sweat at sight of Giles's lean, broad-shouldered body, his flat belly and the bush of golden-brown hair between his thighs only partially hiding his—?

The part was whisked modestly under cover as Giles slid in beside her. Thanks be to the Holy Virgin, the bed was so large that he seemed a safe distance away. There was space for two others where the demanding swansdown rose like a protective bastion between them. But that did not stop the colour seeping from her cheeks, the cold, clammy damp of apprehension prickling her skin. Courage! she admonished herself sternly. Seeing, knowing and doing were such vastly different things.

No one troubled themselves over a trembling bride, one moment flushed as though in a fever, the next pale as death. This maid might be older than most, but such a reaction was only to be expected of a virgin.

Sweet herbs and flowers were strewn over floor, and those thought to induce fertility over the bedcovers; the priest present blessed the bridal bed and the couple in it, praying for their fruitfulness and the gift of many lusty sons and daughters. Flasks of wine were brought in, cups filled and passed around. Henry Bolingbroke raised his and gave the toast. With jovial shouts and great ribaldry, everyone drank to the success of the coming nuptials.

At length it was over and the noisy company filed out, leaving the bride and groom in conspicuous privacy to consummate the union. The instant the heavy door closed behind the last reveller, Philippa struggled up from the shifting swansdown's clutching embrace, swung her legs over the side of the bed, and reached urgently for her chamber-gown.

Before she could grasp it, Giles had moved and, in a swift tangle of silken covers and undulating feathers, gripped her arm in a clasp like a band of steel.

"Where do you think you are going?" he demanded with a wicked lift of one expressive brow.

"To—to…" Philippa ran her tongue round leaf-dry lips, seeking moisture. Giles's eyes darkened to a deep slate-grey at the unconsciously provocative action. "Away from you!" she finished breathlessly, alarmed anew by the expression she read in those vibrant eyes.

She tried to wrench herself free, but Giles simply tightened his grasp, turning her tender flesh white and bloodless where his fingers bit. "You are hurting me," she protested hotly.

"Your own fault, my wife," he murmured. But his grip slackened, though not so much as to set her free.

"Pippa." There was determination, tenderness, a kind of resignation in his voice and expression as he sighed and pulled her closer to him. The silk was swathed about them, the mattress billowing, but, even so, in places she could feel his bare flesh against hers. The comforting bastion between them had disappeared as though by magic.

His now guarded eyes looked down on her intently. He had drawn her so close that the sensitive tips of her breasts rubbed against the fine mat of golden-brown hair covering his chest. Philippa trembled. In her heart she knew that, if Giles had married her sooner, before her father's seizure, before she had branded him traitor, she would have welcomed him as her husband. Already she could feel the tendrils of attraction twining around her heart and emotions, threatening to blot out every other consideration.

She could not allow that to happen! She must hold to her principles! She pushed at his chest, putting space between them.

"'Tis no use, wife," murmured Giles deeply. "Whether you are willing or not, our marriage will be consummated this night. I want no threat of annulment to come between us in the future. You are mine, and what is mine, I hold!"

"You are welcome to my dowry," spat Philippa. "'Tis my person I wish to deny you—"

"I have little interest in your dowry, Pippa. Else, despite your youthful interest in manly pursuits rather than in men themselves, I would have wed you years ago, bedded you and left you, while taking your undoubtedly rich manors into my keeping. But I chose to wait, hoping..." His voice trailed off, and Philippa frowned, wondering exactly what he had hoped. He quickly gathered his thoughts and went on wryly, "But I waited too long, I see that. However," he added softly, his voice a tender threat, "I will not now be denied the delights of your sweet body, my wife. I shall demand and take my husbandly rights."

"Very well." Philippa knew when further resistance was useless. Wives were expected to be submissive and obedient to their wedded lords. No cry for help would be heeded, and Giles was far too strong and agile for her to escape him for long. "Take your pleasure, my lord," she invited coldly.

She flopped back into the swansdown's embrace, massaging the angry red weals which had appeared where Giles had first grasped her arm, and shut her eyes. Men had the right to treat their wives as they willed, could flog them into submission. She doubted Giles would be as ruthless as that. Not, at any rate, the youthful, lively, kindly Giles she had known since childhood. But this new, mature, domineering Giles, the Giles who had become a traitor to his King? Whatever, she preferred not to put his ruthlessness to the test. Indignant, reluctant submission was her best course now.

"'Twould give me greater pleasure—and you, too, Pippa—were you a willing partner, my love."

Giles's voice had become deep, vibrant and coaxing. Like the soft touch of his hands on her breast and neck. Like the tickle of his beard, the whisper of his lips as they brushed her closed lids and then moved down, trailing over her high cheekbone, her hollowed cheek, to find the small mole at the corner of her tightly clamped mouth. There they lingered for a moment before travelling along the line of her jaw to the sharp angle below her ear. His tongue found the nearby hollow, flicked her lobe, probed the orifice itself.

Philippa lay rigid, striving to ignore the persuasiveness of his overwhelming male presence, the heady odour of clean male flesh scented with thyme, the trickles of excitement dancing along her nerves. Determination not to enjoy what had been forced upon her grew. Even when the sudden darting of his tongue made her stifle a gasp, when his clever fingers brought her nipples to stand proud and erect, ready for...for...

She could not help the moan that escaped her as Giles abandoned her face and neck and brought his mouth down to claim one of those treacherous hardened peaks. The hair on his face caressed the tender flesh surrounding it. At the same time his hand inserted itself between her thighs and his fingers began exploring parts of her anatomy previously entirely her own preserve. Her moan became a cry of protest at his invasion of the secret centre of her womanhood.

With a sense of shock she recognised the sensation his probing fingers wrought. 'Twas only of recent years that the sight of animals mating had brought unease to her, strange reactions to assail her womanly parts.

''No!'' she moaned.

''Yes.'' Giles lifted his mouth for just long enough to emit the one breathless word. Then his lips descended again, on the other breast, and the exquisite pain of his sucking shot straight to the place his fingers probed.

Hot, hard, throbbing flesh pressed against her thigh. She felt her muscles weakening. Her limp arms shifted, instinctively seeking to clasp to herself the man giving her so much unexpected pleasure.

Just in time her brain cleared and she remembered. She hated him! She was an unwilling victim! She stiffened in an utter rejection all the more determined because she had almost succumbed, and brought her thighs sharply together to stop her husband's delicate, arousing caresses.

"Get on with it!" she spat. Or would have spat, had her throat not been so closed with emotion that her voice came out in a croak quite unlike its normal self.

Giles stopped his wooing. He had felt her momentary surrender, knew that her rejection was one of will, not of distate. So be it.

"As you command, my lady," he returned icily, his tone quite at odds with the fierce anger which threatened to overwhelm him because of her stupid, wilful rejection and of the hot demand of the blood pulsing urgently through his veins.

He heaved his body over hers, pinning her rigid, resistant form to the bed, his mouth a thin line of determination as he clamped it over hers. His teeth ground against her lips and then her teeth, forcing both apart until he had gained the entry his tongue demanded. Even in his anger he remembered she was a virgin still, and moderated his first thrust, exploring her readiness, thankful to find that her body was still partially prepared to receive him. Once past the slight barrier of her maidenhead he waited a moment, expecting a cry of pain which did not come. Only then did he unleash his body, driving again and again, hard and fast. His release came swiftly. For a moment he lay supine; then, with a single great shudder, he rolled from his still and silent wife and, turning his back, composed himself for sleep.

Or so it seemed to Philippa. She did not know that her husband lay staring into space, ashamed of his punishing outburst while still believing it fully justified.

His mouth had suffocated her, his body crushed her, while his hard tongue and…and other thing had invaded her. She clenched her teeth against the indignity of it all. Hate boiled up and spilled over into the clenched, impotent fists digging into the mattress on either side of her. The knowledge that it could all have been so different, that, had she allowed her muscles to relax as they'd begun to do, had she not angered Giles with her rejection of his tenderness, things would have been very different, did nothing to ease her sense of violation. She ached down below, her thighs were stuck together with something wet. Blood, she supposed disgustedly. The women would be back in the morning to examine the sheets for evidence of the success of the union. Giles would have that one satisfaction, at least. There would be no question of an annulment now.

Some new-born, womanly instinct told her it would be the only true satisfaction her husband would reap from the night's work. He had eased his body, but, she recognised, he had been seeking more than that.

She ought to feel that it served him right. But she did not. Why had she denied him the pleasure he sought, forced him into treating her the way he had? Because she wanted to be able to justify her hatred?

Tears welled in her eyes, rolled down her temples and into the tangle of her hair. Deep down she did not hate her husband at all. She had been fighting a rearguard action against liking him too well, and thus becoming a traitor to her family loyalty.

Chapter Six

Giles had gone when Philippa woke the next morning. The hollow where he had lain felt cold to her touch.

Ida was pottering about the room, filling a small tub with warm water from a row of pitchers just inside the door. The arrival of those had probably wakened her. The tiring-maid turned as she heard her mistress stir, and smiled enquiringly. "You slept well, my lady?"

Philippa blushed. "Er—yes."

"Good." This time the grin stretched Ida's round face into a mask of satisfaction. "Your bath is almost ready."

The dried tears still stiffened her face. Soon after becoming Giles's wife in the flesh as well as in law, Philippa had dropped into the deep, dreamless slumber of emotional exhaustion, from which she had only now emerged.

She moved carefully, flung back the coverlet,

reached for her chamber-gown, slid her legs over the side of the bed, and escaped the soft clutches of that awful bed. Sun streaked through the eastern-facing windows.

"What hour is it?" she asked, slanting a surreptitious and embarrassed glance at the dark stain where her hips had been, as she stepped from the platform to the floor.

"'Tis after the hour of Prime, my lady. You have slept late."

"When did—?" Philippa gulped, swallowed and began again. "When did my husband rise?"

"I do not know, my lady. He had already gone when I arrived, a full hour ago."

He had not sought to linger. To waken her and… Depression settled on Philippa. Nothing would ever be right between them again. She could have loved Giles, she acknowledged, there could have been laughter and happiness and caring in their union, had it not been for Bolingbroke and his quest.

All her pent-up resentment focused, not on Giles himself for some reason, but on the man he followed with such unswerving loyalty, her reluctant sympathy of the previous evening quite gone. Henry Bolingbroke was a threat to the peace of the entire nation! He had ruined their marriage before it had begun. Yes, it was Henry Bolingbroke's fault that she felt abused, deserted and alone.

Isobel and a bevy of other ladies arrived at that moment, greeted her with cheerful cries and exclaimed over the evidence of her lost virginity as they stripped the bed. They soon departed, carrying their booty—all but Isobel, who remained.

She looked intently into Philippa's eyes. "'Twas so bad?" she demanded abruptly.

Philippa met her new friend's puzzled gaze grimly, determined not to admit her new vulnerability. "He used me brutally, Isobel," she declared. Her voice shook on the half-truth. "Look!" She bared her arm and showed the blue bruise-marks left by Giles's fingers.

Isobel frowned, shaking her head in bewilderment. "I would never have thought…but, if you resisted, 'twas his right," she pointed out. "Did you?"

"Only at first." Philippa made the admission reluctantly, her head lowered as she stepped into the steaming tub. Her knees came up under her chin as she sat down, but the herb-scented water was warm and soothing about her hips. "He was taking an age. I told him to get on with it."

"And he did!" exclaimed Isobel, enlightened. "How could you, Pippa?"

"I did my wifely duty," said Philippa defensively. "He should have had a care—"

"Duty makes a cold bedfellow, Pippa. Had you welcomed him… I am certain he did not wish to use you ill."

Philippa shrugged. "It hardly matters now. I fear we shall never find the joy of which you speak so beguilingly."

Isobel looked into the girl's mutinous face and saw some of the true emotions she was trying to hide. Hurt, disappointment and regret lurked in those dark, defensive eyes. She smiled encouragingly. "I would not be so pessimistic, Pippa dear," she advised. "Only those who cast horoscopes can tell what the future holds."

Bathed and refreshed, gowned in a simple kirtle Ida had fetched, Philippa returned with Isobel to be greeted by an exuberant Spot.

"He whined all night," Isobel told her wryly.

"I hope he didn't keep you awake! Poor old boy!" Philippa took his narrow face between her hands, inspected his healing wound with satisfaction, and kissed the top of his head, avoiding his eager tongue with a laugh. "Did your mistress desert you, then?"

Once she had weathered the dog's boisterous greeting, she peered from the window, relieved to observe that the scaffold had already disappeared from the yard beneath.

The State Chamber had been theirs for the wedding night only. No one had mentioned further arrangements designed to provide the newly-weds with privacy. The castle was over-full, space for such a luxury an impossible dream, even had they desired it. So she would continue to share her bed with Isobel and the Countess, all three women separated from their spouses at night. Philippa assured herself that this was for the best. The less she saw of her new bridegroom

the better. He aroused too many conflicting emotions
in her for comfort.

Giles appeared to share her sentiments. She saw
nothing of him all that day. He did not appear for
dinner. Neither did his squire, Walter Instow. Philippa
deduced they had gone off somewhere together. She
sat with Isobel and her knight, Miles—a shortish,
well-mannered man not above thirty years, whose
brown eyes seldom strayed far from the delicate face
of his wife.

Philippa found their obvious delight in each other
painful. It reminded her of earlier, carefree days when
she and Giles had been friends, when tenderness and
caring, understanding and harmony might have been
possible between them. Now, although husband and
wife, they were further apart than they had ever been.
They had been at odds over the last days, but not
completely estranged. Last night had driven a huge
emotional wedge between them that it would be well-
nigh impossible to remove.

If she wanted it removed. Did she really want to
be close to a man so opposed to her family's loyalties? Her father and brother were both prepared to
fight for the King. While Giles was equally ready to
take up arms against his Sovereign, if doing so became necessary to Bolingbroke's cause.

Impossible to change her own loyalties overnight.
Just because she was surrounded by a vast army of
people ready to challenge the King and force his
hand, that did not mean she had to acquiesce in an

act of treachery which would enable her sire and sibling to brand her traitor. It was far better by far to remind herself of her reasons for hating her husband.

Giles appeared late for supper, tired, hot and sweaty. He sought out Henry Bolingbroke and spoke earnestly with him for some moments before he joined her at their board.

He greeted her courteously enough. "You are well, wife?" he enquired, not quite meeting her eyes.

"Well enough, I thank you, husband." Philippa spoke stiffly, covering her embarrassment, which seemed greater than her resentment. The aura of sheer animal strength emanating from him in a mixture of odours—hot steel, leather, horse, fresh manly sweat—stirred her newly awakened senses, made her too conscious of his nearness. She fiddled with the girdle at her hips and tried to make amiable conversation. "I see you have just returned from abroad. You have been far from the castle?"

"Some distance. 'Twas a hard ride. But I was glad of the exercise, which has made me hungry as a wolf!" exclaimed Giles, helping himself to a large crust of bread, and allowing Wat to pile his trencher with a mixture of roast meats. He had indeed welcomed the vigorous physical activity to relieve both his lingering frustration and his irrational sense of guilt.

"You went on Bolingbroke's business?"

He glanced at her sharply. "Aye."

"He was quick to deny us our bridal days."

"Did you wish them, wife?" This time his eyes did meet hers, a startled, enquiring expression in their depths. "I thought you would be content, relieved of my company," he added with a cynical laugh.

Philippa shrugged. She could not allow him to know that she had missed him. That in some way she couldn't understand his absence had hurt her. "In truth, lord, it makes no difference to me," she assured him coolly. "But such days are usually obligatory. I wondered what guile you had used to avoid spending unwelcome time with your bride."

"These are stirring and unusual times, wife." Giles chewed deliberately and swallowed, his expression remote. "Henry had need of my services. I could not refuse to do his bidding." He lifted more meat to his mouth.

Philippa smiled provokingly. "Mayhap you volunteered?" she suggested.

He stopped chewing and his brows arched up until she thought they would disappear into the sun-streaked hair sweeping back from his high forehead. "And if I did? Would that have mattered to you, Pippa?" His voice challenged. He began to chew again, slowly, his questioning eyes on her face. Philippa concentrated on cutting up the portion of roast boar on their trencher. What had possessed her to needle him? But she had discovered that he was not as indifferent as he would like her to think. The knowledge cheered her considerably.

"Not at all," she declared, a little too positively.

"But after last night you would scarce have wished to face me until forced."

They were speaking low. Giles had bent his head, the better to ensure the privacy of their conversation. His eyes were very near hers when she looked up to see the impact of her words. They were opaque, as though he had pulled a veil over them. His Adam's apple shifted as he swallowed his food. His shapely lips twisted into a mocking smile. "You did not enjoy your bedding, my love?" he enquired smoothly. "But then, you have much to learn of the art of ensuring your husband's pleasure, of being a submissive and obedient wife. I look forward to giving you further instruction."

Philippa gasped. His last words had been spoken in a tone that left her in no doubt of his intent. She took a grip on her courage, and tossed her head.

"I warned you that you would find little joy in our union," she reminded him grimly. "You should not have forced me, Giles."

This time he gave a shout of genuine laughter, though he still spoke low enough to keep their conversation private. "Forced? My love, you stated your willingness."

Confused, Philippa said nothing for a moment. He was right, she had… "Only because you insisted on making me your wife against my will," she came back sharply. "I but bowed to my duty."

"As did I. I did but insist on your honouring our

contract immediately.'' He hesitated. ''Don't hold it against me, Pippa. I felt I had no choice.''

Was there just the suggestion of pleading in his voice? Philippa glanced up from under a fringe of long black lashes to catch the frown between his eyes. ''I trust,'' she said coldly, ''that, now you have proved your virility, you will leave me alone. There are plenty to attest the fact that I am no longer a virgin.''

''That fact, I believe, is in no doubt.'' The male arrogance in his voice set her teeth on edge. ''But unfortunately I cannot promise what you wish, wife. You forget, you have yet to prove your fruitfulness. But—'' he paused to take a draught of wine and wipe the back of his sinewy, sensitive hand across his lips ''—I shall not trouble you here. There is scarce a private corner to be found in Bristol.''

''For that small mercy I give you most hearty thanks!'' cried Philippa furiously, and jumped to her feet. ''I have eaten my fill. I will leave you to enjoy your repast alone.''

Giles disappeared again the next day, and for several days thereafter. Philippa began to suspect that he was out gathering information for Henry Bolingbroke, for he invariably reported to his lord immediately upon his return.

Her suspicion was confirmed when, on the first day of August, Henry Bolingbroke gathered everyone in the Great Hall to make an announcement. This Lammas-tide was the twenty-eighth anniversary of Giles's birth. Travel-stained and weary, he stood at his lord's shoulder as Bolingbroke addressed the throng.

King Richard, Henry informed his audience, returning from Waterford in Ireland, had landed at Milford Haven in Wales two days after they had entered Bristol. As soon as he had landed the King had, of course, heard of the defection of his uncle of York, the fall of the castle and the deaths of his officials. He, Henry, had been waiting to see what the King would do.

Now it seemed that Richard had abandoned his initial intention to come to Bristol. According to the latest intelligence, brought by Sir Giles d'Evreux in the last hour, King Richard had ordered the army he had brought back from Ireland to march on Bristol while he himself set off across the mountains of Wales to join John de Montacute, the Duke of Salisbury, in Conway. Salisbury had previously been dispatched there to raise men, some from North Wales, but most from Richard's stronghold of Cheshire.

Philippa knew by now that Cheshire had been a fertile recruiting ground for the King in past years, providing not only his personal bodyguard of formidable Cheshire Archers, but also a large number of men who wore the badge of the white hart as a sign that they had sworn themselves ready to answer his call to arms. If the King could reach them, he would have power at his back. He must be attempting to match his cousin's military strength in the conflict of wills ahead.

"Therefore we march at first light and must make all speed to Chester. A forced march, sirs," announced Bolingbroke in ringing tones. "Let the faint-hearted remain with those who must defend Bristol, should the King's army decide to attack. Who is with me?"

The resounding shout of support almost lifted the thatch high above their heads. The smoke-blackened beams rang with the sound of cheering.

Giles left the dais and strode through the throng, making purposefully for Philippa's side. He bowed. "I march with Henry, of course, and you, my wife, will travel with me. You will need Ida, of course. Bring with you only such things as can be carried by one pack-animal."

"Will Eadulf accompany us?"

Giles grinned, looking suddenly young now that the long days of riding to meet with the agents Henry had sent to scour the Welsh valleys for news, the anxious waiting and watching, were over. And his wife had so far raised no objection to the proposed journey. "Aye. He is one of my company by now, an excellent groom, and he will guard you faithfully should I be otherwise engaged."

Philippa looked him straight in the eye. "Do I have a choice in this?" she demanded. "I would prefer to travel to Fishacre, to be with my father while I wait for my wedded lord's return."

The smile left Giles's tanned face. "Pippa, your father is recovering well; you heard Sir Walter's messenger deliver this welcome news yestereve. You have no need to fear for his welfare. But your family is headstrong, and I do not want my wife tempted to act unwisely in the wrong cause." He reached out and took her hand, folding it between his toughened palms. "Trust me?" he asked her softly. "I want no ill to befall you. Remain with me. 'Twill be an interesting experience for one as fond of action as you are, my love. The ride will not exhaust you, of that I am certain, or I would not ask it of you."

"You are asking it of Ida, too," Philippa reminded him.

"Aye. But she is still young and fit enough to enjoy an adventure. Else she would not have been so ready to accompany you to Evesham," he pointed out slyly.

Philippa nodded. Mention of Evesham brought with it a vision of Reverend Mother smiling and ordering her to go with her betrothed. Were she here, she would now be persuading her it was her duty to accompany her husband.

"Very well." She inclined her head in graceful acceptance of the inevitable. "I believe, husband, that today you celebrate the anniversary of your birth. I wish you well and happy."

For an instant Giles looked taken aback. He had not expected her to remember, let alone mark the occasion with good wishes. In quick response, he squeezed the hand he was still holding. "I thank you,

Pippa.'' He gazed deeply into her dusky eyes. "Much of my future well-being will depend upon my wife."

Philippa saw the ardent light glowing in the depths of his beautiful eyes, the eager curve on his smiling lips, and caught her breath sharply. She had not wanted to arouse his carnal passions! She tugged her hand from his hold.

"We will be ready to ride at first light," she promised stiffly.

Giles, disappointed, let her small hand go as it squirmed in his hold. A sigh of weariness escaped him as he watched her graceful retreat. Her small gesture of caring had led nowhere. But at least it had been made.

Ready at dawn they were, but the logistics involved in getting an army the size of Bolingbroke's on the move meant that they waited interminably to move through the castle gate, and then endured another lengthy delay outside the city walls.

Giles had been trotting around on Panache, helping to organise order out of chaos. He brought the roncey over to where Philippa sat on a low wall awaiting her turn to move off, while her palfrey and Ida's hack both nibbled contentedly at the grass, and Spot sniffed excitedly at every coney warren or badger set he could find.

"We travel with the men-at-arms and archers on foot," he told her, dismounting. "They must be kept moving at a smart pace if they are not to lag too far behind. 'Tis my job to see that they do not.''

"Does that mean we can set off at last?" asked Philippa, pointedly looking at the sun, which had risen high in the heavens.

"Aye." He ignored her sarcasm. "The last of the soldiers are on the road. We travel behind them, but before the camp followers. If *they* lag, 'tis no great loss, though others will keep them moving, else we shall be short of farriers and food. Are you ready to mount?"

"I have been ready since dawn." He grinned at her tone and, catching his amused gaze, Philippa flushed, while her heart knocked diconcertingly in her chest.

"Then give me your foot."

She did so reluctantly. She did not want him touching her.

Wat, who had joined them, held the palfrey's head while Giles helped her to mount. Giles smiled up into her set face, one hand on Blaze's neck, the other lingering on her calf. Even through the layers of her riding gown his touch disturbed her breathing. "Eadulf and my grooms have ridden ahead," he told her, "so our camp will already be made by the time we arrive. Enjoy the ride, Pippa."

She made no reply, but put Blaze into a trot to join the departing column. Giles and Wat took up their stations on either side of her, Ida as usual following closely behind her mistress, her round face beaming. Philippa scowled as she caught a glimpse of her tiring-woman's enjoyment. Ida seemed to have discovered a taste for change to match that which normally drove her mistress. But Ida didn't have to make her pleasure so obvious.

The journey along the Severn valley passed without great incident. For most of the time Giles rode steadily at her side, now and again spurring ahead to join those of his men riding alongside the foot soldiers to chivvy the marching men along. Stops for rest and refreshment were short. By the time they reached the camping place chosen by Henry's scouts, the sun had already set. The van had been established in position for some hours. Pavilions stretched for mile upon mile beside the river. As the first appeared, Giles scanned the camp for sight of his pennon.

Eadulf came running out to meet them, greeting Philippa with a dutiful flourish and a broad smile which disclosed his blackened and gappy teeth.

"Follow me, my lady!" he shouted, and set off at a good pace to lead them to the d'Evreux encampment.

Several tents had been erected. Giles dismounted, and turned to his wife, who, helped by Eadulf, was already out of her saddle. "Come, wife." His smile held intimate invitation. He indicated the largest tent, formed of scarlet silk dusted with golden acorns. His shield, charged with his coat of arms, hung over the entrance, and his pennon fluttered from the central pole. "Our pavilion is ready."

Philippa hung back. "I do not wish to share your

pavilion,'' she told him bluntly. ''Ida and I will lie elsewhere.''

''Where do you suggest?''

The icy fury latent in his voice almost diverted Philippa from her purpose, but she rallied in time. She was perilously near forgetting her hatred of her husband in a reluctant return of her old liking. To share his pavilion would endanger her fragile hold on antipathy still further. His cold anger was preferable to that seductive charm he knew how to wield so effectively.

She stiffened her spine. ''You have several tents here. There must be room in one of them for us.''

''You would share with other men?'' he enquired dangerously.

Philippa tossed her head. ''They can move in with you,'' she told him haughtily. ''Otherwise, I will sleep under the stars. 'Twill be a warm night.''

Giles's lips tightened into a thin line. The flesh around them was white. His fists clenched and unclenched. For an instant she feared he would drag her, kicking and screaming, into his tent. But suddenly he relaxed. The smile he gave her was indecent in its suggestiveness.

''Afraid you will succumb to my virile charms?'' he enquired silkily.

''No!'' denied Philippa instantly. ''My fear is of having to endure your brutal advances!''

''Well, my dear, you have given everyone much entertainment with your quite unjustified reluctance to submit to your wifely duty. But—'' he shrugged expansively ''—I can be a tolerant husband. For the moment. Wat!'' He turned to his squire. ''Bring your pallet into my pavilion, and those of the men sharing with you. Then perhaps you will so good as to show Lady Philippa to her quarters.'' He turned on his heel, and the ring of his spurs jangled on Philippa's nerves. Without a backward look, he disappeared into the glowing crimson pavilion.

Philippa glanced around at the circle of curious, amused faces, felt her own flame, and took a deep breath.

''Come, Ida. Wat, show us which tent is ours.''

Philippa spent a miserable night in a small tent with few comforts, and the following day did little to cheer her.

Apart from a courteous greeting Giles ignored her, choosing to ride alongside the ranks of the foot soldiers rather than behind them with her. Wat accompanied him. Without their presence to restrain the camp followers in the rear, she and Ida were soon overtaken by those loose women possessed of donkeys or mules who wanted to establish contact with their prospective clients before nightfall. Philippa rode in aloof silence, though her curiosity was keen. Although tawdrily dressed in sometimes filthy finery, on the whole they seemed a cheerful and not ill-favoured company.

One of them, riding a mule—a buxom, fresh-faced but wordly wench younger than herself, as far as Philippa could judge—had her eye on Giles.

"There be a bonny one!" she remarked to a companion, pointing ahead to where Giles rode on Niger, his spare black charger, man and beast splendid in heraldic jupon and brilliant horse-trapper. She rubbed her thumb across the tips of her fingers in the age-old gesture of greed. "He'll be good for a nice bit o' siller. He'm mine!"

"Good luck to ye, Miriam. Me, I prefer a bit o' rough wi' me siller. Like that un ower there."

She pointed to a hairy archer, and the girls giggled. Philippa watched the one called Miriam sidle up to Giles whenever opportunity allowed, making ribald pleasantries which he returned with an unconcerned aplomb and chaffing good humour which made Philippa squirm. He was flirting with the lewd wench! How dared he? And within sight of his wife, too!

When they halted for the night she was not surprised to see the girl standing outside Giles's pavilion, crowded close to the knight, laughing up into his face. Giles, grinning, chucked her under the chin, said something which made her pout, and sent her off with a playful smack on her round behind. As he turned from sending the woman on her way, Giles caught sight of his wife's fulminating glare. The suggestion of a smile twitched the corner of his mouth.

Eadulf brought them supper, as he had the previous evening and Philippa settled down for another uncomfortable night. And now she had vivid pictures of

Giles and the whore to plague her mind. Had the wench returned? Or had Giles gone to visit her in the privacy of her own tent?

Her body ached and her mind rebelled. She seemed to be in the grip of some nightmare from which she could not escape. She would not attempt to run away. Some force greater than her own will seemed bent on keeping her with Giles. And, in a strange way, despite all the discomforts of body and mind, she was quite enjoying herself. She'd been lifted from her safe, restricted little world and thrown into the midst of turmoil.

Fleetingly, she wondered how Isobel was coping. She hadn't seen her friend since leaving Bristol. Isobel had joined her knight near the front of the mounted column, and no doubt spent her nights happily sharing his pavilion. As for the Countess of Butterwick, she had decided to follow at a leisurely pace, riding pillion behind one of the Earl's grooms. No camping out for her. She would seek civilised shelter overnight.

Not that her pavilion was that uncivilised, Philippa had to acknowledge. Her discomforts arose more from unaccustomed exercise and a restless mind than actual hardship. Her pallet was well stuffed with straw and the one coffer she had brought was placed in the tent each evening. Eadulf drew water for her and Ida ministered to her needs. In fact, she thought as she turned over with restless energy, the pallet on the ground was infinitely more comfortable than the bil-

lowing down-filled mattress on which she had spent
her wedding night.

The memory of that occasion brought a sudden and
devastating reaction in her body. Her nerves tingled
and a peristent throb began between her thighs. She
groaned inwardly, bit on her bottom lip, and buried
her hot face in one arm while she tried to quell the
uncomfortable feeling by cupping her free hand over
its source.

It died at last, and Philippa fell into an exhausted
sleep aware that her bridal night had changed her in
a way she had not anticipated. However reluctantly,
she had become a woman, and now she had a
woman's needs.

On the second day they crossed the Severn at
Gloucester and turned north-west towards Hereford.
Richard had created Bolingbroke Duke of Hereford
before his banishment, so he had adherents in the
area. Men flooded to join him at every stage of the
march. As the days progressed, they turned from the
city of Hereford itself, heading north for Leominster
and Ludlow.

Ludlow Castle, set on high ground in an angle between the rivers Teme and Corve, was bounded on
two sides by high cliffs descending to the flowing
waters. The east and south approaches were defended
by concentric walls, with the outer bailey between.
Most of the travellers camped in the meadows lining
the banks of the rivers, where rocky outcrop gave way

to gentle slopes, but Giles had been allocated accommodation within the castle itself. Wat escorted Philippa through the outer gatehouse into the vast yard, where the grooms had already erected the d'Evreux pavilions. Philippa would rather have been down by the river, and told Giles so when he punctiliously came to see her safely installed.

"The bailey is noisy and none too clean," she complained. "The grass by the river would have been soft and sweet-smelling—much preferable."

"But then, my lady, you would have been without protection, for my following has been invited within the castle curtilage. I sup with Henry this evening—something of a banquet, I believe. You will not be joining me at the board. Supper will be brought to you in your pavilion."

Philippa stared at her husband. "And who," she demanded quietly, "made that decision?"

"I did," he owned, unabashed. "You have declined to undertake your duties as my wife. There is therefore no reason why you should enjoy the privileges of your position."

Philippa shrugged. "You do not discomfit me, sir. I shall enjoy my supper the better for eating it away from your presence."

"That is what I thought," responded Giles blandly. "Sleep well, Philippa. We have another long march ahead of us on the morrow." He strode away to his sumptuous feast, and Philippa stood watching his retreating back, biting her thumbnail as he strode across the drawbridge and through the inner gatehouse.

Supercilious beast! Had she really imagined she liked him? And as for wanting him… No! Those feelings were no more than her natural womanly desires. She needed to be wed. But not to Giles d'Evreux. Never to Giles d'Evreux!

Chapter Seven

They did not linger at Ludlow, moving off next morning as the first streaks of day lightened the eastern sky. Now they were in hilly country near the border with Wales. That night they camped beside the ancient Roman road just short of Shrewsbury, where the broad way and wide grassy banks of the King's highway wound between distant silhouettes of wooded hills, with the bulk of the Wrekin towering near by.

The Cound Brook provided their water and, after another long day in the saddle, Philippa felt the urge to splash her hands and face in the clear, clean water, mayhap to dip her hot and aching feet in its cooling depths.

Ida was busy about their pavilion, Eadulf away currying the horses. With Spot for company, Philippa decided to make her way to an isolated stretch of the narrow stream and indulge her fancy.

Soon she left the bustle of the camp behind, not

far, but far enough to be alone. Blessed solitude! How she had missed the chance to roam free, to sit idly watching the wild creatures as they went about their daily business. Darkness had almost fallen, but the rustles in the grass, the twitters and hoots in the branches of trees spaced at irregular intervals along the river's banks told her that the nocturnal creatures had begun to emerge as their daytime brethren retired for the night.

A band of long grass and wild flowers interspersed with low bushes edged most of the stream, and Philippa headed for a gap beside one of the trees, where the bank sloped gently to the water. Spot ran off to one side, intent on routing out unsuspecting otters or water voles.

Philippa picked up her skirts and hooked the hem into her belt before squatting to remove her shoes and hose. Her laces were barely untied when she heard heavy footsteps approaching, and looked up to greet whoever had come to intrude on her privacy.

A stout knight approached, made heavy and ponderous by the mailed vest and breastplate under his yellow jupon.

"Good even, sir," She greeted him cheerfully, despite her annoyance at being disturbed. "'Tis a fine evening, is it not?"

He did not answer immediately, but stood watching her. In the dusk it was difficult to make out his features, but something in his manner alerted Philippa to danger. Instead of removing her shoes, she hastily re-tied the laces and sprang to her feet.

He put out a hand to detain her as she began to walk away, and his words confirmed her worst fears.

"So, my pretty," he chuckled, eyeing her tucked-up skirts. "preparing yourself to receive me, I see. How much?"

"No, sir!" gasped Philippa, terrible fear clutching at her vitals. "You mistake me for someone else. I am no lewd woman of pleasure—"

He thrust aside her protestations with a snort of anger. "Don't like the look of me, huh?" His tone had turned nasty. He crowded close enough for her to smell the ale on his breath, see his rotting teeth, his raddled, pock-marked face. "My money not good enough for you, eh? Here!" He threw a silver penny on the ground at her feet. "I saw you among the whores today. You can't fool me with your haughty ways! Come here, woman. I'm eager for my sport."

He grabbed at her, and Philippa let out a small shriek. "Spot!" she screamed.

The dog responded with a warning growl as he burst from the bushes, fangs bared, back bristling. He hunched for a spring. Snarling, he leapt at the man who was threatening his mistress.

The knight had been warned by that growl. Had had time to wrench his sword from its sheath. And as the dog leapt he caught it on its point, spitting it through with one deadly thrust.

Philippa watched in horror as her pet yelped and

dropped to the ground, whining and writhing in a pool of blood. ''No!'' she screamed. ''Oh, Spot! Spot! What has he done to you?''

She gave no further thought to escape, but made to drop down at the dog's side. The unknown knight gave her no chance. He grasped her arm and swung her to him, pinning her struggling body against the unyielding, chafing metal which the thin material of his jupon did little to soften.

His hot, repulsively wet lips closed over hers, and Philippa felt her senses reel under the assault of stinking breath laden with the stench of stale ale and rotting teeth. She managed a despairing wail as she felt herself flung to the ground.

''No!''

The bump as she landed, with that evil bulk on top of her, brought fierce anger to clear her brain. She would not submit to this brute! She kicked and writhed while her fingers fumbled in the folds of her gown, searching for the small knife hanging from her belt. The man was holding her down with one hand and the weight of his body, the other hand fully occupied fumbling with his breech-belt. Philippa brought out the knife and stabbed wildly downwards. The blade danced off his armour. He did not even notice the strike. In a new fury, Philippa lunged again, seeking to find the vulnerable spot above his steel gorget, for he wore no helmet.

This time she succeeded. He let out a bellow of pain and anger and blood spurted over her from his neck, just as the weight of his body was miraculously flung aside.

''Giles!'' She croaked his name in a burst of disbelieving joy. And next moment her husband's sword had finished the work she had begun.

''Pippa!'' He was on his knees beside her. Anxiety made his voice hoarse and somewhat shaky. ''Did he harm you?''

Philippa shuddered. ''No. Not much, anyway.'' She rubbed a breast bruised by the armour. ''But Spot! He killed Spot!'' she wailed, and burst into tears.

Giles muttered an oath under his breath, and issued crisp orders to Wat and others of his retinue who had come running with him when her anguished scream of Spot's name had told them who was calling. No one would have bothered about a whore in trouble by the river. But Giles had been galvanised into action by the cry from his wife.

The man was dead. Would like as not have died of Philippa's stab, but more slowly. Giles almost wished he had not dispatched the brute in such a hurry. But he could no more have prevented himself from striking out at his wife's attacker than he could now help picking up her shaking body and cradling it in his arms as he carried her tenderly back to his pavilion.

Philippa made no demur as the red silk closed about her. In the warm glow reflected by the horn lantern hanging overhead, held fast in her husband's arms, she felt safe and secure for the first time in days.

Giles laid her on his pallet and supported her shoulders while he held a wine-skin to her lips. She drank greedily.

"Better?" he asked tenderly.

"Oh, Giles! Did I kill him? I meant to!"

Giles hesitated. Would it be best for her to think she had, or to believe him responsible for her attacker's death? She was a fierce little thing, who liked to fight her own battles. He told the truth.

"You gave him a mortal wound, Pippa. I but put him out of his misery."

"I'm glad! He deserved to die!" she choked.

Suddenly, the floodgates opened. She flung her arms about his solid, reassuring body, buried her face in the hollow of his shoulder, and wept as though her heart would break.

"What is it, love?" he questioned. "He didn't…?"

"He killed Spot," she gulped. "Spot is dead! What shall I do without him? I—I loved him so much…"

All this grief for a dog! thought Giles grimly. Would she have been as shattered had it been he who had died? He thrust the thought aside. It was reaction, too. Reaction and grief together could very well produce a storm of emotion like this.

He signalled Ida and Wat, who stood enquiringly by the opening, to remove themselves. Then he stretched out beside Philippa, and drew her into his arms. She nestled closer. Giles smoothed down her tumbled hair and composed himself for a long night of discomfort and self-denial.

* * *

Philippa woke next morning to find Giles standing watching her. She sat up abruptly.

Realising where she was, and how she had spent the night, colour flooded up her neck and brought spots of bright red to her high cheekbones. "Oh!" she gasped. Then she remembered why she was where she was. "Spot," she whispered. "Is he really dead?"

"Aye, and buried." Seeing her about to burst into new floods of tears, Giles's compassion found its outlet in anger. "What the devil were you doing down by the river alone, Pippa?" he barked roughly. "You must have realised the risk you ran!"

"No, I didn't! And anyway, I had Spot..." Her voice trailed off and Giles made an exasperated sound under his breath. "He thought I was a whore," shouted Philippa defensively. "Small wonder, since I was left to travel alone among their company!"

"So this is my fault, too, I suppose?"

Giles's scathing anger cut Philippa to the quick. Last night he had shown nothing but tenderness. That had soon disappeared, like his first tenderness on their bridal night. She scrambled to her feet.

"Well, isn't it?" she demanded, equally angry now. "You ignore me, so how was a stranger to know who I was?"

"I ignore you because you deserve to be ignored, wife. But from now on I will brook no more disobedience from you. You will share my pavilion and wear my badge on your horse's trapper. That way there should be no further misunderstandings!''

"So I am to be branded your property!"

"Which you are," he reminded her silkily, his first anger turning to admiration at her show of spirit. God's bones, but taming this wench would bring reward past imagining! 'Twould be a tough task, but how he would enjoy the doing of it!

He smiled. "And now, my lady wife, if you would be so good as to ready yourself, we must move off within the half-hour. I believe you need to change your gown. Your coffer has been brought here for you. I will call Ida."

Philippa, seething, looked down to see the bloodstains spattered across the front of her kirtle. Memory of the previous night's terror returned to send a shudder through her. "Where did they put Spot?" she enquired tightly. "I will not leave without first seeing his grave. I have no defender now," she added plaintively.

"You have me," Giles reminded her quietly.

Philippa met his level, intent stare, and remorse overcame her. He had charged to her rescue, dispatched her attacker and then held her while she spent her tears. Twice now he had shown a tenderness and understanding she would scarce have expected from any man.

"Aye." She gave him a watery smile. "I believe I have to thank you for coming to my aid so promptly.

And for soothing my sorrow. I am not ungrateful, husband.''

"Then let us cry truce." His smile caused her stomach to lurch. "When you are ready, I will show you where your dog lies."

"And—there was no trouble over the knight's death?" she asked rather breathlessly.

Giles shook his head. "There were witnesses enough to his attack. His sword was drawn and bloody. His squires are taking his body home for burial. There will be no further questions asked."

Philippa drew a bolstering breath. "Then send Ida to me. I will be ready in good time."

"That," said Giles softly, "is more like it, wife." And dropped the softest of kisses on her startled mouth.

The cavalcade reached Chester on the ninth day of August at the beginning of the twenty-third year of Richard's reign. The town had fallen without resistance by the time Giles and Philippa arrived. Like the Bristol burghers, those of Chester had no love for Richard. And the royal border castle's garrison, faced with the immense hordes Bolingbroke had brought with him, could see that resistance was useless.

Henry could cry checkmate on the King.

North Wales was now Richard's only source of support. Henry immediately ordered most of his forces across the border to Flint, to challenge the King, who had reached the safety of Conway. With

Chester secure, most were already on their way. So the town and its castle were relatively empty.

Thus Philippa discovered that she and her husband had been allocated a small private chamber in the tower of the castle, which had been built in an angle of the city walls. The windows were little more than arrow-slits commanding a view over the encircling river, the straggling suburbs and the surrounding countryside.

A box-bed, high and relatively narrow, had been fitted into one corner of the chamber. She eyed it disparagingly. And with a certain amount of guiltily pleasurable anticipation.

She had shared Giles's pavilion since Shrewsbury, but not his pallet. Ida and Wat had kept them company. But there could be no escape from sharing this bed. And their attendants had already laid their pallets elsewhere. A shiver of perverse excitement ran along her nerves. She had come a long way, not only in miles, since Bristol. Giles was liked and respected among his peers, almost venerated by his inferiors. She could not help a feeling of pride in being his wife.

And Henry? Never had any leader appeared so popular. Cities and castles fell before his mere presence. Men, great and small, flocked to support his cause. As for Richard…it seemed that men were less ready to rally to his side. Already the southern army, left to march on Bristol, had disintegrated when its leader, Edward of Rutland, the Duke of Albemarle, had declared for Bolingbroke. The Chesire force had failed to materialise. Henry's intelligence was that Richard had reached Conway to find the Welsh army scattered, on a rumour of his death. He had retained the support of Salisbury, but without an army he could no longer challenge Henry.

Most strangely, Philippa found that what happened between the two cousins mattered to her less and less. Whatever the outcome, her future lay with Giles d'Evreux. If Henry prevailed, Giles was likely to prosper. If Richard, by some masterly stroke, regained the upper hand, and Henry's banishment—or worse— was reimposed, Giles would suffer the same fate. And she wanted to be with him.

When the change had come she couldn't truly say. Perhaps during that night spent in his arms after Spot died. Whatever else, she could see things now in a longer perspective. Whoever ruled England, for good or ill, Giles was her husband. She might as well accept the fact. And make the most of it. For he was certainly not repulsive to her.

They mounted the stairs together. Giles went through to the tiny wardrobe with Wat, leaving the bedchamber to Philippa and Ida. "I wish you a good night, my lady." Ida had not been too happy with her mistress's behaviour since leaving Alban, but was too fond of the girl to show it. Sympathising with her situation did not blind Ida to the fact that Philippa's lot would have been eased had she not antagonised her new husband from the first. So, as she helped her mistress to climb into the bed, she patted Philippa's small hand and smiled. "Were I ten years younger I could wish myself in your place," she confided, speaking low because the men were close by with only a skin arras between. "Bed is a lonely place without a man to warm it," she added wistfully.

Ida had joined her service as a young widow. Philippa studied her tiring-woman with new interest. Ida had always been more friend than servant, yet they had never before spoken of such intimate matters. Perhaps I was too young, if not in years, then at least in mind, thought Philippa ruefully. "You miss your husband?" she asked curiously.

"Aye, my lamb. But mayhap, now, I shall meet another." Her face, like her body less round after a week of intensive travel, flushed. "I have enjoyed this march, meeting so many new people. Alban was an isolated spot."

"You have met someone special?" asked Philippa, illumination flooding in. She had been so wrapped up in her own passionate resentment that she had barely noticed Ida's new animation, or taken trouble to wonder what her woman did in her limited free time.

"Mayhap." Ida blushed even more rosily. "He is man-at-arms to Harry Hotspur."

"So you would leave me to travel north?"

"Nothing has been settled as yet, my lamb. Do not fret yourself. Wolfram has not spoken. But I think he finds me to his liking."

"And so he should! He would be a wise man to take you to wife, Ida. I wish you happy."

"As I wish you, my lady. I must leave you now." She hesitated. "Be kind to your lord husband, my dear. He is a good man. You would look far for a better husband."

Philippa bristled at her maid's well-intentioned admonition. Knowing her words to be true did not make them easier to accept. From another. But had she not been thinking much the same thing? So she controlled her irritation, and nodded dismissal. "God keep you, Ida. I'll not need you again until morning."

When Giles came through Philippa was huddled under the cover, lying near the wall. Wat passed through and out. Her husband strode quietly towards the bed, his face grave. He wore naught but his shirt, which he drew off as he walked.

He stood beside the bed, naked, and Philippa peeped up at him from shadowed eyes. Giles reached out for the extinguisher to pinch out all the candles but one, then slid into the bed beside her. No billowing feathers separated them this time. The mattress was stuffed with fresh straw and herbs, clean and firm, so narrow that Giles could not avoid touching her as he stretched out beside his wife. And the wall blocked off her last chance of escape. But she no longer had a wish to escape.

He inserted an arm under her shoulders and drew her to him. "So, wife," he murmured deeply, "at last we have a chamber to ourselves." His other hand came up to smooth the freshly-brushed curls from her high forehead. His fingers trailed down her face and fingered the slight cleft before taking hold of her chin, turning her small face to his.

In the almost-dark his eyes glittered in the strong silhouette of his face. A small sound escaped Philippa's throat, part anticipation, part anxiety, part pleading. Giles seemed to read her mood, and made a soothing murmur in return. "Just relax, sweeting," he murmured. "'Twill not be so bad, that I promise you. You may even enjoy yourself; who knows? I intend to be gentle, and gentle I will be—an you do not try my temper beyond endurance!"

Philippa was not prepared to accept the implied criticism without protest. "So your ill-usage was my fault, was it?" she hissed indignantly.

"As much as your stupidity and Spot's death was mine," came the immediate, sharp riposte. His voice thickened again. "But we have a truce, Pippa. Don't spoil it now."

She pouted in the darkness. "Very well. I am quite ready to do my duty as your wife."

"Mmm." Giles shifted his weight, turning into her and throwing a long leg over her thighs, pinning her to the bed. She presented a challenge, this delightful, difficult, passionate wife of his. He had felt her initial surrender that first night, and knew that if he could wake her dormant womanhood successfully he would win himself a responsive and worthy bed-partner. Silently, he acknowledged his debt to all those women in his past on whom he had practised the art of seduction. They had not mattered. This woman did.

"You are a true beauty, my wife," he murmured, interspersing his words with small kisses on her forehead, her eyes, her nose. "And you have a desirable body—" he ran his palm the length of her arm and torso, on down over her swelling hip until it came up against his own leg "—soft as a kitten, yet beneath your velvet flesh lie steely muscles which can control a lively mount and draw a heavy bow." His hand travelled up again, coming to rest on her ribcage, just below the tender swell of one breast. His fingers splayed beneath it, his thumb caressing the valley between it and its twin, his fingers resting in the warm fold beneath. "Lovely," he growled seductively.

Philippa's eyes were shut, her breathing shallow. One of his hands cupped her head, the other rested intimately upon her body. His breath was soft and sweet on her skin. His lips were feather-light as they explored every crease, every feature, traced the line of her jaw and found the fluttering pulse where neck met shoulder.

Giles raised himself on one elbow and lifted his head the better to see the pale oval of her face, defined by black arching brows, the dark, sweeping fans of lashes resting on her cheeks, the shadow cast by her rather long nose, the curves and depressions of a generous mouth. And the mole at its corner. She wasn't truly beautiful. Yet his wooing words had been no lie.

So absorbed was he in the contemplation of the individual, imperfect, utterly charming parts that gave the overall impression of beauty, that he remained still for some moments. Philippa, missing the intimate touch of his lips, the grazing of his beard on her skin, opened her eyes.

Immediately, in the flickering shadows cast by the single candle, their gazes locked. Giles drew in a sharp breath before he lowered his head again, this time to claim her mouth.

For a long moment he seemed content to savour her lips. But then his tongue began to probe, to demand entry to her mouth. Philippa, swimming against the tide in a sea of sensation, was powerless to resist, though part of her wanted to. She had determined to be submissive, but she had not intended to co-operate quite so enthusiastically. Her mouth opened involuntarily, and as his tongue thrust fiercely into the sweetness of the cavern Philippa felt her whole body respond. She tasted the wine from supper, mingled with the extract of calendula flavouring the chalk he had used to rub his teeth. A low growl broke from her throat.

With a soft chuckle that ended in an answering growl, Giles shifted position again. His hands moved, each claiming a breast. He pushed them upwards, holding the plump flesh in his palms, guiding first one nipple, then the other, to his mouth. As he suckled, the shafts of painful sensation she had come to know speared to the centre of her womanhood. Philippa moved restlessly, not knowing what she wanted—for him to stop or to go on to something else, something more satisfying.

He began to concentrate on one tender peak, releasing a hand to search out the secret places between her thighs. Pleasure flooded her body. As it must be flooding Giles's, if the heated, hard, throbbing flesh pressed against hers was any indication. She had needed to summon up all her hatred and resolve to deny Giles pleasure on their wedding night. She could still do it, she told herself as she let the waves wash over her, but she had decided not to...

Her hands, which had somehow become tangled in the thickness of Giles's hair, dropped limply to her sides as strength drained from her limbs. She began to take deep, gasping breaths, as though she was struggling for air. Giles emitted another low growl, and abandoned her breasts as he rose above her, poised to enter her flowering, expectant body.

"Pippa, sweeting," he whispered, "I want you so much." Gently, he lowered himself. She felt him slide into her sheath, and then lie still, controlling his own ragged breathing. She gasped at the unexpected pleasure his entry brought. Her arms came up and held him, demanding closer union.

He began to move again, thrusting slowly, gently, gradually probing deeper and deeper into the core of her. And Philippa moaned under the onslaught of ravishing sensation. She didn't want him to stop. There was no soreness this time, no true pain. She could have borne his soft stroking of her womanhood for ever. When he stopped to gather his control, she uttered a small cry of protest.

Giles chuckled, and the undisguised triumph in his tone brought a measure of sanity rushing back to Philippa. Her arms slackened as he began the last phase of his journey to completion. She could not let him enjoy complete victory over her traitorous body. Not yet.

He had lost her. Giles groaned inwardly, but maintained the steady, erotic rhythm for as long as he could. When at last he could bear it no longer, he unleashed his body. A few fierce thrusts, and he collapsed over his silent wife as the shudders of fulfilment shook him.

Her arms tightened again. He felt the faintest of soft kisses touch his shoulder. Yet when he regained control and rolled from her she did not seek to restrain him. He gathered her into his arms and pressed her head into his shoulder. She was so quiet. He feathered a kiss on her white forehead. ''Thank you, my wife,'' he murmured softly.

Philippa did not answer. She could not. Overwhelming emotion had deprived her of the ability to speak. Tears choked her throat and threatened to course down her cheeks. She blinked them back. She must not let him see. For these were tears of sheer joy. And of tenderness for the man who had brought it to her.

Chapter Eight

Several days passed without great incident. Giles was kept busy during the day, but the nights were theirs. Philippa began to revel in the sensuous delight she found in her husband's arms, but some part of her refused complete abandonment to her new-found passion, fearing it would be the final act of treachery to her family.

Bolingbroke had sent Henry Percy, Earl of Northumberland, as emissary to the King at Conway. Bolingbroke's terms for a peaceful solution to their quarrel were reasonable. Richard would, of course, remain King. Henry continued to maintain that he had no intention of threatening the throne. But Richard must bow to the wishes of his magnates: clear Henry's name and return John of Gaunt's estates to his rightful heir; rescind the sentence of banishment and appoint Bolingbroke hereditary High Steward; and surrender five members of the council for trial for treason, since they had abused their powers so wretch-edly.

Henry could dictate what terms he chose, since the King lacked effective support. Rumour had it that Richard had reacted to his cousin's challenge with a mixture of self-pitying despair and furious defiance, swearing that Bolingbroke should die a death that would make a noise as far as Turkey.

Philippa wondered what he would do. There must be ships in Conway harbour. But if he sailed to some other land to raise an army, he would be abandoning a throne Henry had promised he would retain. Yet that Henry was now in a position to make such a promise made that throne glaringly insecure.

And what was her brother up to? she suddenly worried. She realised rather guiltily that she hadn't given Roger more than a passing thought in days. She frowned, deeply disturbed now that she did think about him. Any army he could muster would be puny beside that of Henry Bolingbroke. Roger would be risking ruin, even death, if he dared to go to the assistance of his sovereign lord. A shiver of apprehension ran through her. He would as likely try. And, she admitted ruefully, she would once have encouraged him in his loyal defiance.

But the last weeks had taught her things she hadn't dreamt of in her sheltered life at Alban. And since she could do nothing to prevent whatever happened, to Roger or to the King, she did her best to thrust all her uncomfortable thoughts to the back of her mind.

It took ten days for the negotiations to be completed, for Henry to receive word that Richard was prepared to leave the safety of Conway and risk all on a meeting at Flint.

Jubilation in the Bolingbroke camp was reserved. Giles, like everyone else, was fully aware of the magnitude of the events taking place. The future prosperity and safety of England depended upon their outcome. Richard might yet have a trick or two up his embroidered and jewelled sleeve. And if he accepted the terms, could he be trusted not to go back on his word? Richard had a long memory for injuries, and never forgot a slight. His quick wit, physical courage and trickery had brought him victorious through crises in the past. There could be no guarantees where King Richard was concerned.

So it was with severe reservations that Giles collected his wife and followed his lord to Flint.

There, Philippa found herself housed in a pavilion once more, though this time Giles took care to ensure their privacy at night. And she discovered Isobel Fortescue in the same part of the camp.

"The Countess Helen?" laughed Isobel once their glad greetings were over. "Aye, she is here, sharing a pavilion with the Earl. Why?"

"She arrived at Conway some days ago, and was most affronted not to be given accommodation within the castle walls!" chuckled Philippa. "But every inch of space was taken, and her husband here, so she was sent on to join him! I did not speak with her, but I heard her voicing her strong disapproval!''

"But you and your lord husband were given a chamber within the tower, you say?" Isobel paused, glancing at Philippa's blooming face quizzically. "Have you settled your differences, Pippa?"

"Mostly," admitted Philippa reluctantly, suppressing a sigh. "I have come to accept—nay, I must confess, enjoy, my wifely duty." She lowered her eyes as colour rose in her face. "But there is still the question of my father's illness, of our conflicting loyalties, to be settled. I cannot feel truly at peace in this alien camp."

"But you are not as unhappy as you were," observed Isobel with a smile. "And this despite the loss of your hound. I heard of that tragedy, though I found no chance to speak with you then."

Philippa's face dropped into lines of sorrow. "Aye, poor Spot! He died trying to fend off my attacker. I do miss him terribly, though I have had small chance to mourn his loss. Even in Chester there always seemed to be something to take my attention." She shuddered. "Thank the Virgin I had time to replace the gown ruined by that awful man's blood."

"By the time you settle down to real life again, you will be over your first grief," soothed Isobel.

"True. Giles has promised me another puppy. It won't be the same, but I'll have something of my own to love again."

"Mayhap, by then, you will have a babe," suggested Isobel gently.

"Mayhap." Philippa pushed the thought aside. A small Giles to love? The idea confused her. "But have you no children, Isobel?" she suddenly thought to ask.

"Aye, a bonny boy, safe with his grandmother. And I believe another babe is growing in my belly," confided Isobel shyly.

"I am glad for you," said Philippa sincerely. "Look!" she exclaimed. "See, Bolingbroke's herald is riding out again!"

"Heralds and messengers will ride busily back and forth between the two camps until all is finalised!" prophesied Isobel.

And so it was. Eventually it became known that Richard would arrive at Flint on the nineteenth day of August. The denizens of the castle scuttled about making ready to receive him.

Philippa had not expected to find a place in the Great Hall for his reception, but Giles pulled a few strings, and she found herself at his side as Henry Bolingbroke awaited his moment of triumph. His rather heavy but good-looking face looked calm enough under a high-crowned felt hat.

Distant fanfares and the echo of muted cheering announced the King's approach. A bustle at the door, and Richard strode in, high-collared houppelande billowing around him. All dropped to their knees except Bolingbroke, who prostrated himself three times in the traditional act of submission before kneeling at his Sovereign's feet.

Richard's face was pale, perhaps paler than usual, but it was true what they said: he did not lack courage. A tall man, he carried his head high, wore a coronet on thick, long hair the colour of ripe corn, and an imperious expression on his rather womanish face. Exquisitely barbered tufts of beard protruded on either side of his chin, and a slight moustache shadowed the extremities of his lips as though to belie the essential delicacy of his features. As those present began to rise to their feet he looked around and, one by one, as his frosty blue gaze rested on them, men and women dropped again to their knees.

Obeying Giles's urgent tug, Philippa sank back to hers as Richard eyed her carefully braided head with complete detachment. She realised that he was impressing his majesty, calling on the elaborate ceremonial and acts of deference he had instituted at his Court to bolster his exalted notion of his own importance. Giles had warned her. She had scarcely believed it possible that a mere man, even God's anointed King, could demand so much servility of his subjects.

The meeting progressed. Richard graciously acceded to all Bolingbroke's demands as though he were granting favours. Philippa occupied herself observing this King who, over the years, had managed to alienate himself from the vast majority of his subjects, both great and small.

He was thirty-two years old. Had lost his beloved Queen Anne and, though still lacking an heir, married Isabelle of France, a child of eight years, who even now was not old enough to bed. Rumour had it he preferred men. Yet he had truly loved his first Queen, and been desolate after her death, ordering the destruction of their favourite palace of Sheen, where she had died.

He appeared all scarlet and gold. Philippa eyed his costly garments and priceless jewels with reserved envy. 'Twould be wonderful to afford such luxurious adornment, but to pay for these and other extravagances Richard had levied his forced loans and intolerable taxes, had invented the iniquitous fines which came to be known as *La Plesaunce*—payments demanded from any who had even remotely supported the Lords Appellant—those nobles, including Bolingbroke, who had challenged his powers in 1387. Ten years after the event, with unrestrained power in his hands, he had executed some of his old enemies, banished others, and demanded payment from the unspecified remainder in order that they should regain his good pleasure. Individuals and the people of seventeen shires had paid up, submitting themselves to him as traitors rather than suffer the consequences of his grave displeasure. But this stratagem to extort money had endeared him to no one.

The King waved an imperious dismissal which only Bolingbroke and the assembled magnates ig-

nored. Next day they were all to ride to Chester, with
Richard in their midst.

From Chester, Richard sent out letters patent and
writs to summon a parliament to meet at Westminster
at the end of September. He also sent to Ireland, at
Bolingbroke's request, to summon young Harry back,
to be reunited with his father after their long separation.

Then began the lengthy journey to London. Philippa was beginning to long for the quiet life she had
known at Alban! Yet she also knew that she would
not have missed the excitement of this eventful journey. She felt intensely alive, fit and well, the days
seemed brighter, the birdsongs sweeter, the scent of
new-mown hay more pungent than she remembered,
especially after one of the increasingly frequent showers. And the nights were filled with delights she had
never imagined.

The King travelled with Bolingbroke, well guarded
but separated from his own small retinue of servants,
and from Salisbury, his only real friend in that assem-
bly.

As the cavalcade passed by, reapers stopped work
on the harvest to stare. Because the three visitations
of the great pestilence had halved the population since
1348, whole villages on their route lay abandoned.
Sheep grazed where once crops had grown, for there
were not enough labourers to till the land. But from
villages and towns where people did still live, crowds

appeared to cheer their progress. Philippa couldn't help but notice that the name cried out the loudest was that of Bolingbroke. There were few enthusiastic cheers for the King.

Giles had been relieved of his duty of shepherding the marching men, for this was a more leisurely progress. They rode amid the main body of mounted knights, just behind the King and his immediate bodyguard.

Day succeeded day. At Shrewsbury they turned east, following the King's highway to Lichfield, from there dropping down to Kenilworth, one of the Lancastrian castles now returned to Henry's hold.

The stone walls glowed softly rosy in the sunlight, the ancient keep, known as Caesar's tower, and the extensive assemblage of other towers, walls and buildings seemingly rising from the centre of a shimmering lake. The weather had been kind during the entire expedition, with just those light, refreshing showers and the occasional dull day to mar their enjoyment of a ride through a countryside where green was mingled with gold, where spikes of purple loosestrife grew from beds of yellow creeping cinque-foil to paint the way with colour, and travellers' joy laced the hedgerows to fill the air with the heady scents of summer.

Only those of knightly rank were admitted within the walls, the remainder left to camp on the banks of the mere which defended the approach to the castle from west and south. As she queued to cross the long,

embattled causeway which dammed the lake at its
eastern end, separating it from the defensive pool to
their right, Philippa gazed in delight at the wide
stretch of water, at the small barges tied up along its
banks.

"Giles!" she exclaimed. "Could we go out upon
the lake? 'Twould be wonderful to drift lazily in one
of those boats...mayhap we could catch fish!"

Giles smiled indulgently. His wife was full of
youthful enthusiasm for the simple pleasures of the
countryside. "Aye, mayhap. Henry plans to rest here
for two nights, for he wishes to meet with the Lancastrian stewards and check on his inheritance while
he is able. Few will question the delay in such a delightful place! But if you require fish, the stews are
yonder, beyond the Brays!" he told her with a grin,
nodding over his shoulder.

"I just want the fun of catching one!" She laughed
joyously, happy to have won such a hopeful response,
though that grin had left her unaccountably breathless.
"Have you been here often, Giles? Do you know it
well?"

"Tolerably well. 'Twas Katherine Swynford's favourite home, and John of Gaunt had much of it re-
built. The kitchens, the Great Hall and all this nearer
wing, including a garde-robe tower. Henry spent a lot
of time here in his youth, and later visited quite reg-
ularly. I accompanied him more often than not."

"Lucky you!"

She kept the envy, even the resentment, from her

voice with a considerable effort. But Giles read it, and voiced the thought she was trying to suppress.

"I am sorry, Pippa. I was selfish. Had we wed five years since, you would have been made welcome here, too. But then again, mayhap you would not have been so happy to live in exile."

"But yours was voluntary! You did not have to go, and could have returned at any time!"

"And been suspected of spying for Henry? No, once the decision to go with him was made, it would have been difficult to return."

"So you did not intend to honour our contract?"

Giles shifted uncomfortably in his saddle. Niger tossed his great head, and the harness jingled. "I had not given it much consideration."

"Nor how your family would feel."

"My father served and followed John of Gaunt for most of his life. He was with him at Najera—he met my mother in Spain—and later joined many of his campaigns. So he understood my need to support Henry. And at the time we thought it was for ten years only. Richard went back on his word there, too, in extending the banishment to life."

"I," said Philippa deliberately, "would have been nigh on thirty years old by the time you returned. An old and sour maid. Almost too old to bear a child."

"Nay, Pippa, I would have sent for you within a while. The choice would have been yours. I would not, then, have insisted on your honouring the contract. You would have been free to find another husband.''

''Mayhap, then, 'twould have been better had you not returned!'' She couldn't keep the snap from her voice.

''Did you have a candidate in mind?'' enquired Giles mildly as, at long last, they began to pass through one tower gateway and traverse the causeway towards a second.

Her knee knocked against his. She glanced sideways quickly. Caught the devilish gleam in his dancing eyes, and knew that he was teasing her. Mother of God, but he was an attractive devil! Her nerves jumped with the sudden shock of the contact, of his possessive, self-assured smile, of his arrogant—and entirely accurate—assessment of her new dependence on his favours.

''No,'' she retorted haughtily, ''but no doubt my family would have found little trouble in securing one.''

''But none more devoted and amiable than I, my love.'' He hauled on Niger's bit to stop the eager destrier from forging between two horses ahead. ''I fear we shall have to pitch our tent in the outer court,'' he went on casually. ''There will be no chamber to spare in the castle, and I do not fancy spreading a pallet in one of the halls. I have come to treasure the nights in my pavilion spent with my delightful wife.''

Philippa realised she was having a hard job to keep

up the antagonism which had come so naturally at first. All her emotions, her beliefs, seemed to be in some vast melting-pot, and she no longer knew exactly how she felt or what she thought. Only that she no longer wanted to be separated from the strange mixture of security and stimulation she found in Giles's company.

Their pavilion was pitched in the outer court, not far from the chapel of St Mary. Eadulf took Blaze and Niger off to the stables while Ida and Wat saw that their mistress and master had everything they needed.

They ate that evening in the Great Hall. Climbing the flight of steps to the finely decorated doorway, admiring the intricate carvings on the arch and jambs, Philippa caught the rich aroma of roasting meat, the sharp tang of spices, the mouth-watering waft of freshly baked bread coming from the adjoining kitchens. Ventilation shafts from the undercroft beneath the Hall emitted a faint, vinous whiff of oak casks and a fine vintage to mingle with the cooking smells. She realised she was ravenous.

The westering sun glowed through the high, traceried arches of the Hall windows, throwing a golden sheen over trestles laid for a banquet. Grooms, servitors and pages scurried everywhere, carrying laden platters and steaming cauldrons, heavy flagons and slopping pitchers. The carver was at work on the dais, the sewer stood near by ready to taste everything before the King or nobles ate.

Trumpets flourished from the gallery above, and Henry led Richard to the chairs of state at the high table in the centre of the dais. People bowed and made deep obeisance. Richard swept the chamber with his haughty gaze, but no one cringed to his knees. Somewhere along the road he had lost his regal authority to become little more than an honoured noble. A noble who was not free to leave the cavalcade.

He had proved that, yesterday, by attempting to ride off at a tangent. He had been prevented. For his own safety, naturally.

Failing to receive the deference he considered his due, Richard sat back, his face flushed and angry. He extracted an elegant square of fine linen from the folds of his jewelled and embroidered houppelande, and wiped his sweaty forehead before delicately dabbing at his nose. Philippa had never seen such a thing before. People used their fingers, or their sleeve, mayhap a piece of rag. She glanced at her husband. By the sardonic smile twisting his lips she judged he considered the carrying of a hand kerchief unmanly. And so must everyone else, for this innovation of Richard's had not caught on.

Philippa still had sympathy for the King, but she no longer felt deeply indignant at his humiliation. By all accounts, and by what she herself had observed, he deserved no less, anointed Sovereign or not.

She gnawed the last piece of flesh from the leg of a pheasant and licked her fingers. "The King does not appear to be hungry," she remarked to Giles, who was busy dealing with the remnants of a haunch of venison.

Giles glanced to where the King sat, staring morosely at a trencher laden with meat. ''The food is not to his liking,'' he told her with a shrug. ''He prefers his meat ground and spiced, mixed with wine and sugar. 'Tis then fit only to be eaten with a spoon. The cooks here are not accustomed to his tastes.''

''And have not been instructed to accommodate them,'' observed Philippa. ''Giles, what will become of him?''

He shot her a sharp glance. ''What should happen to him?'' he demanded. ''He will remain King.''

''Will he? Have you not noticed, he is virtually a prisoner? Henry has him in his power.''

''But Henry means him no ill,'' affirmed Giles stoutly. Then he shrugged again. ''The only problem is, can he trust his cousin to keep his word? At the slightest sign of Richard's wishing to renege...'' He let the sentence die, a deep frown between his golden-tipped brows.

''The King will find himself without a throne.''

Giles opened his mouth and immediately compressed his lips over the sharp reprimand. ''Do not even think such a thing, Pippa!'' he urged, looking round apprehensively to make sure no one else had heard his too astute wife voice thoughts best left unspoken. ''Who would succeed? Richard named the Earl of March, as grandson of his eldest uncle, although Mortimer's descent was through his mother. But he is dead, his son but a child…''

"And can hardly be looked upon as a desirable monarch," Philippa finished for him. "But Henry…? Next in the direct male line—?"

"Shush! Enough, Philippa! What are you saying? Mind your tongue lest you speak treason!"

Giles's voice was low and harsh. He glared at her, his eyes hot with suppressed anger. And anxiety.

It was Philippa's turn to shrug now. "I but repeat what others say," she told her irate and worried husband unrepentantly. But she kept her voice to a murmur, so that it would not carry to others sharing their board.

"Pippa!" exclaimed Giles in exasperation. "What am I to do with you? You must not listen, must not gossip…"

"You could send me home," she suggested, the picture of innocence, her dark eyes narrowed seductively to linger on his.

Giles was forced into a chuckle. Saucy wench! "Where I am unable to keep an eye on you? Never, sweetheart!" he returned, equally innocent. But his eyes flirted with hers.

Darkness had fallen. With it had come the ladies of the night, flitting from pavilion to pavilion in the intermittent flare of scattered torches. They no longer troubled Giles.

Philippa grinned with satisfaction at the thought as

she threaded her way back to their tent to prepare for the night. Giles was still closeted with Henry, but had promised not to be long. She hummed softly under her breath as she walked, Ida a step or two behind. She never wandered the camps alone now. One bad experience was more than enough.

When a man's voice came from the darkness to accost her, she therefore jumped with both apprehension and surprise. Ida was beside her in an instant.

"Who is it? What do you want?" she demanded, keeping her voice crisp and authoritative despite its attempt to squeak.

"Pippa!"

Her name was repeated, and she belatedly registered what had been said before. Few people called her Pippa. And the voice was familiar!

"Roger?" she gasped. "What do you here? Have you joined Bolingbroke—?"

Her brother stepped from behind the sheltering pavilion, and Philippa saw that he wore a plain black jupon, the distinctive green lozenge of Alban, even his badge—the alban knot, twisted into a fancy capital "A"—missing from his clothing. Her nerves tensed as she realised the implication. She felt slightly sick.

"Roger?" she repeated.

"I'm glad to see you well, sister. Mary told me how d'Evreux pursued you in order to carry you off on his traitorous errand. Like so many others, I have joined Bolingbroke's truimphal procession." His voice dripped scorn. "They allowed me entry here because I am a knight, though no one knows my true identity. I am come to see you."

"To see me?" Philippa grasped at the one sensible thing he had said.

"Aye, sister. I need your help."

"What for?" asked Philippa apprehensively.

"To get a message to the King. You must be able to reach a page with access to him. Give him this."

He held out a small piece of parchment. Philippa eyed it as though it were a viper. "What is it?"

"A warning of our plan to rescue him from his captors." He suddenly realised that she had thrust her hands firmly behind her back. "Here, take it," he ordered brusquely.

"No."

"Now see here, Pippa—"

"No, *you* see here, Roger." She gulped down a bolstering breath and prepared to defy the brother she had respected and somewhat feared all her life. Roger could be frightening in a temper. And, by the look of his square face, the beard at his chin silhouetted against a torch and wagging in outraged aggression, his spleen was rising fast. "I am wed now," she told him firmly. "My first duty is to my wedded lord. I cannot go against his wishes. I cannot do as you ask. I am no spy."

"Would you desert your King? Your father and brother?" demanded Roger bitterly. "Why so? Do you love the churl who forced you to marry him?"

"That," shot back Philippa, ignoring the thrust of some new, agonising sensation in her chest, "has naught to do with anything! 'Tis the law. And besides," she added more quietly, "'tis dangerous to attempt to help the King. You would do well to return to your family, Roger, and let affairs of state take their course."

"I never thought to hear such words from you, Philippa," said Roger harshly. "It seems I needs must find some other way to deliever my message. But make no mistake. Deliver it I will. And if a warning is given," he added menacingly, "I shall know who gave it. I shall know how to revenge your disloyalty, sister."

Philippa brought her hands round and clasped her arms across her chest. Her teeth had begun to chatter, and she clamped them tightly shut. She felt as though she were being torn in two. She did not want to deny her brother, yet she wanted no part in his plots. She did not want to betray him, either, could not. Yet to keep silent over what she knew would amount to betrayal of Henry's cause, which was also her husband's...But she had no choice.

"I will not speak of this. Neither will Ida," she told Roger d'Alban at last. "But do not let me see you here again, or riding in Henry's train, or I may change my mind. Go, Roger. Leave Henry's army, for here you are a spy."

"I'll go, readily enough, once I have found the means to deliver my note. I will see you anon, sister.

I shall ask the King to be lenient with you. I know you do but follow d'Evreux's lead.''

Philippa lifted her stubborn chin. ''And I pray you will not have to lay your head on the block, Roger,'' she retorted tartly. ''Your attempt at resistance is useless, pathetic. Cannot you see that all the great lords of the realm are behind Bolingbroke? Richard threatens them all with his imperious, extravagant ways, and it will take more than your puny efforts to overthrow so many powerful men.''

Roger made a harsh sound in his throat. ''It seems my sister has become tainted by the company she keeps! I never expected to hear such cowardly, traitorous views from a d'Alban.''

''Not traitorous,'' whispered Philippa, ''nor cowardly, but sensible. I have had time to think these last weeks.'' Despite her best efforts her voice broke, and she began to plead with her headstrong brother. ''Think, Roger! Think of the consequences if you are taken! Remember Mary and the children—''

''Enough, sister! Would you make a coward of me, too? I pray you to remember our father, who lies stricken—''

''Stricken still?'' Philippa gulped. ''But Giles has received reports of his recovery—when did you last see our sire?''

''When he was taken from Alban Castle by litter. I kept my eye on things there until the family left, then followed them and their escort to Fishacre. I managed a brief word with my wife before I set about gathering a force of men with loyal hearts who were willing to fight for their King.''

''Then you do not know that he is making a good recovery!'' exclaimed Philippa in relief. ''His speech is slurred and he cannot use his left hand, but otherwise he is almost fit again!''

She saw her brother's shoulders move in a shrug. ''That is as may be. But the Earl our father would have challenged Bolingbroke, and I must do likewise.''

''Did you raise a force?'' asked Philippa faintly. There seemed no arguing with him.

''A small one, sufficient for our purpose. But I waste time, and I believe your husband comes. Farewell, sister.''

He was gone. Dissolved into the shadows like a wraith. Philippa could hardly believe he had been there, except for the new pain in her heart. Deservedly or not, she was now branded traitor by her sibling. And by her father, too, if and when he found out about her change of heart.

Chapter Nine

"Who was that? Was someone bothering you?"

Philippa jumped guiltily. Giles's sharp tones brought her back to an uncomfortable reality. She had to cover for her brother.

"No one," she answered, turning quickly to meet her husband, moving away from the place where Roger had disappeared. "Just a groom searching for his master. He wasn't bothering me."

Giles's eyes glittered in the darkness and he took her arm in a firm though gentle grip. "Come, let us seek our pavilion." His voice held a degree of barely suppressed annoyance. "I would have thought you had learnt not to wander the camp at night, my lady."

Philippa realised that his manner cloaked concern, but nevertheless resented his tone. "I had Ida with me!" she flared.

"Aye, so you did." Much of the tension she sensed in his body went, but she knew his eyes were searching her face in the gloom. She suffered his scrutiny as calmly as she could. It was difficult not to show her feeling of guilt. But he seemed satisfied. He dropped her arm to drape his own around her shoulders. "I worry too much, my sweet," he admitted, pulling her to him, "but I want no repeat of that cursed incident when your hound was killed."

Philippa relaxed in the haven of his hold. "Nor I!" she assured him, in such heartfelt tones that he chuckled.

"Dismiss Ida," he whispered.

In their pavilion, by the light of the guttering candle in the horn lantern, he turned her to face him, his expression intent but gentle. He brushed the back of his hand across her flushed cheek, then let his fingers slide round to bury themselves in the escaping tendrils of hair at the nape of her neck. His other hand dealt with her circlet and the pins holding her braids in elongated coils on either side of her face. When they hung free and he had teased the plaits out with his long, deft fingers, he drew a deep, unsteady breath and moved to undo the large carved wood buttons fastening her cote-hardie.

Philippa began to tremble. He had never wooed her in quite this way before. He had always prepared for bed elsewhere, with Wat to attend him, arriving in their pavilion after Ida had left, and she waiting naked in their bed. But now his every move, nay, his very nearness, brought with it a new, tingling awareness. He had only to look at her with that special light in his darkened blue-grey eyes for her knees to melt, her breathing to become difficult...

But why? His touch was by now familiar, his close presence an admitted source of pleasure. He had regarded her in similar fashion before. Why, then, should she suddenly begin to tremble like the virgin she no longer was, to weaken and melt, wanting to lose herself in the body of this man who was her husband?

She knew why. Her brother's casual shaft had struck a target she had not known existed. The pain in her chest clutched at her heart anew. She loved Giles d'Evreux.

But she could not! Despite her new understanding of all he stood for, still he had neglected her for years, caused her father to act in a way that had brought about his illness, had carried her off by force to a reluctant marriage. And had used her ill that first night.

She stiffened in his hold. Giles, lost in the exquisite joy of at last making real and leisurely love to his wife, felt the rejection and jerked his gold-streaked head from the thyme-scented warmth of her neck, where he had buried his seeking lips. His arms tightened round her like clamps. "Pippa?" he demanded.

She felt the steely strength, the hard possession, heard the sudden arrogance in his voice. And realised something that until then had remained a mystery to her. Since that dreadful night when she had almost killed a man and Spot had died, Giles had shown her nothing but gentleness. Strength, yes. Determination to protect, to possess, yes. But force, hurtful mastery, no.

Yet now... She could feel the beginnings of that intolerant tension in him which would call forth the domineering male. And she was bringing it upon herself. As she had brought it on her bridal night.

The shock of understanding was like falling into cold water. She had evoked some primitive emotion in him which even Isobel had known to be alien. She realised now that she could not deny the desire he had for her without rousing the other, demanding side of his nature. He was too chivalrous, too self-controlled, too nice a man to do her real physical harm. To beat his wife into submission as other men thought it their right to do. But she would be hurt just the same. Because she did not want to be taken in anything other than love.

But that was stupid! She did *not* love Giles d'Evreux! And if she did not love him, then to be taken with tender strength and passion must be what her body and heart desired. She could not deny her husband. Because to do so would be intolerable; she wanted him too desperately.

She shut her eyes to avoid the growing anger in his, and let herself relax. A smile spread across her face, springing from the wells of...of affection...and desire buried deep within. She sighed, and rested her cheek against the cool texture of his satin cote-hardie.

"Nothing," she murmured. And then, with unconscious pleading, "Love me, my husband."

Giles groaned, crushed her slight frame against his chest, hurting yet not hurting, thrust a muscular thigh between hers so that she could feel his hard body pressing against the entire length of hers. "What else do you think I am doing, woman?" he demanded huskily.

Philippa giggled. Reaction from all her secret meditation set in. She did not want to think, only to feel. "You are being terribly slow," she teased, echoing yet not echoing that disastrous demand of their first night.

Her fingers went to the wrought-silver buttons decorating the front of his cote-hardie and began to tease them open. In deference to the temperature he wore no tunic beneath. She felt him catch his breath as she slipped her arms inside the opened garment, revelling in the warm strength of his body, which the thin chaisel shirt did little to shield from her touch. "You have fewer layers than I," she murmured, running her exploring fingers over the bunched muscles of his back.

"Pippa!" groaned Giles. "Stop that, my love, or we'll never reach the pallet!"

She realised the truth of his protest as his body hardened against her stomach, potent with his masculinity despite the layers of clothing still separating them.

"Then let us disrobe at once!" she suggested demurely, releasing him and preparing to step back.

But Giles was not ready for that yet. He let her go, but only so that he could frame her flushed face in his hands. He gazed deeply into her dark eyes, black in the dim light of the lantern, yet full of an emotion he had not seen in them before. He could scarcely believe it! And that secret, seductive smile which had so thrown him earlier! It seemed that his reluctant bride desired him at last!

He heaved in a great breath. Triumph, laced liberally with unbelievable tenderness, welled up in Giles. His dearest wish was about to be realised! This night he would hold a willing and responsive wife in his arms.

But, however much she teased him, he must not hurry. He must woo her anew, rouse the romantic, passionate nature he knew had lain dormant too long in his bride. And the fault had been his. That she had resisted him so long was understandable. She had fought with the same passion he hoped she would now bring to her loving.

He drew another steadying breath. God's blood! 'Twas difficult to leash his need! He had never desired a woman more. His lips descended slowly, tender and teasing before they firmed into demand, clinging to hers, the only contact between them apart from the whisper of his fingers as he drew off her over-garment and began to unlace the ties down the back of her gown. He stroked it from her shoulders, but could not remove it entirely, because her sleeves were buttoned too tightly.

Reluctantly, he took his lips from hers while he dealt with the offending fastenings. While he was working on one arm, Philippa used the other to tug at the strings on his braies, pushing the loosened garment down over his hips. She did not question where her courage, where the instinct to use her hands to discover him, came from. It was just there, in every nerve, every sinew of her quivering body.

Giles shuddered as her fingers touched him. With a protesting groan he caught at her hand and began to unbutton that sleeve. Philippa used the arm he had just freed to drag the cote-hardie from his shoulders.

''Patience, my love!'' he muttered hoarsely. ''How can I deal with your buttons with my arms tied up?'' He stopped work for a moment while he flung off the garment and kicked off his braies, and with them the hose tied to them and his pointed shoes. His shirt followed, landing on the pile of other discarded clothing, a white marker on the turf.

He really was magnificent. Instead of shyly averting her eyes, Philippa gazed boldly at the figure of her husband, admiring the breadth of his shoulders, the narrowness of his waist, the flatness of his stomach, the strength of his thighs. There was scarce a grain of surplus flesh on him; she could count his ribs, an she tried. She reached out to trace the rippling lines spreading from his breastbone, and Giles moaned as he undid the last button and eased the kirtle from her body. Her undergarment was an altogether simpler matter to remove. He lifted the embroidered hem over her head, and threw the finely embroidered linen smock down on the growing mountain of their clothes.

Now she, too, was naked—apart from her pale saffron hose, kept up above her knees by blue ribbon garters. Reverently, he pulled the ends of the bows and slid the stretchy silken material down over her ankles and feet, taking her shoes with it.

Then he simply stood and looked. And she looked back.

"Well, wife."

He was having difficulty in speaking. Philippa opened her mouth, but no sound came. Her throat was parched as a brook in a drought.

But she had no need to say anything. Giles drew their naked bodies together, and held her fast. She could hear the thunder of his heart under her ear, echoing the pounding in her own chest. His desire pulsed against her stomach as his mouth caressed her ear and his tongue explored the intricate contours of the orifice. She shuddered, and found his small, hard nipple, almost lost in its bed of fine hair, and teased it with her fingers, making Giles jerk and suck in a breath like someone gasping for air.

He tore his mouth away and reached up to pinch out the candle in the horn lantern. Darkness enveloped them. Philippa became aware of the background sounds of the camp: the carrying voices, the occasional guffaw of lusty laughter, the clank of armour, the sweet notes of a pipe, the distant shrill of a horse's neigh.

Then everything outside their two selves was forgotten again as Giles ran his hands over her, caressing her shoulders, cupping her breasts and brushing their peaks with tantalising delicacy. Finding the hollow of her slender waist, his hands lingered a while, before travelling over her hips to mould her small buttocks in their palms.

She let her hands wander, too. She marvelled that she had never wanted to touch like this before. She had been content to take. Tonight, she wanted to discover every hidden secret of his beautiful body, to give him the pleasure he was giving her. She slid her fingers along his backbone, feeling the bumps of his vertebrae, up to those wide shoulders, down past the narrowing at his waist to the tight, lean flanks until she held him as he held her.

Mouth to mouth, chest to breast, thigh to thigh, they stood savouring each other's perfection, their breathing fast and uneven. Philippa was drowning in new sensations, Giles wondering how he had ever found pleasure in any other woman. He kept a clear head by sheer strength of will. He must not hurry. Must not frighten away this new and oh, so exquisite response.

He rubbed himself against her, renewing her knowledge of his desire. Then, gently, he lowered their bodies to the pallet. The night was warm, even sticky. They had no need of coverings. His eyes had become used to the darkness; he could feast his eyes on her delectable figure. He began a slow, arousing exploration with fingers, lips and tongue and, to his delight, his wife responded with sweet caresses of her own. She seemed to know instinctively what would please him. But, when she formed a sheath with her hand and held him *there*, he was forced to call a temporary halt. He could not delay much longer. He probed with his fingers and found her ready. But the instinctive arching of her hips had already told him that.

"Sweet wife," he murmured, and slid inside her warmth.

Philippa thought she would shatter into small pieces as the shimmering waves of sensation rippled through her body. She held him fiercely, twining her arms and legs around him so that he should not escape. The waves were just receding when he began to move. She moaned and cried out, thrusting her hips up to meet him, demanding...demanding...

And Giles did not let her down. Not until he felt her muscles contract, felt the shudders begin, did he allow himself release.

Philippa knew she must be dying, floating upwards to the azure heavens above the clouds, and Giles must be dying too, for she was just barely conscious of his racked body and the muffled groans which sounded like pain and anguish...

But were ecstasy.

Philippa's mind rejoined her lax and sated body to find her lord sprawled over her, the groans diminished into harsh breathing and the spasms reduced to occasional shudders. He was still inside her. She tightened her arms and legs around him with renewed strength, determined to keep him there for as long as possible. And smothered his shoulder with hot, tender kisses. She knew she had given him more pleasure than ever before. And, in return, had received it.

Giles lay very still, caught in the tendrils of his wife's allure. He could not have moved, even had she not entwined herself around him as though she were the ivy to his oak.

The simile disturbed him somewhat, for ivy eventually killed the tree it wound itself about. He must not allow himself to become so bound by this woman's seduction that he forgot duty, neglected prudence, was led into actions he would later regret. He must remember that she still regarded him as a traitor.

The following day most of the nobles and knights proposed to go hunting while Henry attended to his business. Breakfast was over, and they were already mounting up.

"You wished to go on the mere, I believe?" smiled Giles.

"Aye, but are you not hunting?" asked Philippa doubtfully.

"Nay, love, I can do that any time—unless you would prefer to join the chase?"

"Oh, no! I do not like hunting, even though it is for meat. I hate to see any wild creature killed."

"Then let us take a boat out on the water." He grinned, expansive and content after the delights of the night. "We will count today a bridal day, my love."

Philippa blushed, knowing why he had chosen that day to be alone with his bride. Until last night they had not been truly one flesh.

"Do we go now?" she asked.

Giles studied the sky from an east-facing window of the Hall. The sun had risen enough to throw its rays across the surface of the water, spangling the breeze-ruffled surface with gold.

"Why not? If it is not warm enough we can always come back and try again after dinner, when the sun will have gained its strength."

"We can wear mantles," suggested Philippa eagerly.

"Aye, 'twill be as well. Come, then, and I will try to borrow a fishing net. Unless you object to killing fish?" he asked teasingly.

"Oh, but I shall not kill it if I catch one," protested Philippa. "You can do that!"

"You eat meat and fish willingly enough." Giles pursued his train of thought with some determination. This was a facet of his wife's nature he had not appreciated.

"Well, 'tis natural. Man has always eaten the flesh

God provides. 'Tis just that I cannot bear to see the killing.''

''So you allow others to do it for you!'' he scoffed.

''Aye, those who do not mind. But I snare conies and net fish at home.'' Home? Alban was no longer her home. Philippa thrust the momentary chill of that thought aside more easily than she would have believed possible only days ago. ''I would kill if I were starving or threatened,'' she admitted defensively. ''I think I have proved that!'' she added, remembering with a shudder that she had been willing enough to kill a man who attacked her.

Giles chuckled. ''You do not make sense, my sweet.''

''I do! Men do not like seeing babies born, but they are willing enough to beget them!''

''''Tis women's work to deliver their issue!''

''As providing meat is men's!''

For a moment Giles looked quite struck. Then his features warmed into a beautiful smile that turned Philippa's heart in her chest. His eyes danced, his shapely lips parted to reveal those slightly crooked teeth as he pulled her hard against his side. ''Your logic is unanswerable, my sweet,'' he admitted cheerfully, planting a quick kiss on the tip of her nose.

Having obtained a net and the use of a small rowing boat, they passed to the water's edge through a small doorway near the gate-tower which led to the causeway. Since the latter doubled as a tilt yard, it was even then being used by several knights to practise their skills. The sound of thundering hoofs and splintering wood echoed across the expanse of the mere.

While a churl held it steady, Giles helped Philippa to step aboard the flimsy vessel. She held bunches of her voluminous azure skirts in one hand and gripped his steadying fingers tightly with the other. She sat quickly on a thwart near the stern, while Giles took his place facing her, and bundled his mantle on the tiny bow thwart before pushing off with one of the oars. Manoeuvring expertly, he soon had the boat pointing the way they wanted to go, and then moved it through the water with strong, steady strokes.

Philippa couldn't help admiring the play of his shoulder and arm muscles, clearly visible through the fine material of his close-fitting tunic. Or the movement of thighs straining against the confines of azure tights. Her stomach tightened as she remembered the feel of his flesh against hers. Last night had been heaven—or almost heaven. If only he loved her…But that was a foolish, romantic dream fit only for a minstrel's tale. Though it did happen. Even Giles admitted that.

But he hadn't said he loved her. So love hadn't grown for him. And her own notion that she loved him was surely born of that same romantic folly. She had already decided that for her to fall in love with him was an impossibility.

The sun rose higher in the sky, hot and bright. Philippa cast off her mantle and dipped a finger in the passing water. The sleeve of her gown caught a ripple, and she brought it out, dripping wet. She shook it, gurgling with delighted laughter, then dipped her whole hand, sleeve and all, into the cool depths.

"This reminds me of my school days at Evesham," she told Giles happily. "The nuns used to watch while we paddled in the river. Some of the younger ones, and the novices, paddled too. I always enjoyed those afternoons."

"Did you swim?" asked Giles with interest, imagining a clutch of nubile maidens sporting in the water.

"Nay! 'Twas not allowed. So I did not learn. Can you swim?"

He grinned. "Oh, yes. So you are quite safe. I'll save you if you fall in."

"I thank you, but I shall not fall in!" asserted Philippa firmly.

Giles made a circuit of the lake, and finished in the middle. He shipped his oars and let the boat drift. "Methinks this will do. Have you seen any fish?"

Philippa peered into the somewhat weedy and murky depths, and shrugged. "No. But they must be there."

"Here, take the net and try."

Philippa shifted, and the boat rocked alarmingly. But she grasped the long handle he held out to her, and leaned over the side, dipping the mesh into the water, and scooping. Giles watched, amused.

Suddenly Philippa squealed in delight. "There are fish! I saw one!"

She began trawling with even more enthusiasm. And caught something heavy. She leapt up to heave it in, and went sprawling over the side of the boat, landing in the water with a mighty splash.

Giles, left alone in a wildly rocking boat, was quick to react. He knelt in the bilge-water and leaned over the side, ready to offer his hand the moment Philippa's head bobbed up again. She clutched thankfully at rescue, spluttering the water from her nose and mouth, blinking it from her eyes.

"I thought you weren't going to fall in," he accused, his eyes dancing blue delight.

"I didn't intend to," gasped Philippa. "Giles, help me out!"

"You'll fill the boat with water," he objected.

"Wretch! Giles, my clothes are dragging me down, and I'm getting cold!"

He pursed his lips and reached for the painter with his free hand. "Here you are. Hold on to this rope and I'll tow you in."

"Giles!" she wailed. "You wouldn't!"

"Why not?" he enquired blandly. "You'll be quite safe." He offered her the rope again.

But Philippa wrapped her chilling fingers round his wrist and clung on for dear life. She knew he didn't mean it, and yet... There was that mischievous look in his eye...He might...

Tears gathered and, instead of cold pond water, warm moisture washed down her cheeks. She stifled a sob. "Please? Giles?"

He relented abruptly. He hadn't meant to make her cry. But the impulse to tease had been irresistible.

"Don't cry, my love!" Contrition made his voice husky. He offered his other hand.

Philippa grasped it, and he heaved. The boat rocked again and almost tipped up, but she was safely in, sprawling in a dripping azure mess in the bottom. Giles wrapped her mantle about her and smoothed the sodden hair from her eyes, removing several fronds of weed in the process. He grinned. "Stay where you are, love. I'll row back as quickly as I can."

Philippa lay where she had landed, in abject misery. She knew she had made a fool of herself. Giles was laughing at her, God rot his soul! And she was cold to the bone.

Good as his word, Giles made the bank in moments, though it seemed an age to Philippa. The churl helped her out, and whined over the loss of the net, which she gathered he would have to replace. Giles promised to pay for it. Then he scooped her up in his arms and carried her back to their pavilion.

He waved aside Ida's twittering concern. "Just find a large dry towel," he ordered brusquely.

He was almost as wet as Philippa. He stripped off her clothes, knowledgeable now about the intricacies of her dress, and swathed her in the soft linen cloth. Then he threw off his own wet things. Philippa's teeth were chattering. Part cold, part shock, part resentment. Giles began to rub warmth back into her limbs, first of all briskly, but as her chill abated so his touch gentled until the act of drying became an erotic massage. She forgot her resentment.

His own body had dried while he worked on hers. He threw the towel aside and lifted an uresisting Philippa into his arms.

"Bed," he decreed, his voice husky. "That will warm you up."

He laid her on their pallet, and threw a light covering over her. Then stretched out beside her, and drew it over himself.

He gathered her to him, burying his nose in the damp hair spread over the pillows. "You smell of pond weed," he told her with a soft chuckle.

Philippa knew she would not remain cold for much longer. But it was not the blanket which would produce the warmth...

Chapter Ten

When the journey resumed the next day Philippa could not prevent a certain nervousness. Hiding it proved an effort. She had seen no sign of her brother since he had disappeared into the darkness, and had successfully managed to forget him during the previous lovely, eventful day; but now she remembered again. He would not be far away.

Plotting.

So what would he do? What *could* he do, without a huge army? Mount a diversionary attack while the King escaped? Try to reach the King at night and spirit him away? Either possibility seemed doomed to failure. But, knowing him as she did, she was certain of one thing. He would not be deterred. So Philippa travelled a prey to apprehension and torn loyalties.

She could not give Roger away. She had promised. Yet she felt guilty at not warning Giles of a possible attempt to free the King, who, although still treated with the greatest reverence and respect, was now quite openly regarded as a traitor to England and its people.

But nothing happened. For days the progress continued without major incident. Philippa relaxed. Mayhap Roger had thought better of his intention after all.

Then, suddenly, some few miles north of St Albans, her worst fears were realised. Out of the blue came the Alban war cry, and a tight body of armed horsemen charged ponderously from the cover of a copse, scattering grazing sheep and cattle as, in a welter of flying turf, they headed across the wide swath of green fringing the highway, cutting straight for the point in the column where the King's standard flew.

Philippa gasped, her shock all the greater for her having been lulled into a false sense of security by Roger's lengthy delay. She glanced quickly in Richard's direction, and caught a glimpse of him between the heads of his mounted guard, attempting to wheel his horse towards the commotion, his face grim and determined. Roger's message had got through. Richard had known what to expect, and when.

While Philippa sat stunned with dismay, Giles reacted instantly. "To d'Evreux!" he roared, and wheeled Majesty from the column.

No one had seriously expected a challenge at this late stage. Roger had behaved with unexpected caution and deviousness. No word of any planned resistance had reached Henry's ears. Lacking the warning she could have given, Giles was only lightly armoured.

Sir Malcolm and Sir William shouted orders, and all the d'Evreux command swept aside. Except Walter Instow, who, cursing loudly, found himself trapped on the far side of Philippa's and Ida's mounts.

The King's guard, far from being diverted, closed in about Richard. His desperate attempt to force his way past the barrier of men and horseflesh failed.

Giles pounded Majesty at an angle towards the approaching attackers. The open swath between highway and screening trees, more than an arrow's flight in width, was maintained by law to prevent ambush. Roger had had no choice but to risk an open charge. He rode at the head of the King's would-be rescuers, his surcoat proclaiming his identity for all to see. He was armoured cap-à-pie, and armed to the teeth. The two men would clash at any moment, and Giles was vulnerable.

Wat had managed to wheel his horse about and pass behind her as space was made by the departure of others. Philippa woke from her momentary trance as he whooped past. There was no time to think. It had all happened in the space of less than ten heartbeats. She dug her heels into the gelding's flanks and put him into a mad gallop which might just overtake Giles before he reached Roger. Majesty was slow and ponderous, heavily laden, Blaze fleet of foot and with only her slight weight to carry.

She had to stop the two men meeting. Had to turn Roger aside and protect Giles. It was her fault he was in danger. She was gaining. But other horsemen were in the way.

Frustration ousted deadly fear until she spotted a gap between two heavy horses and put Blaze through it. Now she was streaking up on the outside, could see Roger clearly, lance aimed straight at Giles. Wat had been carrying Giles's lance, and shields were used only in the joust. Giles had only a sword with which to defend himself.

Fear clutched anew at her stomach, threatened to paralyse her breathing, but she managed to find enough breath from somewhere to shriek at her brother.

"Roger!" she screamed, "Desist! Flee!"

All Giles saw as she shot past was streaming black hair, come loose from its braids, and billowing green sendal. He heard her shriek her brother's name. Whatever it was she was trying to do, she was succeeding in getting in the way and putting herself in danger. And then he had no more time to worry because as she drew level, with her brother only yards away, she jerked Blaze's head round and charged straight in front of Majesty, who, war-trained though he was, shied and almost threw his exasperated, furious rider. The little whore! She had tried to unseat him, to render him helpless before her cursed brother!

Roger, seeing his sister riding straight in front of his levelled lance, swerved violently aside, emitting a heartfelt curse and throwing his following train into confusion. And then they were surrounded by a large section of Bolingbroke's army, led by d'Evreux's men.

It was no contest. The small force of attackers had relied on surprise to spring the King from his human prison cell, so that he could join them and together they could flee, ensuring his escape. The plan had failed and, although some fighting ensued and some of the men evaded immediate arrest, only to be chased over the fields by screaming hordes of Henry's forces, Roger and most of his supporters were captured.

Philippa sat on Blaze's back, weak and shaking, sweating and blowing almost as much as her mount. She had prevented disaster. Giles was safe. But Roger was captured. She didn't want to think what the penalty for his rash behaviour might be. Or why, when forced to choose, she had saved Giles and delivered her brother into his enemies' hands.

Though she had tried to save him, too. Told him to retreat. Had warned him in the first place not to attempt the impossible. He would have been caught whether she had intervened or not. The thought did little to console her uneasy conscience.

She became aware that she was surrounded by horse-soldiers. Lifting her drooping head, she met Giles's gaze. He sat erect on Majesty's highly decorated fighting saddle, staring at her with an expression she could not fathom. Philippa tried a smile, though relief and confusion made it waver, and the ice she saw in Giles's eyes wiped it completely from her face.

"Giles!" She attempted to urge Blaze nearer, but someone took hold of her bridle.

"What in Hades did you think to achieve, my lady?" enquired Giles grimly. "I am not so easily unhorsed!"

Philippa gasped. Giles thought that she… She tried to protest, but no words came. Her mind went blank.

Giles wheeled Majesty away. "See she does not escape," he ordered over his shoulder, and rode off without another glance in the direction of his stricken wife. But there was an unaccustomed set to his wide shoulders. Almost a slump of defeat.

Philippa made no protest when she was led back to join the column, as much a prisoner as Richard or Roger, who sat heavily on his horse, scowling ferociously. Why Giles had assumed she had been trying to aid Roger she could not fathom. Yet perhaps her punishment was just. She had not passed on her knowledge. And mayhap she deserved Roger's condemning looks and muttered curses, too.

Ida came to her in the tent allocated that night. Giles did not. Several soldiers stretched out on the ground, and their snores reverberated around the flimsy shelter. Philippa buried her face in her arms and wished to die.

Everything had gone wrong. And where was that optimism which normally saw her through bad patches? Where was the courage she needed to face the uncertain future, the condemnation of both husband and brother?

Giles would not have been harmed; she saw that now that it was too late. He was far too good a soldier. Had she not rashly interfered, Roger would still have been captured, but she would have been spared the anguish of knowing herself condemned by her husband.

That she did not deserve his harsh judgement scarcely mattered. That, after all they had shared, he could still suspect her of betraying him, did. But she had her pride. She would not plead with him. She would rather die.

This reckless d'Alban pride in the face of adversity kept her upright and apparently calm during the remainder of the journey to London. In truth she shut her mind to any other thought, enduring both hardship and malicious, vengeful glances with equally abstracted calm.

While Henry Bolingbroke and the magnates dispersed about Westminster and the city, Richard was escorted through the crowded, narrow, noisome alleys with their small, dark cottages jumbled on either side, to the Tower. Philippa found herself a part of the same cavalcade, with Roger a few horse-lengths behind. She had barely glimpsed Giles since her arrest.

Her stomach heaved. The stench rising from the streets made the air almost unbreathable even in the cooler temperatures which had followed the humid heat of a week since. There had been little rain, and the cobbles oozed a thick, stinking slime of filth. Stray curs, rats and pigs, rooting in the open sewer running down the centre of the road, scurried from beneath the horses' hoofs. If this was London, its people were welcome to it.

The walls of the Tower closed about them. The King would be comfortable enough, for he was escorted, with due ceremony, to the Wardrobe apartments, from whence as boy-King he had departed for his coronation, and where he had in the past held Court. Now he was surrounded by strangers. Perhaps more so than she was, mused Philippa, for she still had the faithful Ida with her.

She could not help the clutch of cold fear that gripped her stomach as she was led away. Roger was taken to a grim-looking tower, but she was lodged with the Lieutenant, in a small chamber high in his lodging—a timber-framed structure built against the massive curtain-wall, its top storey rising above the stonework. A prisoner still, of course, but her worst imaginings had not yet materialised. She had not been consigned to some dark, dank dungeon. The heavy door thudded shut, and she heard the huge key turn in the lock.

The chamber was barely furnished, but at least there was a bed, even if it was only a straw-stuffed mattress laid on a shelf running along one wall, with a couple of blankets tossed on top. A second pallet, laid straight on the wooden planks of the floor, had been fitted in for Ida. A small table and low stool stood near the glazed window, which overlooked the

River Thames. Her own coffer, which had travelled with her, had been dumped near her bed.

She and Ida were alone for the first time since her arrest.

Philippa looked round the narrow confines of her prison, and the tears sprang to her eyes. The first she had shed since that initial night of captivity. Reality could no longer be kept at bay. There was naught to do but sit and think.

"There is water here, my dear lady. Do you wish to wash?"

Ida's quiet voice broke across her dismal thoughts. Philippa gave her a wan smile, noticing for the first time that all the newly acquired happiness had gone from her tiring-woman's face. She looked pale and depressed. Philippa realised that she had been so sunk in her own gloom that she had spared no thought for poor Ida, condemned to share her mistress's captivity.

"Aye, Ida. 'Twill do us both good to cleanse ourselves of the journey. Would that I could have a bath!"

"No such luxury here, my lamb. Let me unlace your gown."

The green sendal had not been off her back for days. Just to feel the air on her body was luxury. Cold though the water was, it refreshed Philippa, and with the aid of soap from her coffer even cleansed her quite filthy hands.

The azure kirtle which had been immersed in the mere at Kenilworth—a lifetime ago, it seemed—

had dried, and, though creased and somewhat shrunk, was cleaner than the one she had just removed, and did still fit. With her hair tidied, Philippa began to feel better. This nightmare could not last! The truth must become clear before long. No one had questioned her yet, but she was bound to be interrogated. Surely they would believe her when she told them that she had not intended to aid her brother, but her husband?

"Ida," she wondered, "will they believe me?"

"Believe what, my lady?"

"Why, that I did not intend harm to Henry's cause! That I was but trying to protect Giles! Roger would have killed him!"

Ida's face relaxed. "Is that what you were doing, my lamb? 'Twas difficult to make out what you intended, it all happened so quickly!"

"Ida! You did not think I was aiding Roger?"

"Well, it did look like it. And he is your brother."

"Oh, Ida! How could you think such a thing? How could Giles? He knows I lo—I like him, have forgiven him his high-handed treatment of me! God knows, I wish him no harm!" Quite the reverse, in fact. She reluctantly acknowledged the fact that, if anything happened to her husband, life would scarcely be worth living.

Philippa sank down abruptly on the stool. When had she made that discovery? It must have been in the same instant she had plunged so recklessly to his aid. And caused nothing but chaos and heartbreak.

For Giles thought her still against him and his cause. Condemned and hated her.

Would he visit her? Surely he must! He could not abandon her entirely! She was his wife!

Aye, and looked likely to bring disgrace on the name of d'Evreux. He would never forgive her that.

Giles paced his chamber in the lodgings at Westminster Palace, prey to a completely alien indecision. There must be some other explanation for his wife's action! He simply could not believe that she had tried to have him killed, even in a misguided attempt to release the King. She had softened of late, been a willing partner in their delightful lovemaking. And surely she had come to see Richard for the unstable, extravagant despot he really was?

Was she what she seemed: an honest, impulsive child just emerging into rational, entrancing womanhood? Or a treacherous whore who would pretend a passion she did not feel in order to allay his suspicions while she plotted against him?

He really could not believe the latter. She had been virgin on their wedding night. And had fought long and hard against admitting to even her first childish liking, let alone the adult attraction which had flared between them on that first day at Alban. She did not have the experience to fool him into believing a pretended passion genuine.

So why had she intervened? To save her brother, mayhap? That could be. She felt strong family loyalty, for which he could hardly blame her. But now she was married to him—she owed *him* her first loyalty!

Northumberland had witnessed the incident and ordered her arrest. He himself had believed the worst at the time, and done nothing to protect his wife. But now? What did he believe? And surely he owed his wife the same loyalty he demanded from her?

He must talk with her. Resist the undoubted influence of her beauty and the memory of passion, and search out the truth. Only then could he sleep in peace.

He strode from the room and made haste to the river, where the royal barges were moored.

It was almost dusk. Philippa sat by the small window, watching the busy traffic still plying the river below. Little ships from the ends of the earth brought their merchandise to London, ships which looked neither strong nor large enough to venture out into the vastness of the ocean, which she could only imagine, because she had never seen it.

Giles had described the risky crossing from Boulogne to Pevensey, made in one of the small ships Henry had seized to carry his friends and the fifteen lances brought with him from France, and the subsequent trip north to Ravenspur on the Humber, where they had arrived on the fourth day of July. To make for the south coast had been a clever feint on Henry's part. William Scrope had led a royal force to

Dover to intercept the landing and, finding his quarry gone, had returned to St Albans to try to raise an army to cover the approach to London.

St Albans. Why had Roger gone there? He might have thought to rally support more easily in a town that bore his name. Mayhap it was some of the men Scrope had tried to raise that Roger had won to his side! Poor Roger. She dared not dwell upon his predicament; her own was bad enough. Resolutely, she turned her mind back to the train of events Giles had told her of, and which had led to the present confinement of the King.

Only when the Council had realised that Henry was making for the Severn and Wales had they ridden west, where three of them, including Scrope, had met their death.

Philippa shivered at the memory of that day, wishing she had not allowed her thoughts to travel that far. Yet she couldn't have stopped them, and tangled with the horror lingered the memory of the strength, the peace and comfort she had found in Giles's arms. And she had been so determined not to yield an inch to his persuasive charm!

She let out an unconscious sigh. If only he were here now. 'Twas getting late. He would not risk travelling the streets of London after dark. She nibbled fretfully at her thumb nail. He could read. If he did not come tomorrow, she would ask if she could write him a letter.

The daylight was fading fast. They would have to

light their single tallow candle soon. Not that either she or Ida had much to do that needed light. Ida had already done what she could to mend the once splendid new gown, so torn and tattered by the time Philippa had arrived at the Tower. But even a small glimmer of light would help to disperse some of the shadows in the room, shadows which seemed to invade her very heart.

She turned from the window with another sigh. Seeing so much activity going on all around only emphasised her own loss of freedom. People spent their whole lives in prison. Would she be left to moulder into an ancient crone, denied the right to life and love and children? She had begun to bleed again that day. So she was not yet pregnant. She did not know whether to be glad or sorry. They might not behead her if was with child. Yet to bring a child into the world in captivity—that was unthinkable. So mayhap 'twas as well she was not yet carrying the heir Giles would have cherished.

How long she sat in the twilight, sunk in her gloomy thoughts, she did not know. When she glanced out of the window she could see the lanterns gliding across the water of the Thames. The echoing sound of roars and other strange cries from the Royal Menagerie, housed somewhere in the Tower, did little to calm her frayed nerves.

Ida's soft voice broke into her reverie. "Shall I light the candle, my lady?"

Philippa stirred. "Aye, 'twill seem less dismal

with a little light. Poor Ida! What have I brought you to? But you are a free woman. If you wish to leave me to join your lover I shall not ask you to stay.''

"Leave you in trouble, my lamb?'' Ida looked up from striking flint against steel to fix Philippa with an indignant eye. "Of course I will stay! You will not be here for long, you mark my words. Sir Giles will not allow it! Then, mayhap, when you are settled with him and his family, I will seek to join Wolfram Root in Northumberland. He has asked me to be his wife. He is widowed, and his three young children need a woman's hand.''

"And besides, you like him,'' smiled Philippa, cheered by her tiring-woman's happiness despite her own predicament. "Did you not accept him when he asked?''

"I told him I would consider his offer. I did not know whether you would object to my leaving you, my lady.''

"To find your own happiness? Of course not, Ida. If that is what you truly want, you must get word to him, so that he does not leave London not knowing your intention.''

"Aye, though I doubt he can read. 'Twill have to be word of mouth I send.''

"I intend to ask if I can write to my husband. They cannot deny me that privilege. I will request him to send word to your Wolfram Root.''

"Thank you, my lady. 'Twould be a load off my mind.''

"Will the tinder not catch?" asked Philippa, noticing that Ida was still striking sparks without much success. "Let me try."

She jumped up with sudden energy, glad of something practical to do. She had taken only two steps towards the table where Ida was wrestling with the flint and steel when the key grated in the lock and the heavy door began to swing open. Light from a single candle threw a beam across the straw-strewn boards. A flickering glow spread upwards to light the Lieutenant's heavy jowl and ruddy face. He had a deep barrel of a chest and a throaty voice which went with his gross stature.

"You've a visitor," he announced gruffly, and stood back to let his companion past.

The candle flared as the men moved, and Philippa gave a glad cry as she recognised the tall figure who stepped from behind the Lieutenant. Her hands went out in an unconscious gesture of appeal.

"Giles!"

He took the candlestick from the Lieutenant's hand as he passed. "I shall have need of this. It seems the ladies have no light."

"There is a candle on the pricket," rumbled the Lieutenant sourly. "'Tis no fault of mine if 'tis not alight."

"Except that the tinder is damp!" put in Philippa with sudden spirit. Seeing Giles had brought back much of her lost confidence.

"Leave us," ordered Giles curtly. "And mayhap

you can find a place by the kitchen fire for Mistress Ida?''

"Aye, if that is what what your lordship desires. Come, mistress.''

Before obeying the man's summons, Ida looked a question at Philippa, who nodded. Ida bobbed a curtsy at Giles before the door closed behind her and the Lieutenant. The key turned again in the lock.

Before putting it down, Giles lit the candle on the pricket from the one he carried. The twin flames illuminated the small chamber with a golden glow, casting long, shifting shadows beyond everything their rays touched.

He stepped back, and turned to look at his wife. The moment he had entered the room he had been aware of little but her slight figure, clad in the crumpled azure of that mere-soaked kirtle. He needed no such reminder of that day to divert his purpose. His expression hardened as he scrutinised her pinched features.

Philippa stood where she had been when the door opened. Her husband had ignored her outstretched hands, had barely glanced in her direction.

But he was here. And now he *was* looking at her, searching her face as though he sought the answer to some worrying problem. She tried to reach him again, taking a step towards where he stood, though the chamber was so small that the distance separating them was not great. "Giles, husband,'' she whispered.

"I am so thankful you have come. I had planned to ask to write to you…"

She couldn't see his face clearly in the flickering light, but enough to know it was set in harsh, forbidding lines. Gone was the amused lift of smiling lips, the quizzical quirk of a bushy brow, the warmth in laughter-filled, almost-blue eyes. Back had come the haughty lift of the brows, the ice-chilled stare of purely grey eyes, the grim, tight line of a compressed mouth. This was an angry man—the arrogant, domineering Giles who had met her rebellion in their early days. Her heart cried out for the generous, charming, passionate bridegroom of those nights—that day at Kenilworth.

Giles's lips were white. She saw his jaw muscles clench and unclench beneath his beard. "Why, Philippa?" he demanded urgently, "Why did you betray me?"

"But I did not!"

The cry came from her very soul and was echoed by the howl of some captive animal near by. She had had enough of pride, of torn loyalties. She cared not what happened to Roger; her brother had chosen his own path. She knew where she wanted to be. In her husband's arms. To find again the security and peace she had discovered there in the past.

"You say so? How can I believe you, my lady?"

"Ask Roger!" she appealed desperately. "He will tell you that I refused to aid him! He cursed me as loudly as you did when I came between you by the road!''

Giles eyed her sceptically. He had heard d'Alban using some choice language—had it been directed at his sister? ''Why, then, did you attempt to unseat me?'' he demanded, his frigid tone not one whit modified by her pleading.

''I did not! I know it looked like it—Ida said as much; but, oh, Giles, you must believe me! I did feel guilty, I admit that. I should have warned you that Roger was attempting a rescue, but he had made me promise not to! I could not break my word! So you were not prepared for his attack, and I thought he would kill you! You wore only your breastplate... I tried to save you,'' she finished miserably.

''Then why did you not say so at the time?'' His voice had softened, his face reflected his uncertainty. Philippa took heart.

''I was given little chance,'' she reminded him grimly. ''I was put under guard, and no one even asked me why I had done what I did. Even now, you are the first—''

''Henry had other, more important matters on his mind,'' snapped Giles. ''You are to be questioned to-morrow.''

Philippa swallowed. ''By whom?'' she got out.

''Northumberland. He saw the incident and ordered your arrest.''

''Sir Henry Percy.'' Philippa closed her eyes, picturing the tough, fierce northern Earl, and finding little comfort in the recollection. "He will not believe me."

"If you speak the truth he will. He is not an unreasonable man." Giles paused, then took that all-important pace which brought him close to her, so close that she could feel his body-warmth envelop her like a cloak. "Pippa." He lifted her chin, the steel of his fingers more gentle than she had expected. "Did you speak truth? Were you trying to stop Roger's lance?"

She lifted her eyes to meet his squarely. She imagined they had some blue in them again. "Aye," she affirmed. "I spoke truth. I refused to deliver a message to someone near enough to the King to pass it on. But the message got through. Richard was expecting the attack."

"Aye, I know. I wonder who—some page, I suppose, for reward..." Giles abandoned his speculation. Her large, dark, dark eyes shone up at him without guile. He knew suddenly that she was telling him the truth. Relief and anger surged through his body in a hot tide. He longed to clasp her to his breast, to kiss her until they were both dizzy. To shake her senseless. To thrash some sense into her addled brain.

He resisted all three of his conflicting impulses. "Well, lady," he bit out scornfully, "you might have deflected your brother's lance, but you have managed to embroil us both in a wasp's nest of trouble in the process! Did you think me incapable of defending myself?"

"I did not stop to think! Afterwards, I realised you were too experienced to fall to Roger's attack. But…all I knew was that I couldn't bear for you to die. Especially at my brother's hand."

Giles's heart knocked in his chest. She couldn't mean that she cared what happened to him? "So now we come to the nub of it!" he snorted. "'Twas Roger you wished to save from a charge of murder!"

"You twist what I say! I did not even think of that!" protested Philippa desperately. "Giles, sometimes I absolutely hate you! Can you not see that I am innocent of the charge Northumberland has brought against me?"

The lion roared into the silence before he shrugged and answered. "Mayhap," he admitted, "but my opinion is not what matters." Would Percy believe her? That was the important thing. Would Henry Bolingbroke, if Giles sought him out and told him the story? Once an accusation had been laid it was so cursedly difficult to disprove it. It was her word against what Percy thought he had seen… "Pippa," he went on fiercely, "you must stop behaving like some beardless youth. You are my wife!" he finished on a sigh of exasperation.

Philippa flinched as though he had struck her, and the fingers on her chin tightened. "I had begun to doubt you remembered that!" she shot back.

"Oh, I remember." He bent his head, and his lips claimed hers in a brief, hard kiss. "I will visit again on the morrow," he promised, then released her chin and, in the same flowing movement, rapped on the door with the hilt of his sword.

The guard must have been waiting just outside. The key turned, the door opened and Giles left without a backward glance, leaving the second candle behind. She had forgotten to ask him to deliver Ida's message. Never mind. There was always tomorrow.

Tomorrow. What would it bring? Hope of release or condemnation?

Whatever else, it would bring Giles. The ache in her heart, the depression bearing down her spirit, lifted slightly. Philippa stretched out on her pallet and, for the first time since her confinement, allowed her thoughts to roam over their brief marriage.

It hadn't been all grief. But if things went badly tomorrow, she might never know the full joy of being wife to Giles d'Evreux, the mother of his children.

When Ida returned she found her mistress lying with her face to the wall, weeping quietly.

Chapter Eleven

Giles paced the ante-room to Henry's chamber. He had sought audience half an hour since. Such a wait was unusual. Henry was normally quick to admit him to his presence.

Could Henry possibly suspect him of being in collusion with his wife? He had detected a slight remoteness in his liege-lord's manner over the last days. But surely he was the last man Henry Bolingbroke would suspect of treason against his cause? Had he not suffered exile for his lord's sake?

Curse Philippa and her scatter-brained attempt to prevent her brother's doing him an injury! If she had harmed his relationship with Henry Bolingbroke, then he could wish he had never gone to Alban Castle, let alone forced the wench into a marriage against her will.

Yet—he would not be unwed. He could not deny the attraction which had flared in him the moment he had set astonished eyes on his amazingly improved betrothed, standing defiantly in the courtyard of her home. Nor the way she had changed from spitting kitten to affectionate, purring cat, the outpouring of her passionate nature diverted into new channels under his tutelage. He had always liked cats, he mused. A wry twitch of a smile momentarily softened the grim set of his lips as he absorbed the aptness of the comparison. Infuriating, independent creatures!

The thought of her suffering twisted his gut. He halted abruptly, staring sightlessly at one of the brightly patterned heraldic shields hung on the wall. The mere hint that she might lose her life over this affair tore at something much deeper in his emotions, something he refused to acknowledge.

At that point in his cogitations the door opened and a groom of the bedchamber indicated that Giles could enter. It was late, and Henry was abed, though sitting up, propped on billowing pillows which reminded Giles uncomfortably of his nuptial couch.

"Giles! 'Tis good to see you!"

His greeting sounded sincere. "Your Grace." Giles bent his knee as he always did when entering Henry's presence. "I am grateful to you for granting me audience."

"Forgive my neglect of late." Henry made a wry grimace. "I have had weighty matters of state on my mind." He indicated the parchments scattered over the coverlet of the bed.

Giles nodded. "Aye, lord. The fate of this nation

rests on your shoulders. But I crave your attention on a personal matter for a few moments.''

''Doubtless the Lady Philippa, your wife,'' remarked Bolingbroke, his expression of wry regret replaced by a rather grim frown. ''I confess her behaviour puzzles me.''

''As it did me, my lord. But I have just spoken to her in the Tower—''

''Is she lodged comfortably? I have no desire for her to suffer unnecessarily. I did not see what passed, but Henry Percy is convinced she attempted to render you helpless before her brother's lance, and thus aid his attempted rescue of the King. Not that my cousin required rescuing,'' he added grimly. ''An he is reasonable…But that is yet another matter. You have seen your wife, you say?''

''Aye, lord. And I am convinced that, although she acted rashly—I am learning that many of her actions are rash—'' Giles admitted ruefully, ''she meant neither me nor your cause harm. She wished to prevent bloodshed between her brother and myself. A not unreasonable objective, I believe, though her manner of achieving it left much to be desired. And,'' he added with a gesture of lofty dismissal, ''her concern was quite unnecessary.'' He paused to look Henry straight in the eye. ''But I do not believe she deserves further punishment for her foolish action.''

Henry peered at him from beneath knitted brows, and waved an enquiring hand. ''What does Percy say?''

Giles shifted his stance. His spurs jangled in the quietness of the bedchamber. "I have yet to speak with him, lord. But I did visit Roger d'Alban before I left the Tower." He gave a mirthless laugh. "He is in a sullen and truculent mood. He greeted me with invective, which was directed as much against his sister as it was against me. He confirms that he attempted to enlist her help for his scheme, which she refused. And then inserted her person between himself and his target—which at that moment happened to be me."

Henry's face relaxed, and he broke into a chuckle. "Always in the van, eh, Giles?"

Giles responded with a quick smile before he went on quietly. "He considers himself justifiably incensed by his sister's behaviour. Had another led the counter-attack, I doubt my wife would have taken action. She vows she was afraid for my skin, and feeling guilt because she had not broken the promise of silence he had exacted from her and warned me of her brother's intention."

Henry gazed intently at his uneasy courtier for a moment. "Who does she support?" he rapped. "Richard, or me?"

"My lord, I do not think she actively supports either party. Richard is her anointed King, and her family has always been loyal to the throne. As have we all," he pointed out smoothly. "She has now had opportunity to study Richard, and knows you to have been sorely wronged. She is content to let you work

things out between yourselves. But,'' went on Giles
firmly, lifting a determined chin as though to challenge any possible rebuttal, ''her first loyalty is owed
to me, her husband.'' He stepped forward, and lifted
Henry's capable hand from the parchment on which
it rested. He knelt and carried it to his lips. ''And my
loyalty is yours,'' he affirmed quietly. ''My wife will
follow where I lead.''

''Can you swear to that?'' enquired Henry, a sardonic gleam of amusement in his eyes. ''But I accept
your allegiance gratefully; I have never for a moment
doubted it. And I hear what you say. I will speak with
Northumberland in the morning, before he leaves for
the Tower. Your wife appears to be guilty of nothing
but misplaced good intentions. She has a loyal heart,
which should serve you well in the future.''

''My lord, that is my hope.''

''She will be freed. But—a certain amount of questioning, of uncertainty, may prove a salutary lesson
to guide her future conduct. Do you not agree?''

Giles smiled his relief and sprang to his feet.

''Aye, and I thank you, Your Grace. You have my
deepest gratitude.''

''I am glad to see you happy in your union, Giles.
Make sure you guard such felicity. I wasted my
chance,'' Henry admitted with a sigh. ''I wore my
poor Mary de Bohun down with too much child-
bearing and too little companionship. Yet I loved her,
and miss her now she is gone.''

''You are in treaty to marry the daughter of the

Duc de Berry. Mayhap you will find new happiness there, lord.''

''Mayhap.'' Henry sounded doubtful. His would be a political alliance if it matured. ''Thank God Mary was able to give me Harry and the other children, though I should have realised how frail she was, and desisted...'' He sighed. ''But young Harry will be here soon! I have seen too little of my son and heir over the past years. He must be grown almost to manhood! I pray I may have the opportunity to make up for my past deficiencies as a father!'' He held out his hand. ''Rest easy, Giles. Your wife will be safe with you on the morrow.''

''I thank you again, lord.'' Giles took the proffered hand, and hesitated, reluctant to ask another favour, but knowing he had little choice. ''I would like to take her straight to my parents, at Acklane, in Oxfordshire. Will you grant me a few days in which to make the journey and see her settled?''

''Aye, Giles. But do not delay too long. I fancy there will be much to do over the next few weeks before Parliament meets. Negotiations...changes in the highest offices of state... Richard must be made to right his wrongs. And I shall need all the support I can muster.''

''You may rely on me, lord. I will make the journey with as much haste as possible.''

''Then go in peace, my friend.'' Henry grinned, looking suddenly much younger. ''And good luck in your affairs matrimonial!''

* * *

The inquisition was harsh. Philippa, summoned from her chamber to the presence of Henry Percy, Duke of Northumberland, hid her trembling hands in the crumpled folds of her azure kirtle and kept her chin high. She would *not* be intimidated! She had done nothing wrong! Except to act recklessly in defence of her husband.

Giles, hidden behind an arras, silently cheered his wife's courage, the common sense and honesty with which she countered Percy's persistent questioning. Had he not known that Henry Percy was merely putting on a show he might have trembled for his wife. Though she seemed to be holding her own. The old man's tone had softened despite himself.

Percy harrumphed. ''So you do not support your brother, eh?'' he enquired, in a voice which said he didn't believe her, and if he did she was wrong not to.

Philippa bristled at his tone. ''I cannot support my brother against my husband! Believe me, my lord Duke, I desire nothing but peace between them, and in this land!''

''Hmm, well, I am inclined to believe you, Lady Philippa. Mayhap I was wrong to accuse you as I did. But appearances were against you. You may go,'' he ended abruptly.

'''Go'?'' For a moment Philippa felt bewildered. Was she free? Or merely being allowed to return to her prison chamber? ''You mean I may leave the Tower?''

"Aye. All charges dropped. Your husband is waiting near by. He will escort you from here."

Relief made Philippa weak. She concentrated on Northumberland's weathered face as the room swung around her. "Thank you, Your Grace," she managed. She turned and forced her legs to carry her steadily towards the door. Her brain seemed numb with relief, yet before she reached the exit she stopped and turned again. "What will happen to my brother?" she enquired tightly.

"He will be tried."

"On what charge? He was attempting to aid the King. That can surely not be counted treason?"

"The King did not need his aid," snapped Percy irritably. "Do not concern yourself with Roger d'Alban. In due course he will be dealt with fairly and justly. Meanwhile, he is not uncomfortably lodged."

"May I see him?"

"It would be unwise. Go with d'Evreux, child. Thank God, Henry Bolingbroke, and your husband for your release. Do not become further embroiled in your brother's fate."

Philippa nodded. A modicum of warmth began to spread through her body. So Giles had had something to do with her aquittal. She left Northumberland's presence and returned in a daze to tell Ida the good news.

Giles stepped from behind the arras and frowned

grimly at Henry Percy. "You did not spare her, my lord," he accused.

"I was instructed otherwise! She is a taking filly, d'Evreux; you are a lucky man. But do keep her on a leading-rein in future! Otherwise, you are liable to find both her and yourself in deep trouble!"

Giles allowed his relief to surface, and chuckled. "She is too spirited for a leading-rein, Your Grace. And I could not bring myself to whip her. So I shall have to use gentler methods. Treats, and kind words and...ah...the occasional soothing pat and stroke...?"

Both men broke into gusts of laughter, and Giles was still grinning when he tapped and entered his wife's chamber.

Philippa, waiting expectantly for his arrival, observed the amusement on her lord's face and something inside her snapped. She could see absolutely no reason for mirth; her situation had been uncomfortable to say the least—terrifying, if the truth be told. And Giles had not helped the previous evening by his unsympathetic, critical manner. He must have been instrumental in gaining her release, but now he had the gall to laugh at her!

The candlestick, with its burnt-out stub of wax, was to hand. Without considering the wisdom of her action, she snatched it up and threw it into his mocking face.

Giles's reflexes were honed to perfection. He caught the missile easily, and stood looking from it to his wife in pained astonishment. "What did I do to deserve that?" he enquired mildly.

"You…you…" Philippa searched for a bad enough word to use "…you smirking cretin!" she spat. "'Tis no matter for amusement! I was unjustly accused, I have suffered most grievously, and all you can do is laugh!"

"Pippa! I was not laughing!" he protested somewhat guiltily. "I know you have had a miserable time! My love, I am just happy that you are free!"

"Ha!" she scorned.

He stood there with the candlestick in his hand, looking as though he didn't know what on earth to do with it. Suddenly he looked comical, the situation was comical, and Philippa broke into hysterical laughter.

Giles acted instantly. He thrust the candlestick into Ida's ready hand, strode over to his wife and took her by the shoulders. Now he could shake her with good excuse, and he did so.

"Stop it, Pippa! Stop it, do you hear me?"

The laughter turned to great, gulping sobs, and Giles gathered her to him. "My love, it is over! You are safe!" he murmured tenderly.

Philippa rested against him, her hands spread against the solid wall of his chest while the shudders racked her body. She felt his hand stroking her hair, the soft touch of his lips on her temple, gave a last convulsive hiccup, and buried her face in his shoulder.

"I'm sorry," she whispered.

"Nay, wife! 'Tis I who should apologise, for my harsh treatment over the last days. I should have known that you would not betray me. But—you had been so fierce in your father's cause."

She lifted huge midnight eyes, still swimming with tears, to scrutinise his face. "Your doubt did hurt me, husband. After all we had shared... I could not understand how you could question my loyalty."

"I shall not do so again."

He lowered his head and touched her lips with his. Fire seared between them, and Philippa's arms reached up to wrap themselves about his neck. Giles's hold tightened, his lips firmed, and the kiss went on and on until they were both breathless.

They broke apart and stood looking at each other. Something new had happened between them during that embrace, but neither quite knew what it was.

"Come, wife," murmured Giles at last. "Let us remove ourselves from this place. I am taking you to my parents, at Acklane. You will be safe and cherished there."

Philippa gulped as a sudden chill swept over her. "But—cannot I remain with you?"

"'Twill only be until Parliament meets. Until then I shall be kept busy with Henry's affairs. You would be lonely at Westminster, sweetheart, and you need time to recover from your ordeal. After that, I shall have more time, and shall know what the future holds. Then we can be together again."

"Very well." Philippa knew it would be useless to plead further. He did not want her at his side. Would probably find her presence an embarrassment. Mayhap, in a month's time, the scandal of her arrest would be forgotten.

Their arrival at Acklane two days later caused a considerable stir. Giles had sent a messenger ahead to warn of their coming. Philippa passed the great oak which gave the manor its name, rode steadily beneath the leafy branches of an avenue of wych elms, and emerged to rein Blaze to a halt before the gracious manor house Richard, first earl of Wenstaple, had built in the first half of the century, and later given to his half-brother Thomas, Giles's father. The place was alive with servants and dogs. A new wing, built of the same warm, cream-coloured stone, had recently been added to the original building, and it was from there that a man in thick leather buskins and a plain russet tunic appeared on the step to greet them.

"John, my brother," grinned Giles, leaping from Panache's back and helping Philippa to dismount while one of the grooms rushed to hold the horses' heads. Two women had appeared behind his brother, one youthful and comely in a blue linen kirtle with matching velvet bosses holding her abundant chestnut hair, the other older, in a simple grey gown and white kerchief, bearing a baby in her arms. "Constance, his wife," Giles went on informatively, "and that must be the latest addition to their brood in the nurse's arms! The older ones are away for schooling, the younger no doubt occupied in the nursery.''

Ida and Wat dismounted too, while Eadulf brought up the rear, shepherding a pack-mule bearing their coffers. Meanwhile John d'Evreux strode across the neat courtyard to greet them.

''Giles! 'Tis good to see you, brother, and looking well, too! And this must be Lady Philippa, your wife!'' He turned to scrutinise her with searching interest, his serious grey eyes warm with sudden admiration. ''My dear, we are glad to welcome you to Acklane. Giles, you appear, as usual, to be a lucky dog!''

Philippa found herself blushing. ''Thank you,'' she murmured.

Constance, on closer inspection, proved to be less striking in her features and rather older and plumper than the distant glimpse had suggested. Yet good nature shone from her rather pale blue eyes, and she appeared comfortable in her matronly role.

''Where are our parents?'' enquired Giles as they all made for the main entrance to the house, set in an embattled tower, the only sign of defensive fortification visible in a place where doves flew in and out of a cote set at the apex of the thatched roof. ''Well, I trust?''

''Father rode out to inspect the harvest; he had expected to be back before now. Mayhap he has uncovered some slackness,'' grimaced John. ''He does not yet completely trust my stewardship! And our mother is resting. She tires more easily these days.''

''There is naught wrong with her?'' demanded Giles anxiously.

''Nay, brother, do not distress yourself! She has been busy this morn preserving fruit from our orchard, and decided to rest before supper, that is all.''

But Lady Marguerite had heard the commotion of their arrival and, as they moved through the screens to enter the Great Hall, a large chamber made light by the tall, mullioned windows lining one side, she came down the stairs from the solar.

Marguerite de Bellac had aged well. Never truly beautiful but always attractive, her bone-structure had stood the test of time, and her finely drawn face was as well-sculpted now as had been that of the woman of four and twenty years who had captured the love of Thomas d'Evreux.

Her hair, braided and coiled, half hidden under a circlet and veil, was almost entirely grey. She must be—what? Philippa asked herself as she curtsied to the Countess. Well past her fiftieth summer. And thin and straight as a lance. She held herself with dignity and, though blotched brown in places, the hand she extended to Philippa was shapely and strong.

''My dear daughter! Welcome!'' She drew Philippa to her and kissed her cheek. ''And my son! A married man at last! I had despaired of ever seeing this scoundrel honouring his contract and brought to the church door!'' She laughed joyously, and took her second son into a warm embrace, which he returned with a great hug.

She had still not lost the attractive French accent with its Spanish intonations that Philippa remembered from her betrothal visit. She stared in renewed fascination at the French Compte's daughter who had defied convention to marry a base-born Anglo-Norman knight. John had arrived in the world a scant seven months after their marriage. He had not been premature. Philippa had heard only echoes of the scandal which had rocked the Lancastrian court, where Thomas had served John of Gaunt faithfully for most of his life, but she knew the couple had weathered it, and been blissfully happy in their union. As well as their two sons, they had two daughters, who were both now married with children of their own.

She and Giles were escorted to a guest chamber. Philippa gave a crow of delight.

"You had my coffers brought here!" she exclaimed. "Ida! Find me a decent gown to wear!"

Giles chuckled. "I thought you might need a few more things than those you were able to take on the journey."

"But how did you know…when did you know we were coming here?" demanded Philippa, suddenly suspicious.

"I knew we were destined for Westminster. I ordered your things brought here when we left Bristol.

I would have sent for them had you remained in London.''

''Handy,'' sniffed Philippa, suddenly less pleased to see her possessions. ''You managed to avoid that necessity by banishing me here.''

''Pippa, you have not been banished! Do you not want to know my parents? My brother and his wife? They are your family too, now. Your stay here will allow you to forge links which will last a lifetime. Sweetheart, I will come for you the first moment I am able.'' He drew her to him, holding her fast against his warm, vital body. ''You know I will burn for you while we are apart,'' he murmured deeply. ''I do not leave you here from choice.''

His lips covered hers with fierce possessiveness, and Philippa knew that he meant what he said. As the heat between them intensified she cursed her monthly showing, which would prevent their full union for several days yet. If only she could have sent him on his way with the delights of passion freshly imprinted on his mind and body! But she could still make her mark on his awareness. She vowed he would remember the coming night throughout their separation.

She left his arms reluctantly, running her finger down his cheek in a gesture of tender submission. ''Do not doubt that I shall miss you, too,'' she told him softly. ''Thank you for your thought for my comfort, Giles. I was foolish to doubt your good intentions.''

Giles, still breathing rather heavily from the passions aroused by that kiss, lifted her chin and touched her swollen lips again with his, cherishing and soothing them to assuage the effects of his previous assault. ''Where you are concerned, wife, all my intentions are good ones,'' he assured her, ''even if a little primitive at times…''

She chuckled contentedly. ''So I have noticed! And now, my lord, please allow me to bathe and change, so that I may present a more respectable appearance at supper!''

The Earl of Acklane was not one to stand on much ceremony at the best of times, and kept a modest establishment now he had retired to his estates. His ego needed no boost from the lavish ceremonial some of his peers thought essential. So a single herald trumpeted the news that supper was about to be served.

Thomas, dressed still in his riding clothes, rose from his chair on the dais to greet his son and his wife as they appeared. Philippa noticed that he winced with pain as he pushed up on the arms, and limped slightly as he moved stiffly towards them. The joints of the strong swordsman's fingers which gripped her hand were knotted with rheumatism, and she guessed his knees were similarly afflicted. Otherwise he appeared fit and well, his lean face still remarkably attractive under the abundant grey hair and lavish beard which went with his advanced years. He had been the same age as John of Gaunt, whose death earlier that year had precipitated the present crisis.

He greeted her courteously, then gripped his son's shoulders. They were of a height, though possibly the father had lost an inch with age. They smiled at each other, and Philippa thought how alike their lively eyes were, apart from their colour. The Earl's were quite grey. At that moment Giles's looked almost blue. "'Tis good to have you home again, my boy," said the Earl heartily, releasing his son's shoulders to clap him on the back. "And Henry? How does he?"

"Well enough, I believe, sir." Giles returned the affectionate gesture, and then shrugged. "Though he is in two minds as to the King's intentions. Richard promises much, but—"

"Aye. Poor Lancaster had the devil's own job guiding the boy over the years. He was ever devious, and seemingly quite oblivious to the feelings of his subjects. What a tragedy for England that his father died so young." He sighed. "John did his best to keep his nephew in line, but now that he is dead..."

"Richard has run amok," said Giles grimly.

"Aye. Mayhap Henry and their uncle of York, the Percys, and others, too, can instil some sense into his head before it is too late."

"I think it may already be too late. People have had enough," said Giles soberly. "Everywhere I hear the same prayer. God give us a new King."

Thomas looked at his son in alarm. "'Tis that bad? People are openly speaking treason?"

"Aye."

"And Henry Bolingbroke?"

"Is next in the male line. He would be willing, I believe," said Giles quietly.

Philippa smothered a gasp. When she had voiced such a possibility Giles had jumped down her throat. Yet now he was airing the idea to his father!

Thomas frowned. "Be careful where you speak words like that, my son. Should Richard prevail, there are those who would have your head for treason—"

"But here, sir, in the privacy of your manor, I believe I can speak my mind without fear. Henry would make a good King."

Both men ignored the swarming churls and varlets serving and gathering for supper. They would not hear what was said, and if they did would not betray a master they respected, probably loved. Philippa knew the same could have been said of the manor folk and servants at Alban. And the men clearly trusted her not to repeat what she heard. She moved closer to Giles, allying herself with her husband. Never again would she give him cause to doubt her loyalty.

"I have known Henry since he was a babe," smiled Thomas. "Aye, he would make a good King. He has ambition, as had his father, and a wise head on young shoulders. He is shrewd, energetic, an excellent tactician and soldier, a great defender of the nation's rights. John would never have challenged his nephew himself; he had too much sense of the sanctity of an anointed King.'' He paused in fond and respectful remembrance of his old lord and friend, then sighed. ''But things have come to such a pass that I believe he would applaud Henry's stand. And he would be gratified to see his son King. Two of his daughters are Queens, albeit of foreign lands. To have Henry King of England...'Twould delight him greatly.''

''You knew him better than most, Father. I am glad to hear you say so.''

Thomas nodded soberly. ''And you, Giles.'' He pursued the subject on a more personal note. ''You would not lose by his accession. You have been a faithful retainer and companion for many years. He would surely reward you well.''

Giles shrugged, while Philippa studied her husband's face with renewed interest. That thought had not previously occurred to her. But mayhap Henry would appoint him to one of the great offices of State. Or grant him a title of his own.

But Giles was shaking his head. ''I have no ambition for high office, sir, nor to be tied to the King's Court. Lands would be welcome, mayhap, though those my wife brought me would suffice for our needs, I believe.'' He drew Philippa into the crook of his arm. ''We require little more than we already have. Do you agree with me, wife?''

Philippa smiled up at her husband, and the Countess, arriving at that moment, felt a sense of deep relief sweep over her. Margot loved all her children, and their happiness was important to her, but this second son of hers was perhaps more dear than the others, for he was so like his father had been in his youth. Her first-born, John, had become studious and earnest as he'd grown into manhood. At times Margot wanted to stir her eldest from his preoccupation with estates and family, make him seek honour, fun and adventure. But such pursuits were not in his nature, and he seemed happy enough.

Although Giles had undoubtedly fulfilled all her dreams of breeding a courageous, honourable, compassionate son just like his father, embodying all the best attributes of chivalry, he had troubled her of late. So devoted to Bolingbroke, always battling for honour in some joust or another, skipping from one romantic attachment to another, he had appeared reluctant to fulfil his obligations and ignored his young betrothed, who had perforce waited for him these many years.

Margot drew nearer and studied his dear face anew. It held a new expression of contentment as he smiled down at his wife, and her heart lifted. Her son needed the stability an affectionate wife and family could give him. Above all, he needed love. Just as his father had needed love, though he had not known it until it had hit him in the face like the low-hanging branch of a tree slapping a careless rider galloping beneath its boughs. She smiled at the memories, and regarded her daughter-in-law with new affection.

Philippa loved her husband, perhaps without fully realising it, but Margot was certain. That look in her eyes could mean nothing else. As yet Giles was not aware of his wife's deep attachment, and showed little sign of returning it. But he would. He appeared fond and protective, and passion lurked in the depths of his eyes. Love would grow. Margot joined the little group happier about her favourite son's future than she would have thought possible only moments before.

''Nay, husband,'' Philippa was answering, ''I have no desire to become part of a Royal Court. I have seen enough of the scheming and treachery, the dangers which seethe beneath the surface, and I want no part in it.''

Giles squeezed her waist affectionately. ''We may have no choice, sweeting. An Henry orders, I must obey!''

''But he will respect your preferences, Giles, make them known to him.'' Margot's throaty voice joined the conversation for the first time, and Thomas smiled a welcome to his wife while Giles and Philippa bowed and curtsied.

The idea of Henry's becoming King was no new one to the Countess, Philippa noted. She had immediately understood the tenor of their conversation.

John and Constance arrived at that moment, and they all took their places for supper.

''We heard from Dickon today,'' Margot informed Giles once they were seated and Grace had been said.

"He will bide here on his way to Westminster for the Parliament."

"And how does my cousin Richard, the second Earl of Wenstaple?" asked Giles with a grin. "He is getting rather old to be chasing about the countryside attending Parliament, I'd have thought!"

"My dear boy, he is eight years younger than your father, and still fully active! They intend to travel to Westminster together."

"He comes alone, then?"

"Aye. Wenfrith and Wenstaple, not to mention both the Countesses, will be in his son's safe hands while he is away," his mother informed him. "'Tis a pity Matilda is not strong. I know it distresses Dickon greatly to see his wife so weak since the birth of their last child."

"Aye, it must. How is the old Countess?" asked Giles. "'Tis many years since I last saw her—"

"'Tis the same for us. Devon is so far distant," interjected Thomas sorrowfully. "I cannot ride so far these days, and neither, of course, can Eleanor. She was like a mother to me, and I much regret that we are so far apart."

"But to answer your question," said Margot, "she is indomitable as ever, though frail, which must be expected in someone who has just celebrated the seventieth anniversary of her birth!"

Philippa, listening to the chatter, relaxed into the embrace of the d'Evreux family while wondering, somewhat belatedly, what was befalling her own.

Chapter Twelve

Giles departed early the following morning. Before he left he presented his wife with a puppy from the kennels' latest litter.

"He's beautiful," whispered Philippa in gratitude. Giles had remembered his promise, and the realisation brought her more comfort than the actual possession of the tiny creature snuffling and whimpering in her arms.

"Something to remember me by," he grinned, but his voice held a deep note which stirred Philippa's pulse anew.

"I need no such reminder," she told him breathlessly, "but I shall be grateful for his company during your absence." Her colour rose, and she hid her face in the puppy's velvety fur. "Do you remember *me*, husband!" she bade her spouse gruffly.

He took hold of her chin and lifted her eyes to meet his. "Do not doubt it, my love," he assured her softly, and sealed the promise with a kiss both would remember for many a long day.

September had brought an autumnal bite to the air, and a mist lay hazily over the demesne fields as Philippa watched his departure from an embrasure in the battlements above the entrance. The turning leaves were still thick enough on the trees to obscure his figure as he cantered off, azure velvet mantelet flying behind him, Walter Instow in faithful attendance.

Eadulf had remained at Acklane to act as her escort should she wish to ride abroad. Not that there were no horse-grooms at Acklane, but Eadulf was a familiar servant and friend, and Giles, she was increasingly aware, a thoughtful husband.

Philippa lifted the soft furry creature in her arms to kiss its little head. It squirmed round to lick her face, and found the single tear which had escaped to trickle down her cheek.

She swallowed hard, and turned to descend the stairs, heaving a sigh. Despite the company of the d'Evreux family and her new pet she would be lonely while Giles was away. Mayhap he would manage a quick visit before the end of September. Memory of the ardour with which he had promised to return to her bed with all dispatch brought colour to Philippa's pale cheeks. She had astonished—nay, embarrassed—herself with her wanton behaviour during the night, but Giles had not complained. A reminiscent smile curved her lips. She had instinctively found ways to give him all the release and joyous satisfaction he needed despite her condition. And in return had received exquisite pleasure from her husband's caresses.

She prayed he would not wish to bed other women while he was away from her. She would not be able to abide other than her husband's touch, but mayhap men were different. Most wives seemed to think so, and accepted their spouse's faithlessness with resignation. But perhaps most of them did not give their husbands incentive to remain faithful. And mayhap they did not love them.

She tossed that last thought aside as she winged fervent thanks to Isobel, who had been her first instructress on the importance of giving pleasure to one's spouse.

"What shall I call you?" she murmured as she set the puppy down on the rush matting in her chamber. Tail high, yelping excitedly, he immediately set about sniffing into every corner of his new surroundings. "What do you think, Ida?"

"'Tis not for me to say, my lady. But mayhap Ears would do."

"Ears?" asked Philippa in surprise. "Why Ears?"

"They are so big and floppy," grinned Ida.

Philippa laughed, but said, "No, I don't like that idea." She caught the puppy and ran one of his long appendages through gentle fingers while a frown of concentration marked her smooth forehead. Suddenly she exclaimed, "I know! Paws!"

"Paws?" echoed Ida with raised brows. "Is that so very different from Ears? And why so?"

"Because they are big and white, while the rest of him is dun, and it has a better ring. Don't you like it?"

"Of course, my lady!" Ida chuckled. "Paws he must be! Though they won't look so large when he has grown!"

"I know that, but they will still be white!"

The days passed quietly but pleasantly. When it was fine Philippa rode out on Blaze, discovering the extent and beauty of the Acklane estate, but as the month progressed rain became more frequent and she was confined much of the time to the house.

Philippa adored Giles's parents, and liked his brother and his wife, though aware that, content in their marriage as they were, John and Constance would never reach the heights of conjugal bliss that the Earl and his wife had found. *Their* delight in each other, even after more than thirty years, was encouraging to see. It gave her hope for her own marriage, for undeniably Giles was very like his father. And if he should learn to love her…

She spent time with the children and cooed over the baby while the desire for one of her own grew. A dog was not enough, sweet as Paws was. She did not think she was particularly maternal, but to give her husband heirs was her duty. And she had become quite attached to the idea of a small replica of Giles to love.

But she could not curb her restlessness. The thought of her brother in the Tower, his wife and children bereft of his guiding hand, distressed her more every day. She had time to think now. To consider the plight of her father and sister-in-law, banished from their home. And on Giles's orders! However much she might now understand and forgive, and realise by Roger's subsequent actions that Giles's concern had been justified, the fact remained. And nothing had been done to relieve her relatives' distress.

Here she was, comfortably ensconced in the bosom of her husband's family—although John was away, visiting others of the manors which comprised his inheritance—awaiting a summons to the new King's Court. For that, she was by now convinced, could be the only final outcome of Henry's bid to regain the Lancastrian estates and bring Richard to heel.

News did reach Acklane, and they heard of concessions made by the King. The Government was still being carried on in his name, but on the third day of September he had given the Treasurership to John Norbury—another, like Giles, who had been with Bolingbroke in Paris. Philippa wondered whether the office had been offered to Giles, and turned down. Thomas grinned and shook his head, observing wryly, "Giles knows nothing of money except how to win it and how to spend it—and besides, he was here with us at the time!"

Two days later the King had ordered Edmund Staf-

ford to surrender the Great Seal, and appointed John
Scarle Chancellor in his place. Thomas knew Scarle.
He had been in John of Gaunt's Chancellery, and he
reckoned him a sound choice. But both the new appointments must have been dictated by Henry Bolingbroke, and Richard Clifford, Keeper of the Privy
Seal, had kept his office only because he had acceded
to the new administration, and vowed himself willing
to work with those appointed on Bolingbroke's instructions.

Eventually, Philippa could stand the inactivity, the
anxiety, no longer. She knew what she must do.
Travel to Fishacre to see her father and Mary. Why
hadn't she thought of it before? It was only just over
the Oxfordshire border in Gloucestershire—no more
than a day's journey from Acklane for a person travelling light on a good horse and with a minimum of
escort. Ida need not come. Mary's maid would see to
her needs when she arrived. Eadulf could escort her;
she need not trouble Lord Acklane for men to accompany her.

Another thought struck her, which firmed her resolve to make all speed to see her father. He would
have received a summons to Parliament. If he was
truly recovered, he would surely attend to voice a
protest, and would be leaving Fishacre any day now.
If news of Roger's incarceration had reached him he
would have sprung to his son's defence; mayhap even
now he was acting against Bolingbroke, which at that
moment would probably be tantamount to suicide. If

she was not already too late she must try to dissuade him from such a headstrong course.

She had tarried too long! In a fever of anxiety she informed her hosts of her determination.

"But, my dear," murmured Margot in some consternation, "Giles wished you to remain with us! I am certain your father is being well cared for, and your brother's family will not want. Be content, my dear. Wait until Giles can escort you there himself."

"I am sorry, my lady, but I cannot. Mayhap you did not hear the full story of my sire's sudden seizure?" Both Margot and Thomas looked puzzled, so Philippa set about informing them of the truth. "'Twas Giles's coming which brought it on! And then he insisted I leave my father's side to accompany him to Bristol to be wed! I hated him for his arrogance, and what I saw as his traitorous allegiance to Henry Bolingbroke! I wanted to break our betrothal contract, but Giles would not countenance the idea!"

"I had not realised you were an unwilling bride, Pippa! It sounds as though my son acted in a most regrettably high-handed manner!" Margot frowned slightly, remembering the soft glow she had seen illuminating Philippa's eyes when she gazed on her husband. "But he has shown his true gentleness and courtesy since, I am certain! And now, surely...?"

"I have accepted my duty," said Philippa stiffly. Not even to Giles's parents would she admit to her growing affection for her husband. "We deal well enough together now," she admitted, "but I can no longer allow him to prevent my seeing my father! I must warn my sire, beg him to show prudence in his support of the King. Mayhap I have already left my visit too late.''

Margot looked her daughter-in-law straight in the eye, while Thomas frowned, troubled more by the idea that all was not as it should be in his son's marriage than by any possible difficulty Tewkesbury might get himself into.

''Giles is your liege-lord,'' Constance reminded her, aghast at such wifely disobedience. ''You must obey your husband, Pippa!''

''But he did not order me not to leave here! And even if he had I must defy him! He has my true loyalty, but I must retain some concern for my family!''

''I agree! Thomas, my dear, I think we should provide an escort for our daughter. Will you leave tomorrow, Pippa?''

''Aye, my lady, and I thank you!'' cried Philippa in relief. ''But I do not need a large escort. I have Eadulf.''

''Two of our grooms will accompany you,'' Thomas told her with a rather wry smile. ''I tremble to imagine facing my son's wrath when he finds his wife gone!''

''You, my love? Tremble?'' Margot gave a delighted gurgle of laughter. ''I have yet to see you tremble before any man!''

''And only one woman,'' murmured Thomas with

a look which brought becoming colour to his wife's face.

Philippa did not miss the by-play. Would she and Giles be as affectionate towards each other in thirty years' time? So much depended on whether Giles learned to love her. At the moment he was ashamed of her, however much he might deny the charge. She vowed to become more worthy of his love.

Disobeying his wishes would scarce assist in that endeavour, but duty to her family weighed heavily upon her shoulders. Roger she could do nothing to help. However, the others' future might well depend on her intervention. Her new resolve to seek her husband's approval would have to await a more opportune moment, she decided unhappily. Resolutely, she straightened her shoulders and gave her new in-laws a grateful, rather grim smile.

"I will go and prepare for the journey," she told them. "I know you will care for Paws for me while I am away, and see that Ida does not mope. But I can ride faster without her to slow me down."

"The weather has improved today. It should be fine tomorrow. I pray you find your father and the others well," said Margot with a reassuring smile.

The journey was accomplished without incident, though Philippa arrived quite late, with the pale sun already sinking in the west. She would have missed supper, she mused, and was so hungry she could have eaten an ox!

She was not expected, and so the family did not rush out to greet her. Instead, a rather bent man of about forty years stepped out into the courtyard to see who had arrived.

"Buffey!" Philippa slid from Blaze's steaming back into Eadulf's hold, then, clutching her skirts, ran across the courtyard to the steward's side. "How does my father?"

"Lady Philippa!" Surprise echoed in the man's voice as he made deep obeisance. "We had no warning! Naught has been made ready for you!"

"'Twas a sudden decision. All I need is food and a bed. And to see my family! Father is here?" she finished anxiously, but gave the bemused steward no time to answer.

While they were speaking Philippa had led the way into the familiar manor house where she had spent many happy childhood summers, and where she supposed they might live once Giles's future was settled. Like Acklane, the building had only the suggestion of defensive fortifications, for it had been built in the more peaceful years of Edward II's reign.

A fire in the central hearth produced both warmth to dispel the autumnal chill and smoke to choke the lungs. Philippa was still breathing deeply after her exertions, and was caught in a fit of coughing.

"Pippa! Pippa, is it really you?"

Mary came hurrying forward, her homely face, as always framed in frilly white linen, alight with welcome and concern. "Are you well, sister? You are not suffering from a chill?"

"Nay!" gasped Philippa. "'Tis the smoke! After the warmth of the summer, I had forgot how it makes one cough!"

"I'm glad you are well. We had thought never to see you again! Have you news of Roger?" asked his wife fearfully. "We know he was taken; one of those who escaped came to give us the news..."

Philippa pushed the question aside with an agitated wave of her hand. "Later," she said quickly. "Mary, I must see Father. Where is he?"

"There, near the fire. He is well enough."

"Thanks be! I had feared he had left for London."

"He will not be answering the summons to Parliament, Pippa," Mary told her quietly.

Philippa frowned. "Why so? Is he not fully recovered? The last message Giles received—"

"He is well enough physically. But you will find him changed. He has a new passion. Come, he will be pleased to see you." She led Philippa across the smoky Hall to where a man sat on a stool fondling a fierce-looking peregrine falcon lodged on a low perch by his side.

Philippa stopped short. Her sire had lost weight, and with it presence. He looked his age, with added lines to emphasise the new hollowness of his face, but otherwise weather-beaten, active and fit. She ran forward and dropped to her knees by his side. The bird's chain rattled as he moved his feet and stretched his wings, disturbed by the presence of the newcomer.

"Father! I am glad to see you so much recovered!"

"Philippa?" Hugh d'Alban looked rather confused. "I thought you were with that traitor Bolingbroke."

"Nay, Father, I am here, come to see how you do." He spoke belligerent words, but in an unfamiliar, passive voice. "Mary says you have heard the news of Roger's arrest," she said gently. "I am sorry he acted so rashly. I attempted to dissuade him."

"'Twas a lost cause," muttered the Earl, his words slurring slightly. He reached out to stroke the smooth feathers of the falcon. "He should have realised it. You know, daughter, this peregrine is an excellent hunter, and I have more fine birds in the mews. I fly them every day; we do not lack for meat for the pot, do we, daughter?"

He smiled at Mary, a satisfied, lop-sided smile caused by the lingering uselessness of some facial muscles, a smile that tore at Philippa's heart. Her father had indeed changed if his main interest was now to fly his falcons and fill the pot with small game and birds. She did not know whether to cry for the man he had been or to be glad that the man he had become had taken no rash action in his son's defence and was therefore safe.

"Roger is in such trouble," she reminded him gently. "I had feared your concern would cause you to court danger on his behalf."

Her father shrugged. "He must fight his own battles," he told her irritably. "I am too old. I have done with such things. Buffey!" he bellowed. Receiving no immediate answer, "Where is that pestilential steward?" he complained to no one in particular. "Buffey!" And as the harassed steward appeared, "Bring me more wine!"

Philippa rose slowly from her knees and turned to Mary, who stood by with a sad, rather exasperated look on a face which had lost some of its healthy colour and plumpness. The past weeks had taken their toll of her, too.

"He thinks of nothing but his birds," she explained tiredly. "Even news of his son and heir's arrest did not move him for long. He seems able to shut out any unwelcome thoughts. 'Tis sad for one who was so fiery, so fierce and impetuous. But he is happy, so that is something," she added with a sigh.

"But you are not happy!"

"Oh, I do well enough," assured Mary quickly, "though naturally I am concerned for your father, and for my husband's welfare."

It took no seer to realise that Mary was always happier in her lord's absence. In the past, Philippa had noted the fact with faint censure. Now she could understand more readily how a woman could dread being at the mercy of a man she neither loved nor respected. And Mary had married from duty.

"Poor Mary!" she sympathised, feeling a new fondness for her sister-in-law, and expressing it in a swift hug. "I cannot think how to cheer you! Roger is in bad case, incarcerated in the Tower, and I cannot hold out much hope for his future.'' She shook her head in helpless regret while tears gathered in her eyes. ''Why could he not see his attempt to rescue the King was doomed to failure?'' she groaned. ''I warned him! I tried to stop his foolishness, and ended up in the Tower myself!''

''You, Pippa?'' Mary's shocked tone told Philippa that news of her part in the affair had not reached Fishacre.

''Aye, and it was not a pleasant experience, believe me! I attempted to part Roger and Giles, to deter Roger from his purpose, but my motives were mistaken. Some thought I was assisting Roger, and I was accused. Giles believed—eventually—in my loyalty and innocence, and pleaded my cause with Henry Bolingbroke, and I was released.''

The softness with which she said her husband's name caused Mary to scrutinise her sister-in-law afresh. ''You do not now regret your marriage?'' she asked a trifle apprehensively. ''I had wondered whether I did the right thing in sending Sir Giles to the Priory to seek you…''

''I cursed you at the time,'' admitted Philippa ruefully, ''but you did right, Mary. 'Twas my duty, and he is not the monster I believed then. I see now that Father brought this sickness upon himself. Just as Roger has brought his trouble about his own shoulders. Could you not dissuade him, when you spoke to him the day you arrived here?''

Mary shook her head. "Believe me, I tried. But once my husband's mind is made up no one can change it, least of all me," she admitted with a touch of bitterness.

Philippa sighed, knowing the truth of Mary's statement, and recognising rather belatedly that her brother had a touch of the despot in him, demanding absolute obedience from his wife and family. "I know," she admitted wryly. "I have been advised to detach myself from him, and I must, for my husband's sake, even if I did not now think his and Father's erstwhile loyalty misplaced. Richard is a bad King, Mary," she told her earnestly.

"He is God's anointed—" began Mary.

"I know, I know!" cut in Philippa. "But I have seen him, remember—so aloof, demanding quite preposterous reverence and respect, almost effeminate in his love of costly clothes, and so extravagant—almost every lord in the land is against him, especially since he confiscated Bolingbroke's inheritance. I came here partly to warn Father to be circumspect, but I see that I had no need to concern myself." She smiled suddenly, her sombre mood dispelled. "But how are the children?"

Philippa ate while Mary brought her up to date on her offspring's progress. How futile her journey had been! she thought. She had risked Giles's wrath to no purpose! Though she could not have known how much her father had changed, and was glad to have her fears over his possible actions set to rest.

''Where is your husband?'' asked Mary when the subject of her children eventually ran out.

''Giles?'' A dreamy look entered Philippa's midnight eyes. ''With Henry at Westminster. Where else would he be?'' she questioned rather wryly.

But Giles was not at Westminster. He was on his way to Acklane, nearing a manor hourse where he could ask for shelter for the night. He had left Westminster late, and would have a long ride ahead of him the next day, would have to push Panache as fast as the horse could go if he wanted to arrive before the family supped. A smile curved his shapely lips and his heart beat faster as he imagined Philippa lying under him once more. Frustration had made him edgy over the last days, and Henry, with wry acumen, had ordered him to seek his wife and return with her at his side.

As in the past, he had sought to relieve his needs with willing ladies about the Court, for old habits died hard. But somehow the satisfaction he had previously found in such amorous adventures had not materialised. He had succeeded only in making himself feel disgust and guilt, and knew he would not readily seek solace in strange beds again. Pippa, his fiery, independent, passionate little wife, had spoilt him for other women.

He swore softly under his breath, the smile momentarily wiped from his face. He could almost hate her for that! And yet he did not. What mattered variety, the pursuit of other female charms, when his own wife offered him so much more than the mere satisfactions of the flesh? Her body was deliciously desirable—and God knew he wanted it desperately!— yet his need for his wife went much deeper than that.

Panache's hoofs beat out a steady rhythm in the soft mud of the road, Wat's horse travelling half a head behind. The two men rode without speaking, Wat sensing his master's desire for silence.

Giles was struggling with new emotions, a new awareness of just how much he had come to rely on his wife's company, on her approval, her care. He did not just desire her, he was truly fond of her, he thought in amazement. She might spit and scratch on occasion, she might be a handful to manage, but he had known no other woman quite like her, and had fallen victim to her charm.

Did he love her? What was love? He saw it manifested in his parents, but had scarcely expected such a lasting passion would ever come to him, and had not been certain he wanted it, in any case. Such total commitment had its reverse side: greater dependence, greater anguish on separation or loss. Love wasn't necessary. Not at all.

But he could not deny the attractiveness of a future blessed by mutual love. Cold aloofness, perhaps even enmity within a household, did not appeal to Giles's warm nature. But if he admitted to his love for his wife, could he be certain it was returned? The thought that she might one day fall in love with another, if she did not already love him, brought with it a surge of such fierce jealousy that his hands tightened on the reins and Panache jibbed, tossing his head and snorting in outrage.

Giles dismounted at the manor house without having come to any conclusion in his thoughts. But, he promised himself, he would know when he saw his wife again on the morrow! And he would know, too, whether she was truly growing fond of him. He thought she was. She had softened of late, and showed some concern for his comfort. And he remembered the kiss they had exchanged in her bare lodging in the Tower, and the caring way she had pleasured him the night before their present parting. When, later, he dropped into exhausted slumber, his wife's name was on his lips.

At Acklane next day he threw himself from Panache's back, leaving the horse to waiting grooms, and strode rapidly indoors. His mother and father were sitting in the Hall with Constance and several others. The supper-boards had already been cleared away. He had been delayed because Wat's horse had cast shoe along the way.

He looked around expectantly. "Greetings!" he cried cheerfully. "Where is my wife? In our chamber?"

"Nay, my son." Margot's voice was gentle. She watched Giles's face carefully. "She has gone to Fishacre, to see how her father does."

His face darkened; it was like watching the thunder clouds gather. But pain and disappointment, not anger, filled his turbulent eyes.

"Fishacre?" he exclaimed explosively. "I told the wench not to become involved with her family's affairs! How dare she disobey me?"

"She loves her family, Giles. You cannot deny her the chance to see how they are, or to warn her father against taking action on his heir's behalf. She was afraid for him, my son. She had waited for you faithfully until yestermorn."

"She departed only yesterday?"

"Aye, my boy, with our blessing. We have become greatly attached to your wife." Thomas's voice held mild reproof at his offspring's anger. "She owes you duty and loyalty, but has a mind of her own which you will never wholly control," he observed whimsically. "So take my advice, and do not attempt the impossible! Sit down, refresh yourself with small ale, and tell us the news from Westminster."

Giles stepped forward with long, impatient strides, his golden spurs sounding a jangling note into the comparative silence which fell after his father's words. He picked up the jug and drank deeply, passed the back of his hand over his lips to remove the excess moisture, and addressed his father.

"I must beg the loan of a good horse. Panache is finished. I ride for Fishacre within the hour."

But it was several hours before Giles and Wat finally set out, against his mother's pleading, to travel through the night. Giles wanted to be with his wife by the time she broke her fast.

Philippa rose before dawn. She had developed an urge the previous day to visit Alban Castle. No news had arrived from there since the day they had been escorted from its precincts.

The place had been stripped, that she knew. It would be bare and chill now, yet it had been home. She had a longing to see it again. And the manor folk would welcome her; she could see to their welfare. Without the castle to turn to for protection, the inhabitants of Alban were at the mercy of any marauding band of outlaws or cut-throats who happened by.

She would easily find shelter for the night, either within the castle or in the village, or failing that with the Prioress Mary-Luke in Evesham. She lingered only to break her fast and to pick up the saddle-bag packed with spare linen and victuals before going out into the pale dawn to join Eadulf and the Acklane men in the stables, where Blaze and their own horses were standing ready, saddled and bridled.

Eadulf tightened Blaze's girth, and threw his mistress into the saddle. "'Twill be another fine day, my lady," he remarked as he adjusted her stirrups. "We should reach Alban well before nightfall."

They did, arriving while the sun was still quite high above the horizon. The stark walls rose ahead, outlined against its brilliance, but—

Philippa urged Blaze to increase his pace, outstripping the others as she made headlong for the home of her youth. Something was amiss. The familiar outline of the stonework against the sky looked different, but it was not until she was within arrow's distance of the walls that she drew rein and sat quite still, staring.

Much of the edifice was in ruins. The drawbridge was down over the dried-out moat, the gatehouse had gaping holes where the mechanism for its raising should have been housed. The portcullis had gone. And the curtain wall had been breached in several places.

Alban Castle had been destroyed. Tears began to course down Philippa's ashen cheeks, but she did not notice.

Chapter Thirteen

Closer inspection revealed that the main part of the original castle remained largely untouched, though some of the entrance steps had been prised loose and heaved aside, leaving a difficult scramble up to the open doorway.

Silent and grim, Eadulf helped Philippa to reach the Hall, while the Acklane men dismounted and stared about them, taking it all in, though knowing they had no part to play in this drama except to get their lord's son's wife back to Fishacre safely on the morrow and to Acklane soon thereafter.

Philippa wandered through the ancient stone building, and found only ruin and desolation. Sour, evil-smelling rushes in the Hall, where rats and mice had made their nests. In the chamber at the top of the tower she pounced upon a rag-doll kicked among the dusty straw, disturbing a rat, which scuttled to cover. She held the toy tenderly in her hands, a poignant reminder of the little girl and her brother who had sheltered here with herself and their mother on that fateful day, etched so deeply on her memory, when Giles had come riding into the courtyard on Majesty, splendid and disturbing, to turn her world upside-down.

She tucked the doll into the scrip at her waist and went on up to the battlements above. Like the curtain wall, the parapet had been breached, and here all the protective merlons had been levelled, giving the tower the strange, unfinished look which had arrested her attention at that first distant view.

In a remote, unthinking daze, she descended to the courtyard and crossed to the living quarters, there to be shocked from apathy into acute pain. Not only had the rooms been stripped, but also in places, where wood had been plentifully used in the construction, gutted by fire. She stared at the blackened walls, at the open sky striped by the charred beams of her old chamber, and tasted gall.

She returned to the courtyard sick and dismayed, crossing it with dragging steps, dreading what she would find, wandering in a daze of warring emotions from the empty but mercifully spared stables and kennels to the undercroft, with its barren granary and buttery, smashed churns in the dairy, destruction in the brewery. And as for the kitchen…blackened hearths with ashes still in them, empty meat hooks, broken spits, iron and copper utensils left battered and useless.

Marauding outlaws would not have done such extensive damage. Giles must be to blame! How could he have ordered such a thorough dismantling of her past life? Hadn't leaving the place an empty shell been enough? Why had he destroyed so much of the d'Alban heritage? There had been no need for that!

But, yes, there had! No one, now, could use Alban Castle to stand against his liege-lord, Henry Bolingbroke, who had become undisputed master of the Lancastrian inheritance, and probably of England, too. That was why Giles had ordered the castle slighted!

Resentment flooded Philippa, filled her with impotent fury against her husband. She hurled a warped and split wooden bowl into a corner, watching it splinter in a burst of angry satisfaction before turning back into the courtyard.

A murrain on Giles d'Evreux! She drew a harsh breath and lifted unseeing eyes to the pinky golden-edged clouds gathering round the lowering sun. How he had deceived her! Leading her to believe that all he had done was remove her family and their belongings to a safe place while denying Roger shelter from which to gather an army. He had cared nothing for her feelings! Only for the welfare of his treacherous, traitorous, banished master!

All the new, tender feelings she had been nourishing for her husband shrivelled under the searing heat of an anger fuelled by a disconsolate sense of loss and disappointment. She had come to expect better of him. All her dreams of future happiness faded and died. For she could never forgive him this desecration.

She sank down on the chill stone of a mounting-block, and buried her face in her hands. The tears would no longer be denied.

It was Eadulf who heard the fast approach of horses and went to the ruined gatehouse to see who came. Philippa was so lost in her anguish that nothing seemed able to penetrate her misery. Even the stamp of hoofs on the cobbles failed to rouse her.

Giles took in the scene in one all-embracing glance. The destruction, the two Acklane men, strangers to him, slouched against a wall drinking from their flasks, Eadulf with his anxious, tired face. Shock and anger were quickly replaced by concern and pity and a flood of some unnamed emotion which included infinite tenderness as his gaze was drawn irresistibly to the forlorn figure huddled on the block.

He strode across and laid a gentle, comforting hand on her shoulder. "Pippa!" he murmured, all the shocked sympathy he felt clear in that one syllable.

Philippa did not heed it. He had wrenched her from her private grief, had forced his attention on her when he was the last person on earth she expected or wanted to see. She flinched away from his touch, and sprang to her feet.

"Go away!" she spat. "Have you not done enough damage, injured me and my family enough? I hate you! Go away!" she repeated desperately. "I never want to set eyes on you again!"

"Pippa! 'Tis not seemly for you to address your husband so!" Giles's mouth had hardened and his words chided, but his already blanched face took on a stretched, taut look, and his eyes—his eyes looked back at her with a tortured expression which tore at some corner of her heart. Yet he could not possibly be feeling sorrow, anguish, desperation to match her own. He had *caused* this shambles, this death of all the memories and dreams she held closest to her heart.

"I do say so!" she insisted vehemently. "Sir, how could you? How could you order the destruction of my home, of my family's inheritance? How can I continue your wife, when you have done this to me and mine?"

"I seem," responded Giles coldly, while his firm jaw lifted in arrogant challenge, "to have heard this accusation before. Then, I forgave you, for we did not know each other well. But now—now, when we have shared so much, have loved so well, how can you believe me capable of issuing such an order?"

"Love!" scorned Philippa. "You speak of love! Did you believe me, until I pleaded with you to trust my loyalty? No, husband, for days you left me in captivity without lifting a finger to help me. The sharing, the loving meant not *that* much to you!"

She snapped her fingers under his nose. Giles made a protesting sound in his throat, and Philippa gave a fierce snort of laughter which almost broke on a sob.

"I cannot easily believe in your honesty," she declared. "Admit it! You ordered Sir William Grafton to slight this castle! And he did his work well!"

Giles felt all the old exasperation, all the simmering anger rising to the surface again. Impossible wench! Why should he offer sympathy when she threw it back in his face?

He drew a deep, calming breath and managed to keep his temper in check. There was little point in engaging in battle. He knew only too well the searing pain of disillusion, warranted or not. Had he not felt it when he'd thought Pippa disloyal? Was not that why he had kept away from her for those agonisingly long days and nights while she travelled in captivity?

Her pinched, suffering face pierced him like a shaft in his breast. She was shaking, almost as though with an ague. He was forced to clear his throat before he could speak. "Pippa," he began gruffly, "I have apologised for that lapse. I deeply regret it. But that experience helps me to understand your feelings now. I know why you are so upset."

Philippa just stared at him. Her great eyes seemed darker than midnight, red-rimmed, the long black lashes glued together in damp clumps, her nose tipped pink. She had never appeared more vulnerable, more desirable. He longed to crush her in his arms, to erase the pain and scorn he saw writ large on her face.

"Do you?" she wondered derisively. She hardly knew herself why his unwarranted act of destruction should cause her such desperate anguish.

Giles ignored her interruption. "Wife, you must believe me.'' He held out his hands in appeal, but did not touch her, for he knew the time was not yet right. ''I did not order Grafton to slight this place. If this is his work, he exceeded his authority, and shall answer for it.''

Philippa studied her husband from near-dry eyes, seeing him in watery outline still, and distorted by her mind's distress. Yet she could not now miss the concern, the genuine anger in his voice, the sincerity mirrored in those eyes she had learned to read so accurately.

She blinked to clear her vision. 'Twas true. She knew him well enough by now to tell when he was bluffing, when he was lying, when he was evading an issue. He was doing none of those things. His gaze was clear, his eyes intent upon her face. And they held a look of such honest purpose that she could not doubt his sincerity.

''Grafton?'' she whispered. '''Twas his doing?''

''Aye, my love. It must have been, unless others have passed this way. The villagers will know. 'Twas not done on my orders,'' he repeated. ''There was no need—we are not at war, and I knew stripping the place would be enough to deter your brother from lingering here. I will discover who is responsible, and see that restitution is made. I am sorry you found out in this fashion. Had you remained at Acklane…''

He allowed his voice to trail off. Not accusing. Just stating a fact. But to Philippa, emotionally scoured, still half blaming her husband for the condition of

Alban even if he had not ordered its destruction, it came as an accusation.

"I could not!" she flared. "Even your parents saw that I could not remain obediently with them in ignorance of how my father and Mary and the children did! If Father intended answering his summons to Parliament, I had to warn him to desist from his support of the King! Had to make him understand the danger of attempting to side with Roger! Though," she choked, "my brother could well accuse us of deserting him in his time of need. Mayhap we *should* stand by him, ready to share his fate!"

"Not you, my wife. You are too precious to risk your life in your brother's lost cause."

"'Precious'?" Philippa blinked in surprise. The whole bailey was illuminated by the red-tinged light of the dying day, and Giles stood in a shaft finding its way through the ruined curtain wall. She realised anew just where they were. His presence at Alban was as unexpected as the word he had used. She frowned. "How come you here?" she demanded.

Giles held out his hand. "Come, wife. If we are to talk, let us do so sitting down. We can use the edge of that drinking trough," he suggested.

Philippa hesitated only a moment before placing her small hand in her husband's warm, strong hold. The comfort the contact gave her was instantaneous. How could it be, she wondered, that this one man's touch could set her alight, calm her, warm her, protect her, content her, bring her hope, give her peace? She sat beside him, unresisting, and allowed him to retain her hand in his.

"I went to Acklane to fetch you," he told her, once they were settled. "I have secured decent lodgings within the Palace of Westminster, and wanted you by my side." His voice deepened. "I missed you, Pippa," he admitted with a slightly embarrassed laugh. "I had not realised how much I needed you near me."

She made no response, but gazed steadily into his face. So he went on.

"I found you gone, and intended to set out immediately for Fishacre. But my mother persuaded me to rest for an hour or so, that to arrive before dawn would not be convenient. And then Dickon rode in on his way to Parliament, so my departure was further delayed. The journey took longer than I anticipated, since to travel in darkness is to travel slowly, and the horses we borrowed were not as fleet as Panache and Wat's usual mount."

"At what time did you arrive at Fishacre?" asked Philippa quietly. Her heart had leapt at his declaration, and was thudding with renewed hope, but she feared to build too much on his words.

"A good long while after Prime, with the sun already riding high, and you gone! Imagine my annoyance! Such an elusive wife I have!" He grinned suddenly, encouragd by her mellowed mood. "Independent, disobedient wench! I could have wrung your neck!"

Philippa laughed at his affectionate teasing, allowing her new-found hope to surface in a joyous burst of sound which echoed around the courtyard, causing both Wat and Eadulf to look over to where the two sat so closely together, and exchange a knowing smile. And, scrutinising her husband's face, Philippa saw the drawn lines of tiredness around his eyes, put there by days and nights in the saddle with very little rest or sleep. Put there by his pursuit of her.

Was it just possessiveness which had made him chase after her, or something more? He could have rested at Fishacre to await her return on the morrow instead of borrowing fresh horses and riding on. Her free hand went up to touch the signs of his weariness. ''You are tired, my lord husband,'' she murmured softly, ''and there is nowhere here for you to rest.''

''But is that not my own fault?'' he questioned wryly. ''I had thought myself blamed—''

''I believe,'' said Philippa with a small smile, ''that you were as responsible for this—'' she waved an expressive hand as her lips twisted in distaste ''—as for my father's seizure. Both arose from your visit, but neither was truly your wish or fault. And I do not want to quarrel with you further, husband,'' she admitted with a small sigh. ''I would like us to be— comfortable together.'' She paused. ''As your parents are,'' she mumbled low, her flushed face hidden from his suddenly intent gaze.

''But they,'' reminded Giles soberly, ''fell in love with each other. Passionately and deeply. I truly believe that either one would give his or her life for the other's happiness.''

''Aye.'' Philippa sounded deflated, and did not raise her face. ''I...had hoped...'' she began tentatively.

''That we might find a similar love?'' Giles tilted his wife's face to his. His eyes were so intense, so soft, so blue. His beautifully sculpted lips curved within the frame of his beard. ''Do you find it a possibility, Pippa?'' he asked deeply.

Philippa's breath had got caught up somewhere in her chest. Her heart had stopped merely pounding. It was hammering so hard and fast that it had cut out every other function of her body. She couldn't answer. But her eyes were shyly eloquent as they locked with his and the small nod she gave travelled from the fingers which held her chin and on down Giles's arm to wound him anew in his suddenly vulnerable breast.

He drew a harsh breath and swore softly. ''Pippa, I want to love you as we've never loved before,'' he growled urgently, ''to tell you that you have given my life new meaning, new purpose, that I cannot imagine living without you now!'' He grinned suddenly, boyishly, relieving his own tension. ''Oh, I was annoyed when I found you gone from Acklane!'' He sobered again quickly. ''But even more was I afraid—afraid that I had lost you, that you had returned to your father's roof to escape me...''

Philippa's heart had stopped behaving like a farrier's hammer on an anvil, but the blood still coursed hotly through her veins, making her tremble.

"No," she denied breathlessly. "You forget, husband, that Fishacre is yours now. I felt obliged to visit, but went reluctantly, for I knew 'twould anger you, and I wanted to win your love, not your disapproval." She smiled with a radiance Giles had never seen before. He caught his breath in wonder.

"You desired my love?" he asked tentatively. "You have forgiven me my harsh treatment of you?"

"Aye, husband. I know you were driven by considerations I knew nothing of at the time. And I was happy in our union until...until the Tower."

She shuddered, and Giles drew her closer. "And you have forgiven me that lack of faith, too?"

"As I hope you have forgiven me, for doubting your intentions over Alban Castle."

"You cannot imagine," he told her quietly, drawing her so close that she could feel his warmth through the layers of their apparel, "how devastated I felt when I believed you had left me." He paused, then added deliberately, "I do love you so much, Pippa."

She gasped as her heart leapt anew, and drowned in the tender blue pools of his eyes. "You do?" she managed.

"Aye. I had not fully realised it until then," he admitted sheepishly. "Promise me you will never leave me again! And tell me that I can hope for you to love me, too!"

The tears began to fall again. Giles bent his head and gathered them on his tongue. Salty proof of how much his declaration had moved her. His spirits soared, and an urgent desire to show her his love in the only way open to him seized his loins.

"I did not leave you, husband," she whispered. "And I do not think there is anything could drive me from your side now! For I have loved you since…oh, Kenilworth, at least!" The convulsive tightening of his arms brought a new glow to her cheeks as she went on. "Only I would not let myself believe it! How could I love the man who had caused my father's illness, who was allied to Bolingbroke, who threatened to dethrone the King?"

"Aye." Giles's arms slackened, and he shifted uncomfortably, his eyes dropping from hers as a frown drew his brows together. "Will it concern you, wife, if Richard abdicates and Henry is acclaimed King in his stead?"

"Is that what will happen?"

"I believe so. 'Tis mooted." He lifted his gaze to meet hers again, and took both her hands in his. "Richard will not trust his cousin, and Henry holds the power. Had the King proved honourable in the past, 'twould be a different matter. But Henry would be foolish to give credence to Richard's promises now."

"I am wiser than I was a month or more ago. I can see the King's faults, and that many people suffer under his rule. He spends more money on peaceable things than he would on war!"

''Aye. He is a prodigal spender! Henry would make a just and thrifty King, and have the Lancastrian wealth to call on without recourse to confiscation! But—France would not like it. If Richard abdicates, his little Queen Isabelle will lose her throne, and her father will surely declare war.''

''So the truce would end.'' Philippa sighed. ''It seems we may jump from the skillet into the fire.''

''But the die is cast now, my love. For Henry, there can be no going back.''

''Well, we can do little to influence the course of events. But we *can* attempt to find shelter for the night! I had not noticed how low the sun has sunk. 'Twill be dark soon. The days are drawing in fast.''

Giles stirred, tempted to kiss the lips so near his own, yet putting off the moment in a desire to savour the anticipation—and to find privacy. He sprang to his feet.

''Wat!'' he bawled.

Wat came running. ''Aye, lord?''

''Send Eadulf into the village to obtain victuals for us and the horses. Here—'' he dug in his pouch ''—give him this penny; he'll need it to buy them. And see if there is hay or straw in the stables for bedding, otherwise we shall have to ask the village to supply that, too. But first send those idle churls from Acklane to me.''

''At once, Sir Giles.''

Wat ran off, and Philippa stood up. ''We shall need water,'' she reminded her husband. ''Since it is dry,

Grafton must have dammed the stream which feeds the moat. There can be no shortage of water after the recent rain.''

''What of the well? Is there no water in that?''

Philippa lifted her brows and gazed straight at him.

Giles cursed. ''The devil take William Grafton! We cannot know whether he tampered with the water, so cannot risk using it. Is that your view?''

''He was very thorough in other ways.''

''So he was. Ah, you there!'' He addressed the Acklane men, one sturdily built and tall, the other shorter and wiry, who had presented themselves at Wat's request. ''What are your names?''

''I am Alan,'' said the wiry one, ''and this is Ralph, lord.''

''You know me?''

''Aye. You are the Earl of Acklane's younger son, Sir Giles.''

''Good. Then you will not object to carrying out my orders. One of you stable the horses and rub them down. Eadulf, the groom, has other matters to concern him. I sent him into the village, since the people know him, and will be generous with supplies. The other of you must go for water—an he can find a container. The stream is yonder, beyond that line of trees.''

He pointed through a gap in the curtain wall, and Ralph nodded. ''I'll go. My arms are stronger, and Alan will be better with the horses.''

''You'll find buckets in the dairy. They do not appear to have been destroyed. There,'' put in Philippa, indicating the door in question. She grinned at Giles. "I'll go and look in the stew. There may be fish still there."

Wat returned to report a cache of straw, found forgotten in the darkest corner of the loft above the stables.

"Then we may sleep soft tonight! Fetch the saddlebags, will you? Alan is seeing to the horses, Ralph has gone for water, and the straw needs bringing into the Hall—enough to make pallets for us all. Make yourself useful, you lazy varlet!" he grinned, and Wat returned an impudent grimace before running off to do as he was bidden. Giles turned to Philippa. "We will bed in the solar, I think. 'Tis usable?"

"I believe so. Just empty."

"Then come, wife." He held out his hand in invitation. "We will investigate further."

"First I must go to the stew," she reminded him "I'll take a cauldron—I saw a dented one in the kitchen, and I don't suppose we'll find a net. We shall need kindling, too, if I am to cook my catch."

"Then we will go together. I can't have you falling in!" chuckled Giles, reminding them both of her ducking and what had followed.

Philippa skipped along, fizzing like newly brewed ale, euphoric with love, her feet barely seeming to touch the ground. Giles shared her mood, and the excursion became an adventure. They returned singing loudly, Philippa with a huge armful of brushwood and Giles carrying the cauldron, heavy with plump trout.

With the supplies gathered together, Giles declared a feast, to be laid out on the only surface available—a work-bench in the kitchen—and eaten sprawled on the floor. Eadulf had done well in the village, and returned with rough brown bread to cut into trenchchers, small ale, milk, cheese, fruit, cold salt pork, a supply of rush lights and a couple of women eager to serve them.

Through it all, Philippa continued to bubble with happiness. She was with Giles again, and he wanted her. Not just for bed-sport, though he wanted that, too—she could see it in the intense, burning gaze turned so frequently on her—but as companion, lover, wife. She ate with relish, her eyes constantly meeting her husband's, so full of love and desire, each mouthful of succulent trout or tasty cheese bringing nearer the time when they could retire. And, when supper ended, she followed him up the stairs to the solar with an eagerness she did her best to hide. It would not be seemly to exhibit impatience to strange eyes.

Giles had dismissed Wat, and they served each other. A bowl of water stood ready for their use, and Giles turned her disrobing and the removal of the day's dirt into a sensuous rite. He seemed in no hurry to claim her, but intent on showing her how much he reverenced and delighted in her body.

The cleansing complete, he knelt at her feet, hands on her buttocks, moving his lips up her thighs to linger in the thick black hair at their join. Philippa held his golden head, pressing his face to her, her fingers laced in the springy waves of his hair. When he reached higher and touched her navel with his tongue, she shuddered and cried out. Giles growled in response, and drew her down to him, so that they knelt thigh to thigh and he could reach her tender breasts with his worshipping mouth.

She groaned as the thrill of his suckling pierced her through. "Giles, stop!" she pleaded huskily. His clothes still separated them. "Please wait! Let me do for you what you have just done for me!"

Giles lifted his head, his eyes heavy with desire, and succumbed to the temptation he had been denying since first she had declared her love. After all her past enmity and scorn he could still scarce believe it. He must test her response now! He would surely detect the difference if passion was now truly spiced with mutual devotion.

His lips claimed hers in a kiss tender yet passionate, a long, enervating caress that seemed to draw her soul from her body and leave her empty of all feeling but one of wondrous, palpitating, tender love. He lifted his lips. He felt drained yet infinitely satisfied. Oh, yes! There was a difference.

"Anything you want, my love," he promised gruffly.

He had often called her his love, but never before with that special throb in his voice that told her it was no figure of speech, but the true expression of the feeling in his heart.

He helped her with the buckles on his spurs, with his hose, the long boots he had worn for riding, and with his belt and points; but otherwise let her manage alone, revelling in the feel of her small hands on him, caressing as they moved, as his had caressed her. She sponged him carefully, dried him meticulously—even his most masculine parts—and Giles held his breath and clenched his fists for fear of breaking down and gathering her to him, so putting an end to this most exquisite form of torture.

When she had finished, she knelt before him and did as he had done to her until she reached his groin. As her lips whispered tenderly over his body, Giles found he could stand the torture no longer. He bent down and scooped her slender figure up, holding her close to his breast, and carried her to the pile of straw and hay which would make their bed that night.

He had spread her houppelande over it, and drew his larger one over them as he gathered her into his arms.

He had sworn to love her as he had never loved before, and he kept his promise. He subjugated his own need to give her the most exquisite pleasure she would ever know. He clung to his own control, bringing her to an exultant climax and waiting for her to spin back to earth before beginning his strokes again, coaxing her into yet another.

Returning from that high and distant plane to which he had lifted her, Philippa clasped him close, her legs twined about him, and thrust her hips upwards in an endeavour to take him into her very centre, to fill herself with him. For this was what she needed above all else—Giles a part of her, for ever. But to become one indissoluble whole with her lover she knew that she needed to give of herself, as he had given. Love was composed of give and take.

"Giles, my darling," she murmured huskily, "I love you so. Let me show you how much."

She kissed him then. Giles accepted the tribute, allowing her to make love to him, to pleasure him, to urge him to his own release. And at the end they shuddered together in a cataclysm so great that Philippa for one was surprised to find herself still alive when the blood slowed and reason returned.

But it seemed to her that they had truly become one, that they belonged together as the church bade: 'til death came to part them.

Chapter Fourteen

Margot and Thomas eyed their son and his wife with amused tolerance, exchanging satisfied glances. There could be no doubt that the couple had returned to Acklane in a state of loving euphoria—Giles proud and indulgent, gazing at his wife with that in his eyes which spoke of a bewitched adoration, Philippa starry-eyed and pliant with a new softness which only love could have inspired. What had brought about the change was a mystery into which Margot had no intention of enquiring but, as she gently squeezed her husband's hand, careful not to hurt his tender joints, she thanked the Holy Mother for her son's patent happiness. It was exactly what they had wished for him. John could manage with a stable, unromantic affection that would never satisfy the more imaginative, demanding Giles.

Richard, second Earl of Wenstaple, greeted his new cousin with affection, tickling her face with his greying beard and flowing moustache. A tall man who had once been fair, like Giles, Dickon carried his dignity without pretension, and Philippa warmed to him. He had brought his youngest son along—a lively, athletic lad of fifteen, who was to join another household as a squire. Edward had been named for the old King, and was inevitably known as Ned.

Philippa found the boy endearing, not only for his dark good looks and cheerful nature, but also for his open display of adoration for his new cousin, which shone from his ingenuous grey eyes whenever he looked at her. She was flattered by his evident devotion and encouraged his chatter, discovering that his grandam, Eleanor, was in good health despite her years, and virtually ran the manor at Wenfrith because of his mother's indisposition.

"Though she still misses my grandsire," he confided with a boyish grimace of disgust. "And him dead this ten years past!"

"You have yet to fall in love," she teased him gently. "One day you will understand."

Ned coloured to the roots of his straight black hair. His grey eyes reproached her. But he did not declare the love burgeoning in his romantic young heart.

Philippa grinned. "Go and practise your arms," she ordered him gaily. "Do not waste your time while here at Acklane! Wat will oblige you with a contest, I am quite certain!"

Giles viewed his young cousin's infatuation with tolerant amusement. "'Tis obligatory for a squire to fall in love with some unattainable lady," he told his wife with a chuckle. "He would be thought a strange lad were he not to sigh and swoon over the object of his youthful adoration."

"Do not laugh at him," chided Philippa severely. "I find his attentions warm and sweet. Remember your own youth, I pray!"

"Oh, I do! That is why I can laugh at young Ned's devotion. Were he older, I might show rather less tolerance." He pulled her to him and lifted her chin to gaze fiercely into her soft eyes. "Be warned, my love. I will not stand by and see you taken from me."

Philippa wound her arms around his neck. "You need not fear that, husband. I am entirely yours, now and for always, as you very well know!"

"Mmm." Giles tasted her eager lips, then released her, giving her a sharp slap on her rump. "Run along, wench! And behave yourself at Westminster!"

"Of course, my lord!"

Philippa executed a deep obeisance, and ran, laughing, from the room.

The family party travelled to Westminster together, arriving the day prior to the meeting of Parliament. The entire place was buzzing with the latest news.

The King had abdicated! Reputedly with a smile on his face, he had signed a document asking that Henry should succeed him, and as a token had sent Henry his signet ring! But had he truly meant to abdicate, to hand over the Kingship, or merely the administration, as he had been forced to do once before, to the Lords Appellant? *Regnum* or *Regimen*—which had he intended? The words were so similar. Opinions differed, but next day, the last of a rather damp September, when the Parliament summoned by Richard met in Westminster Hall, it was declared in his absence that Richard had abdicated and that Henry had succeeded him as King.

There were protests—even the Percys appeared uncomfortable with the turn of events—but such voices were not heeded. Three and thirty articles were read out, proclaiming why Richard had deserved deposition. Great emphasis was laid on his perjury, on his record for breaking promises.

Then Henry stepped forward and asserted claim to the vacant throne by right of descent vindicated by conquest, whereupon he was acclaimed King by the majority of those present.

Thomas and Dickon returned to the lodging accompanied by Giles, who was not qualified to sit in Parliament, but had watched proceedings from the gallery and was still fuming over the fact that a London mob had managed to gain entry to the Hall to mingle with the Members, while he had been excluded.

"He is without doubt next in the male line—but conquest?" queried Philippa. "I saw no battle!"

"God be thanked!" exclaimed Thomas and Dickon together, for, though neither would shun a fight, both had seen enough of bloody, unrewarding conflict at Najera, in Castile, some thiry years before. Dickon, in addition, had been finally disenchanted when his hero, the Prince of Wales, that "chief flower of chivalry of all the world", as the poet Jean Froissart had written of him in his *Chroniques*, had ordered the sacking of the town of Limoges. Weak and ailing, the once glorious Prince had watched the brutal scenes from his litter. Dickon had found himself defending women and children from the swords of his comrades. He had not sought honour on the battlefield since.

"The huge size of the force which rallied to Bolingbroke's banner deterred active resistance," declared Thomas, rubbing thoughtfully at a swollen knee joint, "so the succession had been achieved without bloodshed."

"What happens now?" Philippa asked.

"The proctors must renounce their homage to Richard. They will do so tomorrow, at the Tower. Then Henry will issue new writs, and Parliament will meet again, in a week's time." Thomas smiled serenely, evidently pleased with the way things had gone. "The new Parliament will proclaim Henry King, and he will be crowned in Westminster Abbey on the thirteenth day of the new month. The ceremony is already being planned."

A slight frown crossed Philippa's face at mention of the Tower, for it reminded her of Roger. But Giles quickly diverted her mind from such grim matters.

"You, my love, will require a new gown," he told her.

Philippa caught her breath. "I shall be present?" she asked in awe.

''An you wish it. Henry will squeeze us in; of that I am certain!''

''What colour shall I choose?'' wondered Philippa, trouble forgotten, excitement bringing a warm flush to her cheeks.

''Azure,'' proclaimed Giles without hesitation. ''Azure and silver, with miniver trim and acorns embroidered on the skirt!'' At that moment a page arrived to summons Giles to attend Henry. ''We will see about it when I get back,'' he promised as he settled his deep blue houppelande on his broad shoulders, set his elaborately swathed court hat on his fair curls, and went to obey his lord's command.

Philippa was determined to have the Alban knot embroidered somewhere on her court dress. Perhaps on the breast. She set about sketching the design for the embroiderers. She could draw it, but she couldn't sew it, for she would ruin the fabric. Ida could work it, given time, and the acorns, too, but perhaps it would be best to leave it all to the court seamstress and her assistants. First have the gown made to her liking!

She was happily engaged in designing when Giles returned. He was having difficulty in repressing a smile, though his eyes held a rather dazed look. Both the older d'Evreux men were present, since they were sharing the lodgings with them, and Philippa had joined them in the lower chamber. Ned had left, gone to join his new lord—a scion of the powerful Mow-bray family—in his.

Philippa had been impressed with the comfort of the dwelling allocated to them, one of a terrace of two-storey, timber-framed, wattle and daub buildings built on a stone foundation and roofed with shingles. There were only two rooms, one above the other, with wardrobe and pallet chambers attached. Every window was filled with glass, and the beds had feather mattresses, satin covers and many a pillow.

"Giles?"

Philippa sprang to her feet, almost tripping over Paws, who had been brought along and was busy chewing an old shoe. She knew something important had happened. Giles held out his arms, and she ran into them.

"Giles," she repeated, "what is it, husband? You have news?"

"Aye, wife." He bent his head and smacked an exuberant kiss on her startled lips, then released her and looked around the company. "You remember Richard introduced the rank of Marquess to honour Robert de Vere?"

"Aye." Dickon answered for himself and Thomas, who merely nodded. Philippa frowned, for the reference meant little to her—the exiled de Vere had been dead eight years. "You were with Bolingbroke and the other Appellants twelve years ago at Radcot Bridge, when the King's force, led by de Vere, was routed, weren't you?" remembered Dickon.

"I was, as Henry's squire." Giles grinned. The memory of that occasion was, for him, one of glorious accomplishment. "'Twas a lively skirmish! Well, I—" he swept an arm, threw up his head and paused for dramatic effect "—God willing, I am to be Marquess of Thame!"

The exclamations of delight interrupted his flow. He gathered Philippa to him again. "How do you fancy becoming a Marchioness, my love?"

"I do not know!" she gasped.

"Will you have lands?" the Earl of Acklane asked.

"Aye, Father, 'tis not an empty honour. Some in Oxfordshire, which march with Acklane, others in several counties, a borough or two—enough to give me an income to meet our most extravagant needs!"

"And you will outrank our fathers and your cousin!" realised Philippa, still trying to take it all in.

The Earl of Acklane laughed, and came to clap a hand on his son's shoulder. "Congratulations, my boy! I always knew you would go far! Wait until your mother hears the news! I must send for her! She cannot be allowed to miss the Coronation."

"Your device will change!" frowned Philippa, fixing her whirling mind on something practical. "My gown…"

"I will keep the acorn as badge—I have always liked it—and my new heraldic coat will be impaled with your father's lozenge now, my love. We will wear coronets and ermine to the Coronation, but the rest can wait."

"I had thought to incorporate the Alban knot..."

"Of course!" agreed Giles expansively. "By George, but I need a drink!" He strode to the table and poured ale from the waiting flagon. He distributed the cups and lifted his. "The King!"

The others echoed his salute and drank.

"You are very certain of all this," observed Dickon, wiping the moisture from his facial hair. "Parliament has still to confirm Henry as King. There may be counter moves—"

"But it will! Surely nothing can prevent it now!" exclaimed Giles. "Henry himself has issued the new writs, and plans for the Coronation are going ahead. You saw the temper of the Members. Few spoke against Richard's removal, and the Londoners—damn their audacity—fairly demanded it! They have already acclaimed Henry King!"

"Aye, Henry is a popular choice," observed Thomas, "I think your doubts are unnecessary, Dickon."

"The honour cannot be confirmed until Henry is finally acknowledged King next week," admitted Giles, "but 'tis certain enough. I will call in the tailor, the seamstress and the goldsmith, my love!" he declared to Philippa.

The next two weeks passed in a whirl. Henry's accession was confirmed, and the Court gathered about him, switching allegiance with little apparent difficulty. Certain things at Westminster Palace changed, however.

Although Henry had cultivated tastes, was sensitive and intelligent, he disliked the messed-about food Richard had favoured. The cooks were instructed to provide real meat, huge roast joints, whole sucking pigs, entire fish and birds for dinner. At supper, the spiced cakes and wine were supplemented by more substantial fare—meats, cheese and fish, fruits and bread. Richard was a gourmet, Henry a hearty eater. Few at Court regretted the change.

After supper, an elderly poet called Geoffrey Chaucer read from his works to amuse the members of the Court. He had been brother-in-law to Katherine Swynford, John of Gaunt's love and third Countess. The first evening he read a new poem he had written to honour Henry, hailing him as "the Conqueror of Brutes Albioun of which, by line and free election, he is truly King". Afterwards, he read excerpts from his *Book of the Duchess*, written to eulogise Henry's mother, Blanche, after her death. On subsequent occasions he entertained them with tales told by an assorted group of pilgrims on the way to Canterbury. He had an attractive voice, and Philippa listened avidly and laughed with the rest at the capers he described.

Many of the women wore elaborate head-dresses about the Palace, some shaped like cows' horns, others like hearts, all made from costly materials, studded with jewels and draped with wispy veils. One

Countess wore a long, steeple-shaped affair, with a fine veil floating to the floor from its point, which, she informed Philippa, was called a hennin. Such fashions were fast becoming all the rage in France, a fact acknowledged by Giles. Philippa wanted a hennin.

"Remain as you are," pleaded Giles, smoothing her forehead. "I like your hair coiled into frets or bosses. To wear any of these fashionable head-dresses you would have to shave the front away to raise your hair-line." His fingers travelled upwards until they mingled with her hair. "'Twould be a grave pity, my love."

Philippa grimaced, and gave way. For the moment. But if they were to remain at Court, she would insist. She did not intend to be labelled an unfashionable dowd, even to please Giles!

They saw little of Ned, and when they did he was invariably with other squires. He always gave her a deep bow and a speaking look, but no longer sat, almost literally, at her feet all day. For one thing he did not have the time, but Philippa thought his passion was wearing off, and surprised herself by feeling disappointed. Giles worshipped her, of course, but Ned had been the first human being to do so unconditionally and without hope of reward, and the novelty had been sweet while it lasted.

To her delight she met up with Isobel again, her belly already beginning to swell, and with less enthusiasm renewed her acquaintance with Helen Cooksey.

She made other friends about the Court, and began to feel quite at home.

Ida had been reunited with her archer, and it was arranged that, when Northumberland and his retinue returned north, Ida would travel with them as wife to Wolfram Root. Philippa knew she would miss the woman who had served her faithfully for so many years, but there would be no difficulty in replacing her. In fact, as a Marchioness, she would need several serving wenches and tiring-women, as well as a court of ladies to keep her company. Giles would also have to increase the size of his household.

Philippa was entranced by her new gown. Embroidered with silver thread and pearls, edged with ermine, it had a long train at the back and trailed the ground at the front, making it difficult to walk, but that seemed a small price to pay for the splendour and dignity afforded. The short cote-hardie fitted snugly into her waist. More ermine trimmed it and formed the long tippets floating from her elbows. Its sleeves ended there, allowing the tightly fitting ones of the kirtle, buttoned to the wrist before flaring out to cover her knuckles, to show beneath. There was a mantle, too, with an ermine cape and a train which rivalled that of her kirtle for length. The Alban knot became part of the fastening across her breastbone.

Giles's white hose and cote-hardie of cloth of gold were covered by a magnificent scarlet houppelande, the sleeves of which were so wide that they swept the floor when he bent his arms. An ermine cape covered his shoulders below the high, jewel-encrusted collar of the houppelande.

"You make a splendid couple," Margot told them with a smile as they paraded before her. She herself had recently arrived to join the Earl, and was magnificently attired for the ceremony, as was he.

"And so do you!" rejoined Philippa sincerely.

On that thirteenth day of October Henry was crowned with great splendour in Westminster Abbey and anointed with the sacred oil reputedly given to St Thomas of Canterbury by the Virgin. He was now King in the sight of both God and man.

All the lords, great and small, attended. Cloth of gold combined with scarlet and purple velvet, ermine and jewelled and padded coronets to make the Abbey vibrate with colour. Henry paraded down the long, arched aisle with all the dignity anyone could require of a King. Behind him, helping to support his train, walked his sons, Prince Henry, the eldest, safely returned from Ireland to a future he could hardly have envisaged a few weeks earlier.

Heir to the throne! Philippa eyed him fondly. He, in his turn, would make a splendid King. A handsome lad, he had the air, the natural authority bred into the Plantagenets through generations of power. Which, in Richard, had turned to overweening pride and arrogance bordering on tyranny. At the moment young Henry was a bit brash, a touch inclined to feel his position and to overact his part, but with his father to guide him he would soon grow out of that.

So this was what that long and arduous journey had led to. A new King, a new heir, a new chapter in the history of England. And her own happy marriage.

Philippa was content.

Philippa, accompanied by two of her attendants, was walking in the pleasaunce of their new manor of Morton. The January snow had long melted away, the sharp, icy, invigorating cold replaced by the grey, damp chill of a dripping February, but she needed air and exercise.

Things had gone well since their retirement from Court. After the excitements of the January uprising, when John Holland and his cronies had tried to capture Henry at Windsor, where the Court had spent Christmas, Philippa had been glad to have Giles safely back from the skirmish at Maidenhead, ready to shoulder his new responsibilities in the safety of his manors.

She walked carefully on the muddy path, her feet kept clear of the mire by pattens, her gown held up in both hands, her mood sombre as she wondered how her brother was faring in France. She had been both relieved and anxious when Giles had brought her the news.

"Banished?" she had gasped. "For ten years?"

"Aye." Giles had been matter-of-fact. "'Tis better than standing trial, mayhap being sentenced to the block. He will still retain his right to inherit your father's estates and, after his own experience, Henry will not be foolish enough to recant his word on that!''

''Poor Mary!'' All Philippa's compassion went out to her sister-in-law. ''I wonder if she will join him in France—I assume that is where he will go? And the children…''

''An she is wise she will remain here with Lionel and Maud, on hand to take responsibility for the Alban inheritance should anything happen to your father.''

''Perhaps so,'' she'd agreed, and shaken her head ruefully. ''I do not think the separation will trouble her over-much. She manages well enough without him. Roger kept her subdued. She has more strength of character than I once believed.''

Giles had smiled and given her a brief kiss. ''Then I am glad I argued for this outcome. Henry does not wish to appear vindictive, and in truth is not.''

The restoration of Alban Castle was already well advanced. Sir William Grafton, challenged, had admitted exceeding his orders, though from the best of motives to his own mind, and been ordered to contribute most of the cost. Philippa could only imagine the anger he had faced from both the King—who had not wished his march to be destructive—and Giles, whose orders he had disobeyed. He had retired to his manors disgraced, while her father, Mary and the children remained at Fishacre awaiting completion of the works.

Her companions were chattering just behind her,

but it was the winding of a horn which brought her thoughts back to the present. A few moments later Giles appeared from the gracious manor house, which was in process of restoration and extension. A frown of concern marred his normally cheerful countenance.

"Bad news, my lord?" asked Philippa anxiously as he drew near.

"Nothing to concern us too nearly," he reassured her quickly. "Come, wife, I will walk with you awhile."

Her companions were left behind. The moment they were out of earshot Philippa stopped and faced Giles, determined to discover what was troubling him.

"Tell me, Giles. I heard the messenger arrive. Was he from Westminster?"

"Aye." Giles took a deep breath. "Richard is dead."

"Richard? But—he was safe at Pontefract! Or so I was told! Giles, I always knew Henry would have Richard killed in the end! How could he? How can you condone it?"

She was both angry and distressed. Giles placed his hands on her shoulders and spoke deliberately. "I do not believe that Henry ordered his death."

"No? Almost everyone else connected with the January rising has already been summarily executed. Four of them were seized by the people of Cirencester on Twelfth Night—after two days of hard riding they had few followers left. They were beheaded in the market place the next morning. Despencer cut his way out, and managed to reach his castle in Cardiff—''

"From whence he attempted to take ship for France—"

"But the ship's master took him to Bristol, where he was beheaded by the burgesses!" Philippa persisted.

They were rehearsing an old tale, an old conflict.

"But not by Henry!" Giles reiterated. "Those events show how solidly behind the new King the people of the Realm were—and are! The stir in Cheshire was put down by local people!"

"But John Holland's capture at Pleshey and his execution later in January were not spontaneous acts by the people!"

"No. Young Tom Fitzalan took his revenge there. Holland was instrumental in the arrest and execution of the boy's father, the Earl of Arundel, remember. Tom is not one to let a grudge go."

"So Henry is blameless?" scorned Philippa. "How did Richard so conveniently die?"

"He starved himself to death."

"So that is the story! He was starved, more likely! Or given putrid food he would not eat. Everyone knows how fussy he was, how delicate his tastes!"

"But not on Henry's orders," insisted Giles. "Pippa, believe me, Henry would not stoop so low! Though mayhap Tom Swynford, who governs Pontefract and so had Richard in his care, thought to help his stepbrother the King. That is not impossible."

"All Katherine Swynford's brood have done exceptionally well for themselves, have they not? Look at John and Henry Beaufort! And Joan, married to a Neville."

"And why not? All are Henry's siblings, in one way or another. Do you blame him for seeing that his step and half-brothers—and sister—are well provided for? Or John Holland for attempting to restore his half-brother Richard to the throne? He has suffered the ultimate penalty, but I cannot truly blame him for his loyalty."

"Oh, I hate you!" muttered Philippa darkly.

"Do you, my love?" murmured Giles, gently pulling her into his arms. He stroked the bulge of her stomach, which had just begun to swell. "Then 'tis a pity we can no longer have our marriage annulled. No one would now believe it had not been consummated…"

Philippa's skirts dropped into the mud as her arms wound themselves around her husband's neck. "Why are you always so right?" she demanded indignantly.

"Because I am your lord and master," he pronounced arrogantly, his face alight with love and humour.

"Mmm…" Philippa enjoyed the rapturous kiss to the full. "Giles," she murmured as they came up for air, "I am a little chilled. Would you fetch my fur-lined mantle?"

He nipped the tip of her nose with his beguilingly uneven teeth. "Wretch! Proving your power, eh?

Why not send one of your ladies? Then we can continue with this much more entertaining occupation…''

As his lips claimed hers again, Philippa gurgled with laughter. She had not truly needed the mantle at all…

* * * * *

The Traitor's Daughter

by

Joanna Makepeace

Joanna Makepeace taught as head of English in a comprehensive, before leaving full-time work to write. She lives in Leicester with her mother and Jack Russell terrier called Jeffrey, and has written over thirty books under different pseudonyms. She loves the old romantic historical films, which she finds more exciting and relaxing than the newer ones.

Chapter One

Summer 1503

Philippa Telford stole a hasty glance at her mother as they stood together with their squire, Peter Fairley, on the quay at Milford Haven. Her mother had been very sea sick during their crossing from the port of Damme, in Burgundy, and Philippa had been very concerned for her. The crossing had been rough and the two women had been almost thrown from their bunks several times; Philippa's mother had not slept for one moment of the time. Philippa had tended her, since they had been unable to bring a maid with them from their lodging in Malines where Philippa's father, Martyn, Earl of Wroxeter, served the dowager Duchess Margaret of Burgundy—the sister of England's late King, Richard III. Now, on dry land at last, Philippa was anxious to get her mother quickly to an inn where she could rest and recover from the hardships of the journey.

She was glad that they had followed Peter's advice and donned their warmest cloaks, since a mist had enveloped the harbour and coastline as they had disembarked and the air was chilly and damp, despite the fact that it was early summer. Philippa sighed as if this inclement weather was a presentiment of misfortunes yet to come.

Peter had already settled their dues with the captain of their carrack, *Le Grande Dame*, and had assembled their saddle bags of extra clothing and necessities upon the greasy cobblestones of the quay. The bad weather had, apparently, caused the town's inhabitants to seek drier quarters and the quay looked bleak and almost deserted, which was fortunate, since it was imperative that their arrival should not be unduly noted.

Philippa could see a huddle of uninviting buildings, behind which were the faintest of blue outlines, veiled by the sea mist; she presumed them to be hills. The prevailing sea mist hid from the travellers the sight of other vessels docked in the harbour, though glimpses of tall masts and the creak of timbers came to them eerily from the dank half-darkness of the early evening. This, then, was Philippa's first sight of the land which had been her mother's home. Again a shiver ran through her. This place seemed exceptionally inhospitable. She prayed that matters might improve with better weather prospects in the morning when they began their journey to her grandfather's manor near the town of Ludlow. Had not this land of Wales been described to her by many fellow exiles as a most beautiful one?

Peter led them to an inn situated at the far end of the quay, having discounted a tavern in the centre of the harbour, from which they could hear the sounds of noisy banter, as being unsuitable for his charges, and also considering the necessity of not encountering anyone from near the town of Ludlow who might be staying here in Milford on business in the harbour. It had

been many years since the Countess of Wroxeter had
been back in her home land, but it was essential that
she should not be recognised by anyone who might
have known her in childhood, before she had left her
father's manor to journey to Westminster where she had
married the Earl and whom she had followed into exile
almost twenty years ago. All three of them were acutely
aware of the danger which threatened them constantly
on arrival; only the dire need to be with Philippa's
grandparents during the serious illness of her grandfather Sir Daniel Gretton had brought them to this dank
unwelcoming shore.

Philippa was wryly amused to see the inn's crudely
painted sign of the White Dragon creaking and swaying
from the corner of the eaves.

"At least it is not a red dragon," she murmured in
her mother's ear, recalling that her father had often re-
ferred to the court of King Henry VII at Westminster
as the lair of the red dragon, contemptuously speaking
of the Tudor King's personal device of the red dragon.
To Philippa's father, the present English King would
always be a usurper who had unlawfully taken up arms
against his true King, Richard III, and, aided by traitors,
had defeated him at the battle of Redmoor near Bosworth, where Wroxeter's friend and liege lord, King
Richard, had been slain. Now Philippa's father was a
proscribed traitor within his own home land, living in
exile, unable to accompany his wife and daughter on
this journey on threat of a hideous death should he be
discovered and arrested.

Cressida made no answer, but Philippa could tell that
her mother also was not impressed by the coincidence
of the somewhat ominous inn sign.

The tap room appeared as crowded as the other tavern

had been, but slightly less noisy. Talk stopped as the eyes of the men gathered round the scratched and stained tables were turned upon the newcomers in open curiosity. Philippa considered that they all looked vaguely alike to her, medium-sized, sturdily built men, dressed in homespun, dark avised; their language, which had come to her in snatches when they had entered the room, was totally incomprehensible to her.

Peter engaged in talk with a slightly taller shambling fellow who announced himself as mine host. He, at least, appeared to speak English, though his accent was very marked and singsong in rhythm.

"I require a private room for my sister, Mistress Weston, and her daughter, my niece. I am escorting them to visit a sick relative who lives near to Ludlow. Can you oblige, master innkeeper?"

The man shook his head emphatically. "I have but one private chamber which is already spoken for. The ladies must make do with the common sleeping room. There are but two women sleeping there tonight. You must sleep down here in the tap room, or the stable if you would prefer that."

Peter turned to confer, but Cressida said hastily, "Peter, I would much prefer to sleep within the stable with Philippa and you nearby. Can that be arranged?"

The innkeeper scowled and the men seated nearby within earshot whispered to their neighbours. It seemed that only certain members of the company understood English and needed a translation of what had transpired. Curiosity increased. Strangers, most likely, some merchant's wife and daughter, were usually content enough to share the women's common sleeping chamber. An atmosphere of resentment seemed to grow within the tap room, making the ale-stinking place chillier than it had been at the outset when they had entered.

"Aye," the innkeeper growled, "if the lady insists, but if it's food ye want you'll have to be fetching it yourself. I can't be waiting on folks across the courtyard. I've customers in plenty in here. You can eat here if ye've a mind to, all of ye."

Cressida smiled politely and once more shook her head. "Innkeeper, I mean no offence. It is just that we are wearied and would eat and sleep in quiet. We shall be glad to see to our own needs, they will be simple enough, some ale, perhaps, and bread and meats or cheeses."

"Oh, aye." The man turned away, then taking a lanthorn from a hook behind him, came from his place nearest to the ale barrel in present use and moved towards the inn door.

"Come this way then, folks and I'll show you the way to the stable. I take it ye've no horses of your own?"

"I intend to buy mounts for the land journey tomorrow," Peter informed him. "We have only lately disembarked from the carrack, *La Grande Dame*, just in from the port of Bruges. My sister's husband had been living there for some years as he has business interests there."

The innkeeper sniffed and moved in his clumsy, shambling walk to the door, opened it and held up the lanthorn so they could see only dimly across the unlit courtyard. "Directly opposite is the stable door. There are only three stalls occupied at the moment. The lord who has taken my private bedchamber has a horse stabled there with that of his squire and my own cob is there as well. There'll be plenty of room for the three of ye, and there's clean straw in plenty for your beds.''

Peter thanked the man civilly and took the proffered lanthorn, murmuring that he would take particular care with it within the stable, then the three of them stepped outside into the mist—shrouded air again.

The cobbles of the courtyard were slick with rain and mist and they were forced to watch their steps, the ladies holding their skirts high to avoid any ordure or refuse from the inn or stable as they crossed.

''My pardon, my lady,'' Peter murmured, ''I had thought to provide you with better accommodation than this poor place this night. God's blood, it appears that what they say about this benighted land of Wales is true, the inhabitants are barbarians. Did you hear those outlandish peasants chattering in their singsong tongue?''

''Peter,'' laughed the Countess, ''remember that I lived in the Welsh Marches throughout my childhood. We had many Welsh servants at the manor and, though I could not speak their tongue, I grew to respect and like them very much. We would have been regarded with just as much outright curiosity wherever we had fetched up. We shall do well enough if the stable is dry and we shall have privacy which is most important.''

''Yes, mistress, but you have had a rough time of it on board ship and I hoped for better conditions for you both than these.''

''I prefer to have you within call, Peter,'' Cressida said quietly, ''and I am sure you and my lord have slept in many worse places than this over the years.''

He glanced at her sharply and Philippa glimpsed a wry twist to his lips as he pushed wide the stable door and held up the lanthorn for them to enter before him. The missions the Earl had undertaken for the Duchess

Margaret in her relentless intrigues against the Tudor king had often meant danger for them both and, indeed, they had many times been forced to live for quite long periods of time in disguise and in vastly uncomfortable circumstances.

The warmth and familiar scent of horseflesh met them and they heard the restless movement of wickering within the stalls as the horses were both disturbed by their unexpected arrival and alarmed by the sudden lanthorn light. Peter held the lanthorn high, glimpsed a hook suspended from the thatched roof to hold it and hung it securely. Surprisingly the place looked well kept. Obviously it had been cleaned that very morning, possibly in expectation of the arrival of the lord the innkeeper had spoken of. Philippa moved to inspect the mounts. Two were sturdy Welsh cobs, she surmised, one belonging to the innkeeper and the other to the lord's squire. The third horse was a black courser, a large, heavy-boned, finely muscled animal, extremely valuable, she guessed. Of the three, this one was the most restive and she moved closer to the stall and spoke gently, reassuringly.

"Steady there, my beauty, we mean you no harm nor any to your master."

Cressida uttered a sharp warning as her daughter reached out a hand to pat the creature's velvet nose, aware of how dangerous destriers could be, bred for warfare as they were, but Philippa turned, shaking her head gently. She was patient and the sound of her soft voice did eventually reassure the animal and it stood docilely while she ran her hand gently down its silky well-brushed nose.

"There, there, I have no apple for you. Perhaps I will

have tomorrow. I will try to find some and reward you all.''

Philippa adored horses and had very little opportunity to ride, let alone own a mount while at her parents' lodging at Malines. Her father had been forced by limited means to hire mounts only when he had need, but he had managed to have his daughter taught to ride and she was glad now that she would have no problem during their journey to Gretton.

Peter had busied himself, piling up clean straw in one of the stalls furthest from the horses and the door for Philippa and her mother. He intended to make his own bed well away from them and near to the door so that he might be aware of anyone entering unexpectedly during the coming night. Possibly the lord's squire would come before retiring for the night to ensure that all was well with his master's horses and might intend to sleep within the stable. Peter frowned as he considered that might pose a problem and hoped the fellow would either sleep across his master's doorway as he himself had been used to do for Lord Martyn or content himself in the warmer and more comfortable tap room. He would meet that problem if and when it presented itself.

Philippa sank down thankfully upon the sweet-smelling straw and watched as her mother took off her cloak and laid it down upon the bed Peter had formed for her.

''There, Peter,'' she said, ''it is as I thought, we shall manage very well here and be spared any awkward questioning we might have to face within the common sleeping chamber. If you could go across and fetch us something to eat and drink, we can settle down soon and get some sleep. We have a long journey in front of us.''

Peter nodded, looked round to assure himself that he had made his charges as comfortable as he could, then moved to the stable door.

"I should keep this barred, my lady. Make anyone wishing to enter declare himself and, even then, I would advise you to wait for my return before admitting anyone."

Philippa smiled in answer. "Be assured we shall do that, Peter."

He left and she snuggled close to her mother, still huddling within her own frieze cloak. "Aren't you chilly? I am still. Why don't you put your cloak back on for a while?"

"No, don't fuss. I am quite comfortable out of the damp air." Cressida looked round the gloomy stable and gave a little petulant shrug. "I shall be glad when we are well on our way tomorrow."

"Grandmère will be glad to see us."

"Yes, indeed. I only hope and pray that we are in time to see your grandfather."

Philippa made no answer. She was aware that her mother entertained little hope that Sir Daniel would continue to survive the collapse which he had suffered some two weeks ago, which had left him partially paralysed. The message which Lady Gretton had managed to send to her daughter in Burgundy had informed Cressida that her father had lost the power of his speech. Philippa knew, as her mother did, that attacks such as these were often followed by others, which, eventually, led to the death of the sufferer. Cressida had pleaded with her husband to be allowed to journey to Gretton to see her father and take with her their only daughter, his grandchild, whom he had never seen. Reluctantly, the Earl had given his permission and allowed Peter

Fairley, his trusted squire and friend, to be their sole protector.

Philippa watched as her mother stretched wearily out on her straw bed.

"You do believe that we shall be safe," she queried softly, "that at Gretton the servants can be trusted and…?" Her voice trailed off uncertainly.

Cressida lifted her head and gazed doubtfully at her daughter in the flickering light of the lanthorn.

"Nothing can be certain, child. The servants have been with your grandparents for years and will, I believe, be discreet. They loved me as a child and they are all aware of the dangers. Travelling under assumed names, we should be safe enough, but if you are afraid I could instruct Peter to see you safe on a ship bound for home—"

"No, no, I insist on going with you. I am most anxious to see my grandparents," Philippa declared passionately. "I am most concerned for your safety. Papa was saying that the King's spies will be extra-vigilant since the Yorkist gentlemen will be in a state of great anger and agitation due to the summary execution of Sir James Tyrell and the lying confession about the murder of the Princes, which was published after his death."

Cressida sighed heavily. "When will this realm be fully peaceful? I doubt if I shall see it in my lifetime, yet the Tudor King holds the state firmly. He should be able to do so," she added bitterly, "he has managed to destroy all the rightful heirs who might have challenged him for power and then he married the Yorkist Princess, Elizabeth, in order to secure the loyalty of some of the disaffected nobles."

Philippa bit her lip as her mother once more lay

down. The journey had tired her so. She needed rest badly. Philippa had rarely seen her beautiful mother so downhearted and distressed, not even when the Earl, her father, had risked himself on hazardous adventures for his patroness, the Duchess Margaret, who had struggled over the last twenty years to bring down the Tudor monarchy.

Philippa's father had made her aware of the situation which had made him a hunted traitor in his own land, even though she herself, now seventeen, had been born after the tragic events which had caused it.

She knew that for over fifty years, since 1450, there had been struggles for supremacy amongst the Lancastrian and Yorkist heirs of King Edward III. In 1461 the weak Lancastrian King Henry VI had proved so incompetent that his cousin, Duke Richard of York, had challenged him for power. He had been killed in the fighting which had broken out, but his son, King Edward IV, had finally won a bloodthirsty battle at Towton in Yorkshire and had then assumed the throne and ruled ruthlessly and competently for over twenty years, despite sporadic outbursts of violence which had threatened the peace. Unfortunately he had died unexpectedly in 1483, leaving the protectorship of the realm and care of his two young sons and older five daughters to the care of their uncle, his younger brother, Duke Richard of Gloucester.

Almost immediately the peace was threatened again due to the minority of the young King, Edward V, who was just thirteen years old when Richard brought him to London to be crowned. On the journey the Queen's relatives made a bid for power which was defeated and two of them were executed. The Princes were placed for safety within the palace of the Tower of London, traditionally used to house the new monarchs before their coronations.

Philippa was aware that her father, Martyn, Earl of Wroxeter, had been a trusted friend of Duke Richard and eventually left his own estates on the Welsh Border to become his confidante and spy master.

The Bishop of Bath and Wells had made a surprise announcement at a meeting at the Tower, revealing that the late King's marriage had not been lawful and therefore his children were illegitimate. He, himself, he had declared, had betrothed the king formally to Lady Eleanor Butler and that lady had still been living when the King had married the widow of a Lancastrian nobleman, Lord Grey of Groby, and betrothals were binding, so much so that a dispensation from the Pope was required to break one. This revelation had thrown the realm into disarray once more and Duke Richard had finally been persuaded to accede to the throne as King Richard III. Philippa's father had served him faithfully and fought for him at the tragic battle of Redmoor two years later when Henry Tudor, descended from the Lancastrian, Prince John of Gaunt, and his mistress, Katherine Swynford, had arrived in England in a bid to seize the throne. The King had been treacherously betrayed by Lord William Stanley, who was married to Henry's mother, and his brother, Sir William, on the very battlefield and had died in a last courageous charge.

Since that time the Earl's fortunes had been totally destroyed as he lived in almost penniless exile in Burgundy. Philippa knew, only too well, that her chances of finding a husband, since she had no dowry, were hopeless.

This business of Tyrell's execution had heightened their danger, she knew. Sir James, like her father, had been a member of the late King's household, but had been on a mission for King Richard to France at the time of Redmoor so had taken no part in that battle. He had made his peace with the new King, Henry, and had served the Tudor house, though his estates had been confiscated and he had been deprived of his official posts in Wales. He had been later appointed Governor of Guisnes and, for the following sixteen years, had remained in France, then, suddenly, he had been accused of treasonable correspondence with the Earl of Suffolk, the late King's nephew. He had refused to surrender himself, but had allowed himself to be lured from the safety of his castle and on to one of King Henry's ships in Calais harbour by the promise of safe conduct. He was then captured and taken to the Tower of London and, later, unceremoniously executed. After his death it had been announced that he had confessed to the murder of the Princes, King Edward's young sons, who had disappeared from the Tower, on the order of their uncle. This slur upon the honour of the dead King Richard had naturally angered many of the late King's former supporters. A little shiver ran through Philippa's body, for she suspected that her father knew more about the fate of those young princes than he would ever divulge, not even to his closest family. Was this the reason why King Henry hated him so much and wished to have him in England directly in his power? She knew, only too well, that in the dungeons of the Tower men could be forced to divulge their closest-held secrets. If the King could hold the Earl's wife and child as hostages, would not her father come to their help and surrender himself, as Tyrell had done? The secret of their journey to Gretton must be kept at all costs.

Her thoughts ranged to her friends, Richard and Anne

Allard, who had been her companions four years ago when she had gone to Westminster to serve King Henry's queen, Elizabeth of York. They had all been forced to flee together from England when Richard had involved himself in trying to help the young Earl of Warwick, who had been a prisoner in the Tower. Philippa sighed deeply as she remembered how that unfortunate young man had been executed with another pretender to the throne, Perkin Warbeck. Richard and Anne had been pardoned and returned to England. Philippa would have dearly liked to see them while she was here but knew that would be dangerous for all of them.

Peter appeared to be taking his time, she thought, and rose to go to the door and unbar it. After moments her eyes became accustomed to the darkness and she could see that the courtyard appeared to be deserted and she could see in the distance the dim glow of candlelight in the windows of the inn. Surely it would not have taken the innkeeper so long to provide Peter with a flagon of ale and bread and cheese? He would not linger, she knew, being always concerned for the safety of his charges. Philippa turned and looked anxiously towards her mother, who had sat up the moment she had heard her daughter stirring.

"What is it? Can you hear someone coming?"

"No, it is just that it is taking Peter rather a long time."

"Has it? I must have dozed." Cressida frowned. "It is unlike Peter to delay."

"I think I should go and look for him."

"Philippa, no. He warned us—"

"I know all that, but I don't think we have a choice. I fear something might have happened to him."

Cressida rose and joined Philippa at the stable door. Together they peered anxiously into the dark courtyard.

"It is indeed very strange that he hasn't returned before now. Had it been anyone else but Peter..." Cressida shook her head worriedly. "He is not the man to allow himself to be drawn into some gambling ploy."

"He would never leave us unprotected for so long. Something must have happened to him."

The Countess shook her head again and bit her lip doubtfully.

"Mother, I must go back to the inn and ask after him."

"I do not like that idea at all."

"I don't myself, but if anything has happened to Peter we have to know about it, even—" Philippa broke off abruptly, averting her face so that her mother should not see how very alarmed she was "—even if we cannot do much about it."

She dared not put into words the fear that harm could have come to their squire and, if it had done, what they could possibly do without him as escort.

"You stay here by the door and keep watch." Philippa put up her cloak hood and drew its comforting warmth about her. "I shall not be gone for more than a moment or two. The landlord is bound to know what has occurred. It may be that Peter heard of some suitable mounts for hire or purchase and thought it imperative to go immediately to find out about them."

"At this late hour?"

"I know that it seems unlikely, but it is the only reason why he might have left us for so long." Gently Philippa shook off her mother's detaining hand upon her wrist. "Do not be anxious. I shall come back immediately and will not allow myself to be drawn into talk with any of the men in the tap room. At all events, most of them do not appear to be able to talk English." She made a little wry twist of the lips in her attempt to humour her distraught mother.

Reluctantly Cressida released her and stood back as Philippa pushed the heavy stable door further open and, with but one reassuring glance behind her, stepped out into the yard. It seemed very black, but she could not take the lanthorn and leave her mother in darkness and she could just make out her way ahead by the flickering light of the candles within the inn building.

She was about halfway across when she heard some slight movement. She stopped dead still and listened, but her frightened heartbeats sounded so loud within her breast that she knew any other sounds would be drowned out by them. Reproving herself for cowardice, she crept forward cautiously. She was not wont to be so foolish. The sound could easily have been made by a night-prowling cat. She could hear the noise of talk now from the inn and she stopped again, calling upon her courage to enter the tap room alone. The outright impudence of the customers' curiosity when they had first arrived made her hesitate. As Peter had said, the travellers had certainly not been welcomed. So intent on her determination to proceed was she that she went sprawling suddenly across something directly in her path. The breath was shaken out of her and she stifled a sudden cry, recovered herself and turned to stare down at the body of the man who was lying senseless, his head in a puddle. Her eyes had become more used to the darkness now, though it was a moonless night, and, as she crouched to examine the injured man, she knew instantly that it was Peter Fairley.

He made no sound as she carefully explored his

clothing, wet with the damp mist, and she gave a little gasp of fear and pity as her fingers, when lifting his head, discovered some fluid more sticky. The wound was bleeding copiously. No wonder he was unconscious and made no answer to her softly uttered urging to answer her. Had he stumbled and fallen in the darkness? Like her he carried no lanthorn and it was just possible, but Peter was a cautious man and he would have waited before proceeding to cross, allowing his night vision to develop. Unless he too had stumbled across some obstacle in his path, it was unlikely. Terror struck her forcibly as she thought he must have been deliberately struck down, but by whom—and why? Surely it had been obvious to everyone in the tap room that they were not wealthy travellers—yet Peter had made it known that he was carrying a considerable amount of coin in order to hire or buy horses for their journey. To men living in poverty that would have been invitation enough to attack and rob him. She half stood up after her efforts to rouse him had failed and looked round apprehensively. Peter was a big man. She could not lift or drag him to the stable, but dare she call for assistance from the men in the inn?

As she stood for moments, irresolute, she was taken totally by surprise as brutal hands suddenly pulled her backwards and caught her wrists in a cruel grasp, thus freeing one of her attacker's hands to clasp over her mouth before she could draw breath to call out.

"Softly there, my little beauty," a voice, speaking in English, though with a singsong lilt she had come to identify as that of a Welshman, whispered in her ear. "There's no call for you to be making a scene and, like as not, you'll not end up as your servant there if you're wise."

She was trembling with anger as well as fear and tried desperately to free herself from the man's grasp, but he continued to drag her backwards, her heels trailing helplessly on the cobbles. The fellow appeared to be alone and yet he was so strong that she feared he would be able to drag her where he wished and that she would be helpless to prevent him. Even in her desperation she feared for Peter. If she were unable to help him, he could die there in this dank straw-spattered courtyard, an ignominious end for a man who had faced often far greater dangers. And she—she could not doubt her own fate and knew with blinding clarity that her attacker would be unlikely to leave her alive after he had finished with her. Would he make for the stable? If so, her mother, also, was in deadly danger, but no, he was aware that the stable was inhabited and he would not risk her mother screaming for help and the possibility that in the ensuing chaos his prey would perhaps manage to free herself. She tried to keep calm. He obviously knew of some other shelter where he intended to drag her. If she waited for the opportunity, surely she would then manage to free herself momentarily, at least to shout out a warning to her mother. Yet, even so, she coolly debated the wisdom of that. Her mother would have a better chance of escaping this fellow's attentions if she, Philippa, remained quiet and allowed him to do what he wished. As these thoughts raced through her mind there was no time for hysteria or panic. Her fear was absolute, but for the present, she was helpless to affect her own fate. The time it took to drag her to some secluded spot seemed elongated. In actual fact it could only have taken moments, yet she appeared to have opportunity to think out rationally what she could and could not do and what would be best for her mother's safety. It would be only minutes now before she was pulled into shelter and she did not doubt that her molester would free her mouth only to render her senseless with a blow to the face.

She prayed to the Virgin and to St Catherine, the patron saint of maidens, to give her the courage to face what must be. Then, suddenly, miraculously, another voice spoke menacingly behind her. She could not understand the words for they were uttered, presumably, in Welsh, but the import was unmistakable. Abruptly she was released to fall forward onto her face.

Sobbing with terror, she scrambled up and half-turned to find her attacker had been seized from behind, as she herself had been, and, even in the dim light of the darkened courtyard, she could see the dullish gleam of a dagger held against the fellow's throat. She staggered back, unsure if she were being rescued or had fallen into the hands of another merciless attacker. The man who had first seized her was crouching awkwardly, making inarticulate sounds of rage and fear. Unceremoniously he was dragged to his feet, still with the dagger menacing his throat, and pulled some distance clear away from her.

She could not see the man she hoped was her rescuer clearly, but by his bulky shape, wrapped in a dark frieze cloak, she realised that he was a big man, towering over his prisoner, who was now continuing to babble incoherently in Welsh, his terror only too apparent.

The newcomer spoke again commandingly and the blubbering ceased. Another sharp command, in English, this time, alerted a third man to the scene who, apparently, had been waiting his opportunity to come to the newcomer's assistance.

''David, come, take possession of this fellow and cart

him off to the nearest constable. I've felt him for weapons and found only a single dagger, but take care." He tossed the weapon down at their feet where it clanged on the cobbles. "You can never tell with these ruffians where they manage to conceal others. Hold him for a moment while I secure his hands."

Still trembling, Philippa felt unable to move, let alone run. She could not see clearly what her rescuer was about, but guessed that he had used some belt about his person to make her attacker secure. The fellow was still murmuring promises and pleas, which were abruptly cut short, so she thought he had been unceremoniously gagged.

The man addressed as David, also a well-muscled fighting man, judging by his lumbering bulk, jerked at his prisoner's bound arms and dragged him away. Since he had made no answer to her rescuer's orders but instantly obeyed them, Philippa gathered that he was used to doing so and was, probably, his servant.

She managed to let out a little, breathless gasp at last and the man who had come to her rescue came instantly forward and put out a hand to steady her.

"Are you hurt? You are, I take it, one of the English travellers just arrived at the inn and taken up residence with my horses in the stable, or so the landlord informs me?"

"Yes," she whispered throatily, "I thank you, sir. My mother is in the stable and my..." she hesitated, then recollected herself suddenly and the need to guard her identity "...my uncle lies injured some paces off. No, I am not hurt, that fellow had only just grabbed me as—as I was trying to help my uncle. He—he took me by surprise but—but he had no time to—hurt me."

"Thank the Virgin," he said curtly. "Show me

where your relative lies and I'll summon assistance from the tap room, then you must go to your mother."

She was feeling even more trembly now and she staggered and would have fallen had he not once more put out a sturdy arm to catch her. She felt an unaccountable tremor pass through her at the touch of his fingers and struggled a little to pull free, but he continued to hold her firmly.

"What is it? You are not afraid of me, are you?" The voice was clear, slightly lilting—as all voices, she thought, must be here in Wales or even on the Border, her mother had told her—but it was also hard, uncompromising, authoritative, and she wondered just who he was and if she could trust him. He had come to her rescue seemingly, but her attacker had known him or recognised his authority and she feared that he might question her, demand proof of her identity. He could well be a magistrate and answerable to the Crown for the good behaviour of those within his district.

"No, no." She was afraid that reaction had set in and that she was liable to break into tears. That she must not do before this commanding stranger. "I am sorry, sir, that I have not yet recovered my balance, it seems. Please…"

She led him to where Peter lay and was thankful to see, as they approached, that Peter was slowly coming to himself now and giving sharp little cries of pain.

Philippa's rescuer gestured her imperatively to stand slightly aside and dropped to one knee beside the sufferer and examined the head wound gently, as she had done. She marvelled at the gentle, sensitive touch of those strong large hands.

"It appears that he was struck from behind, possibly with the hilt of a dagger, mistress. Fortunately the wound does not seem to be too serious as already he is coming to himself. Head wounds can be dangerous and unconsciousness can sometimes last for hours—or even weeks.''

He stood up and removed his cloak so that now she could see that he was, indeed, a tall, muscular man with massive shoulders, though she thought by the hardness of his body, as he had held her momentarily against his chest, that there was not an ounce of surplus fat upon him. Obviously he kept himself in superb fighting form. Was he a soldier, a mercenary?—but his commanding manner gave her the impression that he had some standing in the district and was more than likely a knight. Could he possibly be the lord the landlord had spoken of?

As if in answer to her unspoken question he addressed her as he rose to his feet once more. ''Allow me to introduce myself. I am Sir Rhys Griffith and, like you, I am accommodated at the inn.''

So her surmise had been correct. He was indeed lordly. No wonder the innkeeper had not offered to request that he vacate, for her mother's use, the private room he had bespoken.

He was continuing. ''You can leave this man's care in my hands, mistress, and go to your mother. She will be frantic for news of you both, I am sure. I will see to it that your uncle is conveyed to the inn and then I will come and inform you what is best to be done.''

Philippa still felt that her limbs would let her down if she did not find some support soon and she had the strange feeling that she must not allow this stranger to touch her again, let alone hold her as closely as he had done formerly. She was close to tears again and inwardly she castigated herself, since her immediate dan-

ger appeared to be over and she had no outward reason
to distrust this man—nor yet her own feelings regarding
him. It was just that he had taken over so completely,
overwhelmed her by his compelling personality. Yet he
had said little to her to bring out this strange, dubious
excitement. Certainly he had offered her no discourtesy.
She struggled to find words to thank him adequately.

"I am—most grateful, sir. I do not know what would
have happened had you not come…" She swallowed
and averted her face from his hawklike gaze.

"I think you must certainly have realised what would
have happened, mistress," he said a trifle harshly. "I
can understand your concern for your uncle but, really,
you should not have ventured out of the stable alone."

She was a trifle angered by that suggestion. He was
reproving her for what had happened, as if it had been
all her own fault. What would he have had her do, leave
Peter to die out there while she remained in cowardly
security within the stable?

"I had to go, sir," she said haughtily, "there was no
one else. As for the attack, it all happened so suddenly.
My uncle left us to fetch food from the inn and he was
such a long time gone that I was forced to believe something had happened to him—which, indeed, it had. I
stumbled over his body and, while I was kneeling by
him, I suppose I was so frightened and intent on my
uncle's fate that—that I did not hear anyone approach.
This fellow grabbed me from behind before I could so
much as pull away or cry out and—and…"

She sensed that he had relaxed his grim demeanour
now, as he said more gently, "Best not to think about
it any further as no real harm has been done."

He put out a hand to offer to lead her towards the
stable. She attempted to draw away from him so that

he might not touch her again, but he would brook no denial and took her hand firmly and turned her towards the stable door.

"It was fortunate that I happened to come along when I did," he said. "I have been visiting a friend in the town and came into the courtyard by the back way. Providentially we—that is, my squire David and I—heard noises, which indicated all was not well. I heard the man threaten you and instructed my squire to stand back while I came to your assistance. On rounding the gate post I saw at once that you needed it fast."

She still could not see his features clearly and was glad that he must not be able to see her. She must be in a fine state after that terrible struggle. She could feel her hair straggling about her face and she wondered if she had transferred blood from Peter's wound and filth from the cobbles on to her cheeks. Certainly her hand felt sticky and dirty and he must be aware of it. How stupid, she told herself, to concern herself about such paltry matters at such a time, yet her desire to remain aloof from all strangers on this journey and the strength and determination of this man made her acutely uncomfortable in his presence. She was also anxious that he should not get too close a glimpse of her mother or guess at the real reason for their need to sleep apart in the stable.

She had felt the fine wool of his sleeve and had smelled the tang of a good-quality leathern jerkin when she had been close to him and judged that he was, as he claimed, a knight. With luck they might never meet again, but she had a strange desire to see his face clearly before their final parting. Surely that was natural, she thought, simply a wish to see the features of the man who had saved her honour and her very life.

They were approaching the stable door and he released her hand. "I should go and give assistance to your uncle. Everything will be done for his comfort and I will ensure the future safety of you and your mother." These last words were spoken in so stern a voice that she wondered if he suspected her attacker had been given information about the latest guest from someone inside the inn and was determined to investigate the matter further. She gave a little shudder and did not envy the men whom he would face in that tap room. He was one man, alone, yet he would deal with any rabble, she was sure of that.

A voice called anxiously from the opened door of the stable, "Philippa, is that you? Whatever is wrong? Peter has not returned and I am—frightened." It was so unlike her courageous mother to sound so querulous and pitiful that Philippa's heart bled for her, alone in that stable, fearful, dreading the worst for her daughter and her squire.

Sir Rhys gave a slight bow to the shadowy woman in the doorway. "Your daughter and—your brother have encountered some difficulties, lady. Your brother is injured and I intend to see that he is cared for. Please remain together in the stable until either I or my squire can come and inform you that all is well."

Falteringly the Countess said, "But who are you, sir, and how—?"

"Your daughter will explain. Do not be alarmed." He bowed also to Philippa. "Sit down upon the straw and recover yourself. I can see that you are still trembling. I will send you both some strengthening wine. Do not concern yourself about your attacker. He will not trouble you again. My squire will see to that."

Before either woman could reply he had strode off in

the direction of the inn doorway. After the stress of all that had occurred, Philippa fell sobbing into her mother's arms.

Cressida forbore to question her daughter until the anguished sobbing had stopped, then she drew away from her, gently holding her at arm's length, and stared into Philippa's eyes searchingly.

"Tell me truly exactly what happened. Do not be afraid to do so. Whatever it is, I shall understand."

Philippa drew a hard breath. "I was attacked but he— the attacker—could not finish—what—what he hoped. That gentleman came to my rescue in time. His servant carted the man off to the constable so—so I expect the knight must be well known here. He—he handled the whole episode with such authority—" She broke off and dabbed at her streaming eyes with the knuckles of one hand. "Mother, it was all so dreadful and now— now I do not know what to make of the rescuer. If he is important here, he might well demand to know more about us and—"

"Child, calm yourself. I could not see him well, but he appeared civil enough. I thank all the saints that he was able to help you in time. Who knows what—what would have occurred had he not come so promptly."

"He—he frightens me and—and I do not know why. He was kind and courteous, yet..."

"Philippa, you are naturally upset by everything that occurred and you are alarmed for Peter."

"I know." Philippa took a hard grip upon herself and tried to stop the trembling and deadly chill, which had seeped into her body and sapped her strength. "I am not usually so foolish. I am safe and unharmed but— but I cannot help thinking that this man could be dangerous to us."

"But why? He came to our assistance and, once given, he will most probably forget our very existence."

Philippa whispered, "I am not so sure of that. He said he would call on those people in the inn to help Peter. He was attacked as I was. I found him lying unconscious and his head was bleeding. I could not rouse him and then—and then—" Her teeth began chattering again as the full sense of shock assailed her. "I heard nothing. He must have been very practised in his trade for Peter to have been overcome like that." She buried her face in her hands. "All the time I knew—knew what he—and afterwards that he would kill me and I did not even try to bite at the hand he held over my mouth and call out because—because—"

"You were afraid he would render you unconscious and then find me," Cressida said quietly. "I know, child, I know." She, too, drew a shuddering breath as she realised fully how close both of them had come to disaster and now—they must wait to discover if Peter would recover.

As if in answer to that unspoken fear, a voice called softly from the stable doorway, "May I come in, ladies?"

"Yes, yes, of course." Despite her recognition of the rescuer's voice and the readiness of the invitation, Cressida stood protectively in front of her daughter as he entered and stood limned against the door post.

Stepping slightly clear of her mother, Philippa could see her rescuer more clearly now as the lanthorn light played on his tall, massive form, broad shoulders and slim hips. He was equipped with heavy broadsword and dagger and, though his clothing was of good quality, as she had felt when he had touched her, he was not richly clad, being in serviceable travelling garb of leather brigandine over homespun dark doublet and hose. He had a broad, open face with a dominating beak of a nose and firm chin, dark brown eyes set well apart, beneath a mop of dark hair curling to his shoulders. He had, apparently, scorned the present fashion of curled fringe, nor did he wear the new sleeveless long gown, lately worn at court. His tanned complexion spoke to her of a life spent mostly out of doors. There was an imperious air about him, but his manner towards them could not be judged arrogant. It was difficult for her to guess at his age, but she imagined that he must be in his middle or late twenties, for his massive form had not yet run to fat; she thought he had spent his life in soldierly pursuits and continued to keep fit by hard exercise.

He was unsmiling as he bowed to them courteously. ''I do not think your escort has come to any real harm, my lady. He took a bad bang on the back of his head, which has bled profusely, but he had fully regained consciousness when we carried him into the inn and his wound has been dressed. He is resting in the tap room, concerned now about you both, naturally. I have made arrangements for you to be accommodated within the chamber allocated to me. You will be much more comfortable there and I shall do very well in the tap room where I can keep an eye on your—uncle.'' There was a slight, sardonic curve of the lips as he uttered the last word and Philippa frowned, in doubt. Did he believe that her mother was travelling with her lover and wished to conceal the fact? She blushed darkly and averted her gaze from those piercing dark eyes of his. She was truly grateful to this man for his assistance, but he had no right to judge them contemptuously; however, he was putting himself out for their welfare and she felt constrained to utter words of heartfelt gratitude.

Though her immediate thought was to refuse his offer of the use of his private bedchamber, she knew it would be better for her mother if she accepted graciously.

"I have to thank you again, Sir Rhys, for all your kindness to three strangers and we accept most gratefully your kind offer." She gave a little shiver of horrified remembrance. "Indeed, I think we could not remain alone here in the stable without feeling apprehensive after—after what happened."

He nodded. "Naturally. Please, will you follow me and I will see you settled."

He unhooked the lanthorn from its place and stood by the stable door to light their way. His free hand he proffered to the Countess as she stepped into the darkened courtyard. "Allow me, my lady. It is dark out here and the cobbles slippery. If you take your mother's other hand, mistress, you will be less likely to slip."

The landlord was obsequious as they entered the inn and Cressida went hastily to Peter, who was sitting up in a hard-backed chair by the fire looking pale and anxious, but, otherwise, his true self. Philippa was thankful that the blow did not appear to have affected his memory for he was lucid enough.

"Do not fret, sister. I am feeling better already after imbibing some of the landlord's best wine. I'm only angered at myself for being less cautious and rendering you both without protection and leaving you open to danger."

"This good knight has proved to be our saviour," Cressida said reassuringly. "Now, rest, Peter and get well. We must see how you fare in the morning before we decide to travel."

He was about to argue, but she prevented him with a gentle squeeze upon his hand.

Sir Rhys led them above stairs, after ordering the landlord to serve them with the best supper he could provide.

The room was surprisingly large and comfortably appointed. Philippa looked round appreciatively. "I am sorry, sir, that you must be put out...."

He laughed as he picked up a saddle bag which, presumably, contained a change of clothes and necessities for travelling. "I assure you that David and I have slept in far worse places than the tap room of this inn and, as I said, it will be wiser, considering that it appears to harbour thieves, a matter which I shall take up with our host. Please make yourselves at home and try to rest and, at last, sleep after your trying adventures. I will send David up with your belongings."

He brushed by Philippa in order to reach the door and she felt herself trembling again at his touch. He bowed to her mother. "Please, Lady Wroxeter, accept my apologies for these unfortunate events, happening so soon after your arrival back in your native land after such a long absence."

Philippa saw her mother give a great gasp of surprise and shock and she herself put a hand to her mouth in dismayed astonishment.

"Sir—"

He stemmed Cressida's attempts at denial with a lordly wave of his hand.

"Sir Daniel Gretton's beautiful daughter could not be mistaken for any other, my lady. Her fame spread through the Marches and I had the advantage of seeing you once with your father in the market in Ludlow. That was considerably before you married my lord Earl." He smiled broadly. "I was merely eight years old then but, like all the other males in the district, I fell completely under the spell of Gretton's faery princess.'' His gaze passed to Philippa and dwelt on her slight form, trembling now with another fear that he was aware of their true identities. ''Your daughter, my lady, has been blessed in inheriting your golden loveliness. I am honoured to be of service. I will pay my respects in the morning. Please excuse me now.''

He withdrew and closed the door before either of the astounded women could say a word in answer.

Chapter Two

Philippa woke to find sunlight coming through the unshuttered casement and almost blinding her. She slipped from the bed, careful not to waken her mother who was still sleeping beside her. She went to the window and found, to her delight, that the mist and dampness of the previous day had disappeared and the sun was already well up. She gave a sigh of relief. Provided that Peter was well enough to travel after yesterday's misadventure, they would be able to make an early start and be well on their way before midday.

She had slept well considering how frightened and disturbed she had been last night. Exhaustion had taken its toll of them both. Her thoughts went to the stranger lord who had come to their help. It had been extremely kind of him to put his private chamber at their disposal, but she recalled her mother's alarmed expression when he had announced that he had recognised her. It would be well if they could avoid seeing him again, though Philippa doubted that that would be possible.

A sound from the bed alerted her to the knowledge that, despite her care not to disturb her mother, Cressida had woken and was already sitting up.

"Is there something wrong?" she enquired doubtfully. "Have you heard someone at the door?"

"No, no one. The inn servants are already about their
business. It is a fine day. We should be able to leave
soon after breakfast as long as Peter is well enough."

Cressida thrust back the bed covers and stepped from
the bed. "I'll dress at once. We must call a physician
to Peter if there is need."

Philippa went to her mother's side to help her dress.
Since they had decided it would be best, for this journey, to travel without a maid in attendance, it had been
necessary for them to help each other with back lacings.

Once her mother was dressed she hastened to dress
herself and was relieved that she had done so when she
heard a knock on the door.

Peter Fairley's voice called softly, "It is I, my lady,
Peter. I have brought you some breakfast."

Philippa hastened to let him in, relieved to see he
was up and about.

"Peter, how are you this morning?"

He set down a tray on which was laid fresh manchet
bread, a small pot of honey and a plate of ham and cold
meats and a stoup of ale.

"I'm very well except for a bump on the back of my
head as big as a pigeon's egg." He rubbed it ruefully.
"I blame myself for total lack of caution. I could have
put us all in danger."

"You mustn't blame yourself," Cressida reassured
him. "Who would expect to be attacked in the inn
yard?"

"To speak truth, anyone should, my lady. My only
excuse is that we were all tired and chilled and I was
in haste to see to your needs."

"Well, all is well." Cressida smiled. "We will breakfast quickly and try to make an early start." She frowned in thought. "I have some coin left which, fortunately, I kept in a money belt beneath my gown, but the loss of some of our funds in the robbery is dire. We shall have to be careful on the journey and settle for accommodation not of the best." She had already put out a small pile of coin upon the bed. "Take that and make the best bargain you can over mounts, Peter, but first, have you eaten?"

"Yes, my lady. I shall get off at once. Sir Rhys's man, David, speaks of a reasonably honest horse coper, who has a stable in the street behind the harbour."

"Good." Lady Wroxeter nodded her approval.

Then Philippa said thoughtfully, "Did you discover anything about our rescuer of last night, Peter? Unfortunately he appeared to recognise Mother and we are anxious to avoid his company now." She coloured. "That seems to be very ungrateful, but you understand the need better than any of us."

With his hand on the door latch, Peter turned, clearly hesitant to speak. "Sir Rhys Griffith, my lady, is master of the greater part of my lord Earl's estates. His father was granted them following the battle of Redmoor, for his services to the new King. Sir David was killed in a hunting accident a year ago." He grinned somewhat wolfishly. "He was somewhat appropriately gored by a boar and did not recover from the wound which festered, and his son, Rhys, who had been knighted the year before, inherited."

There was a deadly silence as the three exchanged alarmed glances.

Philippa exclaimed hotly, "So the man has robbed my father of his lands and—"

"He cannot be held responsible for what his father

did at Redmoor,'' Cressida reproved her gently, ''but I confess this news is catastrophic. The man could prove a very real danger to us, indeed.''

''He has enquired after you both,'' Peter said grimly. ''I'm afraid that it will prove very difficult for us to leave the inn without encountering him.''

''And his manor is far too close to Gretton for our peace of mind,'' Lady Wroxeter said regretfully.

Philippa paled. ''Do you think our going there could put Grandmère and Grandpère in danger?''

Lady Wroxeter shook her head. ''I do not think so, though it will not enhance their reputation as Yorkist sympathisers. They are not proscribed and are in no danger of arrest.'' The fingers of one hand tightened on the bedpost. ''I am so very anxious to see them. It has been so long since—'' She broke off, her voice choked with emotion, ''Neither of them has ever seen you. I think we should take the risk.''

''But this man does know we are going there?''

''I imagine so. Since he lives so close I would think he is aware of how ill my father is. It is to be hoped that he will have enough humanity to leave us in peace and not inform the court authorities of our presence there.'' She sighed. ''Our visit will only be a short one. We dare not remain long.''

''You miss your home at Gretton, don't you?''

''I always loved it dearly and when I heard of the proposed betrothal to your father I was most reluctant to leave it. Of course, then there was every possibility of being able to come home on frequent visits but since Redmoor...'' She shrugged helplessly.

''You gave up everything to be with my father in exile, a safe secure home, money sufficient to fill all your needs, everything.''

Cressida smiled fondly. "When you fall in love, Philippa, you will understand that nothing is important save being with the one you love."

Philippa bit her lip uncertainly. The way matters stood that possibility seemed very far off, if at all.

Her mother suddenly remembered that she had given Peter Fairley no instructions about settling their score. "I should have asked him to settle with the landlord on his way out to the horse coper," she said. "The sooner we can leave the better."

A decisive voice from the doorway settled the matter for her. "You need have no doubts on that score, Lady Wroxeter, I have already paid the landlord and the moment your man returns with your mounts we can leave immediately. It will be well to do so since the day promises to be a fine one."

Sir Rhys Griffith stood poised in the doorway which Peter must have left slightly ajar in his agitation on leaving them.

"I beg pardon for the intrusion, but the door was open sufficiently for me to overhear what you said, my lady. May I come in?" He bowed courteously and Cressida, somewhat startled and flustered, nodded hastily.

"Please do so, Sir Rhys. This chamber is yours, after all, but I cannot allow you to stand our score. We have slept in this chamber, and most comfortably, I thank you, and have eaten two meals. I…"

He had advanced slightly and was regarding Philippa smilingly though he must have seen at once that her manner was somewhat hostile.

"You have no choice, my lady. I have already settled the matter. Under the distressing circumstances of last night it was the least I could do as a gentleman knight and for a neighbour." He undid the purse suspended from the military-styled leather belt he wore round his waist and proffered a small leather bag to Philippa.

"There, mistress, is the coin that rascally thief stole from your man. I rose early, called on the constable with instructions as to charging the fellow and retrieved your money. You will need it when you arrive at Gretton or later on your journey home. You need not concern yourself about expenses occurred on the way to Gretton Manor since it will be my most pleasurable duty to escort you there."

Philippa gave a great gasp of shocked surprise and anger. "That will not be necessary, sir. Peter Fairley, my father's trusty squire, is perfectly capable of seeing us safe to Gretton."

Her tone was now unmistakably hostile and his dark brows rose in assumed or real astonishment.

"Forgive me, Lady…?" He paused and looked enquiringly at Lady Wroxeter.

"My daughter is Lady Philippa Telford, Sir Rhys, and she owes her safety from molestation and her life to you," Cressida put in hurriedly. Though she herself was anxious to be free of this man's presence, she had no wish for Philippa to antagonise him deliberately.

He bowed again, smiling. "Forgive me again, Lady Philippa, but I must point out to you that neither you nor your squire appeared last night to be perfectly capable of protecting yourselves. It is my desire and my bounden duty to provide a suitable escort. Both my cousin David and I are soldier-trained and with your squire, who is too, we should prove a sufficient force to keep off any opportunity-seeking robbers on the road." He shook his head, gently reproving, "I fear the roads of Wales are no more safe from thieves and outlaws than any other rural community, though preferable in many ways to the hazards of London town or even Ludlow after dark.''

Philippa looked to her mother for support in her rejection of the idea, but Cressida shook her head gently. ''We shall be grateful for your continued care of us, Sir Rhys,'' she said quietly.

Sir Rhys glanced round the chamber to see if their saddle bags were packed and nodded his satisfaction.

''I will inform your man Peter when he returns with the horses and send him up to you. I should not advise you to come down to the tap room until there is need. The clientele of this place is hardly salubrious, as yesterday's misadventures bore out.'' He bowed again and withdrew.

Philippa said angrily, ''Why did you agree to his escort? We do not need or want his company.''

Lady Wroxeter sighed. ''I do not see how we could refuse. To do so would only appear ungrateful and incur his displeasure, if not his downright anger. We cannot afford to antagonise the man, not only for our sakes but for those of your grandparents as well. Since he is well aware of our destination he could inform on us after our arrival, so it makes little difference.''

''I would have preferred not to have his company,'' Philippa said sulkily and her mother turned on her in sudden irritation.

''You were glad enough of Sir Rhys's services last night, young lady. Be good enough to acknowledge our debt to him.''

''I doubt if he acknowledges any debt to my father,'' Philippa snapped in answer and turned away to see to the final packing.

Philippa was forced to acknowledge Sir Rhys Griffith's need for caution, however, when they were eventually called downstairs by his squire, who informed them that Peter Fairley had arrived with their horses and his master had declared himself ready to leave. The atmosphere in the tap room was decidedly frosty; the small number of men seated at the ale-spattered tables stared at the women in open hostility and the landlord was surly. Obviously news concerning their imprisoned companion had reached them and the blame for his likely fate placed at the women's door. Sir Rhys received them cheerily and conducted them to the door with a show of deliberate courtesy. Philippa shivered in spite of herself and was glad of his presence.

Peter had managed to procure an elderly palfrey for Lady Wroxeter and two sturdy Welsh cobs for himself and Philippa. To her irritation, Sir Rhys insisted upon inspecting them before allowing his charges to mount. As if Peter was incapable of judging good horse flesh when he saw it, Philippa fumed inwardly. She watched, frowning, as Sir Rhys ran his hand down the legs of each of the mounts and inspected their chests and mouths. Apparently satisfied, he came back to the waiting group and nodded his approval.

"You have made as good purchases as possible under the circumstances," he informed Peter.

"If you were not sure of his abilities, you should have accompanied him to the horse coper," Philippa murmured under her breath and he turned and grinned at her. She was not sure if he had actually heard, but he made no comment.

"It is necessary to have good mounts for our journey," he explained. "We have almost a hundred miles over undulating country, some of it mountainous."

Cressida nodded. "I travelled it only once when—

when I left England in 1486 and we were somewhat hurried,'' she said quickly.''

''I imagine you have not ridden a great deal over the last years?'' he enquired.

''No, there has been little opportunity or need,'' she agreed.

Peter stepped forward to help his mistress into the saddle and Philippa was chagrined to find Sir Rhys at her side to do a like service for her. She found herself swung up lightly, the touch of his hand gentle yet firm upon her body. Confused by such close contact, she turned and fumbled awkwardly with the reins, only to find them deliberately placed into her hands.

''You are used to riding, Lady Philippa?'' he enquired. ''If not, you can ride with me.''

''That will certainly not be necessary, sir,'' she said coldly. ''Though I do not ride often in Malines, my father has been at pains to see that I learned well and had adequate practice.''

''Good. As I said to your mother, we have a hard ride in front of us.''

He stood back to confer with the two men, then gave a signal for all to mount up and swung himself lightly into the saddle of the courser an inn groom held ready for him. He moved his horse beside that of her mother's as they rode beneath the courtyard arch and Philippa rode behind with the two squires flanking her.

The day was pleasantly warm and she flung back her cloak and slipped back her hood, allowing the sun's gentle warmth to touch her body. Her new mount seemed amiable enough and soon became accustomed to her touch upon the reins and she leaned forward to pat the cob's shaggy neck. Peter smiled at her encouragingly and she grinned back, thankful, at last, to be away from the inn.

Soon they were out of the mired streets of the harbour and free of the unaccustomed smells of sea air and tar and the green undulating countryside stretched before them. Yesterday's misty dampness had refreshed the air and Philippa began to find the ride pleasurable.

She could hear Sir Rhys in talk with her mother and rode slightly forward so that she could catch everything which was said.

"I would suggest that we make three stops upon the way at inns known to me," he said.

"But, Sir Rhys, I had thought Philippa and I might be accommodated at two nunneries I know of." Lady Wroxeter hesitated, her colour rising, as she went on, "You must understand that expense is a feature of my decision…"

"I think not, my lady," he brushed aside her objection. "Nuns are notoriously curious. They lead such sheltered lives that they are fascinated by the backgrounds and news brought from the outside world of everyone who comes to stay. I imagine you are anxious to avoid as much gossip as possible. Do not concern yourself about expense. I have already made provision for David and I upon the journey so it will be no extra drain upon our resources."

"But surely—"

Philippa saw him lean towards her mother and place a restraining hand upon hers. "Please, Lady Wroxeter, place yourself in my hands and, I assure you, you will reach Gretton without either incident or undue notice."

Philippa considered what he had said and raised an enquiring eyebrow in Peter's direction. He merely shrugged his shoulders in answer. They were in this man's power and she realised they were helpless to change the situation.

She regarded his unyielding back as he rode ahead and mentally reviewed the encounter of the previous night. Her mother was right. Had this man not come to her rescue, they would not be travelling this road today. A great shudder ran through her at the thought. Had she not discovered that he was a loyal Tudor supporter and, worse than that, had inherited her father's confiscated estates, she would have been more than ready to acknowledge her debt to him. What was his motive in offering them protection? Would he lead them into some manor upon the way where they could be arrested and held during the King's pleasure in hopes that her father would come to England to plead their cause and try to obtain their release, so placing his head on the block? It was a likely prospect—yet how could they manage to evade this fate? Peter had clearly accepted defeat—for the moment. She must wait patiently until he was able to suggest some way of escaping Sir Rhys's vigilance, but even should they accomplish this—and it would be difficult and hazardous—their plans to visit her dying grandfather would have to be abandoned and she knew her mother had set her heart upon this visit. She sighed a little too loudly and Sir Rhys turned in his saddle to regard her, eyebrows raised.

"Are you tired already, Lady Philippa? Do you wish to stop? I know that unaccustomed riding can cause saddle soreness."

She blushed hotly at the thought and shook her head. "No, no, sir, I was just—considering the length of the journey facing us."

"I shall try to make it as easy for you all as possible," he returned mildly.

* * *

Their first stop for refreshment was in the Tudor stronghold of Pembroke. Philippa looked up at the looming castle apprehensively. Here, surely, Sir Rhys might well achieve his aim and put them in the hands of the King's officers. More than likely he would obtain the King's favour by so doing though, knowing the Tudor monarch from her days in attendance at Queen Elizabeth's court, she doubted that he would be paid in coin or lands. King Henry kept a very tight hand on the treasury purse strings. Nevertheless all his supporters were well aware that to be in the King's debt would be advantageous.

Sir Rhys drew his small company off the main street which was crowded with carts and market stalls, their proprietors calling hoarsely the worth of their wares to passers-by, into a street behind where he drew his mount up before an inn displaying the sign of the Red Lion. Despite her assurance to Sir Rhys that she was not weary, Philippa was glad to have Peter lift her down and to join her mother in the inn's one eating room where a sweating landlord came obsequiously forward to enquire what service Sir Rhys required.

Curtly the knight ordered a dinner of meat and vegetable broth, pease pudding and what tarts the fellow had to offer which would please the ladies. Philippa and her mother were escorted up the rickety stair to a small dark chamber where a slatternly maid brought them water and towels, plus chamber pots, so that they might refresh themselves. Thankfully they returned to the eating room to find the food already upon the table. Philippa, who had been dry-mouthed with alarm at what might transpire in the next hour or so, discovered that, despite that, she was hungry and was glad of the hot tasty food and the rye bread which accompanied it. This inn was not apparently able to provide the fine white manchet bread to which Sir Rhys was more usually accustomed.

Her mother was rather quiet over the meal and Sir Rhys accepted her need for silence in courtesy. Above stairs, away from his presence, Philippa had thought it best not to alarm her mother with her fears. Catching her eye across the table, she understood that her mother had already considered the danger.

Nothing happened, however. They completed the meal, then David, Sir Rhys's squire, rose to pay the score. Peter had already gone to assure himself that their mounts had been fed and watered. Sir Rhys offered his hand to Lady Wroxeter to lead her outside to the courtyard.

"I considered it wiser to chose a less frequented inn, this being market day," he explained. "The fare was nourishing but hardly acceptable to finer palates used to food prepared in the Duchess Margaret's establishment at Malines."

Cressida shook her head. "The food was excellent and the place unexpectedly clean," she replied.

Since Peter was engaged in mounting his lady upon her palfrey and David was still about his business in the inn, Sir Rhys lifted Philippa once more into the saddle.

"These merchant's clothes form an excellent disguise, and were well chosen," he remarked as he fingered the wool of her russet gown.

Angrily she flashed back at him, "These garments are no disguise, sir. We live in virtual penuary at Malines while you live in luxury on my father's estates."

He looked from the tip of her proudly held young head to her little booted foot resting in the stirrup. How very lovely she was, even dressed, as she was, in these

dull, outmoded clothes. Her golden curls peeped pro-
vocatively from beneath her simple linen coif, for she
had thrown back the hood of her travelling cloak.

He had said earlier that she possessed the same
golden loveliness of her mother, but in Philippa now
that beauty was enhanced by vibrant youth. Her skin
glowed with health and her green-blue eyes, almost tur-
quoise in the sunlight, sparked with angry vitality.
There was a seeming childlike fragility about her in her
exquisite petiteness, which he had noted when he had
come to her rescue in that darkened courtyard. It had
brought out a protective tenderness in him, yet now his
pulses raced as he thought how much of a true woman
she was. He sensed the intensity of her bitterness towards him, read it in the set of her little pointed chin,
in that hauntingly elfish, heart-shaped face, in the hard-
held line of her lips, despite their sensuous fullness,
which now he longed to lean forward and kiss.

He had met and known many women at court, and
other, more earthy voluptuous beauties who had lived
on his estates and granted him favours, daughters of his
tenants and servants, but none had stirred him as this
woman did.

When Philippa had risen, trembling, from her attacker
and he had felt her quivering fearful young body
pressed against his heart, he had recognised the inner
strength of her, the courageous determination to recover
quickly so that she could rush to her mother to warn
and protect her, her genuine concern for their squire,
even under the stress of her own ordeal.

She was in fighting form now, and amused admiration for her warred within him with the sudden surge
of desire which ran through him.

He chuckled inwardly. She would need to be managed—for her own safety and that of those she might imperil if she gave way to rashness brought on by her own contempt for him.

"Ah," he murmured, his dark eyes flashing in understanding, "so that is the rub, Lady Philippa, and the direct cause of your suddenly adopted hatred for me. Your man has informed you about my estates and how my father obtained them.

"I hate no one, sir," she said coldly. "That would be against the teaching of Holy Church. Contempt would be nearer the mark to explain my feelings towards you."

"You think I should have refused to accept my inheritance?" He gave a little dry laugh. "I would have thought you would have gained a better knowledge of the ways of the world than that, Lady Philippa. I am quite sure your father's many services to the late King won him the preferment he both desired and earned."

She went white to the lips and, seeing her unwillingness to reply to that shot, he bowed and moved towards his own mount.

Lady Wroxeter had not been able to hear their conversation, but, feeling instinctively that Philippa had insulted their escort, she turned in the saddle and gave her daughter a warning look.

They travelled for the rest of the day without incident and arrived at dusk at an inn on the outskirts of Carmarthen. Sir Rhys had chosen one less fashionable but apparently clean and respectable. He arranged for a private chamber for the ladies, informing the landlord's wife that Lady Wroxeter was a cousin of his, who was travelling with her daughter and brother to visit a sick relative who lived in the Marches. He, himself, he said cheerily, would make do with the common chamber and, as Peter Fairley announced his intention of sleeping with their horses in the stable, he ordered David, his squire, to join him there.

After a hearty meal the ladies retired and assisted each other to undress.

"Philippa," Lady Wroxeter said, wrinkling her brow in concern, "you have not quarrelled with Sir Rhys, have you? I asked you to have a care. I thought there seemed something of an atmosphere between you after our stop for dinner. We are in enough danger as it is. Do not antagonise the man."

Philippa shrugged irritably. "I merely made it clear to him when he passed an opinion on our state of dress that our straitened circumstances are due in part to his enrichment at our expense."

"But that is hardly true. King Henry would have granted your father's lands to, if not Sir Rhys's father, then another one of his supporters after your father became a proscribed traitor."

"But Sir Rhys's father turned traitor to his rightful king at Redmoor," Philippa snapped.

"I doubt if Sir Rhys was quite old enough to fight for the Tudor either at Redmoor or Stoke and can hardly be blamed for what his father did," Cressida reminded her. "In all events, those battles were over long ago and we have your future to consider now."

"You wish that my father was not so concerned with the Duchess Margaret's machinations?" Philippa posed, somewhat shocked by such a suggestion.

"Like most women, I wish your father would sometimes consider the cost of his outdated allegiance and think a little more of us," Cressida rejoined tartly. "I love your father with my whole heart and will remain loyal to him whatever he chooses to do, but I do have you to think about.''

Wearily she climbed into bed and Philippa thought it best to say nothing further.

She lay wakeful. Her fears had been thoroughly aroused in Pembroke and would not be put to rest. Her mother had not been present during that dreadful journey to the coast, four years ago, when she had been forced to flee from England with her friends, the Allards. The King's body squire, John Hilyard, had followed them and attempted to take Philippa prisoner, to hold her hostage for her father's compliance to King Henry's will. It had been a hard fight when he had overtaken them and Philippa had been little more than a child then, but she had known real heartstopping fear that they would be killed. John Hilyard had paid the price and lost his life as a consequence of that encounter and his body had been thrown over a hedge. In retrospect she recalled how they had all set their teeth and struggled on, their friend, Sir Adam Westlake, severely wounded in the fight and Richard Allard still suffering from the effects of the torture he had endured as King Henry's prisoner in the Tower of London. Report of Hilyard's death must have reached the King. Philippa doubted if she would ever be forgiven. If she could be captured now, on this visit, how great a prize she and her mother would be if Rhys Griffith decided to hand them over. Somehow she must convince her mother of their danger and try to escape from Rhys's clutches.

Cressida had fallen into an exhausted slumber at her side. Cautiously Philippa climbed from the bed and pulled her gown over her head, but was forced to leave it unlaced at the back. She thought it most likely that, despite his avowed intention of staying with the horses,

Peter had more than probably stolen back to sleep nearer to his charges. She must seek him out and confer with him about their next move.

She looked back to see if her mother had wakened but Cressida stirred, then turned over and went back to sleep again. Philippa gave a little sigh of relief, stole to the door and carefully undid the latch. She had not dared to light a candle and found herself in total darkness on the landing when the door opened. The crack in the shutter had lightened her chamber sufficiently well for to see there, but now the blackness appeared absolute and she hesitated for moments to allow her eyes to adjust. After a second or two she could begin to see dimly in greyness and was about to step forward when she stumbled against something soft and yielding right before her feet.

"Peter," she called softly but, before she could bend to examine the sleeping form further, her ankles were caught in a tight hold and she fell backwards into the arms of the man who had risen, cat-like, into a crouch at her advance. A hand fastened cruelly over her mouth and almost cut off her breath.

A harsh whisper came from the darkness. "God's Wounds, mistress, what are you about? Not again! Did your previous hazardous encounter teach you nothing?"

She struggled ineffectively in her captor's arms, realising, in fury, that she had been caught by the very man she had wished to avoid.

"If I remove my hand, will you cry out and waken everyone in the inn?" he demanded softly. "If not, shake your head and I will oblige."

She shook her head vigorously and he released the gagging hand so that she could draw in ragged gasps of breath again. Her knees felt weak—she feared they would let her down and leaned against the door for support. He had risen to his feet fully now and was still holding her by one shoulder, then he urged her silently but imperiously down the stairs where he pushed open the door of the tap room in front of her and thrust her inside.

"We can talk more privately in here."

She made to argue hotly but he lifted a hand impatiently to prevent her, and stood facing her, hands on his hips.

"Now, mistress, I demand to know what business brings you from your chamber half undressed." His eyes passed insolently over her body on which her gown hung loosely and one shoulder was bared to his hard gaze. "I take it that your mother is unaware of this escapade? What are you doing, Lady Philippa? Are you in search of Master Fairley?"

She was about to agree that she was until she understood by the hard gleam in his eyes that he thought her reason for doing so was quite unacceptable. Her cheeks flamed and she went hot with embarrassment and anger that he might have so little regard for her sense of propriety.

"How dare you question me!" she snapped impatiently and turned to hasten towards the door again in order to make her escape, but he caught her by the arm again and pulled her towards him roughly.

"I have every reason to do so since I have made myself responsible for your safety."

"No one asked you to," she flared back.

The room was, of course, deserted and she was aware that her voice had risen and that she might well have awakened someone upstairs who might come to discover what was causing a disturbance in the night. The

room seemed chilly and she turned towards the fire
where the embers had been banked down but a residual
warmth was still being given out. Despite the day's
summer warmth, it had been kindled to allow mulled
ale and spiced wine to be produced for travellers and
customers who requested it. She realised suddenly that
she was quite alone with this man she regarded as an
enemy and knew that her shivers were caused by something other than the chilliness of the summer night.

Tiredly she said, "Allow me, sir, to return to my
chamber now. I am wearied."

"Not too wearied to be wandering about. I will allow
you to go, mistress, when you provide me with a suitable explanation for this wanton behaviour."

"It does not concern you. I do not have to answer to
you, sir."

He did not favour that remark with an answer, but
released her arm and stood dominatingly before her, feet
apart, arms folded.

His very attitude and the fact that he had dispensed
with the courtesy of affording her her proper title but
had addressed her as "mistress", rather than "my
lady", fired her to anger once more.

"If you must have an explanation, yes, I was, indeed,
looking for Peter."

"Why?"

The single word was uttered without any courteous
preamble.

"As I have said, it is of no concern of yours. I—
I—" She flailed about in her mind for an acceptable
reason. She dared not give him the true one. "I—I simply wanted to talk with him—about the problems of the
journey and—and did not wish to alarm my mother."

"You are sure you have no other reason for not

alarming your mother?'' The question was disconcertingly blunt, so much so that she gasped aloud.

"Are you suggesting—?"

"I am suggesting nothing. The facts seem plain enough. You get up in the middle of the night, half undressed, in order to see your father's squire. It requires little more speculation on my part."

In sudden fury she lashed out at his cheek, but he caught her hand before it could do damage and held it in a punishing grip, so that she cried out in pain. "Little hell cat," he murmured softly and deliberately.

She struggled to free herself. His grasp was delivering real pain and she knew there would be bruises to show for it in the morning. He released her at last and she stumbled backwards.

"How dare you!" she stuttered, very close to tears. "How dare you imply that Peter and I would—" Her breath ended in a splutter of unutterable rage. "Why, Peter, unlike you, is the soul of honour. He is totally devoted to our interests and discreet and my father trusts him with all our lives…"

"I do not doubt that, mistress," he said grimly, "but can he trust him with his daughter's honour? Last evening, as I recall, you were supposedly out looking for him then because you said he was late returning to you and you were worried about him."

"That was the truth," she retorted, sparks flying from her lovely blue-green eyes. "Perhaps you would like to question my concern for his welfare and put that down to a dishonourable reason. I imagine you are less concerned about the welfare of your own retainers."

He was silent for a while, not rising to her taunt, watching the angry rise and fall of her breasts, the looseness of her unfastened gown more than normally revealing. Once more he marvelled at her loveliness, so exquisitely formed, like a faery sprite, more beautiful than he had remembered her mother to have been when she had captivated his boy's heart so long ago. He felt an ungovernable anger. Philippa Telford might look like a child, but she most certainly was not. He had the evidence of that before his eyes. She was radiantly lovely, enough to seduce the whole of the male population within the Duchess Margaret's court, he thought, yet she was here in search of her father's squire, a man surely too old and unworthy to be her lover. Was he judging her too harshly? Was she really innocent at heart, simply anxious to talk with the man, as she had said, about the difficulties of the journey ahead? Unaccountably he found himself wanting to believe her. She was so young—sixteen, seventeen perhaps—and he believed her parents had kept her well chaperoned. Yet, the thought came to him that, beautiful as she was and well born, she had not concealed how poverty-stricken they were in exile in Burgundy. She must be fully aware of how difficult it was going to be for her father to provide her with a suitable husband. How galling that must be to her…

He sighed heavily. In her present mood he was going to find it hard to convince her that this rash behaviour was indiscreet, if not downright dangerous.

"Lady Philippa, you know, I am sure, that this is a difficult and dangerous time for your mother and you. It behoves you to be circumspect." He lifted a hand imperiously as she made to interrupt him. "No, hear me out. I cannot imagine why you should wish to seek out your father's squire at this hour of the night, but there must be no more of these escapades. Do you hear me?"

"I hear you," she grated through clenched teeth. "I

would like to know just why you were sleeping outside our door rather than in the common chamber where you said you would be.''

"I have already explained. I regard myself as your protector,'' he returned mildly. "Though the wars are over, the times are still troubled. King's men are everywhere and soldiers, off duty, can pose problems for vulnerable women. I am sure that I do not have to explain that to you.''

"Are you our protector or our jailer?'' she said stonily and his eyes opened wide and darkened to obsidian.

Hastily she added, somewhat lamely, "I meant that— I do not understand why you should appoint yourself our guardian.''

He shrugged. "Perhaps because Fate or the Virgin cast you both before me as being in need. Is that not a good enough reason, mistress?''

Haughtily she shook her glorious hair, which lay unbound in heavy red-gold waves upon her shoulders. He felt an irresistible desire to pull her towards him and run his fingers through it. What was she doing, he thought savagely, appearing before a man in the night like that? Had she no sense of decorum? Didn't she realise what temptations she could arouse in men? He took himself firmly in hand. She was young, vulnerable, and under his protection. He must hold himself in check.

"I am not sure,'' she said icily, "whether either my mother or I are gladdened that fate decided to take such a hand in our affairs. Now, sir, will you please stand aside and allow me to return to my mother?''

He nodded slowly and stepped aside from the door so that she might move towards it unhindered. He could not allow himself to touch her, not again.

He said a trifle hoarsely, "Certainly, Lady Philippa, but be assured that I shall resume my post outside your door the moment you are settled inside."

She did not deign to reply, but sulkily moved past him and mounted the stairs back to their chamber.

He followed and settled himself, seated with his back to their door. He was bewitched as if she had thrown faery dust before his eyes and taken possession of his very soul. How could this have happened to him and so suddenly? Not only was she so beautiful that just to look at her caused an ache within his loins, but she had spirit and courage. He could only pray that those very virtues he admired in her did not bring her into further dangers.

He pondered upon her reaction to his unvoiced accusation that she was wandering out to meet her lover. She had rejected it out of hand and with considerable indignation. Could he believe her? Would she not, if caught out like that, react in exactly that way? And had he any right to be angered by her behaviour?

He allowed himself a little secret smile. Certainly she had made no bones about admitting the fact that she despised him. Why? Simply because he was in possession of her father's former lands? Had she expected to arrive in England and find those estates and manor houses empty and neglected? Was it not usual for the victor in any combat to hand out spoils to his supporters? At Duchess Margaret's court, intrigue-ridden as it was, she could not be unaware of those situations.

He had recognised Lady Wroxeter on sight and on impulse offered her his protection on this journey. He knew of the distress of her parents at being so long parted from their daughter by circumstances they were powerless to alter and of the present serious illness of

Sir Daniel. It had seemed reasonable and his duty to assume responsibility for the safety of his neighbour's kin. He had not expected such a hostile reaction from Lady Philippa. He sighed. They would be thrown together for several more days. In honour he must control his growing feelings for her. He had gravely insulted her by his suggestion that she had acted wantonly. There would be time for him to discover if he were, in fact, mistaken and, if so, to attempt to repair the damage.

The darkness upon the landing was beginning to lighten to grey. He settled himself more comfortably, yet in a position to continue his nocturnal watch.

Philippa stole back to her bed, careful not to disturb her sleeping mother. Her cheeks were still hot with embarrassed fury directed at the man who was separated from her only by the thickness of the chamber door. Her plan would have to be abandoned. Rhys Griffith would not move from his post this night. She would have to try to find some other opportunity to have talk with Peter away from the man's insufferable vigilance.

She punched the straw-filled pillow violently to relieve her feelings and wriggled down in the bed. Yet sleep evaded her. The vision of the man's dark presence continued to dominate her thoughts. She tossed and turned restlessly. She had never before encountered a man so bluntly and insultingly spoken. No one in the Duchess's retinue, nor even any nobleman at Queen Elizabeth's court at Westminster, would have dared to question her so accusingly. He was hateful and she had no way of proving to him how shamefully wrong he was in his suspicions. Peter was a dear and trusted friend whom she had known from childhood. Never could she think of him as—she blushed inwardly at the thought—as a lover. Even if they had had more intimate feelings towards each other, neither would have behaved so indecorously. Peter would have regarded such desires as a blot upon the knightly honour to which he had once aspired. Knowing how vulnerable her position was at court, she had been particularly careful that she was never alone in any man's company, since her dowerless state would have made it impossible for any man to offer her honourable marriage.

Rhys Griffith had immediately jumped to the wrong conclusion. Indignantly she asked herself what business it was of his? He had no hold over her. It was as if he were—jealous! The idea was laughable.

Once more she pounded her pillow in impotent fury. Somehow she must convince him that he had accused her falsely, but without alerting him to the true reason for her determination to meet with Peter privately for that could put them all in danger. Strangely she was most anxious that Rhys Griffith should not think ill of her, though, for the life of her, she could not understand her own reason for caring.

Chapter Three

They travelled by easy stages through the lovely Welsh countryside, through Carmarthen, Landovery and Buith Wells, and stayed at last at an inn in Leominster. The weather stayed fine. The rain, which had fallen before their arrival in Wales, had laid the dust and the roads were reasonably comfortable as a result, neither too miry or too dusty and hard ridged.

As on the stops they had made previously, the inn Sir Rhys had chosen was comfortable and clean without being luxurious or fashionable. Philippa had had no opportunity to speak with Peter Fairley privately during the journey. Though they had ridden side by side, she was conscious that Sir Rhys, riding with her mother only some yards ahead of her, could hear anything they had to say and, therefore, she had had to talk of everyday things, the comforts or disadvantages of the inns they stayed at, the beauty of the scenery, or the weather. At all times, whether he was looking at them or not, Philippa was aware that she and Peter were under close scrutiny and it irked her.

At Leominster she had an excuse at last to follow Peter down to the stables, hoping to find him alone. Her little Welsh cob, of whom she had grown very fond, was limping just a little by the time they arrived and she expressed a desire to go and ask Peter to discover, if he could, the reason and pronounce his opinion on whether she were well enough to proceed next day. Sir Rhys was absent from the eating room for the moment and Philippa's mother nodded her agreement.

Philippa was fortunate to find Peter alone and he was, as she entered the stable, examining the cob's right fore hoof.

He looked up, smiling, as he saw Philippa. "She has gathered a small stone. It isn't serious. I'm removing it now."

"Will she be able to carry me tomorrow? I don't want to further lame her."

"Yes, my lady, she will be fine when she's rested."

Philippa approached him and looked back to see that no one was near the opened doorway.

"I've been anxious to speak with you alone since we left Milford Haven."

He nodded. "It has proved difficult. I would have preferred to have closer access to your mother, also, but it seemed unwise."

"Peter, do you think we are in danger from this man?"

"Sir Rhys? I doubt it, though he is the King's man. Had he any intention of betraying us he would have done so before now."

"Yet he could involve my grandparents in the crime of harbouring us if we are discovered there after we have actually settled in at Gretton. Should we not try to part from his surveillance after we leave Ludlow and, perhaps, postpone our arrival at Gretton?"

Peter scratched his chin thoughtfully. "Neither you

nor your mother are proscribed traitors. There can be no real reason why you should not visit. I, on the other hand, could find myself arrested both for having fought at Redmoor and at Stoke and for being in your father's service and close confidence. However,'' he said, smiling. ''I do not believe that Sir Rhys Griffith thinks I am important enough for him to concern himself about my doings.''

''I am not so sure of that,'' Philippa replied coolly.

He glanced at her quickly. ''Oh?''

''He thinks you are my lover or that you aspire to be.''

Peter's expression of alarm was so comical that Philippa burst out laughing and she quickly explained to him what had occurred when she had attempted to slip out on that first night in Pembroke to see him.

''I hope you disabused him of that idea. Your mother would be scandalised and as for your father's reaction to such news—'' He broke off, horrified.

Teasingly she said, ''Don't you find me attractive, Peter?''

His brown eyes surveyed her somewhat myopically. ''You are the most beautiful girl I have ever seen, Lady Philippa, barring your mother when she was the age you are now, but I would never betray your father's trust, you know that. I love you as a...'' he sought blindly for words ''...as a beloved sister perhaps. I would gladly die for you if there were need, but—''

''You do not love me in the way the troubadors sing of. I understand,'' she said blithely, ''and that is just as well for I, too, regard you as a dear, elder brother.'' She frowned, considering. ''Then you do not think we should try to escape Sir Rhys?''

He sighed. ''It would prove impossible. If he should

decide to call out a search for us, all roads to any coast would be blocked.''

She bit her lip uncertainly. ''Then we can do nothing?''

A cool voice from the doorway answered her with another question. ''What is it you wish to do, Lady Philippa?''

She turned guiltily to face Sir Rhys as he entered, his cold gaze passing from her to Peter.

''We were conferring about my mount, sir,'' she retorted, staring back at him defiantly. ''You may have noticed she was limping when we arrived and Peter tells me she has picked up a loose stone which he has removed. I thought we might require the services of a smith.''

''Ah.'' He did not take his gaze from her for moments and then turned to Peter. ''Will she be fit to carry your mistress tomorrow, think you?''

''Oh, yes, Sir Rhys, there should be no difficulty about completing our journey.''

''Good. We do not wish for any delay as I am sure your grandmother will be anxious to see you, Lady Philippa. Now, if you will come at once, supper will soon be served and your mother will wish you to join her.''

He held out his hand commandingly and she was forced to take it and allow him to lead her from the stable after a murmured ''thank you'' to Peter.

Outside she snatched her hand from his grasp and rasped. ''I wish you would not insist on spying on me when I am with Peter. I have told you before, he is my father's trusted squire and companion and nothing more to me than a friend.''

He regarded her quizzically. ''Since you give me your word on that, Lady Philippa, I must believe you, but I do regard it as my duty to keep you safe from…'' he paused, thoughtfully eyeing her speculatively ''…all harm.''

She flounced ahead of him into the inn and hastily went to join her mother at the table. Lady Wroxeter was puzzled by the strange gleam she saw reflected in her daughter's eye. She had known throughout the journey that Philippa had strongly resented their need to accede to Sir Rhys Griffith's desire to escort them to Gretton, but tonight she thought something further had passed between them. She sighed inwardly but said nothing. This problem would soon resolve itself. Tomorrow they would arrive at Gretton and she doubted if they would see more of their protector. Her father had written on several occasions that his neighbours were inclined to shun him, since he was found to be under the displeasure of the King and her parents had become virtually isolated on their own manor.

Philippa was particularly interested in the small market town of Ludlow next day as they rode in. This was their nearest town and her mother knew it well. Unlike Milford Haven, it seemed relatively clean and peaceful in the afternoon sun since today there was no market and no vociferous traders. Most of the shops were closed apparently over the dinner hour and there was a sleepy air about the place, dominated as it was by the former Yorkist stronghold of Ludlow Castle. She glanced at the grim walls curiously as they passed through. Here it was that Edward, the elder of the two Yorkist princes, had finally ridden out to meet his uncle, Richard, on his momentous journey to London to be crowned. It had never happened. He and his brothers and sisters had been declared illegitimate, the two boys placed in the royal apartments of the Tower of London from which they had mysteriously disappeared. She thought how furiously angry her father had been to learn only days ago that a proclamation had been made that Sir James Tyrell, recently executed, had confessed to their murder on the instructions of their uncle. She bit her lip uncertainly and cast a glance at her mother, who had turned in the saddle, finding her also tight-lipped. Did her mother believe the slanderous tale, despite her father's avowals that the confession was a lie which had either been forced from Sir James while in Tudor hands or fabricated after his death, a lie which could not be denied? Sir Rhys had reined in his mount in order to allow the two ladies to view the castle. Philippa cast him a venomous glance. Undoubtedly Sir Rhys believed it.

As they left the town Philippa was impatient to reach their home manor, but her anticipated pleasure was shadowed by the fear that they might not find her grandfather alive.

Sir Rhys gestured her forward as they entered her grandfather's lands so that the two women could be together. Philippa saw that her mother's eyes were bright with unshed tears and she reined in close and, reaching out, took her gloved hand in her own encouragingly.

"We have come as soon as we could, *ma mère*, I am sure we shall be in time to—" She broke off, too emotionally choked to continue.

Sir Rhys said quietly, "I saw your grandfather just before I left for Milford Haven. I was able to conduct some business for him there. He was incapacitated but able to talk and was as well as could be expected. Your grandmother informed me that the physicians had told her they had no reason to fear the worst.''

Lady Wroxeter nodded, grateful for his reassurance. So he *did* visit her parents, apparently, undeterred by his neighbours' unpopularity. Her mother must have had cause to be grateful to him during those recent difficult and anxiety-ridden weeks.

Philippa was filled with surprised delight when she caught her first sight of Gretton Manor. The evening sunlight caught the mellow building with its strong rays. The undercroft was stone built, with an upper storey of timber and plaster lath painted yellow which showed to advantage against the dark-stained oak beams. The manor house itself was approached through a gatehouse arch which at one time had housed a guard room but, probably due to the settled times and King Henry's proscriptions against the keeping of retainers, was now disused. From the front it was not possible to see the outbuildings and stables but, as the small party approached, grooms ran quickly forward to take the lead reins of their horses. One gabbled to Sir Rhys in Welsh, which he answered fluently. Any hopes Philippa might have had that he would leave them now, having delivered them safely home, were dispelled as both Sir Rhys's horse and his squire's were led off with their own. Peter Fairley lifted her down and she turned, a little flustered, to see a woman standing upon the top step leading to the hall to greet them. She came down immediately the moment she recognised the new arrivals. Cressida, who had been assisted to dismount by Sir Rhys, ran to her with a little choking cry of mingled delight and anxiety. Philippa could see little of her grandmother's features as her head was bent over the shoulders of her weeping daughter. She could just distinguish that Lady Gretton was of no great height, like her daughter and grandchild, and was plumply rounded in build.

Philippa came hesitantly towards the two and just caught the whispered questions each gave to the other.

"Father, is he…?"

"Well enough, child, and very anxious to greet you, but not sufficiently recovered to come from the hall yet."

Lady Gretton had posed her question even more softly.

"Martyn, is he safe?"

Philippa's mother's answer was even softer, barely whispered. "He was safe in Malines and well when we left him a sennight ago."

Lady Gretton gave a little satisfied sigh. "Good. It was unsafe for him to venture with you. Times are troubled here, even yet."

She looked up and held her arms wide for Philippa to run into them. "Come, child. You will never know how long we have waited to have a sight of you."

Philippa was enveloped in a motherly embrace, scenting the fresh, country fragrances of rosemary and lavender. She was hugged so tightly she could hardly breathe and withdrew finally a little breathless, half-laughing and half-crying in the sudden emotion of greeting.

Now she could see that Mildred Gretton was indeed short and plumply attractive still in late middle age, but with nothing about her of her daughter and granddaughter's famed ethereal beauty. Her pleasant features were relatively unlined except for the little crinkles around her round, dark eyes, which betokened good humour. She was dressed in a dark green silk gown, somewhat outdated but of excellent quality, and she wore a small tight-fitting linen cap, but had not yet adopted the new French fashion of attached velvet veil Philippa had seen worn at the English court.

Still holding her grandchild by one arm, she turned smilingly to Sir Rhys Griffith.

"Rhys, how good to see you here, and in the company of my loved ones. As always you are very welcome to Gretton. Daniel will be so pleased to see you."

He bowed courteously. "Thank you, Mildred, but I will not stay. I have business to conclude at home and you both will wish to have this time with your loved ones alone. I found them on the harbour at Milford Haven and made it my business to see them safe to Gretton. How is Sir Daniel?"

"As you saw him a week ago, Rhys. He frets that he cannot yet walk well or sit a horse. He sleeps below stairs as getting him above to our bedchamber has proven irksome, but the physician has hopes that he will soon be able to proceed further afield with the aid of a stick."

Philippa gazed from her grandmother to Sir Rhys. So, they were obviously on good terms, which she found puzzling. She could but hope that Sir Rhys would honour his acceptance of their need for privacy and stay away from Gretton for some time. He was bidding farewell to her mother and she came to herself with a sudden start as he came to her side and held out his hand.

"I must make my excuses, Lady Philippa. I am delighted to hear that you will find your grandfather in good health considering his infirmities. I shall call on you all soon to assure myself that you want for nothing."

She surrendered her hand a trifle unwillingly and

murmured a polite word of gratitude for his care of them during the journey and he bent and kissed her palm. She found herself doubtfully regarding his retreating back as he left with his squire to move to the stable to retrieve his mount after it had been fed and watered. Her feelings were strangely mixed and bewildering, as if she was unsure when or if their paths would cross again and whether that would please or alarm her.

She followed her mother and grandmother up the entrance steps, through the screen doors and into the manor's hall. A man sat near a fire, which was burning on the side hearth despite it being mid-summer, and rose with difficulty at their entrance, leaning hard on a sturdy oaken stick. An elderly woman standing behind the chair clucked at him warningly as Cressida ran to him and he rocked on his feet with the suddenness of her fierce embrace.

"Now, master, be careful. Mistress Cressida, mind your father's condition." Her admonition was unheeded as the two, locked together in the first joy of their meeting, were unconscious of the presence of any other within the hall. Philippa stood back a little shyly as, finally, tears streaming down her cheeks, her mother, helped by the elderly attendant, assisted her father back into his chair. Lady Gretton stood some little distance away, holding her granddaughter tightly by her hand. At last Cressida turned and stood aside a little from the seated figure, who was now leaning forward eagerly to view the newcomer.

"And here, Father, is Philippa. Come, child, and kiss your *grandpère*."

Philippa, released by her grandmother, came forward and dropped to her knees before the old man. She saw that despite his illness his large, big-boned form had not withered. He had a shock of white hair reaching in curls to his shoulders and his broad, open countenance was still weatherbeaten as if, previous to the stroke which had laid him low, he had enjoyed an active, outdoor life. Like her mother, there were tears upon his cheeks and he bent and took Philippa's face between his two large hands, scrutinising her carefully, then he looked up at his daughter and wife who had come closer to the chair, and smiled.

"I had the most beautiful daughter in England and this, her child, and Wroxeter's, looks like being as lovely, and I can see spirit here in her eyes and courage. You have your mother's looks, child, but I think there is something of your father's courage and intelligence in the steadiness of your gaze and the intentness of your concern, aye, and stubbornness in the tilt of your chin, too." He looked upwards to the elderly attendant who was standing behind his chair. "Don't you agree, Alice? She's the child of both of them right enough."

The woman gave a little snort and stared down at Philippa, who returned her scrutiny curiously.

Her grandfather chuckled. "This is Alice, your mother's nurse and your grandmother's maid now, aye, and, over these last weeks, my nurse too, though I could wish her in purgatory some days when she bothers me with her strictures."

"For your own good and you know it," the woman scolded. "The doctor says you'll do well enough if you take your time, but you will rush to do things." Her expression was kindly, though her voice somewhat harsh, and she went scarlet with pleasure as Cressida seized her by the shoulders and planted a hearty kiss upon her lined cheek. She hugged her former charge, grinning at Philippa over Lady Wroxeter's shoulder.

"It's fair good to have your mother back again, sweeting, if only for a little while." Her expression grew sad. "The Virgin knows I wanted to go with her after—well, after—but there, it wasn't possible. It's true, lassie, you be right like your mother in appearance and like to be as much trouble in handling as she was, I'll be bound."

"She is, Alice, she is," laughed Cressida, "but hardships have given her more common sense than I ever had at her age, so that's as well."

"Aye, well, we'll see about that." Alice turned to her mistress. "I'll be about seeing to a meal for you all and away to the kitchen. Did I not hear Sir Rhys Griffith? Will he not take supper here with us?"

"No, Alice, he excused himself. He's just come from Milford. There are bound to be matters needing attention on his own manor. He'll be here again soon," Lady Gretton announced.

Alice cast a quick suspicious glance at Philippa. "Aye, I warrant he will," she muttered as she stalked off towards the screen doors.

Cressida drew up chairs for her mother and herself as Lady Gretton informed her, "We have no pages or squires, now, of course. I gave the servants warning to leave us alone together for the first hour or so. I knew there would be much to discuss."

Philippa remained seated at her grandfather's feet while her eyes roved the hall. She understood his need for a fire. Enforced inactivity, she knew, often caused a chill of the limbs and the blazing logs added an air of cheeriness to the large hall. Despite her grandmother's hint that they were short of the customary number of servants, due, she thought, to the fines they had been forced to pay shortly after the King's accession, the fur-

niture was well kept, though sparse. There were court
cupboards, on which a few remaining pieces of silver-
ware gleamed, several finely carved chests, three arm-
chairs, several backless stools and, in the upper part of
the hall, a single trestle was covered with linen ready
for the promised supper. The fine hangings which
adorned the limewashed walls were brightly coloured,
totally unfaded, and Philippa guessed that they had been
only recently executed, and that embroidery was most
probably her grandmother's chosen pastime during the
formerly long days when her man had been out hunting
or away from the manor on business in Ludlow. Philippa gave a little shocked gasp as something cold
touched her hand and a shaggy head was thrust towards
her, almost knocking her off balance.

Her father gave a little throaty chuckle. "Is Bors
bothering you? He's getting to be an old deer hound
now, but he's strong still. Down, old fellow. This is
your newest mistress come to visit."

Philppa stretched out a hand to pat the shaggy head
and a rough tongue caressed her cheek. "Nay, Grandpère, he does not bother me, I love all God's good creatures and must go soon and see to it that my little cob
isn't missing me or needing attention."

"Aye, it's well you're a country mouse at heart despite all this life in palaces," he said gruffly but fondly.

Her mother had been telling them both about their
encounter with Sir Rhys Griffith at the inn at Milford
Haven and their subsequent journey together. "I was
somewhat concerned that—" She broke off awkwardly.
"Since it is difficult for Pippa and I to be here, I feared
he might pose a danger, but he appears to be a welcome
visitor to Gretton."

"Since he inherited he has proved himself a friend."

Philippa's grandmother paused and looked anxiously towards her husband. "Though we are cautious as to what we say to him. His father was loyal to the Tudor and often at court, but Rhys is in London less often." She frowned a little. "People arrive at this house sometimes whom—well, whom we would rather young Rhys does not see." She shook her head as the door behind the trestle table opened and two serving women entered with trays ready to serve supper. She changed the subject quickly. "I have arranged for one of our young serving girls to be Philippa's maid Gwenny. She's a good girl but inexperienced yet. Alice will want to attend you, Cressida, as she used to do, as she serves me now." She called to one of the women who was busied setting out wooden platters and knives upon the trestle table. "Nan, will you show Lady Wroxeter and Lady Philippa to their chamber and call young Gwenny?"

The two ladies followed the serving woman up the newel stair, along the landing, and into a chamber behind Lady Gretton's solar. The woman smilingly indicated a further chamber beyond. "That is much smaller, my lady, but the mistress thought Lady Philippa would like to have a room of her own. Gwenny can share it with her for there is a truckle bed which can be pulled out." She made a little bobbed curtsy. "I will call Gwenny and we'll come back soon with an ewer of warmed water and fresh towels, my lady."

Cressida smiled her dismissal and turned to survey the chamber with bright tears in her eyes which she hastily brushed aside. "Forgive me, child, you must think me a ninny to be so close to crying all the time but these are tears of joy, believe me. This was my chamber in the old days and I so very reluctant to leave it to go to court and meet your father." Cressida took in all the familiar things she had loved—the testered bed of solid cherry wood with its holland sheets and embroidered woollen covering, the carved oak chest for her treasured belongings which were not accommodated within the press in the garde robe, the prieu-dieu with its embroidered seat cushion lovingly done by her mother—and then she ran to the casement window with its well-used seat cushions upon the wide low sill. Unlatching the glazed casement, she leaned down to gaze at the lawn below with its rose bushes and, beyond, her mother's herb garden and pleasance.

"Oh, Philippa, it is just as it always was. I hope you will come to love it as I did and that—" her throat worked oddly "—that, one day, you will be able to spend more time here."

Philippa joined her and breathed in the heady scents of roses, sweet marjoram and rosemary, which came wafting up from the sun-soaked garden. "Oh, but I would never wish to leave our lodging at Malines with you and Father," she said fervently.

Her mother gave her an odd little glance, her head tilted on one side. "I thought just like you, Pippa," she mused, her lips curving into a strangely sweet smile, "but then—then I met and married your father and was content to live wherever he was."

Philippa broke away suddenly and turned back into the centre of the room. "It is unlikely that I shall find a suitable husband," she said stiffly, "at least, not a man I could love as you love my father."

"No?" Cressida's lips curved into an even wider smile. "Do not be too sure, Pippa. We have already met another man who is taken with your beauty."

"But we have met no one but—" Philippa broke off in horror. "You cannot mean...?"

"Oh, but I do," her mother said lightly.

"But you could never countenance a match so—" Philippa drew a hard breath "—so completely outrageous."

"You could not?"

"Certainly not," Philippa returned hotly.

"No, of course not." Lady Wroxeter was still smiling when the serving woman came back, followed by a gangling, awkward young girl whose strands of red hair were straggling untidily from the sides of her cap. They were laden with an ewer of hot water, a basin and clean towels. The girl, who could not be much more than thirteen or fourteen years old, stood regarding Philippa with rounded eyes until water began to slop from her ewer onto the oaken boards at her feet and she was hastily reprimanded for clumsiness by her older companion.

Philippa nodded to the older woman and asked, "Is this my new maid Gwenny?"

"Indeed it is, my lady, and I hope she will soon learn to be less clumsy."

"I'm sure she will. Put the ewer down, Gwenny, on that chest over there and then you can come into my chamber with me and see that all is ready for tonight when I retire."

The girl bobbed a clumsy curtsy that nearly had her falling over, but Philippa waited patiently until she recovered herself and led the way through into her own private chamber.

It was very small, containing only a bed, a chest and scarcely room enough for the truckle bed underneath hers to be pulled out for Gwenny, but Philippa was delighted with it. She bit her lip thoughtfully as she glanced round. Why was she suddenly so anxious to be private within the night hours, separated from the mother she dearly loved? Was it because, already, she sensed in her mother's manner towards her a different approach, a determination to get her ineligible daughter married? But to whom?

Philippa shivered as she considered her mother's last words. Not Sir Rhys Griffith, surely. He was an enemy, a Tudor supporter who could prove a danger to them all. She shook her head to try to dispel the vivid image she had of him, of the tall, upright, unyielding body, the flashing dark eyes, straight, dominant nose and the mop of luxuriant black curls. She had been less than gracious to him throughout the days they had spent together—and after he had saved her from rape and death. The man could not be attracted to the slip of a girl who had constantly taunted and insulted him. She wondered what he and her mother had talked of on that ride, on the occasions when she had been too far back from them to overhear. She looked up to find the girl waiting anxiously for her to decide what she was to do next.

"Everything seems well in order, Gwenny. Your bed is under mine. I will go now and wash in my mother's chamber and you can return to the kitchens and get your own supper. I'll send for you when I am ready for bed and you can help me to undress and brush my hair after first tidying away the toilet articles."

The girl nodded timidly, curtsyed again, less ineptly this time, and hastened out of the chamber. Philippa returned to her mother who had completed her toilet and was drying her hands.

"Will the girl do, do you think?"

"Oh, yes, she is a frightened little rabbit, but she will soon get used to my ways. You will be glad to have the services of your Alice again."

''Indeed. I have missed her sorely since Redmoor.''
Cressida laughed. ''She has always kept me firmly in
hand and will do you, too, if she has half a chance.''

''And now my father manages you.''

Cressida touched her daughter's bright hair affectionately as she removed her hood to brush and tidy her
dishevelled locks. ''While I found that annoying at first,
I was glad to surrender—in the end.''

Cressida regarded her thoughtfully and they both
knew that Philippa was thinking of her dislike for Sir
Rhys Griffith. ''Differences of opinion have a way of
becoming settled in the marriage bed,'' she said very
softly.

Philippa gave a little cluck of dissent and completed
her toilet before she accompanied her mother down to
the hall for supper.

Next morning when Gwenny was assisting her to
dress, Philippa asked Gwenny, ''Have you been in service at Gretton for long?''

Gwenny, who was feeling very self-conscious about
her new duties, tugged clumsily at the laces of Philippa's gown. ''Oh, yes, my lady, most of my life really.
My mother works in the manor kitchen and I have been
working there for the last three years, but Lady Gretton
thought I was the right age to serve you.''

''And does that please you?''

''Oh, yes, my lady, if I can prove satisfactory.''

''I'm sure that you will, especially if I can rely on
you to be—discreet. I do not wish you to gossip about
me—in the kitchens or with any of the other servants.''

''My mother has told me that over and over, my
lady.'' Gwenny hesitated. ''We all know that you and

your lady mother are here on a very private visit and it is not to be spoken of—in the district.''

''Yes. Sir Rhys Griffith is well aware of it. Does he come often to Gretton?''

''Quite often, my lady. He plays chess with Sir Daniel, especially since the master has been unable to get about.''

Philippa digested this information and added, ''How far is his own manor, Gwenny? Isn't there a castle?''

''Oh, yes, my lady, but that is near to Wroxeter. When Sir Rhy's father became master he considered it very cold and draughty, especially in winter, and he built a newer manor house about four miles away off the Ludlow road; very comfortable it is, with a smaller hall and proper bedchambers, even for the servants, and all the windows are glazed. The furniture came from London, they say. None of the local craftsmen were engaged to make it and it was brought by road all that way. You'd think it would have got damaged, wouldn't you?''

''So Sir Rhys lives at the manor house?''

''Most of the time, my lady, but sometimes he goes to Wroxeter Castle. The hall there is used for the district court and there are dungeons for felons. I 'spect it's a much grimmer place than the manor though Jake, one of our grooms, worked there a long time ago for the Earl and he said it was a fine place.''

Philippa's heart contracted as she thought how her father had been cheated out of his birthright. Would he have deserted the ancient castle, the home of his and her ancestors?

Tartly she said, ''It seems that Sir Rhys has become a very wealthy and fine gentleman indeed since the new King's accession.''

At her reference to the King, Gwenny looked blankly at her again and Philippa realised that the child had no notion of who had ruled in England before the decisive battle of Redmoor or, in her limited, youthful life, thought very much about kings at all.

At breakfast she discovered that her mother had already eaten and was in her father's chamber with her grandmother. She finished her own meal and went in search of them. Her mother came from the small curtained space behind the hall, which had been prepared for Sir Daniel since his illness, to speak with her.

"Your grandfather has had a bad night, I'm afraid, Pippa. He has been excited by our arrival and I think it best if you wait until this evening before you see him again. I shall remain with my mother to tend him. Can you find some way to occupy yourself until later?"

Philippa could see by the worry lines between her brows and the shadows beneath her eyes that her mother was extremely worried about her grandfather's condition.

"Yes, of course," she hastened to say. "There is not the slightest need for you to worry yourself about me. I am sorry. I thought he looked very well last night, considering…" She broke off and bit her lip.

"I know. I allowed myself to become over-hopeful. We shall send for the physician from Ludlow and hope he gets over this set-back." She smiled a trifle distractedly and went behind the curtain again, leaving Philippa doubtful and more alarmed than she had first thought. She moved away from the curtained-off alcove to allow the three complete quiet and sat for a while before the fire, which the manor servants had apparently kindled against need.

Abruptly she rose and made for the screen doors where she encountered Gwenny returning to the hall, apparently in search of her mistress.

"Is there anything I can do for you, my lady?"

"What? Oh, no, thank you, Gwenny. I have decided to go for a ride. Do not disturb Lady Gretton or my mother who are with Sir Daniel. He is less well this morning. Occupy yourself with completing my unpacking and see if anything requires mending or pressing. Can you tell me how to reach the stables?"

She had gone with one of the servants last night to see her little cob but it had been dark then and she had taken little heed of the way. Gwenny pointed out the archway which led to the courtyard and outbuildings, offering to accompany her, but Philippa declined.

She found Peter Fairley emerging from the stables, in talk with an elderly groom. The man touched his forelock at sight of Philippa.

"Good day, my lady."

She nodded coolly. "I would like to ride out as it is such a fine morning. Can you accompany me, Peter, or should I take one of the grooms?"

"Certainly I can come with you." Peter looked enquiringly back towards the manor house. "Is your mother aware…?"

"No, but she is occupied in tending my *grandpère*. She will not mind if you are with me." She glanced down at her gown. "I am suitably dressed, and you appear to be."

As usual he was dressed in serviceable homespun jack and hose without a cloak since the day was already heating up.

The groom called back into the stable for one of his underlings to bring out their mounts saddled and ready.

When her cob was brought to the mounting block, Peter lifted Philippa to the saddle and settled her comfortably.

"You have visited Gretton before, in the old days," she said as she took the reins. "I would like you to show me my father's lands."

Peter glanced at her searchingly but passed no comment. Together they passed through the archway and rode towards the long road which led to Gretton village.

The little place looked prosperous and was almost deserted, most of the labourers busy with the harvest, and they rode together companionably.

Peter said quietly, "Lady Philippa, you know it does no good to think how things might have been."

"I know," she said calmly. "I just want to see how it was for my father and—and I hear Sir Rhys's father built himself a new manor house and would see it for myself—from a distance, of course."

He glanced at her sharply, but nodded and led the way towards the Ludlow road. Soon she could see evidence of well-tended strips and fields on both sides of the highway and labourers working in the distance. The animals, too, appeared to be in excellent condition and Peter grunted.

"It seems Griffith handles his labourers well. Your father would be relieved to know his lands are in the hands of a capable master."

"I'm sure that my father would prefer to have his lands under his own control," Philippa snapped and Peter looked at her again and grinned mirthlessly.

"That is indeed true, Lady Philippa, but as things are the Earl does well to keep his head on his shoulders, as you know well."

They rode on in silence while Philippa took in the continuing evidence of the demesne's prosperity. She was so intent upon her survey that Peter was forced to give a shout of warning as a riderless horse veered suddenly across her path. The animal was limping badly and had, clearly, recently thrown its rider. Alerted to the danger, Philippa pulled sharply on her own lead reins and moved her own mount out of the frenzied creature's path. Her little cob stumbled to a halt and was startled by the suddenness of her move so that she was shivering violently. Philippa leaned down to pat her shaggy coat encouragingly, looking back to see the uncertain progress of the injured animal. Peter, coming up close, pointed with his whip to a huddled form lying in the road some yards ahead of them.

Together they eased their horses steadily forward and Peter jumped down to investigate. The fallen rider looked unconscious but, as Philippa scrambled awkwardly to dismount and joined Peter, he looked up from his crouching position to confirm, with a nod, that the man was still breathing.

"He's not conscious, must have hit his head on that boulder," he said, gesturing towards a rough granite stone a foot or two to their left. "His leg is lying at an awkward angle and I believe it to be broken. Don't try to move him, my lady, not until we've examined him further."

She looked back anxiously to where the riderless horse had floundered by them. "His mount must have been startled by a hare or bird or put its foot in a rutted hole. How badly is our man hurt, Peter, can you tell?"

"He struck his head, as I said, and it's bleeding, but not too seriously. We can only hope he will come to himself soon. It's the leg which gives concern," he said dubiously, cautiously moving the injured limb in an attempt to straighten it. "It is as well he is not conscious, for the moment. See if you can find me a long branch from in the hedgerow and I will try to splint this before he comes to. Then he must be got back to the village, or, preferably, the town. I'm not sure how many miles that is but he may need the attention of a surgeon.''

Philippa did as she was bidden and hastened to search for a suitable branch strong enough to act as a splint. She was finally successful and brought it to Peter, who cut away the lesser branches with his knife and laid it gently alongside the now straightened limb. The sufferer moaned slightly and Peter grunted his approval. ''He is coming to himself so there is no serious brain damage, by the look of it. It's best for us to complete this before he feels more pain.''

Philippa had already torn several strips from her linen petticoat and was kneeling in the road beside Peter, steadying the branch, as the squire went about his task of securing it to the injured leg with the improvised bandages.

Now she could see that the injured man was young, or younger, she thought, than Peter—perhaps in his middle twenties, she considered. He was a merchant, by the look of his dress. Peter had turned him over so that she could see that he was pleasantly featured, his skin without disfiguring pock marks. His fair hair was worn fashionably in a curled bob to his neck and clustered into a long similar curl on a forehead that was dappled with bright blood, but was broad with level, fair brows. His nose was very slightly tip-tilted; his mouth, held in tightly against the pain as he began to regain his senses, was well shaped with a slightly over-full lower lip. Thick fair lashes flickered and grey eyes regarded her wonderingly as she bent close over him.

''Hush,'' she warned gently, ''you are quite safe.

Your horse threw you and we think you have broken your right leg. Lie very still for a while.''

The lashes flickered again and the man attempted to lift his head, then gave another groan as blood trickled down his forehead to drift into his eye.

Philippa dabbed at the trickle with another torn piece of her petticoat, but was unable to pad the head wound for fear of moving the patient.

"It's all right," she added soothingly, "you hit your head when you fell, but we don't think that the wound is serious. We'll deal with it in a moment when the splint on your leg is fixed."

He gave a little relieved sigh and sank back again, a faint smile forming about his well-shaped mouth.

Peter rose and stood, regarding his patient, frowning in thought. "We need to get help now. A broken limb can be…" He shrugged and avoided Philippa's eye. Only too well she knew that fractures could cause the death of the patient or a necessary amputation of the limb and she compressed her lips in alarm. Peter was shading his eyes as he looked to his left to where a small thicket, about a half-mile away, was split as if a lesser road or track ran through it.

"That may lead to the manor house, where we could get assistance. See. It probably joins the road some miles back. I'd best ride and see if I can find some labourers who could provide a rough bier of some sort to get him to a house or to the outskirts of the town. Will you feel concerned about being left alone with him?''

"No, of course not. He needs help as soon as possible. You will not be long gone. There are bound to be labourers or servants within a short ride.''

She was giving her full attention to their patient and

Peter had moved off and was about to mount up when a stern voice, calling for them to halt, arrested him in the action and Philippa turned hastily to face the newcomer. She gave a little gasp of annoyance and surprise as she saw that Sir Rhys Griffith was riding up to them, attended by two retainers. His gaze swept coldly from her dishevelled clothing, dust-stained and bloodstained, to Peter Fairley and then to the injured man.

"Lady Philippa, you are about early, considering your very recent arrival at Gretton. What is this?"

One of his men had jumped down and was holding his rouncey still for him to dismount. He was dressed, as she remembered him, in riding clothes, a leather jerkin over brown hose, and was hatless. He strode up to the three and stared down with marked disapproval at their patient.

"Who is this fellow and what is he doing on my land?"

Philippa was so startled by his hostile manner that she rounded on him instantly. "He is on the highway, Sir Rhys, and you must be able to see clearly enough that he has been thrown from his horse and lies injured."

He stood frowningly regarding the sufferer, tapping his riding whip against his thigh impatiently.

"So it would appear. Actually, Lady Philippa, this is not the highway, but a lesser road cutting through my demesne, and I cannot imagine what he was doing on it, but, there, it seems he has fractured his leg and will need help to be moved." His dark eyes were still regarding the stranger dispassionately. "I do not encourage strangers, poachers, particularly."

Philippa was almost incoherent with anger. "You can see the man is no local poacher but, apparently, some merchant's apprentice or journeyman about his business, probably making his way towards Ludlow to seek accommodation.''

One dark brow rose in amusement. "Here's heat. You take me to task, Lady Philippa, for lack of Christian compassion, but I will see to it that this fellow is tended and then conveyed in a cart to Ludlow town where there are several excellent physicians and surgeons to treat him.''

He turned now to Peter and she saw that her father's squire's presence, alone in her company, rather than one of her grandfather's grooms, had again displeased him. She compressed her lips against uttering further explosive words to dispel his suspicions.

"I take it you were about to go looking for some assistance…" his gaze went again to Philippa "…and about to leave your mistress alone once more.''

"There appeared to be no help for it,'' she said tersely, "since there is no one else in sight—at least, there wasn't until you rode up.''

Their patient had come to his full senses now and was trying to sit up. "My apologies for invading your demesne without permission, sir,'' he said in a low, pleasant voice, "but I thought no harm and was riding towards Ludlow. I have business there. My master is a wool merchant in the Steelyard in London town. My name is Roger Maynard. I regret that I must give you trouble. My horse stumbled in a rut, I think, and threw me. Someone must try to find him and check his headlong dash. He could prove a danger to any child in his path.''

So he had heard Sir Rhys's ungracious comments, Philippa thought, and looked towards him, her own brows raised in condemnation. She was surprised to see that Sir Rhys was staring at the newcomer as if he knew him, but then he shook his head as if he had discovered he was mistaken and inclined his chin in acceptance of the man's explanation.

"So, it was like that, was it? Never mind. We will see to your comfort and find your mount."

He turned to issue orders to his two retainers who had stood silently attentive throughout the exchanges, their faces expressionless, as if they were used to hearing their master put in his place by some slip of a girl.

"You two, get back to the manor and summon some men with a bier. He'd best be accommodated in the gatehouse lodge until he is fit to travel on into Ludlow. In the meantime, I will escort Lady Philippa to the manor house where she can take refreshment and—tidy herself."

Peter said, respectfully, speaking for the first time, "I think it would be best if I accompany you and Lady Philippa, Sir Rhys, and perhaps one of your men here can be detailed to stay with our injured friend until help arrives."

Sir Rhys cast him a challenging glance. Obviously he had thought to command Peter to stay with his patient, but he thought better of that and barked, "Yes, certainly, that would be best."

"Once I am assured that this man is tended, Peter and I could ride home to Gretton," Philippa put in.

"I do not think so, not in that state," Sir Rhys replied, his eyes passing again over the state of her dirtied gown, "you will alarm your mother and grandparents. I take it you were riding to review my demesne. Allow me to welcome you to my manor house."

She flushed hotly and was about to refute his accusation then, catching Peter's eyes, let out a little frustrated sigh and bent once more to reassure Master Maynard before walking towards her own mount.

"I shall make enquiries about your welfare, Master Maynard. I am sure you will soon be safe and in good hands. I wish you a hasty recovery, but I think it will be some time before you will be able to leave Ludlow. I will try to discover your lodgings there and reassure myself about your condition."

The fair young face flushed and he bowed his head. "I shall pray and thank the Virgin for sending an angel to come to my help, mistress. May I know to whom I am indebted?"

Before she could answer Sir Rhys cut in, "Mistress Weston will be staying a short time in the district and it is unlikely that you will see her again."

Philippa smiled at Master Maynard and moved towards her own mount, which Peter was holding ready. She approved Sir Rhys's caution, but wondered if the man could have heard him address her as Lady Philippa earlier. He had appeared to be just recovering full consciousness when Sir Rhys had arrived on the scene. She dismissed the thought, feeling that Maynard must have been confused and dizzy with pain at the time and so, for the moment, her identity was still unknown and could not be talked of in Ludlow town.

Sir Rhys had already dispatched his man to fetch help. He gave orders briskly to the other man, who was waiting by Master Maynard, then he indicated to Peter that he was ready to leave, mounted, and took the lead in the direction of the small thicket Peter had noted earlier.

Philippa had feared he might insist upon taking her lead rein, but he allowed her to ride beside him, with Peter only slightly in the rear.

"I think it best if you do not communicate with this Maynard fellow directly," he said crisply. "I will ascertain where he is finally lodged and inform you of his condition."

She glanced at him sharply and he continued, "I know you consider I was harsh with the fellow but, as matters are in the county at present, and, particularly considering your mother's visit, not to say your grandparents' danger, it is wiser if we do not encourage strangers on our land."

"But Master Maynard is surely no spy. He said he was a merchant's journeyman and…"

"I know what he said. Strangers cannot always be believed."

She eyed him thoughtfully. "But now that the wars are over, the King does not employ spies…"

He smiled grimly. "All the time, Lady Philippa, that is why I urge you to caution. I grant you this Master Maynard appears to be what he seems and looks harmless enough, but he had no real need or right to be riding this way. As for the King's policy—Henry trusts no one, not even those whose loyalty he is most assured of. His creatures are everywhere, making sure the correct tallies are made of properties and taxes. Have you not heard how the new Court of the Star Chamber is kept busy?"

She was forced to give him a smile in answer. "But, surely, you pay your own taxes on time and give true accounting of your revenues."

His answering smile was broad and Philippa heard Peter give a chuckle behind them.

She fell into a reverie as they took a well-marked path through the thicket. Could she have misjudged Sir

Rhys? Was he as genuine as he seemed to ensure her mother's and her own safety?

He gave a sudden shout of warning, as a riderless horse veered across their path and, this time, he reached over and snatched at her lead rein as her little cob squealed in terror and rose, forelegs high in the air, so that Philippa had all she could do to stay in the saddle.

"That was Master Maynard's horse," she said shakily. "Thank you, I wasn't prepared for that."

"Aye, and limping badly, by all appearance. Master Fairley," he barked, "I must leave you to try to retrieve the animal before it causes an accident. Stay with your lady. Continue on this path and veer left as you emerge from the wood. In a mile you will see the manor house ahead of you."

Before Philippa could properly catch her breath he had ridden off at a gallop and Peter came quickly alongside. He noted her paleness and gave a gasp of concern.

"Are you all right?"

"Yes, but I was nearly unseated. I hope he manages to catch the poor creature and return it to the stables of his manor."

Peter's eyelashes flickered oddly and he shook his head, then before she could object, he took her lead rein firmly as Sir Rhys had done, and took the path the knight had indicated.

Chapter Four

The manor house was moated and approached over a static bridge then through a gatehouse, which appeared as they passed under to be guarded. They entered the courtyard and Philippa gave a little gasp of wonder as they passed by a guard sergeant who seemed to know at once who she was and that she had a right to be there. The house stood squarely before them, built entirely of Welsh blue stone with mullioned windows and a central door of solid oak. The sunlight glittered on the glazed windows and she recalled Gwenny's description of the place and acknowledged that it was, indeed, very fine.

Peter gave a slow whistle of appreciation. "Though the place is guarded there is no drawbridge or portculis on the arch and no crenellations." He peered upwards to the sloping roof, and saw no guards upon the leads. "Griffith expects no trouble from his neighbours. The moat appears to be decorative more than useful to deter unwanted visitors."

"Sir Rhys seems to be well able to do that by his own innate power of authority," Philippa commented drily, "but, as you say, the manor house is very fine and must have cost his father near a fortune to build."

Before she could comment further a steward appeared at the opened door and descended the steps to the courtyard to greet them. Already grooms were running to take their mounts.

The steward bowed. "Welcome to Griffith Manor, Lady Philippa. Sir Rhys's messenger, sent to obtain help for the injured man, alerted us to your imminent arrival." He appeared to be in no way put out by the fact that his master was not with his visitors but led the way into the hall which was lime washed and colourful with painted coats of arms and then he took them along a corridor into a winter parlour beyond. "I will summon servants to fetch toilet articles for you, Lady Philippa, a servant to deal with your soiled garments and a page to bring wine and refreshments. Please make yourselves comfortable. Sir Rhys will present himself very shortly."

He bowed himself out, backwards, as if he was dealing with royalty, Philippa thought wryly. Since the man had not mentioned a lady as chatelaine, she presumed that Sir Rhys's mother was not present at the manor or possibly had died. She knew so little about him, only that he was, as yet, unmarried.

She found herself staring, round eyed, like a recently appointed servant, at the luxurious comforts of the new manor. The windows were wide and let in an abundance of light, the walls were oak panelled and adorned with what she believed to be French tapestries and embroidered wall hangings. Here the fire had not been lit in the great stone-manteled hearth, but a large earthernware jug held a wealth of sweet-smelling roses. The furniture was of highly polished oak, with several high-backed chairs upholstered in Spanish leather and there were embroidered cushions upon the deep window seats. This room had been furnished for a lady, probably Sir Rhys's mother. Philippa stared enviously down at the bright rugs from the East which replaced the rushes of her grandmother's own home. Everything within this room spoke of wealth and settled prosperity and she gave a little sigh. Peter eyed her comically and she burst into a little laugh. "No wonder Sir Rhys has abandoned my father's castle as a place of residence."

"Not abandoned it entirely, Lady Philippa," Sir Rhys said as he entered, pulling off his riding gauntlets. "I spend a great deal of time at the castle, which you must visit, before you leave England, but I am here for the present to give what aid and comfort I can to Lady Gretton, should she need me in any emergency."

He approached her smiling, as again, she felt a sudden stab of guilt that she had once more misjudged his motives.

He looked round to see if his orders concerning their comfort were being obeyed.

"Your steward has gone to summon servants," Philippa put in hurriedly, fearing his frown of displeasure for the unfortunate subordinates. "Everything is being done to make us comfortable." She glanced at him anxiously as he waved her to a chair and Peter to another. "Did you find the runaway horse? Have you returned it to the stables here? I'm sure Master Maynard will be prepared to pay for the services of a smith, should they be required."

He shook his head sadly, "I'm afraid such services will not be necessary, Lady Philippa."

She gasped in horror. "You—have dispatched it?"

"The poor creature's leg was so badly fractured that

nothing could have been done for it. You would not wish it to have suffered further, surely?''

Her hand was at her mouth in a distressed gesture, her eyes wide with sorrow. She could only think how badly she would have grieved if her own little newly acquired Welsh cob had been lost to her. She swallowed and turned slightly away so that he might not see her tears. ''No, sir—of course not. It is just that...''

''You cannot bear to see dumb creatures suffer pain or die. That is another point in your favour, Lady Philippa. I admire most a gentle heart in a woman.''

She flushed at the compliment, feeling, vaguely, that he was teasing her, yet when she looked full at him, his dark eyes were grave and his mouth sensitive and she knew he had found his self-appointed task distasteful.

A servant knocked and, on his call to enter, a girl advanced with a ewer and bowls for washing hands, and another older woman, who bore the keys of the household suspended from her belt, curtsied and looked deferentially towards Sir Rhys for further information.

''I think it would be better, Sir Rhys, if I conducted my lady to a bedchamber to repair the ravages to her gown as best I may.''

Like all the women in the Welsh Marches, her accent was soft and singsong. She was dressed plainly in a gown of dark blue wool and her linen cap was spotless.

''Certainly. Do your best, Mistress Cheswick,'' Sir Rhys replied smoothly. ''If you are wearied or distressed by this recent incident, you could lie down and rest for a while, Lady Philippa.''

She shook her head emphatically. ''It was not I who suffered harm, Sir Rhys. Thank you, but I shall be ready to depart for Gretton as soon as our horses have been rested and summoned.''

He nodded, seating himself in a chair opposite to Peter, throwing one long leg over the other at ease. "After you have sampled my hospitality, Lady Philippa," he said mildly. "Do not cheat me of your charming company for an hour at least."

She felt that her flounced exit in the wake of the housekeeper was somewhat churlish but, try, as she might, the man brought out all the contrariness within her.

The airy light-filled bedchamber overlooked the pleasance and herb garden as one would expect. Like the winter parlour it was luxuriously furnished with a wide-testered bed, curtained in blue and silver damask and there were priceless rugs upon the polished floor, elaborately carved chests and press and an exquisitely carved prieu-dieu.

Philippa looked thoughtfully round at the limewashed walls and bright tapestries in appreciation.

"This is a beautiful room. Was it furnished for Sir Rhys's mother?" she asked.

The housekeeper had already set out a small bowl of liquid upon one of the chests and she came to Philippa with a linen towel and cloth.

"Yes, my lady. Unfortunately she died a year before the house building was completed, of a tertian fever. Sir Rhys completed the furnishings and oversaw the setting out of the pleasance in her memory. He loved her very dearly."

"Sir Rhys has no sister? There is no other mistress of the house?"

The housekeeper shook her head. "No, Sir Rhys's only brother was killed in a border skirmish four years ago, leaving him to inherit after the master was killed in a hunting accident."

''I heard about that. How sad! Then Sir Rhys is alone without close kin?''

''Indeed, we shall all be glad when he provides us with a new lady.'' The housekeeper's face crinkled in a little smile. ''He has been lonely of late—not that he and his father always saw eye to eye.'' She avoided Philippa's eye then, realising she had gossiped too freely, and bent to rub at the blood and dirt upon Philippa's gown.

Philippa considered that she had asked too many questions of the woman and allowed her to finish her ministrations, encouraging only light chatter about the weather and general household matters.

A page had brought wine and comfits when she was returned to the winter parlour and Peter and their host appeared to be conversing without the hostility she had detected in Sir Rhys's previous attitude towards her father's squire. Both rose courteously at her entrance and she came to sit in a high-backed chair beside Peter.

''I thank you, Sir Rhys. Your housekeeper has made an excellent job of making me once more respectable. I had not realised how badly my garment was blood-stained. As you remarked earlier, the sight would have alarmed my mother.''

He poured wine for her. ''You are welcome to my hospitality at all times, Lady Philippa. If I should be absent, my housekeeper and steward will see to your comfort.''

She inclined her head graciously, watching him covertly over the rim of her wine goblet. He was a very handsome man who exuded a spirit of pure confidence and authority. Despite her antipathy to him, she recalled with a little involuntary shiver the warmth of his body as he had lifted her to the saddle during the journey and the clean, male scent of him. So he had not been the elder son. The housekeeper had inferred that there had been a certain coolness between Rhys Griffith and his father. She wondered why. Had he been opposed to his father's sycophantic attitude to the Tudor King? Surely not. She found his opaque dark eyes looking at her questioningly and hastily lowered her own.

"I have to thank you, sir, once again, for your timely assistance to Master Maynard and to ourselves," she said, somewhat lamely.

"I shall see that he is cared for. You can safely leave his welfare in my hands." His lips twitched slightly, "I know that you considered me harsh on my first meeting with him but, I assure you, my suspicions will not colour my need to care for him, if only for your gentle sake."

"I wish you would not tease me, sir," she murmured, confused. "You know I only offered what help any passer-by would have done."

One dark eyebrow swept up questioningly. "I am by no means sure of that. I only ask you to be cautious in your dealings with all in the district, for the sake of your mother and grandparents."

She felt a sudden rush of warmth towards him for his consideration. "I promise that I will, sir, truly." She looked towards Peter for guidance. "We should go, Peter. My mother will be worried."

"Indeed." Sir Rhys rose. "Allow me to conduct you to the courtyard."

As Peter moved towards the stables, Philippa said impulsively, "I saw from your mother's bedchamber the wonderful pleasance. What a lovely thought to have had it set out as her memorial. Mistress Chiswick told me of her—untimely death. I was sorry to hear of the deaths of both your parents and brother and so close to each other.''

Peter had disappeared inside the stable and Sir Rhys offered her his arm. ''Allow me to show you the roses. They were my mother's favourite flowers and they are especially splendid this year. There will be no impropriety. Gardeners are at work there all the time. We shall not be alone or unobserved.''

She flushed rosily. She did want to see the pleasance at close quarters. From the distance she had observed that it was much larger and finer than the one at Gretton and her mother had always sighed over the fact that they had no garden behind their lodging at Malines. They were able to walk in the Duchess's gardens, of course, but they were always crowded with courtiers and visitors to the palace.

They passed through a flowery arch into the pleasance proper and Philippa exclaimed at the beauty. As Sir Rhys had commented, gardeners were at work, cutting away at the low yew hedges, clipping away dead flowers and generally tidying. The lawns were well scythed and watered and standard trees grew from the grass. Further on a rose garden held a variety of fragrances and colours and were alive with the heady buzzing of bees. She saw lavender and gilly flowers and lilac trees, fairly new to this country, as she knew they'd only been introduced some hundred years earlier by King Henry IV who had brought trees back from his visit to the Holy land. Her father had told her of how he had obtained a cutting from one of the royal gardens at Kenilworth.

''It is truly beautiful,'' she said softly, ''What a pity your mother could not have walked here. You must have loved her very deeply.''

"Aye."

She turned as she caught a little catch in his voice on the utterance of the single word. "Forgive me. I should not have spoken of her and given you pain."

"You would never mean to give pain, Lady Philippa. She would have admired the beauty she would see in you. She appreciated all lovely and sensitive things—and people."

"Your father must have grieved sorely, particularly after losing your brother."

"Oh, he did mourn the loss of my brother. They were two of a kind." She could not fail to notice the true note of bitterness now.

She was silent for a moment, then murmured, "Your mother was not happy?"

"She was not happy," he repeated. "My father was blessed with a gentle obedient wife but—alas—he did not consider her a beauty and beautiful women were a passion with him—and a weakness. Oh, I could have forgiven his neglect of her. He married her on his father's command, as so many men do, and they take opportunities to seek consolation elsewhere—but he flaunted his mistresses before her—at Wroxeter and in Ludlow—everywhere."

"And your brother?"

"Was of like mind. He was courageous and reckless and died because of it. Had he one moment's consideration for his own skin and, incidentally, for the lives of his men, he would be master here today. He loved wine and hunting—and women—many women. He showed little affection for our mother either and it broke her heart."

Philippa was visibly shaken. She looked away, sensing his emotional distress. She swallowed and said very softly, "I am very sorry for your loss."

He moved slightly forward, away from her. "Yes, life has been—difficult, but there has been much to be done."

She sensed that during his father's time much had been neglected and thought how it might have been had his brother lived to inherit.

"You will soon bring a wife to Griffith Manor," she said. "Your mother would have wanted that—and she will bring you comfort."

"If she is the right woman, yes."

He was gazing at her very directly now and she flushed under his scrutiny as she very often found herself doing.

He said suddenly, a little harshly. "Are you in love with Fairley?"

She started and said indignantly, "I have told you, there is nothing between us. You misjudged my motive that night you found me from my chamber..."

"That is not what I asked."

She swallowed hard, finding herself trembling. "No. I am fond of Peter, but not in the way you imply."

"Or in love with any man?"

"No," she said evenly. "My father cannot offer a dowry for me. The men like my father—exiles of Yorkist leanings at the Duchess of Burgundy's court—are as impecunious as he. They could not, in honour, request my hand—and I am no wanton, sir."

His mouth twitched betrayingly. "I humbly beg your pardon, Lady Philippa, if I ever gave you the opinion that I believed such a possibility."

She inclined her head graciously.

"Then—what will you do?"

''You mean will I enter a convent as so many unmar-riageable maids do?'' Her lips were curving now into a slightly bitter smile.

''That would be a tragedy indeed—for all the men in the world who were deprived of the chance to look on you.''

''Then you need not concern yourself, sir. I have no intention of so doing. I have no vocation for life as a bride of Christ.'' She lifted her chin a little defiantly. ''I shall make my own way in the world, do not fear.''

''But if your father should die?''

She gave a little gasp of horror as the implication of what he had said struck her forcibly. Always, every-where, when away from the protection of the Duchess's court, her father, the Earl, was in danger. And lately it had become apparent that Margaret of Burgundy was ailing. She knew her mother feared the withdrawal of that support and protection. Her father could look after his own interests, she knew that well enough, he could become a soldier of fortune, a mercenary, if needs be, but he needed constantly to be assured that his wife and daughter were well provided for. She bit her lip and gave a little nervous shrug.

''Then Peter will support us loyally as he always has.''

''Why were you seeking him out if not for…?''

She avoided his eye, then said steadily, ''I was con-cerned for our safety during the journey. I wanted to discuss matters with him.''

''You feared I might betray you and your mother to the King's cronies?''

Again she gave a little helpless shrug. ''The thought crossed my mind. To do so would enhance your stand-ing at Court.''

''I think you have mistaken my motives for those of my father,'' he said curtly.

She was silent for a moment, then said, ''Yes, Sir Rhys, I believe that I did. You must understand that to hold both my mother and I would be a strategic triumph for the King. He knows well enough that my father would surrender himself in order to free us.''

He frowned slightly. ''Your father has been a thorn in the King's flesh for some time. It is well known in the district and I cannot conceive of any reason why he is so desirous of having your father within his hands, not now, after so long.''

''Perhaps because my father could divulge matters his Grace wishes to keep secret.''

His dark eyes flashed. ''About the Princes, you mean? But now Tyrell has confessed to their murder the King has little to fear on that score.''

She flashed him a withering glance. ''Tyrell's confession cannot be refuted. Do you think all men believe it? Do *you* believe it, Sir Rhys?''

There was amusement and some doubt in those dark eyes of his now. ''If your father knows the truth concerning the fate of the boys, why has he not spoken out? Even such a statement, coming from such a dubious source as the Burgundian court where all in Europe know how biased the Duchess is in the late King Richard's favour, would draw some considerable attention— especially from the Spanish court at this time when the King is so anxious to further cement the alliance between our countries and marry young Henry to the Infanta, Catherine.''

''My father may well have his own reasons which I have never sought to question.''

His lips twitched again as he moved towards her.

"Come, your escort will become impatient. I will send two of my men with you to Gretton. For one thing, I need to discover the condition of your grandfather. Fairley told me earlier he was not well this morning."

She felt suddenly contrite that she had dallied so long away from Gretton and nodded, her lip trembling somewhat. He led her from the garden into the courtyard, where Peter stood waiting impatiently beside the horses.

Rhys Griffith stood watching wistfully as she rode away from him. God, how very beautiful and desirable she was! Had she any understanding of her own sensuality? He ached for her, had done since the moment he had laid eyes upon her.

That brief childhood vision of her mother he had had as a child had remained in his memory over the years as if he had known, even then, that he must wait for the woman of his dreams—and then he had encountered her at the inn in Milford. He bit down savagely upon his nether lip. He must have Philippa Telford for his bride, yet there was so much between them to make such a union unattainable. He held her father's lands, for which she must hold him in utter contempt. Yet, surely, he reasoned, making her his bride would be the one way of returning those properties if not to Wroxeter, to his descendants. But would she consent? He smiled a trifle grimly. If he knew her mettle, she certainly would not. Resentment of him and all he stood for he read in every line of her impressive, beautiful young face, in her poise, her very bearing. No, Philippa Telford regarded him as her enemy and he could not, as yet, see any way of convincing her otherwise.

He knew her mother was aware of his interest. How would she view an advance from him? The Countess must constantly be alarmed for her daughter's future.

That was evident. Sir Daniel and Lady Gretton had made it plain that they too were well aware of the pitfalls to be negotiated before Philippa could be wed. In all events he would require her father's consent—and the sky would fall before Wroxeter would give it.

Moodily he moved to a bench within the rose arbour he had lovingly created after the manner his mother would have so delighted in. Seated there, he viewed those intertwining blooms of red and white above his head, heady with fragrance, emblems which the Tudor King had chosen to join in the new badge of the Tudor rose. Red and white roses decorating the streets of York had greeted the victorious monarch on his entrance into the city. Those two great houses of York and Lancaster and their loyal adherents, locked in mortal combat. The effects had lasted even after nearly twenty years, and continued to hold him apart from his desire. The King had managed to unite them, for political purposes, in his marriage to Elizabeth, the daughter of the Yorkist King. Could the Telfords be convinced in the same manner that he would prove a suitable husband for their headstrong daughter? For certainly Philippa would prove no docile bride—nor did he wish her to be. He admired her passionate espousal of her father's cause. He wanted, *needed* a mate who would match him in strength of will and purpose. The saints knew he would never neglect her as his own gentle mother had been neglected.

He rose as his steward appeared in the pleasance archway, apparently in search of him, and another thought struck him. If he could accomplish a match between Philippa Telford and himself it would not please the King.

Sir Rhys's steward bowed. "The carrier has arrived, sir and asks to see you."

"Did you put him in my study?"

"Yes, sir."

"I'll come at once. See we are not disturbed."

He passed through the courtyard and into the house, noting that the carrier's cart was standing, waiting, the horse's head held by one of the grooms.

"We shall be some time. Unhitch the horse and take him to the stable. Care for him well."

He went into the house and passed to a small room near the winter parlour he used as a place of business. A man was standing near his desk, who turned and bowed obsequiously as he entered.

"Sir Rhys. I hoped you would be at home."

The visitor was a small weasel-like individual with sparse carroty-coloured hair, in his middle years and with the awkward stance of a man who spent most of his time seated upon the driving seat of a wagon. It was clear that he was stiff from travel and Sir Rhys nodded towards a stool which faced his desk and seated himself in the high-backed chair behind it.

"I have ordered your horse cared for. After we have completed our business, you can take your dinner in the kitchen."

The man grinned, well pleased, and leaned slightly forward.

"I thought you should have the news I have as soon as possible."

"You have come from London?"

The man gave a bob of his head in answer.

"I saw my usual informant in a tavern in the Chepe. He tells me that the lord you asked news of had recently left the Duchess Margaret's court at Malines."

"Where bound, had he any idea?"

The man shrugged, "Only that he was seen to take the road for Bruges."

"Ah, then your informant has obviously had very recent news. By carrier pigeon, do you think?"

"It would seem likely, Sir Rhys. It's known that the King's agents in Burgundy use such a method."

Sir Rhys tapped his teeth with a quill. "Then Wroxeter may well be heading for the port of Damme. Interesting."

The little carrier wriggled on his stool. "I also have news that a certain Master Allard has arrived in Milford Haven, or was there a sennight ago. You may know, Sir Rhys, that this Allard has Yorkist sympathies. His father is…"

"Yes, yes, I know well enough. His father is Sir Dominick Allard who fought for the late King at Redmoor and been an intimate with King Richard since childhood. Richard Allard was four years ago in London in service with Anne Jarvis who, with Lady Philippa Telford, was in attendance on the queen. She is the daughter of another Yorkist, Sir Guy Jarvis. She was married to young Allard some three years ago."

"Then, sir, it is likely that he has gone to Milford Haven to meet some prominent Yorkist…"

"Aye, likely Wroxeter." Sir Rhys leaned back irritably. "What can the man be thinking of to risk coming to England now, when Henry's spies are watching every Yorkist in the country?"

The carrier's little rheumy eyes glistened. "Do you wish me to head for Milford Haven, Sir Rhys? I could pick up enough good quality wool upon the way to make my journey both profitable and excusable."

Again Sir Rhys tapped his teeth thoughtfully. "Yes,

if you can manage to make fair speed. Do you know what this fellow Allard looks like?''

''Aye, sir. I was given a description.''

''Good, then do that. You may encounter him on the road back. I am anxious to know if he intends to come to Gretton and, particularly if he is accompanied by a companion—or even a servant.''

''Aye, Sir Rhys.''

''Then get you to the kitchen. My steward will see you are suitably rewarded.''

The man rose and touched his forelock respectfully and edged his way out of the study.

Some moments later Sir Rhys's steward knocked and requested permission to enter.

''I have paid the man off, Sir Rhys. Is there any further action you wish me to take?''

Sir Rhys shook his head regretfully. ''We can do nothing but wait, Crawley. He brought disturbing news which I half feared, that the Earl of Wroxeter may be intending to visit England secretly.''

''Then he will join his lady.''

''I certainly hope not.'' Again he sighed heavily. ''When you have made arrangements to have that fellow, Maynard, conveyed to Ludlow, see to it that I am informed where he is lodged and...'' he hesitated slightly then continued ''...and further, put someone in the household you can trust into Ludlow to keep an eye on the place and report the comings and goings of any strangers.''

The steward smiled and bowed slightly. ''I will see to it personally, Sir Rhys.''

Rhys sat on, his eyes narrowed. This Tyrrell affair was likely to fire up the realm. His confession, that on the late King's orders he had secretly suffocated the two young Princes placed in the Tower for their own safety, was dubious in the extreme. Rhys, himself, was sceptical about the truth of it. Why had King Henry waited nigh on twenty years to press Tyrrell to confess? He had certainly had the means to force the truth from all those purported to be in on the secret. When he had entered London victorious after Redmoor, surely the servants in the Tower could have been made to divulge the graves of the murdered Princes and produce their bodies. And what of the Queen? What did she know about the fate of her brothers? Rhys shook his head in doubt. The late King had had no reason to kill his nephews. He had already been crowned King and his other nephew, the young Earl of Warwick, who could have been said to have had a greater claim on the throne than the two Princes, had not been harmed by his Uncle Richard and had continued to live until four years ago when he had been executed on a trumped-up charge of treason, simply to facilitate the marriage of the Spanish Infanta to the late Prince Arthur. Her parents had refused to allow the marriage until they had been assured that all Yorkist heirs were no longer living—young Warwick had been sacrificed. And now she was a widow and the King was anxious that she should marry his younger son, Prince Henry. Was that the reason for this hastily conceived ruse of the doubtful confession?

Rhys's loyalty to King Henry had been severely tested then—and now this possibly lying confession which could not be refuted by the accused, since Tyrrell was dead.

Philippa had indignantly denied the truth of it and Rhys was inclined to agree with her. King Henry had kept the peace for almost twenty years and this Rhys had staunchly admired, but now his stomach turned at this ruthless extermination of all harmless Yorkist heirs.

Did Wroxeter know the truth about the fate of the Princes, as Philippa had implied, and was this the reason why the King had stoutly refused to pardon him as he had other Yorkist gentlemen? If so, he, Rhys, must find some way to protect him and aid his escape if need be.

He had to find some way to convince Philippa that he acted only in her best interest, that he was not her enemy.

He believed he had detected some softening towards him in the rose pleasance. Her gentle heart had been touched by the story of his mother's suffering and she had not withdrawn from his touch when he had led her back into the courtyard.

She needed to regard him as a true friend she could trust. Later he would be able to reveal his more passionate feelings towards her.

Chapter Five

It was considerably less hot than it had been for the previous four days, and Philippa was enjoying the ride about the Gretton demesne. Her grandfather had insisted that she leave the manor house and get some cooler fresh air. Today and for the last two days he had been much improved and she had spent much of the time with him, talking of the old times when her mother had been a child at Gretton before her marriage, and reading to him from the new printed books he had ordered from Master Caxton's shop in Westminster. Her mother had left them alone together for the most part, knowing it was essential that Sir Daniel had ample opportunity to get to know the granddaughter who had been so cruelly kept from him over the years by force of circumstance. He'd enjoyed their time together; that was plain to see to all in the household. A healthier colour brightened his cheeks, his ability to talk had returned again and, though he had lost the greater part of his movement in his lower limbs, his servants had been able to carry him in his favourite armchair, now equipped with two long sturdy poles attached to the sides for easy carrying, out into the garden or where ever he wished to go on the ground floor of the manor house.

Today he had chivied Philippa into leaving his side for a while.

"Now, go, child. You have been cooped up with me for far too long during this warm weather and I want you to be able to explore the demesne. Your father's squire will go with you as usual. We know we can rely on him to keep you safe, but, in any case, no harm can come to you on my own land. I will see you again at supper and afterwards, we will talk together once more and I will tell you some more of your mother's youthful misdemeanours."

He chuckled and waved her away after she stooped and kissed his cheek.

She had been heartily glad of the respite and went into the courtyard where Gwenny had informed her that she had last seen Peter Fairley. She found him chatting with one of the falconers and when she told the man she had no wish to take out one of his birds, she dismissed him back to his duties in the mews.

"Grandpère has commanded me to ride out for a while and I will enjoy that but I do not wish to be gone from him too long." She sighed. "Who knows if I will ever see him again after we have left here again for Burgundy."

Peter's comely features expressed his own regret for the need. He knew, only too well, that it would be unwise for the Countess and her daughter to stay very much longer at Gretton.

"I will ride with you."

"No, Peter, I have another task for you. I wish you to ride into Ludlow and enquire for me about Master Maynard. I would like to be sure that he is being adequately cared for and discover where he has been lodged.''

Peter looked thoughtful. ''We shall have to be discreet. Sir Rhys Griffith expressly warned you not to do that.''

She bridled. ''He has been most kind to us all here, at Gretton, but he is not my master and I fail to see why I should obey him as if he were. He has been to Gretton every day to see Grandpère but I have not actually seen and spoken to him on any one of those occasions. If so I would have asked him myself about Master Maynard. No, I will take one of the grooms. It should be quite all right on Gretton land and you can be off to Ludlow and back with your report before supper. I would prefer not to send one of the household servants.'' She looked at him a trifle doubtfully. ''That, as Sir Rhys said, might not be wise.''

Peter pursed his lips. ''If I find him, do you want me to visit him?''

''I see no harm in it. Do you?''

Peter shrugged. ''The young fellow seemed genuine. If I can have some time to chat with him I shall, no doubt, be able to find out more about his business, the name of his merchant master and so set our minds at rest that he can be no spy.''

''I think Sir Rhys is being over-cautious, though,'' she said thoughtfully. ''This present King appears to be very determined to exact every ounce of tribute from all his subjects. I imagine they are sensitive on the issue and are determined to ensure no King's commissioner has set men to spy upon them.'' She smiled. ''Henry's parsimony was often discussed at the court.''

''Which does not make him popular.''

''He does not need to be popular, Peter, only successful in handling the power and security of the realm, which makes him dangerous.''

He looked at her sideways. ''I am just wondering why you are so anxious to know about Master Maynard.''

''Is it not natural? We did find him in a distressed state and—and Sir Rhys was not particularly sympathetic to his needs.''

''And he is very personable, young Master Maynard,'' Peter retorted drily.

She went a little pink. ''Really, Peter, I am hardly acquainted with the fellow. This is a courtesy I would do for anyone. You are as bad as Sir Rhys with your suspicions.''

''He has been suspicious, questioned you—about me?'' He was gazing at her very intently, his eyes narrowed and her own eyes widened in response and embarrassment.

''I think that he fears—'' She broke off awkwardly.

''I am sure that you set him straight.''

The remark was so coldly uttered that she turned sharply to look at him again. Surely, Peter, dear Peter, whom she had known all her life could not be harbouring... She shook off the disturbing thought hastily.

''Please go, Peter, quickly, and do what I ask. I'll go and ask for the services of a groom to ride out with me.''

''I'll arrange for that, but we must make sure the lad is utterly reliable. The head groom will advise me. I'll go and get my own horse saddled. See that your mother is informed that I shall be away for an hour or so in case she has need of me.''

''I will, but she is busied sorting linen with Grand-mère so I think you will not be missed.''

She went slowly back to the house to change her gown for one suitable for riding and to seek out her mother. As he turned towards the stable she thought his reluctance to perform the task she had set him was very palpable.

When she returned to the courtyard she found that one of the younger lads, Tom, was standing waiting, holding the bridle of her Welsh cob and those of his own mount.

She smiled at him as he led her pony to the mounting block and helped her mount. ''We shall not be gone for long, Tom. I merely wish to explore Sir Daniel's lands and visit some favourite spots my mother has spoken of.''

He saw to it that she was comfortably settled and mounted up and soon they had left the courtyard and ridden across the rich sheep-rearing lands away from the manor proper. She saw the labourers at work on their own strips of the two large fields of wheat and barley and laughing, happy people haymaking. All seemed in order, despite the fact that the master was unable to oversee the work personally. Obviously the bailiff was competent and she wondered if Sir Rhys Griffith had made himself responsible for inspecting the work from time to time. She would not be in the least surprised to find that. She pursed her lips thoughtfully. At Gretton they had much to thank their neighbour for, yet—there was a nagging doubt at the back of her mind which made her uneasy about the fact that he was aware of Sir Daniel's danger in harbouring the kin of a traitor. She shook her head to try to dispel the unworthy thought. Her father's warnings and constant need to be on his guard, particularly of all strangers and known King's men, made her unduly suspicious of all men's motives. All the time they remained at Gretton they were, undoubtedly, putting her grandparents in danger of arrest. She shuddered at the thought of her sick *grandpère* and vulnerable *grandmère* being so ruthlessly questioned if that were to happen. Whatever gratitude and admiration she had for Rhys Griffith must be laid against her need to be wary of him.

Her mother had spoken longingly of the woods at Gretton where she had often ridden alone and she asked Tom to take her on the main woodland path towards Ludlow.

He obliged and soon they were riding along a broad track shaded by stately oaks and elms. It was pleasant here, a slight breeze adding to her delight, and she resolutely thrust aside all disturbing thoughts as she slowed her horse to a gentle walk.

They had been upon the track barely more than a few minutes when the noise of a disturbance ahead, and slightly to their right, brought her up sharply. She saw that Tom was visibly alarmed and he drew up close and urged her to return the way they had come.

"Mistress, I think we should get back to the manor, now."

"But, Tom, we are on my grandfather's land. What can be going on? If someone is in trouble we should discover the cause and report back to the steward at the manor house."

He shook his unruly mop of fair hair vigorously. "My lady, I was entrusted with your safety. I will take you back and see to it that someone is dispatched from the house."

She caught a sudden sharp cry of pain, then a kind of roar as if a small crowd was giving utterance to its combined anger.

''Tom, that might be too late. Someone is hurt. I am the lady of the manor here and I should know what is happening.''

Without further arguing she spurred her pony forward in the direction of the commotion. A lesser track led off from the main one and she had to bend low in the saddle to avoid hampering branches. Her pace was urgent in spite of the uneven ground here and she had to encourage her pony forward with gentling words of reassurance and encouragement. She could hear Tom's horse blundering in her wake and the sound of his heavy breathing which told her of his mounting concern.

The noise was growing louder and she could distinguish deliberate shouts of abuse. Someone was in real peril. She turned to encourage Tom to faster progress and plunged on until, suddenly, she found herself in a manmade clearing in the wood, in which had been built a small cottage of mud daub and thatch. An angry crowd was milling round the rough-hewn fence and several brawny fellows had broken down the gate and were hammering on the door. One turned round to shout a word of frustrated fury towards his companions by the fence that he was being denied entrance.

Tom caught at Philippa's arm as she sprang to the ground without his help but she impatiently thrust him off.

''Let me go, Tom. I demand to know what is going on here. My *grandpère* would be horrified to hear of this rioting. Who lives here?''

Tom gave a hasty gulp as several members of the crowd around the fence, hearing her upraised voice, turned to view the newcomer. Their gaze did not strike her as being unduly hostile, merely curious.

She could see that they were peasant labourers,

dressed in homespun, several of the men carrying pitch-forks as if they had been drawn from their task of hay-making. There was also a fair sprinkling of red-faced women among their number and Philippa realised at once that they would not be easy to pacify.

Tom whispered urgently in her ear. "My lady, we should return to the manor at once. The mood of this crowd is ugly indeed."

Her demand had silenced them for moments, but now they ignored her and turned back to shouting and screaming and waving fists and farm implements. The owner of the cottage had undoubtedly raised their ire and was stoutly refusing to come out and face the mob. The imperative hammering upon the door continued and one of the men kicked it hard so that the sound of splin-tering could be heard. It would not hold for long.

Philippa advanced, head high. "What is all this? You are disturbing the peace. Desist from this, at once."

Again the crowd by the fence turned and viewed her now with distinct hostility. One woman, brawny elbows revealed by her rolled-up sleeves, stood, hands on hips, her whole pose insolent.

"Hoity toity, what brings you here to interfere with our concerns? Be off with you, mistress, and leave us to our own business."

"I will when I am assured that this unseemly com-motion stops. Who lives here? What is this all about? Whatever it is I'm sure it can be settled without the breaking of heads. If you have some legitimate grudge against the cottager, one of you send for the village constable."

"He'll do nowt," one of the older men spoke up defiantly, hiding himself behind the buxom woman who had accosted Philippa first. "He's afeared—like we all are."

"It doesn't appear to me that any of you are afraid except the poor soul who lives within," she rejoined tartly.

While she had been having words with the villagers she heard a definite crack as the flimsy cottage door yielded and, with triumphant yells, the men round it surged inside. There was a great deal of jostling and pushing and, eventually, the self-appointed leader emerged, holding an ancient crone by one arm, two of the others urging her ungently from the rear. A second triumphant roar of applause came from the motley watchers by the gate.

Philippa attempted to shoulder the leading woman aside so that she could obtain a clearer view of the victim of all this furore, but was angrily pushed back. Tom thrust a strong shoulder forward and cleared a path for her and, after a hastily muttered word of recognition that he was one of the manor servants, those in front gave way abruptly so that Philippa and Tom were standing slightly ahead of them on the path.

She was shocked to see how fragile and vulnerable the object of their fury was and she advanced indignantly to demand that the old woman's captors unhand her at once.

Sullenly she was obeyed, as if the innate authority in her tone was recognised and noted, but Philippa had to run forward hurriedly to catch the old lady by the shoulder as she was about to collapse. She stood supporting her, angrily facing the mob.

"Now, one of you tell me who this old lady is and what she could have possibly done to make you so angry."

"'Er's Nan Freeman," one of the women by the fence volunteered and the tone of her voice was insolent in the extreme. "Mistress, 'taint none of your business. You leave 'er to us."

"To do what?"

"Well, to duck 'er for a start. She'm be a witch."

"What nonsense," Philippa said briskly. "Anyone with eyes to see knows she's just a sick old woman who needs help, not abuse."

"If 'er be sick it be but justice," one of the men who had dashed into the cottage snapped. "Er 'as made others sick. My lass is 'bout to die 'cos of 'er—and what's more," he bellowed, "she'm be 'bout to pay for it. Let's take 'er to the duck pond in the village—now."

Screamed imprecations followed his words and Philippa was forced to stand her ground before the hapless old woman as the two men surged forward and tried to snatch the frail old body from her. She placed her arms comfortingly about the victim and said softly, "Do not be afraid. I'll not let them hurt you. I'll send Tom for the village constable. He'll restore order."

To her surprise the woman's answer was stronger and more vibrant than she could have believed possible.

"It would be foolish for you to stay here, mistress, and dangerous. These louts be too worked up to see sense at the end of their noses. They'll not listen to you. Don't involve the constable. He'll not be able to help. I shall be well enough. They'll most likely 'ave calmed down by the time they get me to the village."

"But I can't stand by and let them duck you. Have you harmed someone?" Philippa's tone was doubtful now. She told herself that these charges of witchcraft were nonsensical, yet she knew that many people, even those more learned and of the nobility, were inclined to listen to such talk. Why, King Edward's queen, Elizabeth Woodville, had been thought to be a witch and her mother, Jaquetta. And Jane Shore, the King's mistress, had been condemned to do penance as a witch at St Paul's Cross, yet she could not believe this ageing, frail old woman could be guilty of such heinous behaviour.

The old woman shrugged. "Like as not the silly wench didn't listen to un properly and took too much of the potion. 'Twould be better if they'd let us see un but they wunt, not in this mood."

She was right, for, already, the crowd round the fence was getting angrier by the moment. The fence was broken down in one place, then several at the front began to surge forward. The two men behind who had been the leaders of this affray were looking decidedly disgruntled. They recognised that this unknown woman had some gentility and were reluctant to cross her but, on the other hand, they were frustrated at the challenge to their right to deal with their victim as they thought proper. One of them moved menacingly nearer and Tom called peremptorily to him to stay back. They were not, however, likely to listen to some young whippersnapper from the manor stables and, after a hesitant move with sidelong glances towards his companion for support, the man advanced again, lifting one arm to shove Tom impatiently aside.

"'Taint none of your business, this," he growled. "You'd best take yourself off to your betters and leave us to deal with this old witch."

Further angry shouts echoed his demand and Philippa began to tremble. She could see she was not to be obeyed and she would either have to abandon her protégée or fall with her in any attack—and there was little time to consider the matter. In all events she was not about to play the coward. This old creature should be under Sir Daniel's protection and she, Philippa, had a duty to stand up for her, if only as far as demanding that authority should be consulted in the person of the village constable. Tom moved nearer to shield the two women with his body, but Philippa could almost smell his fear.

Nan Freeman buckled in their grasp and croaked, "You'd best go, mistress, ye cannat do any good 'ere."

Philippa turned despairingly towards Tom. "We can't leave her—"

Her words were cut short as a flying stone caught the old woman full on the forehead and blood actually splashed on to Philippa's sleeve. The mood of the mob was becoming more and more ugly by the minute and she knew she was about to suffer as the object of their combined fury. How dared she interfere in the rightful punishment to be dealt out to their captive!

Soon more stones were flying, many, thank the Virgin, missing their targets, but some were finding their marks. Tom let out a sudden yelp as one caught him on the ear and Philippa felt the sharp sting of another on her own cheek.

She gave a little sob of despair, and, as if in answer to her prayer, an authoritative voice broke across the baying of the mob.

"What in God's name is this? Are you all mad? Cease this rioting at once or I'll have the lot of you in chains before sunset."

It was the voice she knew only too well. Rhys Griffith's voice, and the crowd, who had ignored everything but their own lust for blood, recognised it too and that it threatened retribution and could not be denied. They fell sullenly back as he nudged his horse close to the fence and impatiently moved aside with his riding crop those who were tardy about clearing his path. He sat coolly, reviewing the scene and, for a moment, he appeared not to have noticed Philippa standing there, badly frightened and, as usual in her meetings with him, dishevelled and bloodstained.

"So," he said, as he slid from the saddle, and flicked his riding crop against his thigh, "there appears to be some grounds for complaint. I hope that it truly warrants my attention and is an excuse for the lot of you abandoning your work for half a day. It had better be worth it."

He walked through the now silent group to the cottage doorway and, gently but firmly, took the old woman, now in an almost collapsed state, into his hold. "Tom, let us help Mistress Freeman into her cottage." He looked coolly towards Philippa who was leaning weakly against the cottage doorpost. "Are you hurt?"

She shook her head. "Very little, just a scratch."

He raised his voice only slightly. "All of you, get back to your work and your womenfolk to caring for their brats. I want to see none of you here by the time I come back to the door."

One of the men, the accredited leader, Philippa thought, found the courage to speak up. "Josh Carter's lass is like to die from a potion yon old witch sold 'er. 'Er deserves to suffer for it."

"I will look into the matter; meanwhile, Mistress Freeman is under my protection. Mistress Weston here is kin to Sir Daniel, so mind your manners. If she makes complaint of your behaviour, and rightly so, you could all be before me in Wroxeter Castle hall in the morning court. Now, get you gone."

There was a mutter of disgruntled complaints as the group began to disperse reluctantly. As they did so, Sir Rhys called, "Get the apothecary from Ludlow to Josh's daughter. Tell him I will pay for his services. Get about it quickly. She could be worsening by the moment."

He had held the old woman in his arms, effortlessly, as if she were a doll. He then moved calmly into the cottage and set her down upon a bed of rushes covered with skins and rough homespun blankets which had been set against one wall.

Weakly Philippa followed and gazed down at her. "There is water in the crock there on the shelf. I will find some cloth and wipe her face. I do not think she is badly hurt. They wanted to duck her."

He watched her as she went about her task, Tom standing guard by the doorway. "It is always so at these times. More than likely Josh's silly wench took too much of the penny royal Nan gave her and has made herself really sick. She should recover. Nan rarely mistakes the amount of herbs she deals out."

"You know her, then?"

"Oh, indeed. She has been wise woman and herbal healer in these parts since her childhood and her mother before her. It is not witchcraft but experienced knowledge. The villagers are glad enough normally to depend on her services, but it is probable that Josh's lass got herself into trouble with some lad he disapproves of and this has made him more angry than usual. Her own blind panic has made the situation worse, but the apothecary should be able to save her." He regarded Philippa steadily. "I should not speak so openly on so delicate a matter, but—"

"I know well enough that penny royal is used to

abort unwanted babes,'' she said coolly. ''I am no delicate flower, Sir Rhys, as you know well enough.''

He laughed. ''Indeed I do, Lady Philippa. I am becoming used to finding you in some distressed state and with your clothing torn and blood-spattered. Most of the women of my acquaintance would be swooning at the sight of you, let alone get themselves into such situations. My lady, you appear to attract trouble as a flower attracts bees.''

''Would you have had me leave her to the dubious mercy of the mob?''

''Certainly not.'' He took the dampened cloth from her and very gently began to wipe her own dirtied and bloodstained face. ''You have a nasty cut on your cheek which will require some healing salve. I doubt that it will leave a scar.''

She shrugged. ''I have taken worse knocks in childhood. Thank you''—this stiffly as he completed his ministrations. ''Will Mistress Freeman be safe here now?''

''Not for a while with the whole village stirred up against her. I will leave Tom here with her and take you home to the manor house. Sir Daniel will dispatch a couple of his men to take her to my manor where she can stay until she mends and the villagers calm down. I doubt if she will consent to stay there much longer than that.'' He chuckled. ''Like you, Lady Philippa, Nan Freeman has a well-developed stubborn streak.''

Philippa went to the old woman and took her hand. ''Goodbye. I am assured that you will be safe now.''

''Oh, aye, Lady Philippa, Sir Rhys will take good care of me though he mightn't have come in time. My thanks and blessings are for your timely help.''

''You know me?''

''I knew your bonny mother, my lady. You could be

the child of none other. Do ye take care and for those ye love most.''

Philippa wrinkled her brow. "You mean Sir Daniel?"

"Aye, 'im. He 'as been a good master to me but I mean—others." Her pale lips writhed in a smile and Philippa squeezed her hand comfortingly.

"Are you not too old to live here alone now? Would you not be safer and better cared for nearer to the manor?"

"The mother will care for me, my lady, and take me easy when the time comes."

Philippa's brow wrinkled again in puzzlement for the strange words but Sir Rhys drew her gently to the door. "They will be sending men out in search of you. We must go." He addressed Tom. "I'll despatch the men quickly. You won't be alone with her for long."

Tom nodded and knuckled his forehead and Sir Rhys drew Philippa towards her pony and lifted her effortlessly into the saddle as he had carried the wise woman. He felt her trembling in his grasp and her small hand was chilled to his touch as he handed her the pony's lead reins.

"You have been truly shocked by this. I will get you home and into your mother's care. You are quite safe with me, my lady."

She smiled gamely back at him. "I know that, sir. It seems I must always be in your debt. You handled that mob so confidently. Were you not just the slightest bit afraid that they would defy you and turn on you too?"

He raised one black eyebrow and grinned at her. "It did cross my mind that I had no stout men-at-arms at my back, but they know me well. I am the magistrate for these parts; if heads had been broken, there would have been fines and imprisonment to follow. Once the first fury cooled they were aware of that.''

"Yet you did offer to care for the sick girl.''

"She is one of your grandfather's tenants and warranted our care as much as Nan.''

"I think you are a strange man, Sir Rhys,'' she said soberly, ''but I discover new facets to your character every time we meet.''

She urged her pony forward and they rode steadily back towards the manor. After a moment she strove to wipe the ugly scene from her mind momentarily by engaging in more general conversation.

"We talked of my family the last time we were together, Lady Philippa. Have you found it lonely at Malines? You are your father's only child. Were there other children with whom you could play at Malines?''

She shook her head, smiling. "Very rarely. We moved about quite a lot during my childhood while my father travelled on the Duchess's business. There were servants' children sometimes but, largely, my mother and I were forced to fall back upon each other's company. I think, perhaps, I have been indulged too much as a consequence,'' she said, sighing. "My father must have found it a hard fact to face that he has no son. In the early days I think he had hopes that he might be able to return to England and regain his lands, so he must have hoped for a son to inherit. He has never uttered a word of complaint on the subject. My mother had two miscarriages and then one little son, who was stillborn. That was a terrible tragedy for them all and now—'' she looked bleakly ahead along the woodland path ''—my father ails often. He took a bad wound at Redmoor and another at Stoke and his life has been hard since.''

"And there has been little money?"

Her smile was a little wistful as she turned back to him. "It has been sufficient. The Duchess has been good to us, but all the late King's friends and supporters have suffered misfortunes over the years."

He did not answer and they continued their ride in silence.

He was still considering her words when he found himself alone in the hall with Sir Daniel later. Lady Wroxeter had clucked her concern at the sight of Philippa, once more in a distressed condition, and hastened her away to their apartments to deal with the small wounds made by the flying stones and to comfort her. Lady Gretton, after a hasty greeting to Sir Rhys, hurried after them.

Sir Daniel eyed his neighbour quizzically after he had detailed the steps he taken regarding his plans to ensure the continued safety of Nan Freeman. Already two of Sir Daniel's men had been dispatched to join Tom in her defence.

"I have to thank you again, Rhys, not only for your prompt dealing with this sorry affair, but for once more coming to my granddaughter's assistance." He sighed and then chuckled. "She appears to have inherited an overactive conscience and needs to come to the help of every lame dog she comes across. My Cressida was just the same at her age and I was glad to hand her into Wroxeter's care when the time came, never thinking that he, too, had this deep-rooted need to remain loyal to his principles and that Cressida would find herself in distressing circumstances so soon after the marriage. I would to God I could ensure Philippa's welfare, since her doughty spirit requires a strong and reliable mentor, but I fear that might prove difficult considering her lack of dowry."

Rhys was silent for moments as he drained a goblet of malmsey an attentive page had placed on the trestle table at his elbow.

"Can I ask if you are in direct contact with the Earl, her father, Sir Daniel, or would that be too delicate and dangerous an enquiry?"

Sir Daniel stared back at him thoughtfully. "I imagine you have a definite reason for posing such a question and not merely wanting to probe my own loyalty to the King."

"If I could reach the ear of Wroxeter, I would beg him for his daughter's hand in marriage."

It was so blunt an announcement that Sir Daniel blinked in astonishment. He hesitated and played with his own goblet, moving the base in circles upon the table top.

"I cannot have failed to notice your interest in my granddaughter," he said at last, slowly, "but have you considered the consequences of such an alliance, even should it prove possible?"

"You mean I would lose the favour of the King, even come under his strong displeasure, so much so that I could suffer for it? Yes, I have done."

"And you would still wish to proceed with such a marriage, were Wroxeter to prove willing?"

"It is the greatest desire of my heart." He leaned forward eagerly. "I think I fell deeply in love with Lady Philippa the first time I encountered her in the courtyard of the inn at Milford. Since then I have discovered much more about her that pleases me. As you say, she is headstrong and impulsive but her heart is warm with sympathy for those she meets, especially those requiring her help. He gave a great gasp of longing. "She is as beautiful as some faery creature. Sometimes I look at her and can hardly believe she is of this earth. I long to possess her, Sir Daniel, and to keep her safe from all possible dangers, and, as you and I have both observed, she is likely to put herself into peril as often and as naturally as a bee pollinates flowers. I know there are obstacles to the match. I have the misfortune to possess her father's lands, and for this she holds, quite naturally, a decided grudge, but surely that very fact has an advantage. Only just now, as we rode in, she expressed what she believed must be her father's regret that he had no son to inherit his title and lands, but, as my wife, she would do so and our children after her, Wroxeter's descendants."

Sir Daniel nodded gravely. "You and I can see the advantage of that, Rhys, my friend, but will Wroxeter? And, most important of all, will Philippa?"

Sir Rhys shook his head. "I think he will consider what can be gained. Did you consider Lady Wroxeter's wishes when you arranged her marriage to the Earl of Wroxeter or were you constrained to make the best alliance possible for her?"

Sir Daniel gave a wry smile. "In all honesty, I was forced to give my consent. It was the late King's express wish and I can tell you I had my doubts, for Cressida was every bit as headstrong as her daughter, but Wroxeter proved the right man for her and she fell deeply in love with him, a love which has endured through all the dangers and hardships of the last twenty years." He looked away from his guest, across the hall, his eyes narrowing in thought. At last he said slowly, "I will talk to Cressida on this matter and send to you when I have received her own opinion."

"And she has means of reaching her husband?"

"That may take some time."

Sir Rhys nodded. He understood that since the Earl of Wroxeter was in the Duchess of Burgundy's service he must be off upon his travels often so that his wife was unaware of his whereabouts. He said softly, "And may I know your own thoughts, Sir Daniel?"

Sir Daniel turned back and regarded him steadily. "I have a deep admiration for you, Rhys Griffith, as both a man and as a fair and right-minded magistrate and lord. I have to say that since you, too, have undoubted determination you could find my Philippa something of a handful." His lips twisted in some private amusement. "But I believe you could manage her and that goes far in my consideration of her future. Cressida has spoken of her fears regarding the Duchess of Burgundy's health."

"If she were to die, Wroxeter would lose her protection and patronage and, more than ever, he would need to secure his daughter's welfare."

Sir Daniel inclined his head.

Sir Rhys said quietly, "Has Lady Philippa spoken of me to you?"

Again Sir Daniel gave that little wry smile. "She has asked questions about you but, no, she has not expressed an opinion of your character."

"Do you think she hates me?"

"No, I think she has a certain respect for you, somewhat tempered by her concern about your loyalties."

Rhys sighed. "That will ever come between us."

"I fear so, yet—" he waved one hand dismissively "—I have known successful marriages based on even more difficult grounds."

"Then I must be content to wait."

''I fear so. Time and force of circumstances, only, can affect Philippa's attitude towards your offer.''

Rhys saw that his host was beginning to tire. He rose, bowed and made his excuses. He decided he would not attempt to speak with Philippa again today and took his leave of his host and rode from Gretton.

Philippa was relieved, later that evening, to learn from Tom that Nan Freeman had been conveyed to Griffith Manor by two of Sir Rhys's stout men-at-arms.

''She will be safer there, under Sir Rhys's protection, than here at Gretton, mistress,'' Tom assured her. ''While Sir Daniel is so ill and unable to get around the demesne.''

Philippa understood that and was content with the arrangement. She wondered how the poor lass who had taken too much of the old woman's potion had fared and if, should Sir Rhys be right in his assumptions, she was so deeply unhappy, having been abandoned by her light of love. Philippa sighed inwardly. It was ever the way of the world for women to receive no consideration from their menfolk. She pushed aside the unworthy thought that Sir Rhys had shown her every consideration. Rhys Griffith could be considered a fine, upright man for the right woman—that was, the one who shared his political sympathies.

Wistfully she wondered how things might have been had he not been master of her father's lands and she a fugitive. She could not dismiss the sight of him from her mind. How wonderful it had been to see him at that cottage, just when she had been in darkest despair! She had known then, instinctively, that with him beside her she had nothing to fear. And yet—always at the back of her mind was that nagging doubt: could she really trust him?

Her heart yearned to acknowledge that she could. Resolutely she put aside that treacherous longing. Soon she would be gone from Gretton and from England and would never see Rhys Griffith again.

Despite her determination to face that fact squarely, her lip trembled and she felt ready to break into tears as she had so many times lately. During these last days when he had come to Gretton and made no attempt to see and speak with her...

It was all so bewildering. Never had she felt like this before—not even when she had been most afraid.

There could be no more thoughts such as these. If not her enemy, Rhys Griffith was certainly her father's. There would always be too much between them. She must never harbour thoughts of love towards him. To do so would spell disaster for all of them.

When Peter Fairley sought her out later she learned that the injured Roger Maynard was considerably improved, his broken leg set, and was comfortably lodged at an inn near Ludlow Castle.

"It seems," she said thoughtfully, "that Sir Rhys has done his best for the man in spite of his earlier suspicions."

Peter looked dubious. "I doubt that the fellow could learn much to Sir Rhys's discredit in Ludlow where all seem to respect Griffith for his fair dealings."

"So," she said lightly, "the knight is a paragon. What a pity he is one of King Henry's cronies."

Since her grandfather insisted that, after her perilous adventure, she keep to the manor, Philippa saw no more of her rescuer for the next few days. Once or twice she was puzzled to see her mother closeted with Sir Daniel and, afterwards, Cressida seemed somewhat abstracted and followed her daughter with her eyes as if she would read her very soul. Philippa waited patiently for her mother to impart to her the source of her disquiet but Cressida appeared secretive about whatever had been discussed with her father. A sergeant was dispatched from the household on some mission, which was not discussed, and Philippa wondered if her mother was attempting to contact Lord Wroxeter. Knowing how dangerous a move that could be, Philippa was more than ever disturbed. Only something very serious could bring her mother to seek to be in touch with the Earl, her husband, while she was under the Gretton roof. Such a move, were it to be discovered by one of the King's minions, could be hazardous for all of them.

Philippa found her own mood to be restless and distracted, also unusually crotchety. On several occasions she had been touchy and unduly imperious and critical, so that she had brought tears to the eyes of young Gwenny. She castigated herself, knowing the girl was doing her utmost to please her young mistress. What was wrong with her? Certainly she was still worried about Sir Daniel's condition, everyone in the household was, her *grandmère* most of all, but that did not entirely explain her own sense of disquiet. She was not at peace with herself and that she found alarming. Though there had been times when she had been fearful of what the future would hold for herself, her mother and father, Philippa was generally optimistic by nature. She knew these moods of near despair were connected with the knowledge that she could not share in the contentment of many young maidens of her acquaintance, since her dowry was almost non-existent and her father's position made it unlikely that he would find a husband for her. She had always put on a cheerful countenance whenever she was in the presence of either or both her parents, but she was aware that her outward calm hid a passionate nature. Inwardly she yearned for love, for a man who could raise her to the heights of ecstasy she had read of in the troubadours' tales, for a home of her own, for children, but all this was likely to be denied her. She was a burden to her father. Would it be simpler to profess a desire to enter a nunnery? She dismissed the thought, knowing her father would reject such a suggestion immediately, and she knew herself only too well. Such a life would be a constant torture.

She was busy the next afternoon helping her mother to sort linen when Gwenny came into the chamber.

"Lady Philippa, your grandfather requests that you go to him. He is sitting in his carrying chair in the pleasance."

"Yes, of course. Perhaps he wishes me to read with him as we often do. May I leave you to finish this, Mother?"

"Certainly." Cressida smiled fondly at her daughter. "Gwenny will help me here."

Philippa moved to curtsy, but her mother pulled her to her and kissed her gently upon the forehead. "Listen well to your grandfather, child. Remember, we have not too long to be here. Savour the moments we have together."

Philippa nodded and ran lightly down the stair towards the courtyard, pausing only to rid herself of her linen apron as she hastened through the hall.

She found her grandfather reading one of his falconing manuals and he looked up, smiling, as she approached. It was a warm day and the pleasance was comfortable in the slight breeze blowing without the need for them to seek shade. Someone had placed a joint stool near his chair and she ran to him, kissed him on the cheek and sank down upon it.

"How are you feeling this afternoon? Did you want company? I thought that perhaps Sir Rhys Griffith would visit today."

He took her hand in his huge paw. "No, perhaps later. He must be busy on his own manor, overseeing the final bestowing of the harvest."

She nodded and reached for his book. "Perhaps soon you will be able to take out your kestrel, Grandpère."

He smiled wryly. "I think those days are well behind me, child, but I still enjoy contemplating the pleasures I had." He noticed that she wrinkled her nose and bent to ruffle her bright hair, free for once of her headdress since they were sitting comfortable *en famille*. "You do not like falconing or the hunt?"

"Not really, I think few women do. I went on several during my days at Court at Westminster and Richmond, but I do not like to see creatures hurt, though I know it is necessary to provide meat for the winter months. Does Sir Rhys accompany you when you hunt?"

"Yes, he has done." He was holding her hand lightly but she noticed that he did not seem willing to relinquish it. "What is your opinion of Sir Rhys Griffith, Philippa?"

Again she wrinkled her nose, this time in thought, unwilling to answer too readily. "He has been good to you and Grandmère. On the few occasions I have watched him deal with villagers and labourers he seem fair and kindly, though firm. He has come to my rescue

on one or two occasions and he does not lack courage.''
She gave a little bird-like nod of her chin. ''I respect
and admire him.'' She was looking away from him
across the pleasance at the rose bushes, remembering
the time when she and Rhys had talked informally in
the rose arbour at Griffith manor. ''I think…'' she said
slowly, ''that he is often lonely. He did not appear to
have a happy time with his brother and father. Did he
tell you of them?''

Her grandfather inclined his chin. ''We all knew in
the county—what went on—and pitied Rhys's lady
mother.''

''He must miss her. He loved her greatly, I believe.''
Philippa shaded her eyes with one hand. ''I hope he
will soon find a good wife, one who will respect and
love him and deal well with his household as he would
wish.''

''And could you be that woman, Philippa?'' The
question was put very quietly and she turned and stared
at him, mouth slightly open.

''Grandpère—you cannot mean—he has asked for
me?''

''He requested that I sent messengers to your father
begging the right to formally ask for your hand.''

She jumped up, startled. ''And you granted it—and
you have sent—I saw a messenger ride out and wondered but—I did not think—Grandfather, you are mad?
You must not allow Sir Rhys Griffith to know the
whereabouts of my father. Even in Burgundy he is not
entirely safe. You know that. How could you—?''

''Calm yourself, child.'' He lifted a restraining hand.
''There can be no harm done. My messenger will simply return with an answer if and when he finds your

father. Nothing will be divulged about his where-abouts—or the business he is engaged upon.''

Her eyes were wild, her hand hard against her breast. ''But you cannot contemplate that my father would consent to such a monstrous alliance. He—the man is our enemy, he holds my father's lands. He—''

''His father may well have been our enemy, child, but Redmoor was almost twenty years ago, before you were born. We must all live as we can. Your father knows that well enough and, like me, he must be anxious to ensure your future. Rhys Griffith could provide for you more than adequately. He is a wealthy land-owner and what better than that your children would inherit your father's land in God's good time?''

She stared at him blankly, ''Then you—you see some wisdom in this—*alliance*.'' She ground out the final word. ''Have you—have you discussed this with Grand-mère or—'' the enormity of it struck her forcibly ''—with mother?''

''Yes, your mother is of our opinion.'' Again his answer was very quiet but direct. ''She knows the necessity of providing for you in the event of any accident happening to your father. You know the Duchess of Burgundy ails. The fortunes of you all could take a decisive downward turn if she were to die. We must think ahead, Philippa. Rhys Griffith professes his deep love for you. He asks no dowry.''

''And my father,'' she murmured brokenly, ''have you had his answer? What does he say to this unspeak-able proposal?''

''I have had no answer as yet, but your mother and I thought it best to put this to you. Who knows how long you will be able to stay here or if your father can be reached in a hurry?''

"You want me to accept, don't you?"

He was silent for a moment, then he said, "We have pondered over this for a long time and, yes, we believe it could assure your future. I trust Rhys Griffith to provide well for you. I know this must be a shock to you, Philippa, but you must have noticed that he has had no eyes for anyone but you since you met at Milford Haven. While I realise you cannot, as yet, entertain any fond feelings for him, he is young, personable—"

"And wealthy," she put in bitterly. "Like most other maids of my acquaintance, I am to be sold for the best price at market."

"Philippa, you know that is not so," he said, looking up earnestly at her as she sprang to her feet and stepped away from him, blue eyes flashing dangerously.

"No," she said, stepping yet further back and lifting her hands as if to ward him off, "I thought you loved me, Grandpère, but you ask this terrible thing of me. All of you have conspired against me, knowing it would be against my will. Even if I were to harbour tender thoughts for Rhys Griffith I could never—never marry him. He is my father's enemy. How could I live with such a man, fearing for my father's safety, knowing that King's officers might call at our manor at any time demanding to know the whereabouts of my father, waiting for me to lead him into a trap? I would be forced to cut off all contact with those I love best. You know all that and yet you put this to me—for—for gain alone. Rather would I run away from you all and trust myself to a nunnery—"

She broke off in this wild tirade as she saw her grandfather attempt to rise from his chair to go to her. He fell back and again struggled to rise, then he clawed at his throat and made some terrible unintelligible animal noise. She stood rooted to the spot, horrified, as she saw his eyes roll upwards. The dreadful noise continued until suddenly it stopped and she saw he had fallen sideways in his chair. Terror impelled her forward then and she ran to the chair and knelt before him.

"Grandpère, I did not mean any of that. Please, please, you know that I love you, realise that you were trying to do your best for me. What is it, Grandpère? Oh, please, please—answer me…" Her voice rose to a shriek of despair when he did not move, as she shook his shoulder urgently, tears raining down her cheeks. She spoke to him, continued to shake his unresponsive shoulder, implored him over and over again, not knowing what she said or what avail her efforts could possibly do to rouse him.

Abruptly her own shoulder was taken in a firm clasp and a well-known voice spoke very gently. "Leave him, Lady Philippa, let me see. Allow me to help you up."

She turned an anguished face to Rhys Griffith. "He—he will not answer. I—I caused this. He was—he was trying to persuade me to—Oh, Sweet Virgin—I would not listen and he—he—please, oh, please, tell me he is not…"

He lifted her gently but forcibly from her kneeling position and half-carried her to a wooden seat some feet away. "Sit, Lady Philippa. Leave this to me. Do not try to move. Trust me."

She buried her head in her hands as he strode away, back to the carrying chair with its stricken inhabitant. It seemed an age before he returned to her side and dropped to his knees before her, taking both her hands, now wet with her scalded tears, into his own.

"My dear, you must not weep. It happened so quickly that he had no time to fear even. I have sent for a priest. Everything will be done reverently. It is good he had you with him at the last.''

She stared at him blankly. "He is dead?" she whispered at last. "He is really dead?"

He inclined his head gravely.

"He cannot be, not—not now when he and I were— oh, no.'' She burst into a storm of weeping and he drew her up into his arms, holding her close so that she could feel the roughness of his homespun jerkin against the silk of her gown. She sobbed against his shoulder in an access of grief and self-blame. He could feel her shuddering form pressed close to his heart and he murmured gentle words of comfort until the worst of the storm was past and still she clung to him blindly, finding some inner strength which he, and he alone, could impart. At last the shuddering stopped and he drew her down to the wooden seat again, his arm about her so that she was able to cry more naturally.

"It was all my fault," she said again as the weeping eased somewhat. "I knew he was ill and must not be angered or upset and I—and I—and I thwarted him and…''

"Hush now," he said softly, though he made no attempt now to stem the renewed storm of weeping. "None of this was your fault. He suffered a stroke months ago, Philippa. We all knew it could happen again any time and that it could prove fatal. Your mother brought you here so that he would have a chance to see you at last and his wish was granted. You were everything he hoped for. He died as he wished, with you at his side. Now I shall leave you for a moment and summon your maid. Your mother and grandmother will be busied for a while. As I said, I have already sent a messenger to summon a priest. All is in hand. When

Gwenny comes, you must go to your chamber and pray
and try to calm yourself. In time your womenfolk will
need your support. I will arrange everything. You can
trust me.''

He longed to stay beside her and continue to try to
comfort her desperate grief and yet there was much to
be done and he must not, at this time, take advantage
of her need. He could not imagine what had passed
between the old man and his beloved granddaughter that
was so terrible in her eyes that it could not be faced.
He frowned slightly as he rose to his feet.

''Pippa?''

In her agony of mind she did not notice the use of
her mother's pet name for her. She tried to stem her
tears with the back of her hand and looked up at him
wonderingly. ''Yes?''

''I will send for the physician, naturally, but I know
he can do nothing for your grandfather. Do you feel ill?
Can you manage alone until Gwenny comes? You are
shocked and should not try to stand up and walk without
help for a while. The physician will mix you a posset
if he feels there is need.''

She shook her head vehemently. ''No, no, I am being
weak and foolish and in a time of crisis when I am most
needed to be strong. Thank you, Sir Rhys, for your
kindness. My grandmother will—will—'' she swallowed back yet more hot tears ''—will be very grateful,
I know. It was just that—that he and I...'' She broke
off in terror that she might have let fall to him the hub
of the quarrel between her *grandpère* and her: those
bitter words that had caused him such hurt—had made
him try to rise—had caused the seizure that had killed
him. Further words were frozen as if her tongue clung

to the roof of her mouth without the will or ability to release itself.

He nodded, then bent and took her hand, squeezed it in a final act of attempted comfort, then gently released her, stood up and slowly backed away.

She watched him go wonderingly. Though she was not aware of it, the tears were still raining unchecked down her cheeks. Always, it seemed, he was here by her side when she had most need of him. Had he come for his answer? If so, what had he heard? Did he know how strongly she had rejected his offer for her hand?

She stared blankly into the distance, not hearing the sudden commotion nearer the house when the members of the household were told of the master's death and began to react in stunned silence to the news and to prepare themselves for what needed to be done. There was stifled sobbing and running footsteps, but, for the present, Philippa was unaware of it all. She could only think of her own culpability, for, however she told herself inwardly that she could have behaved in no other way, she blamed herself for the tragedy which would now strike at them all. She had refused outright to listen to him, castigated him for the very suggestion and yet—and yet—the stark horror of the situation was now facing her. If circumstances were different—if Rhys Griffith were not what he was—she would have welcomed his proposal. Even now she could feel the strong heartbeat that had moved against her own terrified fluttering one. She had been grateful for the strength of his arms, as he had carried her away from that disastrous scene of death. She had known, instinctively, that he would deal with the crisis: comfort her mother and *grandmère*, as he had striven to comfort her; deal firmly but kindly with frightened servants and competently with the household concerning the services, which must be performed; greet the priest when he arrived. Could any man do more for his neighbours and friends? For all the this time, since they had met in Milford haven, she had fought against the deepening feelings she had for this man, flailed at her own weakening emotions, when she had thrilled at his nearness, known the wild excitement, when he had held her close, or simply lifted her to the saddle, in a simple act of courtesy only.

Her grandfather had said Rhys Griffith had professed his love for her. Was it true? He had offered for her, knowing that she could bring nothing of monetary value to the marriage bed. Was that proof that he truly loved her? Could she trust him? Was his interest in her—and in the Grettons—heightened by the knowledge that their secrets could be invaluable, if revealed to his sovereign? And yet her grandfather knew him, must have considered his own danger and yet—he trusted him. Could she do the same? Could she allow her longing heart its way at last? Was it possible that she could lower her defences and give Rhys Griffith the right to penetrate to her most secret desires? Dare she admit, to herself, that she loved him?

It was what her grandfather had wished for her—his very last wish. Could she deny him? What would her father's answer be? She must, of course, wait for that.

She stood up woodenly when Gwenny, her cheeks tearstained, and eyelids red with weeping unrestrainedly, approached.

"Oh, mistress, what can I say? We all loved Sir Daniel and—"

"I know, Gwenny," Philippa said quietly as she put her hand within that of her maid. She was beginning to control the first wild passion of grief and she took, gratefully, the white linen kerchief which Gwenny offered, and ineffectually began to dab at her eyes. She could remove the stains and wetness, but her own swollen and reddened lids would proclaim to the household how terrible had been her ordeal.

Resolutely she thrust to the back of her mind the inner struggle, which had been the cause of her despair. "We must go to my mother. They will wish me to help with—with the laying out," she whispered brokenly, "then the priest will be here and we must offer the services for the dead."

"There will be others to do that for him," Gwenny murmured soulfully. "Sir Rhys said I was to take you to your chamber for a while, that you were dreadfully shocked, the first person to realise—oh." She began to sob again piteously. "Oh, mistress, how terrible for you that you were alone with him."

Philippa compressed her lips. Would Rhys Griffith reveal to her mother that she had been so terribly distressed because she and her *grandpère* had quarrelled? If so, her mother would be aware of the cause of his excitement and the following seizure. Would she ever be forgiven?

She began to walk slowly and reluctantly towards the house, turning to try to catch a glimpse of the carrying chair and its silent, motionless figure but, already servants had arrived and were preparing to carry their dead master indoors. She gave a little shudder and turned back to Gwenny.

They were passing the stable when a sudden flurry of hoofs alerted her to the fact that a visitor had arrived at this most inappropriate moment. A single groom came to take the newcomer's leading rein as he sprang down. Philippa half-turned, curious, then stood stock-still, eyes widening in yet more shock. There was no mistaking that tall figure, imperious in bearing, despite the homespun and workworn garments of a messenger. The man handed his horse into the care of the stable boy and followed him inside. Gwenny was staring at her mistress, puzzled as she gently urged her with a light touch upon her arm further towards the door of the house.

Philippa forced herself to move from the spot, to walk on as if nothing more unusual had occurred, as if the man who had arrived was of no interest to her. Her whole body screamed out its need to rush into the house and seek out her mother, blurt out her news with its stark warning.

The Earl of Wroxeter, her father, had just ridden into the courtyard—and Rhys Griffith was still in the house.

Chapter Six

Philippa found her mother and grandmother in the hall overseeing the setting up of a trestle table to receive Sir Daniel's body. Two of the older women servants had already arrived with an ewer of warm water, towels and sweet-scented salve for anointing. She hastened to stand beside her mother, looking anxiously around for sign of Sir Rhys Griffith. Then she discovered that he was at the door, beckoning in the men bringing in the carrying chair with its sad burden. It had been a more difficult task than usual lifting it up the steps before the hall door, since the men were afraid to jar it unduly. Philippa gave a little smothered sob and her mother reached out and touched her arm in comfort. The Countess and Lady Gretton appeared calm, though it was plain to see that both women had been weeping.

Philippa watched while the chair was brought close to the trestle and the body of her beloved grandfather carefully lifted and laid out reverently upon it. Lady Gretton bent to kiss the already cooling forehead. Sir Rhys nodded to the two men to retreat with the chair, acknowledging the sorrowing womenfolk with a grave little bow.

"Ladies, I will leave you now to your sad task and wait in the courtyard for the arrival of the priest, acquaint him with the full circumstances of what has occurred and bring him to you here."

Lady Gretton nodded her gratitude. "I am thankful that you were here to order matters for us in such a seemly manner, Sir Rhys," she said quietly. "I am sure there must be much to be done on your own manor. Please do not think you must linger here."

"I shall remain until I am satisfied that all is done which must be done and am sure you have no further need of me."

He bowed again, his eyes passing to Philippa's forlorn little figure, longing to put his arms about her openly and comfort her, yet knowing that could not be—yet.

She acknowledged his presence with a wan little smile. "As ever we are in your debt, sir."

He moved to the screen door and when he had withdrawn she put a hand upon her mother's arm and shook it gently but with a real sense of urgency.

"Ma mère, I would speak to you within your chamber."

The Countess frowned. "Child, you can see that it is impossible for me to leave your grandmother at this time."

Lady Gretton shook her head sadly. She put out a hand and touched Philippa's hand reassuringly. "This is a difficult time for you, child, one to which you are not accustomed. I pray the Virgin such an occasion will not come to you again for a long time. You must be deeply shocked, having been with him when—when it happened."

"Nevertheless, Philippa must realise how necessary

it is that I stay with you now, Mother,'' the Countess said firmly. ''She should go to her own chamber until she is more in control but I see Gwenny is with you, child, and you must manage alone, for a while at least. I will come to you when I can.''

Philippa looked at her piteously. ''My need is urgent, ma mère. You must know I would not ask else.''

Lady Gretton glanced hastily at Philippa and recognised that her pale face was not only revealing signs of shock and grief but real alarm. She said quietly, ''I think you should go with her, Cressida. Philippa is no foolish child to have a fit of the vapours whatever the cause. Go and speak with her.''

The Countess shrugged helplessly, then bent and kissed her dead father upon the cheek, nodded to the two silent attendants and pushed Philippa gently towards the spiral stair which led upwards to their bed chambers. Philippa turned at its foot and dismissed Gwenny, who was wringing her hands within her apron and hovering nearby, uncertainly.

''Gwenny, go and find Master Fairley and ask him to come to the Countess's chamber as soon as he can.''

Glad of something to do at such a difficult time Gwenny sped off, thankfully, upon her errand.

Once within their chamber, Cressida Telford faced her daughter almost angrily, then, yet more irritated as Philippa waited to bar the door against any possible intruder.

''Philippa, what can possibly cause you to act in this way now?'' She broke off abruptly as, like her mother, she saw also how pale and frightened Philippa truly was.

Now Philippa wasted no more time, having established that they were closeted together in private. ''Father rode in as I crossed the courtyard. He is dressed as a serving man and is unlikely to be instantly recognised, but Rhys Griffith is still here and soon the priest will arrive and many other notables from the district to pay their respects. Some of our neighbours may well remember the Earl from past dealings.''

Cressida's face whitened and she sank down upon the bed, a trembling hand to her lips.

''You are sure—?''

''Of course I am sure. How could I be mistaken— even under such grievous circumstances?''

''Is he alone?''

Philippa nodded. ''He went into the stables. Does the head groom know him?''

''Yes, and will take precautions to see that your father remains well hidden for the present, be assured of that, but, as you say, this is the worst possible moment for him to arrive and we must take every care.''

There was a knock upon the door and Philippa hurried close to it to call, ''Who is it?''

''Peter, my lady.''

She fumbled to unlatch it and let him in.

He bowed to them both. Clearly he had been hurrying. ''My apologies, my lady, for being absent from the manor at this time of grief. I have just ridden in.''

''Did you go into the stable?'' Philippa interrupted him.

''No.'' He looked from one to the other of them, sensing something was wrong, even of more moment than the sudden death of Sir Daniel. ''Gwenny was in the courtyard and she insisted I come at once to your chamber. She it was who informed me—told me that Sir Daniel had died very suddenly. I left my horse in the care of a groom and came at a run. I could see that

Lady Gretton was in the hall—'' He broke off, averting his eyes from the naked grief he saw reflected in the gaze of the two who faced him.

''My father rode into the courtyard less than an hour ago, when they were—carrying my *grandpère*...'' Philippa turned away then hastily back to him. ''Sir Rhys Griffith is still here and there will be other visitors arriving soon, the priest...''

Peter nodded hastily. ''Where is he now, Lady Philippa? Have you spoken with him?''

''No, I had no opportunity. Gwenny was with me. He is disguised, but—''

''But there will be many notables hereabouts who will still remember him,'' Peter agreed.

''Our head groom will keep him within the stable for now, but—'' the Countess said distractedly.

''I will go at once, my lady, and make arrangements to get him to safety, at least until nightfall.'' He considered. ''There must be trusted servants who will shelter him. He came here once or twice after your marriage and was well loved.''

''Indeed, yes,'' Cressida breathed. ''Our blacksmith, Rob Taylor, lives within the manor precincts. I am sure he would shelter my lord Martyn for the moment, but while the funeral arrangements are in prospect he should be got away soon, from the house, to Ludlow possibly.''

Peter smiled somewhat ruefully. ''My lord will not go without seeing you both, I wager, my lady, but he will see the need for added caution.'' His brows drew together. ''I cannot imagine what has brought him here, now, when all in the country are talking of the recent death of Prince Arthur and how the King, desirous to make a new marriage for the Infanta, has ordered his officials to ensure that all is quiet within the realm and any malcontents arrested. My lord is well aware of that.''

Philippa was about to answer, then bit back her suggestion. She knew that her father was angered by the scurrilous report of Sir James Tyrell's alleged confession to the murder of the Princes, but her father had known of that for some time. Had he come to the manor to investigate, in person, the possibility of an arranged marriage between herself and Rhys Griffith? If so, she had placed him in danger. Her *grandpère* had said something about consulting him, yet he must have been very near to Gretton to receive such a message so soon.

Her mother turned to her, noting her increased distress. ''Philippa, you will be the best person to keep Sir Rhys Griffith occupied and well away from the stable while Peter makes arrangements for your father's safety.'' She had made no attempt to wrap up the fact that the family was well aware of Sir Rhys's determination to make her his bride. Philippa bit her lip uncertainly. She had no wish, at this moment, to deliberately play to his desires, yet she knew well that at this hazardous time everything depended upon her. She bowed her head obediently as Peter ducked his head courteously to her mother and hastened from the chamber. He had had no time to offer his formal condolences. These normal courtesies must be set aside in face of a possible disaster. The Earl of Wroxeter must not be taken at Gretton—for the sake of everyone within the manor, as well as his own.

Cressida appealed to Philippa wordlessly as she took both her daughter's hands within her own. ''Be very careful. Keep Rhys Griffith from the stable as long as you possibly can. Naturally he will announce his intention to depart soon and—''

Philippa squeezed her mother's hands reassuringly. "Do not be worried. Go back to Grandmother and act normally. When all is clear and Sir Rhys gone from Gretton, I will return to the hall to pray with you before the bier."

She hated deception in any form but, for now, she must behave as the distressed woman he had seen in the garden, a woman who needed his comfort. Not that I do not, she reflected inwardly, but I am not so poor spirited a creature that I would break down now, when all have need of me.

A brief glimpse into the hall, as she sped towards the screen door, told her that her grandmother and the two attendant women were still engaged in their melancholy task.

Sir Rhys was still in the courtyard, apparently waiting for the priest to arrive, and in talk with Sir Daniel's steward. Gwenny was emerging from the dairy and Philippa thought she had probably been gossiping with one of her friends. She summoned her as she approached Sir Rhys.

He turned at once and issued some instruction to their steward. He could see the marks of recent tears still upon her cheeks and came to her at once. "You should be resting, Lady Philippa."

She gave a deliberately hasty glance, first at the steward and then at Gwenny. "I—I would have talk with you, sir, in private," she faltered, "perhaps within the garden…"

He took her arm at once sympathetically and led her through the rose arch, nodding to Gwenny to keep some distance behind them.

"Is your grandmother unwell, or your mother?"

She gave a little shuddering breath. "They are obviously deeply upset but—are engaged in the laying out…'' She half turned away. She had no need to assume deep distress. She could still not come to terms with the way her grandfather had died, believing that she was the cause, and her heart was pounding within her breast as she realised how close to arrest her father could be. She could not lose them both in one day. That would be too cruel.

She turned back to Sir Rhys. ''They are both so dreadfully shocked that I would not have them discover…''

He took her to the bench where he had conducted her first after his discovery of Sir Daniel's body. ''Sit down, Lady Philippa, you must be feeling faint. Your maid is within call.''

''I must beg of you…'' she turned a piteous countenance towards him ''…not to reveal to my mother and *grandmère* just how—how you found me.''

''I will not say anything which you do not wish me to say, Lady Philippa, but I say again, you have no call to reproach yourself. Your grandfather's death was brought about by nothing you did.''

''But it was,'' she insisted. ''I—we—quarrelled. I upset him by countering his wishes. He got agitated…''

He sighed. ''Unfortunately, in your grandfather's state, any small incident that occurred which might have annoyed him could have brought about severe agitation…''

''There you are, then, I did cause his death. If my grandmother were to discover that she would be further hurt…''

''I assure you, she will discover nothing of this from me.'' He frowned slightly. ''Though I confess, I am at a loss to consider how anything your grandfather de-

manded of you could have caused such a violent revulsion to the suggestion.''

She took further refuge in tears, unwilling to provide
him with an answer to that question. ''It was just
that—'' she gulped ''—you know how anxious he was
to ensure my safety and, after what happened to poor
Nan Freeman, he ordered me to remain close to the
manor house. Foolishly, I argued with him about it.''

''I see.'' He gave a faint smile. ''I can understand
your unwillingness to be confined, Lady Philippa, but
this was such a small matter. I am sure that had he not—
had things turned out differently, he would have relented and allowed you more freedom, provided that
you were accompanied by a responsible servant or, perhaps, by your father's squire.''

She detected, as usual, a faint note of disapproval
when he mentioned Peter. He looked down her at
gravely and she avoided his eye. She could not let him
know that she was aware of his offer for her hand—
certainly not now. Her heart was pounding again and
she felt a real physical ache in the knowledge that his
nearness was agitating her. Earlier, in the first full, terrible access of her grief, he had held her close and she
had never felt so safe with any man, save her father. At
this moment she longed for him to put his arms around
her again and hold her close, assure her that nothing
else could possibly go wrong, that he would keep her
and hers clear of all harm. She could have appealed to
him, she knew that. One tiny gesture, one word of
weakness on her part and he would do so, but she could
not. She must keep him at arm's length, while encouraging him to believe that she relied upon him, needed
him. She must do this until she was assured that her
father was ensconced in a place of safety, or until Sir

Rhys left the manor. Only then could they all breathe again. Grief and terror were tearing her apart.

He was standing before her, looking deeply into her eyes, and she knew he was uncertain how to behave at this moment, longing to take advantage of her distress yet unwilling to give rein to this base urge which he thought unworthy of him. She looked slightly to his right, not wishing to meet his anxious gaze and saw with relief that Peter had arrived at the rose arch and was talking to Gwenny. Her maid was gesturing towards the bench and Peter started towards the two of them. Hastily Philippa rose to her feet at his approach, her eyes appealing to him for reassurance.

"The priest has arrived, Sir Rhys," Peter said quietly. "I came in search of Lady Philippa, thinking she would wish to be present when he begins his prayers for the dead."

"Indeed," Sir Rhys replied, "and I do not wish to intrude. Assure Lady Gretton that a messenger to my manor can bring me the moment she has need of any service I can render her."

He bowed to Philippa and tentatively she offered him her hand, which he turned over and kissed upon the palm. "Try to accept what happened as natural and right, Lady Philippa. Your grandfather loved you dearly, as he has told me many times. Your presence here had given him joy. He would not wish you to make yourself too unhappy in the future. He would want you to look back on this short time you had together with pleasure. I know it does not seem like that to you now but later, I am sure, your lady mother will be able to convince you that it was so."

Her fingers trembled within his hold. He bowed

stiffly to Peter and strode off towards the entrance to the stables.

Philippa let out a pent-up breath. "I tried to keep him occupied until—until—"

Peter took her chilled fingers and began to guide her back to the manor house. "All is well, the Earl is safely hidden. I will conduct your father to see you both when it is safe to do so. Come now back into the hall."

At the door to the hall they could hear through the screen doors the murmur of voices together in prayers for the dead, led by the village priest. Peter bent very low to whisper in Philippa's ear as she was about to pass through, "You should be too distressed to sleep without your mother close tonight. Remain with her in her chamber and keep Gwenny in yours."

She glanced at him searchingly and he nodded, then he led her into the hall and, together, they approached the bier.

It was a simple matter to do as Peter suggested. Gwenny readily accepted Philippa's avowed need to sleep in her mother's bed. When the thick oaken door was closed on the maid, Philippa was convinced she would soon fall asleep and allow her mother and herself private talk with her father. Lady Gretton had gone to her own chamber, worn out with grief and worry about the future and Cressida drew her daughter into her bed and held her close. Both wept silently and Philippa was glad of her mother's nearness as, despite the summer evening, she felt chilled.

When she heard Peter's soft scratching upon the outer chamber door she slipped from the bed and let him and his hooded and cloaked companion in.

The Earl swept his daughter into his arms then gently,

hurriedly, pushed her away and went to the bed where his wife sat waiting. Over his shoulder he said softly, "Keep watch outside, Peter."

His squire hastened to do his bidding and Philippa watched him leave, then anxiously barred the door from within. She stood back a little, her heart beating so fast she thought it would burst from the cage of her ribs as she watched her parents embrace hungrily. She had always known how deeply they loved each other and the sacrifices Cressida had made, cheerfully, in order to remain with her husband in exile. Dully she wondered if she would know such happiness, even if she should only have it for short snatches of time as her parents had.

At last Wroxeter turned to his daughter and, seated upon the bed with one arm tightly clasped round his wife's shoulder, drew her, also, into the embrace. "My two darlings," he whispered hoarsely, "how I have longed to hold you close and comfort you from the moment I arrived and heard the news. I had hoped to speak with Daniel before—" He shook his head angrily as his wife made a conscious effort to stem her tears. He addressed Philippa, glancing towards the door between his wife's and daughter's chamber. "You have a maid?"

Philippa nodded. "I am sure she is fast asleep. She is very young and always does so quickly. The door is very stout, as are all the walls, and I doubt she could hear us if we speak softly. Are you safely bestowed?"

"Yes, with Taylor, the blacksmith, he would never betray me, nor, I think, would Daniel's steward or many of the household, but it is as well if the fewer, rather than the many, know of my presence here, for their own sakes." He grimaced. "My timing is bad. The house will be full of county nobles by the morrow until after the funeral. I need to get to Ludlow and find quiet lodgings as soon as possible. Young Richard Allard is there; he met me when I landed and has been with me since. He will arrange a safe lodging for me if Peter can reach him there tomorrow. He must find some errand which necessitates him leaving the manor house.''

While he was speaking Philippa was taking in the beloved lineaments of his face; the dark hair, still thick and plentiful, but greying now at the temples, the long face with the thick, black brows and the heavy-lidded eyes that gave their owner a sleepy appearance, which belied the brilliance of the man. How big he was, and strong still; so reassuring to be held close in those muscular arms which had lifted her high and swung her round in play during childhood. Tears came thick and fast as she thought how much she loved him and feared for his peril, yet it was so good to have him here, if only for so short a time as they dared manage together.

Her mother said quietly, ''You know how wonderful it is for us to see you, Martyn, especially at this time of sorrow, when we need your love so badly, but tell us why you are here. Is it for political reasons? If so, when my father says the King is over-anxious concerning security, was it not unwise to venture here?''

''Yes, my heart, and you know well I do not always consider my own safety as paramount, not even when I should spare you your fears. I came for two reasons: first, to test out the reaction of our Yorkist friends to this scurrilous and baseless accusation against the late King which was published following Tyrell's execution. The Duchess Margaret, naturally, is deeply distressed by it and needs to know how it will affect the loyalty of those who profess themselves still true to us.''

Philippa murmured, ''More than likely Sir James was tortured while in the King's hands and forced to sign a confession. You know that Richard Allard was, and could have been, more badly manhandled had not the Queen come to his rescue. If such was the case we have to excuse Sir James, surely.''

''Of course, if that were the case, I would be the first to do so,'' her father said, tautly, ''but I think it more likely the confession was never made at all. It would be a simple matter for the King's minions to say what they liked after the man was safely dead and could not refute the accusation. Tyrell was never my favourite person, but he served the late King faithfully and for a time was entrusted with the security of the young Princes. I am here to ensure our friends know, without a semblance of doubt, that both Princes were living until after the fatal summer of 1485 and that I can personally assure them of that.''

Philippa said, ''I believe that Richard Allard was convinced that Perkin Warbeck was the younger Prince. He saw him with young Warwick and said the likeness was uncanny, even though he had doubted earlier when he had served Perkin in the field.''

''Mmm.''

Philippa noted that her father neither refuted nor accepted the comment and she added, ''Richard also said that there was a possibility that another Prince was still living in secrecy in the north. He mentioned it because Jake Garnet and his son-in-law, Josh, from the Golden Cockerel inn, which served as a Yorkist safe base, were headed there when we were forced to leave London after helping Richard escape.''

Her father shot her a frowning glance at this and she flushed doubtfully, fearing that she had touched on some fact he would rather she had not known. He gave a slight shrug. ''Who knows? There were many ru-

mours, as we are all too well aware. I only know that
their uncle certainly did not murder them. Indeed, why
should he do so when young Warwick, his nephew, who
some said had more rightful claim to the throne, was
left living to challenge him for it at some later date?''
He gave a little irritated moue. ''I wonder that any sensible soul can believe such a tale? Would it have been
possible to conceal the bodies when Henry took possession of the Tower so soon after Redmoor and all
servants and officials questioned and threatened with
torture, as they assuredly must have been? But folk have
ever been ready to listen to scurrilous gossip about their
betters, especially gossip so ardently fed to them and
concerning murder! If Henry is so sure now, having
obtained a confession, why has he not had the bodies
exhumed? Apparently the tale appears to tell where the
murderers put their victims? No, it is my work to seek
out the truth of all this and know whether or not the
confession was indeed fabricated or obtained, as you
say, under duress, as the Warbeck confession undoubtedly was.''

Cressida gave a great start. ''But to go near any of
the officials at this time would be putting your own head
in the noose, Martyn. Now that my father is dead…''

''I know,'' he said gravely. ''Under the circumstances, I must put your safety first and get you and
Philippa back to Burgundy the moment the obsequies
are over—that is, unless…'' he turned to Philippa
searchingly ''…what Daniel informed me in his letter
is true, which was that Rhys Griffith has offered for
your hand and that you would be willing to grant it.''

Philippa put a hand to her mouth to cover her sudden
cry of distress. ''You came to see for yourself…''

''I did indeed. You are very precious to me, Philippa.

I had to know from your own lips what you wished me to reply to this request.''

"You cannot be serious, Father. The man's father fought for King Henry…''

"I know that well enough, Philippa, but Rhys himself was scarcely more than a boy at the time of Redmoor and you not even conceived. What we have to consider is what is best for you now—in the present.''

She said, dully, "And you consider this best for me, to be wed to the man who inherited your lands, those which were won by his own father's treachery?''

He reached forward and ruffled her bright hair. "Your grandfather indicated that he believed you had some tender feelings for the man. Can that be true?''

She was about to refute the assertion then found she could not, and be true to herself.

"I believe him to be a good man,'' she said falteringly, "fair to his servants and those under his command and—and he has been good to me, rescued me from several dangerous situations. He has never…'' she hesitated "…offered me any discourtesy nor even spoken of his desire—'' She broke off, confused.

"And you, what are your feelings? It could be a fair match, Philippa, despite all considerations to the contrary. You would have a secure future and I could wish you to be able to stay here in your native land and live in peace, but I would not force you to this. If you could live in amity with this man, of whom I have heard many good reports, I would be willing to give my consent, though parting with you will cost me dear.''

"I should not be able to see you and Mother again, be parted from you for ever,'' she murmured brokenly.

"Not necessarily. If you obtained your husband's consent, you could visit us in Burgundy.''

"But there would be a risk. If at any time I should unwittingly betray your confidence to him…"

His expression became grave. "So, you have considered that, therefore you have also thought of a possible future with Rhys Griffith."

She hung her head. She could never lie to her father nor yet avoid a direct answer. "Yes," she whispered so softly that he had to bend close to catch her answer. "Yes, if I am honest with myself, I have found at times that—that his nearness excites me and against my own will I am stirred to tender thoughts of him. Whatever is decided, I wish him happiness."

His touch upon her hair was gentle and affectionate. "I think, already, I have lost you, child. No loving father is ever willing to give away his chick, especially if that chick is his only one and doubly precious, but no loving father puts his own desires first either but must give way and decide what is best for his beloved." He bent and lifted her chin so that she was gazing up into his eyes. "This is a time of deep emotional turmoil, Philippa. You must make no hasty decisions while your heart sorrows, but your final yea or nay must be soon. I would have your answer before I am forced to leave the realm. You understand?"

She nodded and he released her chin and turned to his wife, who had remained thoughtfully silent throughout the exchange between father and daughter. "You have met this man and would approve the match?"

"Yes, Martyn, I would. Rhys Griffith loves Philippa deeply, I am convinced of it and, from what I have observed of his conduct, I am sure he would make her a loving and considerate husband. But," she added, "like you, I would not have her over-pressed to accept him against her own strong convictions."

He took her into his arms and kissed her again. "I must go, my heart. I will try to see you both again before I leave the country."

"Take no foolish risks…"

"I swear I will not." He sighed. "I would that I could stand beside you openly at this time of sorrow, but I should only endanger you all. Daniel knew well in his heart how I trusted and admired him. He will rest in his grave knowing he kept faith."

Philippa ran into her father's arms, wetting his rough homespun jerkin with her tears, then she unlatched the door and stood back as it was opened. Peter Fairley appeared and nodded that all was well. The Earl took one quick glance backwards, saying, "Send me word of your decision soon, Philippa, and the Virgin guide you well in your choice." Then he was gone and mother and daughter sank back again on the bed clinging tightly to each other for comfort and weeping bitterly.

Both women slept badly and Philippa was in a sorrowful and distressed mood as she went down to breakfast. Her grandmother, naturally, had much upon her mind and appeared distracted. There was still much to be arranged and the moment the hasty meal was over she left them to go to the kitchens to ensure that guests arriving for the funeral on the morrow would be well provided for. The Countess was silent. She sat, nervously pleating the skirts of her black mourning gown. A similar one had been provided for Philippa, but it had had to be altered in haste for it was far too large, having been her grandmother's and a tearful Gwenny had been left to complete the stitching. The girl did not appear to have noted anything unusual during the night and repeatedly said how she had slept heavily, worn out by the stresses of the day before.

"Oh, mistress," she whispered forlornly, as she dressed Philippa's bright hair, "who would have thought your visit would have ended so badly? Sir Daniel, he could be strict, but he was a good master for all that, and we all loved him."

"Thank you, Gwenny, it is good of you to be so consoling. It will be a difficult time for all of us over the next few days and we must try not to distress Lady Gretton by our own show of sorrow any more than we can help. She has much to bear and will need our practical help."

She went down into the hall and viewed her grandfather's corpse, now decently clad in his best and washed and anointed. Her mother knelt with other members of the household at his side and Philippa bent and kissed the stone-cold features. Her tears came freely again as she felt convinced she had brought about his hasty passing by her own stubbornness.

She whispered in her mother's ear, "I would like to go into Ludlow with Peter, if I can be spared."

The Countess rose and moved away from the bier with her. "There is little you can do here today, but is that wise?"

Philippa avoided her mother's gaze, staring across to the glazed window above the small dais where the family sat at meals.

"I feel so—confused," she said wretchedly. "I cannot come to terms with any of this and—and I feel I cannot meet Sir Rhys again so soon until I—I have made my decision. His presence—disturbs me. He will be here soon to support Grandmother, I am sure of it, and I need to be away—just for a little time."

Cressida considered and finally nodded. "Yes, perhaps that is just as well. I know, from experience, how momentous such a decision can be and—and you have much to bear at present. Peter is to see Richard Allard and that may cheer you somewhat. He will be able to tell you news of Anne. I know you miss her companionship sorely." She hesitated then said quickly, "You would be enabled to see more of Anne and Richard if—if you agree to remain in England."

Philippa turned back to her, gazing up into her mother's lovely eyes directly, then she gave a heavy sigh and inclined her chin. "Our first need is to ensure Father's safety. Do you think he will endanger himself with his need to meet with other Yorkists at this time?"

"I fear so, but I am used to living with this danger." Her mother's smile was a trifle bitter. "It is the price of true love, Philippa."

Philippa recalled, as she made her way to the stables to discover if Peter had yet left the manor, that her dear friend, Anne, had been equally reluctant to give herself to Richard for the same reason and had confessed to Philippa that this constant fear for the safety of the loved one had torn her own mother apart and would do the same for her if she was foolish enough to give way to her heart's wish. Yet she had done so. She had married her Richard and gone into exile with him, parting from all she loved at home, for the first months at least. Could, she, Philippa, commit herself to Rhys Griffith, allow the first stirrings of desire to grow and be fanned in to flames of passion? For today at least she must stay far from him while she carefully worked out what her answer to her father would be.

She found Peter and, though he was reluctant to take

her with him, he agreed finally and they rode out together. He seemed preoccupied and she did not press him to talk. Either his thoughts were concerned with arrangements to take his master to a place of safety or he had been told of one of the reasons for the Earl's presence at Gretton and was disturbed by the thought of Philippa's impending decision. Guiltily she remembered that Rhys Griffith believed Peter Fairley entertained tender thoughts towards her and, since she could in no way return them, she was uncomfortable in his presence for the first time since childhood. She was deeply fond of Peter, but always had considered him as friend, almost the brother she had never had, and thoughts of love between them had simply never entered her head.

Ludlow was busy since it was market day and Peter led her to an inn near the castle, the Golden Fleece. A whispered discussion with the burly innkeeper was followed by his return to her side with the information that Master Allard was lodged in the front private chamber and believed to be there. They climbed the stair and were admitted after a knock and an announcement of their identities.

Philippa was overjoyed to see Richard, after an interval of almost four years and he hugged her warmly. He did not appear to be changed, only the little laughter lines around his eyes had deepened and, as usual, his abundant brown hair was unruly and needed a comb.

He seated her upon the bed, for the chamber was small and cramped and boasted little furniture and, after asking after her need of refreshment and discovery that she required nothing, turned his attention to Peter.

''I imagine some crisis has arisen or you would not have sought me out so soon.''

Peter put him in the picture immediately and Richard's normally jovial expression became grave.

"I am so sorry about your grandfather," he said, turning to Philippa, "but I can see the urgent need to get your father away from Gretton. There must be many of the guests expected to attend the funeral who know him."

Peter said brusquely, "That is all very well, Richard, but you know my lord Earl. He is determined to complete his mission. There are several people in the area he wishes to see and I cannot persuade him to leave for the coast at once which I consider advisable."

Richard Allard stroked his chin thoughtfully. "Sir Owen Lewis owns a manor some twenty miles from here. He was my father-in-law Sir Guy Jarvis's squire and, though he later fought for the Tudor at Redmoor, he was sufficiently loyal enough to his old master to help me when I was in trouble at Westminster. It might be possible for me to go and sound him out and discover if he would be willing to accommodate the Earl and I just for the next few days. His house would be the safest place possible. He has served the present King and would be regarded as thoroughly trustworthy, unlikely to receive a company of officials poking their noses into his business."

"But can he be trusted?" Philippa burst out.

"Sir Owen could very well refuse outright to shelter a man he considers a rebel, but I do not believe he would betray us," Richard said bluntly. "I can think of no other safe house for the present. Like Peter here, my advice to your father would be to leave the district at once but I doubt he would heed it."

Philippa swallowed hard. She was only too well aware that what both said of her father was true. She said awkwardly, "Peter, could you go below and order dinner for us all here later? I—I would talk privately with Richard for a while."

Peter cast her a hasty glance, but rose at once to do her bidding.

Richard Allard noted the marks of recent tears upon Philippa's cheeks and her somewhat hunted expression, which puzzled him. Grief he expected, but this strange bewilderment he could not understand. He said gently, "Are you in some trouble, Philippa, which you would rather Peter is not aware of?"

"I need to talk to someone who—who knows me and would understand," she said wretchedly. "Since you and Anne are so very dear to me I thought I might confide in you and feel you would advise me as well as Anne would herself."

"Then let us walk for a short while in the town. Will Peter object?"

She shook her head. "I do not think so. He knows—that something is wrong and—and that I cannot unburden myself to him."

He took her arm and led her below stairs. Peter was engaged in talk with the innkeeper and Richard called to him of their intentions. He turned and acknowledged them but made no objection, as Philippa had hoped.

They walked for a short while in silence then Richard said quietly, "Is Peter in love with you, Philippa?"

"I do not know, but I fear he is becoming too aware of me as a woman."

He glanced at her, smiling. "The Virgin knows that would not be difficult for any man. I recognised your growing maturity when we first met in Westminster Palace four years ago. Anne was decidedly jealous, though she would never confess it." He chuckled and Philippa smiled also. She was well aware that though Richard Allard would admire her beauty, his heart was given completely to Anne, his wife, and to her alone. He added reflectively, ''Then if it is not Peter's desires which concern you, who is it?''

She gave a little gasp at his perception. ''Sir Rhys Griffith is our neighbour. He has—proved himself a good friend to my grandparents and has been a constant visitor to Gretton since the day we arrived there; indeed, he happened to meet us first at Milford Haven and escorted us home.''

''Does he know who you are?''

''Yes, and he has asked for my hand. My grandfather wrote to my father requesting an answer and that is one of the reasons why he has come to the manor—to see me in person.''

''And what is his opinion of this match?''

''I think—believe—'' she floundered ''—I think he is in favour of it but—but he leaves the decision to me.''

''And you have some dislike of Griffith, or is that feeling stronger—revulsion, perhaps?''

''No, no, Rhys Griffith is very—personable. He is wealthy and owns my father's lost lands and I—I believe he loves me.''

''And you, what are feelings for him?''

She was silent and he waited patiently for her answer.

''I cannot marry him. He is the King's man,'' she whispered at last uncertainly.

''But that is no answer to my question.''

She turned at last and faced him squarely. ''I am not sure,'' she murmured miserably, ''but—but he excites me and...''

''Oh, indeed?'' Richard's heavy brows rose in

amused interrogation and she turned upon him indignantly.

"Do not tease me, Richard, I implore you. Can I trust him? Would I have to part with my parents for ever?"

He gave a faint shrug. "Who knows, *chérie*? Times change. The King cannot live for ever and, after all, young Henry is Edward IV's grandson. While he will not, I vouch, restore your father's lands, he could well pardon him, as I was pardoned."

"But all the time you must be circumspect—and my father is never that."

"Never," he agreed, a little smile playing about his mobile mouth. "I take it you would be agreeable to the match if you thought you could trust your groom with your father's safety?"

Again she turned away and he waited, then he said, "You know Anne was at first reluctant to trust herself to me because she was afraid of my dangerous activities?"

"Yet you have not changed."

"No, I have not changed, yet she loves me still. Her heart is torn when I am absent from her side, but life with me is preferable to life without me, I imagine. I am a lucky fellow and so is this Griffith, if he has your love."

Her cheeks were colouring rosily and she was about to answer when she found herself accosted by a familiar voice.

"Lady Philippa, I did not expect to find you in Ludlow this morning."

To her dismay, Philippa saw Rhys Griffith across the street and striding determinedly towards them.

Philippa panicked. If Rhys Griffith saw her talking to Richard Allard, he might well suspect that she and Peter had come into Ludlow to meet with him and, worse, guess at the reason for that. As if in answer to her silent prayer, a man's voice at her side said gently, "How good it was of you, Mistress Weston, to come into Ludlow to see how I fared."

She turned, her eyes widening in surprise, to find the young merchant, Master Maynard, leaning heavily on a cane by her side. He still appeared pale and his leg looked to be tightly strapped to some sort of splinted support, but he was smiling and walking gamely though slowly. Rhys Griffith reached them at the very moment she opened her lips to reply to the merchant's greeting. She saw that he was frowning but, obviously prevented from questioning her, as she feared, by the presence of her two companions.

Master Maynard addressed him. "I understand, Sir Rhys, that I am under an obligation to you for the care afforded to me. I am most grateful. Unfortunately it will be some time yet before I am able to leave Ludlow but, as I am sure Mistress Weston here is anxious to discover, I am progressing very nicely."

Rhys Griffith forced a smile. "So I see," he observed. He looked pointedly towards Richard Allard who was silently waiting to see how matters progressed, surveying the newcomer with interest. Philippa could hardly avoid introducing Richard to Griffith.

"Master Allard, Sir Rhys Griffith, our neighbour, who has been most kind to us at Gretton, especially during the unfortunate circumstances of my kinsman's death. Master Allard is an acquaintance, his wife my very dearest friend. I was amazed to find that he is here in Ludlow on business. I came, as Master Maynard observed, to see for myself how he is."

She was surprised to find that her voice had not trembled, though her legs felt like water, and she met Rhys Griffith's challenging stare directly. "Since Peter and I were the first to discover Master Maynard injured, I felt it incumbent upon me to see how he was."

Rhys Griffith bowed somewhat frigidly to Richard Allard who responded, smilingly, his grey eyes twinkling. Philippa had observed from experience that Richard could behave with perfect aplomb during difficult and dangerous encounters.

Rhys said tartly, "You will realise that Mistress Weston is in mourning and will be unable to stay from Gretton long. You say that you were escorted by your squire, Master Fairley? Where is he?" The note was steely and she forced a confident smile. "He is enquiring in the Golden Fleece for Master Maynard, but I came out to get some air and happened to see him walking and was delighted to note how well he is. Master Allard also happens to be lodged at the inn and we were exchanging news of our families."

Rhys Griffith nodded. "I imagine you have business in Ludlow, Master Allard. If I am not mistaken, your father's lands are in Yorkshire."

Richard inclined his head. "Yes, and my mother inherited lands in the Cotswolds, near Tewkesbury. I am visiting some acquaintance of hers, who lives in this district."

So Rhys Griffith was well aware of the circumstances of Richard's father's standing in the Yorkist community and was making it clear to them.

Maynard's wide, guileless blue eyes regarded the group jovially. "I am sorry to hear of the death of your kinsman, Mistress Weston. It is a kindness indeed that you found that you could spare the time to enquire after my trifling injuries."

Philippa found herself wondering why the man was so anxious to cover up for her. Had he merely observed her unease when she had seen Sir Rhys approaching and, by quickness of thought, decided to help her? She shot him a relieved glance and found him smiling at her in a friendly but not too familiar manner, though she thought Sir Rhys would probably regard the man's demeanour as insolent. Sir Rhys had been so openly hostile when he had discovered the injured man upon his property that it was no surprise to her that Maynard had guessed at her discomfiture. She herself had been amazed and yet pleased to learn that Sir Rhys had put himself out to attend to the fellow's needs. However, he had warned her against meeting the merchant again and she knew he was displeased if not downright angry to discover her disobeying him and present in Ludlow.

However, he regarded Roger Maynard dispassionately and said, "You do not appear well enough to be out and about at present. Should you not be back at the inn? Are you not comfortably settled?"

"Certainly, Sir Rhys. Your arrangements for me are excellent. Since it is market day I came to see if the horse coper could provide me with a docile mount for my journey. Alas, he had nothing suitable which I could afford."

Sir Rhys sniffed. "What you need is a sturdy little Welsh pony. I will see that the blacksmith in the village finds you one to carry you home. You need not concern yourself about the cost. Since I was forced to dispatch your horse I am prepared to provide a mount for you to travel."

Philippa was puzzled as to why he should go to so much trouble for a man he apparently still mistrusted, but she could only admit that he was being generous in the extreme. For some reason he was determined to be rid of the man as soon as decently possible.

Sir Rhys said abruptly, "Perhaps, Master Allard, you would assist Master Maynard to the inn. I am sure he has been on that injured leg for too long as it is." Pointedly he added, "I will escort Mistress Weston to the Golden Fleece in a few moments and then, once she is reunited with her squire, back home."

Philippa's heart sank. Not only was she to be deprived of Richard's company and assurances that he would make arrangements for her father, but she would have to account to Rhys Griffith for her absence from Gretton at a time when she would have been expected to be there, assisting her mother and grandmother with all that needed to be done before the funeral. Richard bowed and his grey eyes met hers deliberately. She read in them the assurance she needed and made a little curtsy in reply.

"Convey to Anne my love and good wishes for the future, Richard, and kiss your little one for me."

He nodded, smiling, outwardly unaffected by the unwelcome encounter, then he offered an arm to the limping Maynard and turned towards the Golden Fleece.

Before she could move to follow, Rhys Griffith caught at Philippa's arm, his grip hard, and she thought she would see an ugly bruise upon her wrist later.

"What are you doing in Ludlow?" he grated harshly. "Do you not know that the proprieties require you to remain sequestered on the manor at this time?"

She was seething with fury at his assumed domination of her. "I came," she said tartly, "as I explained, to see Master Maynard. Peter was sent to buy more black cloth, which will be required for the servants attending the funeral, and I took the opportunity to accompany him.'' She turned away from his accusing stare. ''You must realise how oppressive it is for me— at—at Gretton at the moment. I needed to get away, if only for an hour or two. There was nothing I could do there.''

He made some slight explosive sound and stood firmly before her, fingers gripped aggressively within his sword belt. ''I warned you not to associate with that merchant.''

''It is not your business to order me, nor yet to issue warnings,'' she flashed back. ''You have no responsibility for me, sir.''

''Not yet,'' he returned grimly. ''Has your mother not informed you that—?''

''Indeed, she has,'' she snapped, ''and let me tell you, sir, the notion does not please me, and less so, having regard to your attitude this morning.''

He relaxed his aggressive stance slightly, reddening, whether with anger or embarrassment she could not tell.

''It is unsafe for you to be associating with known Yorkists,'' he said more mildly. ''Master Allard was forced to leave the country, I understand, following the execution of the Earl of Warwick and the imposter, Perkin Warbeck, under suspicion of trying to arrange their escape from the Tower.''

''He was later pardoned,'' she said acidly, ''and allowed to return to England. His father, Sir Dominick, was wounded at Redmoor and has never completely recovered. He needed Richard's services to run the manor.''

''Nevertheless, you must realise that he will be under constant surveillance,'' he retorted, then more earnestly, ''I have only your safety and that of your mother and grandmother in mind when I remind you of these matters.''

She was somewhat mollified by his change of tone and nodded rather coolly. ''I understand, sir, and I thank you, but say again you have no responsibility to me or mine.''

''But it is the most earnest wish of my heart that I should have, Philippa,'' he said quickly and he reached out and drew her close by the shoulders this time, though less cruelly. She felt the frantic beating of his heart through the thick velvet of his doublet and the thin silk of her gown and she was almost unable to draw breath. She could never understand this strange excitement which gripped her when she was close to him. Other men had admired her beauty and remarked upon it, for, like her mother, she had learned to accept, from an early age, that she was an object of men's desires, and, they, too, had tried to hold her, even to steal illicit kisses, but she had always been able to manage them before. She had laughed good-humouredly at their foolishness or flayed them with her tongue for their insolence, but she felt quite helpless now as Rhys Griffith held her close to his heart. She had not even the strength of mind to struggle and was horribly near to tears, though she had no explanation for this sudden, unfamiliar emotional weakness.

She said at last, ''Please release me, sir. I—I—have no answer for you yet. I—I must have time to think. This is no time for hasty decisions.''

He released her obediently, though he kept still a light grasp upon her arm. ''I love you, Philippa, I cannot help myself. I want you,'' and more thickly and harshly, ''I will have you, whatever the cost.''

''It could be high indeed, sir, consisting of the loss

of royalist friends and, more seriously and dangerously, the loss of the King's good will.''

''Do you not think I have not considered that?''

Knowing him, she was sure he had done so. She said softly, ''But what of the sacrifices I must make?''

''Your father must soon be lost to you. Indeed, every married maiden must part from her family. I know your parents must remain in exile, but if you become my bride I shall allow you to visit them when it is possible and expedient. Your mother will agree to the match, Philippa and I have even sent messages to your father to beg for his consent. Will you not give me your hand in marriage and become mistress of all your father's lost lands?''

She could not reveal to him that her father was only too willing to give his consent. She could only stare back at him dumbly. Perhaps when she knew her father was safe, then—then she might allow the longing within her heart to overcome the fears, which battered at her brain. She shook her head and turned away. ''Take me to the Golden Fleece. Peter will be anxious and we must return to the manor quickly, as you have reminded me, sir.''

He turned towards the inn and then they saw that Peter Fairley was standing at the door surveying the street, obviously concerned about her.

''Very well, I see I must wait for a while longer and this time of grieving is no time to press you, yet I must assure myself of your safety. You must not come again to Ludlow and meet with those who could bring you into danger. Promise me that you will not do so without me in attendance.''

She looked back at him, puzzled. ''What have you against poor Master Maynard?''

"I have no proof of anything, but strangers are suspect at this time. Heed my warnings. I shall be glad when the man is long gone from this district."

"You think he may be a King's official spy?"

He shrugged. "Who knows whom to trust? The King sits still uneasy upon the throne and his eyes and ears are everywhere. You, above all, should be aware of that."

They reached the inn and she smiled at Peter. There was no sign of either Richard Allard, or of Roger Maynard.

"As you see, Peter, I am safe under Sir Rhys's protection. He has offered to escort us home."

That Peter was not pleased she could read in his expression, but he could make no objection. Sir Rhys strode off to order their mounts brought round and Peter mouthed, "Richard will attend to your father's safe lodging. I will bring him to Ludlow under cover of darkness."

She nodded, relieved, as Sir Rhys returned to them, followed by a groom with their horses.

They mounted and took the road together for Gretton Manor.

Chapter Seven

Philippa knelt in the chancel of the parish church beside the newly laid blue slab of Welsh stone which covered her grandfather's grave. Soon the brass designer would come from Bristol to work on the memorial which would show her grandfather in armour as he had been at Redmoor. She had placed a bouquet of late roses on the stone, of several colours, for she'd not dared to put the white roses she would have wished to place there. In these suspicious times that might well have revealed his past allegiance too clearly. She'd begged leave to come alone for it was but a short step from the manor house and her desire to pray before her grandfather's grave by herself had been very pressing.

Lately the house had been full of visitors attending the funeral and solemn requiem and the feast, which had followed. She'd longed to see her father's face though, just once, and when she had visited the grave with her mother the day following the funeral, she had glimpsed a shadowy figure dressed in homespun hovering near the bell tower. Neither she nor her mother had dared to approach the man but her mother's hand, gently pressing her own as they had knelt there, had told Philippa that the Countess was well aware that her husband had risked himself in coming to see for himself where his father-in-law had been bestowed and had hoped to see his wife and daughter there.

Sir Rhys had been present, of course, throughout the solemn proceedings, close to her grandmother's side, ready to offer help and support whenever it had been required. Though he had treated Philippa courteously, he had not once during these early days of mourning pressed her for her answer to his offer of marriage and she knew that he would respect her need for privacy at this time.

Philippa had needed, desperately, to be alone now. She had still not come to terms with what she believed to be her own culpability for Sir Daniel's death. Certainly he had been ill and it was not unexpected but she could still visualise, vividly, their altercation, her own violent reaction to the proposed marriage he had planned for her. She would always feel guilty, though she was aware that she could have acted in no different a fashion.

She gave a sigh as she rose from her kneeling position. There was little chance now for her to have further words with her father. For his own safety he must remain hidden. She and she alone must make this momentous decision and her awkward meeting with Rhys Griffith in Ludlow had only added to her confusion of mind. She was sure that Richard Allard would do everything in his power to ensure that her father reached Sir Owen Lewis's manor and that Sir Dominick Allard's former squire would be willing to offer Wroxeter a safe haven until he could be smuggled to a port and out of England.

She murmured a final hurried prayer and lit a candle

with another prayer to the Virgin, begging for interces-
sion for the safe repose of her grandfather's soul, and
prepared to leave the church. She turned hastily from
the chancel as she heard the sound of booted feet approaching and knew two men were entering the church,
one, or both of them, a knight, by the ring of metal
spurs on stone. For moments they were hidden from her
view by the bulk of the huge ancient stone bowl which
formed the baptismal font.

A familiar voice informed her of Sir Rhys's presence.
"Mistress Weston, I had not expected to see you here
and regret if we have interrupted your most private moment of prayer."

She moved towards him. "Thank you, Sir Rhys, but
I have concluded my prayers and am about to leave."

Her gaze passed to his companion, a tall handsome
man, past his youth but still personable, clearly a knight
by his spurs and attire. He bowed to her as Sir Rhys
presented her.

"Mistress Weston and her mother are kinsmen of Sir
Daniel, Sir Howell. You may well have heard them
mentioned during the days when you were well acquainted with Sir Daniel and Lady Gretton."

"I did not have that pleasure." The voice was pleasant and the stranger eyed her with frank appraisal and
curiosity. He was, perhaps, a little older than Philippa's
mother, a tall, well-built man with a square, tanned,
open countenance, and strong jaw, whose hair was beginning to grey at his temples.

Sir Rhys said, "Sir Howell Prosser was formerly a
neighbour to Sir Daniel and Lady Gretton. He was from
the neighbourhood and, indeed, rarely visits his parents'
manor these days since his marriage and so has only

recently heard of Sir Daniel's death and has come with me this morning to pay his respects.''

Philippa's heart gave a little jolt of alarm. If this man had known her mother in the old days, and it seemed that he had done, could he fail to note her resemblance to Cressida, Countess of Wroxeter, and was his knighthood a mark of his past allegiance to King Henry? If so, her mother must be warned and she herself be wary of what she said to him.

She curtsied. ''Lady Gretton will be pleased to receive you at the manor, Sir Howell. She is still in deep mourning, of course, but all friends are welcome. My mother and I are on a short visit only and have delayed our departure naturally out of her need for company.''

He bowed his head as his eyes roved towards the chancel and she pointed to the new grave slab. ''There is no inscription yet, sir, and a brass will be laid there soon.''

His voice was pleasantly low-pitched and expressed regret. ''I am truly sorry to hear of Sir Daniel's passing. I visited Gretton often in the old days and he was good to me as a boy. Like his daughter, Cressida, I was an only child and often lonely.''

She half-smiled in answer. He had ceased to regard her directly and turned to Sir Rhys. ''I will stay within the church for a while and pray for Sir Daniel's soul. Thank you for your escort, Sir Rhys but I know you have business on your manor and I will not delay you. Mistress,'' he addressed Philippa once more, ''would you please inform Lady Gretton that I will call on her to offer my condolences formally before I leave the district again.''

She curtsied again and, as Sir Rhys moved towards the church door, she was forced to accompany him.

Outside the sun was bright but low in the sky and she was reminded that autumn was on the way and that she and her mother had stayed too long at Gretton and should soon be on their way into exile once more. The village church, of solid Welsh stone, and the cluster of thatched cottages which huddled close beside it was pleasing to her eye as was the rolling hills beyond and she felt a spasm of regret that she must return to the flatter, less visibly interesting, countryside of Burgundy.

Sir Rhys was regarding her with a curious intensity and she flushed hotly under the scrutiny.

"Always I have to thank you, sir, for the kindness you have shown to all of us at this sorry time. I hope..." her voice faltered a little "...that you will continue to visit Gretton from time to time after we have left. My grandmother will have need of you, I am sure."

"And you will not?" he queried.

She lifted tear-brimmed green blue eyes to his dark ones. "Yes, Sir Rhys, I shall continue to have regard for you and deep—gratitude."

He said, a trifle harshly, "I cannot press you at this point, but you know that I hold in my heart far stronger feelings for you than regard, Philippa, and I shall not give up. I shall see you again before you depart and, by that time, I hope you will be in a less distressed state and more ready to accept my suit."

She shook her head, turning from him.

"I regret that our last meeting was less than cordial," he continued, "but I must insist that you take due care. Your presence here, without the protection of my name, could bring you all into real danger. I think you are only too aware of that."

She nodded again.

"Allard has been pardoned, but he will always be carefully watched. He knows that, as well as I do."

"Master Maynard will soon be leaving Ludlow," she said defensively.

"Yes, and I shall not be sorry to see the fellow go."

He turned from her abruptly. "I will not press my attendance upon you for you have only a step or two to go before reaching your manor and there are plenty of servants about to watch over you."

He bowed courteously and moved off towards the fence to which his horse and that of Sir Howell Prosser had been hitched. She watched him go regretfully. Her feelings were so mixed. As he turned once in the saddle to acknowledge her, she forced a smile and began to walk slowly back towards the manor. She hoped she would not see him again. It would be too painful. Her brain was too full of the fear of betrayal while she stayed here and now a new threat had materialised in the person of Sir Howell Prosser.

Her mother and Lady Gretton listened gravely to her tale.

"If he were a constant visitor to the manor he cannot fail to recognise you, ma mère," she said distractedly. "He looked so closely at me, so much that I trembled for fear he would see my likeness to the girl he had known. With Father so close..." Her voice tailed off doubtfully.

"Howell Prosser was a dear friend to all of us," Cressida said thoughtfully. "Indeed, he may well have been a suitor for my hand had not the King dangled an Earl before my father's bedazzled eyes as a better marriage prospect."

"Your father had no choice, Cressida. It was the King's wish."

The countess turned, smiling, towards her mother. "I have no regrets, you know that, Mother. I love Martyn with all my heart, but during our childhood I was beginning to have tender regards for Howell Prosser. Remember, he was the man who helped me leave England following Redmoor in order to join Martyn in exile. That was not the action of a malicious or vengeful man. He continued to care about me and did his best to ensure my happiness. I doubt that he would deliberately endanger me or mine now."

Philippa drew a hard breath of relief. It seemed that much of the time she was finding it hard to breathe these days. So many threats and fears assailed her. She was, however, much less sure than her mother that Sir Howell Prosser would regard the presence of his former successful rival within the country as favourably as did the Countess if he should guess at the truth. She could only pray that neither he nor Sir Rhys had any suspicion that a traitor was within their grasp. They must take no risks.

"I still think it would be safer if you withdrew when Sir Howell comes to Gretton," she said. "We are here under assumed names and that would not augur well with the authorities should they come to hear of it. Sir Howell might well gossip, however well meaning he might be."

Both Lady Gretton and Cressida agreed, Cressida reluctantly, as she would have liked to see her childhood companion after this lapse of time and she questioned Philippa eagerly as to his appearance, pondering over the changes time had wrought in both of them.

Sir Howell did call later that day and, when he was announced, Philippa and her mother took to their chamber and remained there until he had left. If he expressed disappointment in not meeting her kinswomen, Lady Gretton did not mention it to them later.

To Philippa's relief Sir Rhys did not put in an appearance next day and she proposed that the following day they should begin to make arrangements for departure. Peter was summoned and sent into Ludlow to sound out any news of Richard Allard and if he had returned to his lodging at the Golden Fleece. Before they left both women were anxious to hear from him again and be assured that the Earl was safely ensconced in a place of safety.

The terrifying blow when it came struck all of them with utter amazement.

Four days after Sir Daniel's funeral, the women were busied within Lady Gretton's still room when they heard the sound of arrivals from the courtyard. Philippa hastened to the small horn window and pushed the casement wide. There were several horses, she was sure, and caparisoned in military fashion; her ears told her that before she caught her first horrifying sight of them.

Five men-at-arms in leather jacks and salets, mounted on destriers and accompanying a lumbering, covered wagon, drawn by two sturdy percherons, of the type used to convey noble ladies from place to place, were dismounting within the courtyard. Their leader looked up towards the manor house before the steward came hastening from the hall steps to greet the arrivals. Philippa's heart raced upwards into her throat, restricting her breathing, or so it seemed, at sight of him. The man wore the rose and portcullis livery of the King's force.

She informed her companions, then said in a breathless whisper, "What shall we do?"

Her mother took charge of the situation calmly.

"There is nothing we can do until we know what is required of us. There would be no point in hiding as every one of the servants here knows of our presence." She removed her apron and folded it. "We can descend to the hall and wait to see what transpires." Philippa and Lady Gretton removed their own aprons and smoothed down their skirts. Philippa could see that her grandmother's lips were trembling, as were her own. They had dreaded this; the arrival of the King's men could not be said to be unexpected They glanced quickly at each other, as if seeking support, and then unhurriedly did as the Countess had suggested and descended to the hall to greet their unwelcome visitors.

The steward was clearly alarmed and stood by the door as the sergeant-at-arms advanced to greet the three ladies, his booted feet sounding unusually loud on the stone flagged floor.

He bowed to Lady Gretton. "My lady, I am informed that you have staying here with you a Mistress Weston and her daughter."

Lady Gretton acknowledged his courtesy coldly and nodded, tight-lipped. "My kinswomen are here, as you see, sergeant. They came to be with me during my husband's illness and have remained for his obsequies. I cannot see that their presence should alarm the King's officials. They will be departing soon for their home near Bristol."

The sergeant's gaze passed briefly and dispassionately over Philippa and her mother who were standing ramrod still beside Lady Gretton.

The Countess said tonelessly, "I am Mistress Weston, sergeant, and this is my daughter. What business can you possibly have with us?"

"That, mistress, I am unable to disclose at present. I

am instructed to take you in charge. You will accompany me without question and I must also command you—'' here he turned towards Lady Gretton ''—to allow no one in your household to discuss anything concerning our arrival here with any person outside the manor house or demesne…'' he paused as if for maximum effect ''…on pain of dire punishment. Do I make myself clear? I would suggest that you confine your household servants to the house for the present and send your steward to convey my orders to any of the other servants or labourers working on the demesne.''

His words were so commanding and uttered in so harsh a tone that the steward, standing near the door, gave a great gulp of fear.

Lady Gretton moved a trifle nervously. Her eyes revealed her very real alarm, but her voice was steady enough when she replied, ''Certainly you make yourself very clear, sir. Am I to take it that my kinswomen are under arrest? If so, I would like to be informed on what charge they stand accused.''

The man's gimlet gaze did not shift from her. ''I did not say anyone was under arrest, my lady, merely that I have instructions to take the ladies into my charge.''

''And convey them where?'' Lady Gretton demanded, not to be deterred by his stern demeanour.

''That I am not at liberty to tell you.''

''And can I be assured that they will be returned to Gretton soon?''

He gave a slight shrug. ''Possibly. In any event, you will say nothing of what has occurred to anyone—that is, to no passing caller.''

Cressida said quietly, ''I take it my kinswoman is under no threat of punishment, whatever may happen to my daughter and I?''

"At present, no, mistress. I have no instructions to take any steps regarding Lady Gretton."

"I see." The Countess moved towards her mother and held out her hand. "I am convinced we shall be back shortly," she said as confidently as she could. "See to it that our servant, Peter, is not unduly alarmed and tell him to wait here for our return."

White-lipped, Lady Gretton nodded and the two embraced formally since she dared not take her daughter into her arms as closely as she longed to do. Philippa was similarly embraced and felt the touch of her grandmother's chilled lips upon her forehead. She curtsied and squeezed the gnarled hand reassuringly.

The sergeant addressed the steward. "The ladies will require cloaks and hoods as it may turn cold later. Summon a servant to bring them. There will be no need for further necessities."

Philippa gave a premonitory shiver of apprehension. At least they were to be afforded warm garments within any prison to which they might be headed. She waited, woodenly, until a very frightened Gwenny appeared, carrying the requested garments. With stiffened fingers she donned the cloak and put up the hood, more to hide her face from the sergeant than because its warmth was needed as yet.

With the nervous steward in tow, the two accompanied the sergeant through the screen doors and down the steps leading below to the courtyard. The men-at-arms were waiting stolidly for further orders beside the wagonette. The sergeant assisted the Countess to climb aboard and take her seat upon one of the wooden benches, which stretched along each side of the interior. Philippa mounted without assistance, imperiously shrugging aside any proffered help. She seated herself opposite her mother and the sergeant drew to the leather curtains so that they could not be afforded any glimpse of the countryside on the way to their destination, nor could they be seen by any passers-by on the road. Silently the two women faced each other and, in the dim light, Philippa could see that her mother's lips were moving in prayer. She averted her gaze, not wishing her mother to see that she was close to tears. She heard the jingle and creak of accoutrements and felt the slight movement of the wagonette as one of the men mounted to the driving seat. There was a crisp command from the sergeant and his men could be heard mounting up; soon the heavy, unwieldy vehicle began to lumber towards the courtyard arch. They were denied a last sight of Lady Gretton and the frightened servants standing watching the departure from the manor steps.

They dared not speak least they were overheard by the driver. Each was busy with her own frantic thoughts. Where were they headed? Philippa thought it might be Pembroke Castle, though that was many miles distant, and the sergeant had not insisted that they pack for the journey or require changes of undergarments, which would indicate a prolonged stay. Was their identity known? Common sense told Philippa that must be so, since, otherwise, two unknown kinswomen of Lady Gretton would not have been arrested. It was obvious, too, by the closed curtains, that the sergeant had been given instructions to conceal their presence in the wagonette from prying eyes. Why? Were they to be questioned about her father, the Earl? Cold fear broke over her like a douche of icy water. Her mother's fears looked likely to be fulfilled. They were to be held as hostages for the Earl's voluntary surrender and Philippa knew well that, should Wroxeter hear of their arrest, he would undoubtedly come to their assistance. The vehicle rumbled along what appeared to be a main road, to Ludlow perhaps, on the way to a nearby town where officials of the King had their quarters—and likely some prison where suspected persons might be held and interrogated.

The men rode beside the wagonette without chatter. Obviously they had been warned to remain silent to keep their prisoners unaware of their destination or the reason for their arrest. The silence within the closed vehicle was uncanny. The light was dim and the only sounds that reached them were the creak of harnesses and the sound of the horses' hoofs of their wagonette and of their escort. Philippa reached out and took her mother's hand within her own and squeezed. She could feel the cold smoothness of her mother's betrothal and marriage rings and knew what agonies of fear for her beloved husband the Countess was suffering. He was so near to them—and yet so far. Philippa prayed silently that he would have the sense to remain there. Surely, when it was made clear that neither woman would speak of his presence in England, they would be released. Then memories of how Richard Allard had suffered while briefly a prisoner in the Tower of London flooded back. He had been racked, not badly, but sufficient so as to render him unable to walk for days. Women, she knew, were not protected by their sex. If necessary they could be as ruthlessly questioned as he had been and her legs trembled on the planked floor of the vehicle as she wondered if she could withstand such terrible pain.

In order to force her mind from that threat, she wondered who could have possibly betrayed them. Could Sir Howell Prosser have done so? Her mother doubted that possibility and he had not been told of their identity, had not even seen either of them closely, during his visit, only that brief glimpse of her, Philippa, in the uncertain light of the village church. Could the young merchant, Master Maynard, be responsible? But he, too, had not known their true identities—yet Sir Rhys had distrusted his alleged reason for being in the district. Rhys Griffith! Always her tortured mind returned to the possibility that he might betray them. Bile rushed into her mouth at the thought. Had he so resented her apparent rejection of his advances that he had stooped to this?

Now she could hear sounds of the town, the hustle and bustle of people and the rumble of iron cart wheels upon the road, the cries of apprentices. Could they now be in Ludlow? It was the nearest town and it would have taken longer to reach another. The noises grew louder and their passage was halted momentarily by some obstruction on the road ahead. Philippa heard the sergeant shout a brusque command and, after a short pause, their vehicle began to move slowly forward again and she heard some members of her escort move in more closely. Now it was imperative that the prisoners should not be seen on the crowded thoroughfare.

She could not gauge her mother's expression. The Countess moved restlessly on her seat and Philippa leaned forward to reach out to her and offer silent comfort.

The wagonette came to another sudden halt and, again, the sergeant called out an order, instantly obeyed, for, after a short pause, they lumbered on once more. The side of the vehicle had pressed against something. Philippa was sure. So they had passed through a gate!

Now the sounds of the town were hushed, but she could hear other, familiar noises, the mewling of hawks from the mews, the rustling of wings and the gentle voice of the falconer reassuring his charges, the heavy repetitive beat of the blacksmith's hammer as he plied his trade, the restless movement of horses in a nearby stable. They had arrived. She caught her breath hard. They could only be in Ludlow and, if so, then this must be the castle courtyard.

The sergeant called a halt and then an order to dismount. Already the wagonette had stopped and the driver was climbing down heavily from his seat. The leather curtains were hastily drawn back and Philippa blinked in the sudden entrance of sunlight and saw the sergeant waiting to hand down her mother. She gazed round and realised that her surmise was correct. They had drawn up within the inner bailey of Ludlow Castle. She took the sergeant's hand and found herself stiff as she stepped down the portable wooden steps brought for the purpose. She had been sitting too tensed upon the hard wooden bench.

They were given little opportunity to look round. Philippa had only a moment to recognise the castle chapel nearby before they were hustled up the keep steps and into the most guarded and fortified part of the building. Immediately they were in gloom again and bewildered by their hasty arrival and their fears for the outcome.

Two of their former escorts accompanied the sergeant and his prisoners as he led them down several gloomy corridors and into a larger room, which received direct sunlight from several glazed windows. A man rose to his feet from a high-backed chair and faced them. Obviously he had been waiting for their arrival. Philippa gave a sharp cry of disappointment and fury, but she had no time to speak one word to Rhys Griffith before two guards, armed with crossed halberds, standing before a heavy oaken door, lowered their weapons at the sergeant's low tone of command as he knocked. The door opened and a youthful page, clad in the silken livery of the court, bearing the device of the Tudor rose and portcullis, appeared in the opening and ushered them into the inner chamber.

Philippa turned just once and directed a glance of pure hatred towards Rhys Griffith. He moved forward slightly, and held out one hand, as if in entreaty, but the page was waiting impatiently for her to follow her mother, and the sergeant and his two men-at-arms stood impassively beside the door, obviously on guard until the judgement given inside the chamber should be concluded, and their services required to direct the prisoners to their place of confinement. She was forced to follow the boy.

She had only a moment to take in the appointments of the chamber, which was furnished richly, with a central oaken table, several high-backed chairs and stools and a court cupboard on which silver and pewter dishes were displayed. Philippa felt the thickness of carpet beneath her feet and noted the bright colours of the tapestries upon the lime-washed walls in the full sunlight, which flowed in through the glazed oriel window opposite.

A woman rose from the padded window seat within the embrasure and came slightly towards them, handing her embroidery tambour to another, younger, lady who had been seated with her. With one dismissive wave of her hand she dismissed the girl, who curtsied deeply, then moved to the door and exited.

Cressida gave a swift exclamation as the woman held wide her arms and she ran into them, murmuring brokenly her joy and relief at sight of their hostess.

"Oh, your Grace, this is such an honour and delight. I had not expected ever—to see you again."

Philippa's lips curved into a smile of joy as she recognised Queen Elizabeth, her former mistress, and she brushed back emotional tears as her mother stepped back slightly and she, too, was drawn into the Queen's embrace.

"Come, sit with me. I have ordered the fire lighted as the evenings are beginning to grow chill and I find myself feeling the cold more and more lately."

The Queen sank into a padded armchair before the hearth and gestured for Cressida to sit beside her on a high-backed chair nearby. Philippa sank on to a joint stool close to the Queen's chair. Elizabeth was smiling at Cressida and holding her hand tightly and Philippa remembered that she and her mother had formed a close friendship long ago when Cressida had been briefly attendant upon Queen Anne, the wife of the late King, until her death in the spring of 1485.

The two said nothing for moments, overcome by the pleasure of their renewed acquaintance and Philippa was able to assess the changes in the Queen's appearance since their last meeting four years ago.

Now Elizabeth was mourning the death of her first-born, Arthur, Prince of Wales, and was clad in the deepest of black mourning velvet, as were her two visitors. Only a golden pendant from which depended a crucifix and the small seed pearls embedded in the gilt-braided cloth of the Queen's gable headdress relieved the sombreness of her garments.

There were lines of suffering upon the formerly serene and smooth features and the pale gilt hair she had inherited from her famed mother, Elizabeth Woodville, showing one smooth band upon her forehead, had faded and was touched with silver.

Philippa's mother frowned and Philippa knew that she, too, had recognised the signs of deep unhappiness in the Queen's demeanour.

She said quietly, "I feel for you deeply, your Grace, in the loss of your first-born and heir."

The Queen's answer was very low. "It has been a terrible blow to both of us and unexpected as…" she hesitated, turning away "…the loss of my uncle Richard's child must have been to him."

It was a strange comparison and both women were a little nonplussed by the Queen's thinking.

After a moment Elizabeth continued. "Henry has been very good to me. He came to me when—when we heard the news—to be with me and console me." She turned back to her two companions, her eyes brimming with tears. "You know, Cressida, Henry is not usually demonstrative."

Philippa, who had witnessed some of the King's visits to his wife in her apartments at Westminster, was well aware of that. She recalled the occasions he had complained bitterly and querulously about the expenses of the Queen's court and she compressed her lips in silent anger.

The Queen was speaking tonelessly, "I have come to Ludlow to be near to Arthur, since this where he spent most of his life. I saw little of him, you see. It is a Queen's lot to be parted from her children too early."

That was a reference to the custom of placing royal princes in households of their own while extremely young and the necessity of making marriage alliances with foreign princes for the young Princesses of the court. The Princess Margaret was already given in marriage to the King of Scotland and the young Princess Mary Rose would soon be leaving her mother's side.

Philippa put in eagerly, "Your Grace, how fares Prince Henry and Princess Mary? It is long since I saw them and that time when I accompanied the hunt with the King and Prince Henry, the little Princess was ailing."

The Queen smiled brightly. "Henry grows daily more personable and confident. You know he took a very active part in arranging the celebrations for his brother's wedding to the Infanta of Spain, the Princess Catherine. Despite his youth he made an excellent job of it," she said proudly. "Henry has a fine mind and is strong of physique. He will make a good ruler when the time comes." She added wistfully, "He reminds me much of the King, my father. How fortunate it was that young Richard Allard was present at the hunt that day and managed to save Henry from that charging boar. Henry was always too adventurous for his own good. Mary grows yet more beautiful—and wilful, I fear. She and Henry are much of a kind and have deep affection for each other."

Philippa guessed at what was not said, that the Queen's children were drawing more and more away from her and she was feeling isolated.

Abruptly the Queen leaned towards her former friend. "How is Wroxeter, Cressida? I must offer my condolences for the loss of your father. It seems we are all suffering loss at this time. It makes it more difficult for you that Martyn cannot be with you at this sad time."

The Countess nodded. "And even more difficult, your Grace, because I cannot remain here to comfort my mother. She knew, of course, that the possibility of losing my father was near. He had already had one bad seizure which was what brought Philippa and me to England, knowing that time might be short for him, but we hoped we could be together for a little longer, but it was not to be…'' Her voice tailed off sadly.

The Queen turned to Philippa. ''I believe you had not seen your grandfather until these last weeks. If I remember correctly, he and your grandmother were about to come to Court when you were forced to leave.'' She closed her eyes momentarily, recalling the urgency of that leave-taking and her sadness at losing her two youthful ladies-in-waiting, Anne and Philippa. She smiled slightly. ''I am glad Richard and Anne have been allowed to return to England in safety and I hear that she is a mother. I suppose you have seen nothing of them. You will regret that.'' She was looking searchingly at Philippa and the girl was forced to lower her gaze so that the Queen would not read in her eyes the knowledge that she had, indeed, seen Richard recently and in this very town. It might be dangerous for the Queen to be aware of his presence here and so close to the hiding place of her father.

''No, I have seen nothing of them,'' she said softly. ''I miss my friends, but Anne has been able to write and send messages to me from time to time.''

The Queen sighed. ''Perhaps, one day, all these troubles will be over and meetings between friends from the old days will be possible.''

There was a moment of silence then the Queen said, in a little rush, ''You have not spoken of Wroxeter. Is he well?''

''He suffers the ill effects still of the wounds taken at Redmoor, but he is much improved recently.'' Cressida paused, then added, ''He keeps busy on the Duchess Margaret's business.''

The Queen exchanged a knowing glance with both of them. "This—alleged confession of Tyrell's will have given him much pain," she murmured. "You must know, Cressida, that it distresses me, too, greatly."

The Countess gazed around hurriedly as if she might detect the presence nearby of someone eavesdropping upon their private talk, then she said very softly, "Your Grace does not believe—"

"Of course not…" the Queen's blue eyes became steely "…and, if the truth is known, neither does his Majesty the King. We do not discuss the fate of my young brothers—ever—and it is my belief that he is as bewildered by those events so long in the past as we all are but—" she drew a hard breath "—it is necessary at this juncture to again reassure the King and Queen of Spain that no obstacles would lie in the path of young Henry's accession to the throne and, also, that he obtain a dispensation from the Pope and their consent to Henry's betrothal to the Infanta."

"And it is the Prince's wish?" Philippa said wonderingly. Her remembrances of the madcap young Prince did not lead her to believe that he would be over-willing at this stage to be betrothed to any one, least of all to his brother's reputedly staid young widow. And there would, of course, be some considerable opposition to young Henry's marriage with his late brother's wife since such a union was forbidden by Holy Church, despite the fact that the marriage would be desirable for the welfare of both countries. She had heard it rumoured that the Princess Catherine had sworn upon Holy books and reliquaries that the marriage with Prince Arthur had never been consummated, and that physicians had examined her and confirmed the truth of her oath. If that were so, there were no obstacles for the marriage to take place, as the King wished, but Philippa doubted whether most people would believe it. She could not resist a small inner grin as she remembered grimly what terrible steps King Henry had taken to ensure the alliance with Spain in the first place. Both the young Earl of Warwick and the hapless Perkin Warbeck had gone to the scaffold in order to convince King Ferdinand and Queen Isabella that their daughter would, in time, become Queen of England and that no shadowy heir lived to counter the Tudor's undoubted right to that throne. Certainly the death of his heir, Prince Arthur, had been a terrible and untimely blow to King Henry.

She came from her reverie to find that the Queen was regarding Cressida, her mother, very intently.

"When I discovered that you were here in England, Cressida, I was concerned that Martyn might have followed you. I know he is prone to rash acts—valorous they might be, but extremely dangerous to him and to your family. Henry will brook no opposition to his will at this difficult moment and would deal ruthlessly with anyone who sought to frustrate his plans. You must see that Martyn does nothing foolish."

Philippa said hurriedly, "What makes your Grace fear there is any possibility of that? Could we be informed as to who betrayed us?"

The Queen's slightly myopic blue eyes fixed themselves in a puzzled expression upon her former young lady-in-waiting.

"You use a strong word, Philippa. No one betrayed you. Sir Rhys Griffith—"

"I thought as much," Philippa said through clenched teeth, her eyes stormy. "Who, on our manor, would betray us? And no one else knows of our presence here. What has he been promised in payment?"

The Queen gave a little sharp gasp. "You mistake the situation, Philippa. I have known Sir Rhys Griffith for some time. He came to Court two years ago following the death of his father and gradually showed himself to be in sympathy with my situation...."

"Your Grace should take care that he does not betray you as well," Philippa cut in.

The Queen reached out and took Philippa's hand within her own. "Child, what makes you so hot against this man? I came to Ludlow to be near to Arthur. He spent so much time here that I feel curiously close to my son here. Sir Rhys is aware of that and of my despair. He believed that a meeting between myself and two very dear friends and attendants would comfort me, as indeed it has. He revealed to me, in utmost secrecy, your presence nearby and arranged for you both to be conveyed here, again in utmost secrecy. I understand that no one was allowed to see either of you upon the journey. My captain is fiercely loyal to me and his men-at-arms were chosen for their loyalty to him. You will be returned to Gretton in the same fashion. Only my most intimate companions will ever be aware that you came here." She turned back to gaze into Cressida's hurt and bewildered eyes. "You cannot believe that I would ever seek to do either of you harm or place you in any real danger."

"Of course not, your Grace."

The Queen's facial muscles relaxed and she smiled and squeezed Philippa's hand. "I had thought to see you happily wed by now, like Anne and Richard, but, knowing what I know now, perhaps that it is as well that you are not contracted in marriage as yet to one of your father's impoverished companions in Burgundy." She said brightly, "If you will ring the little silver hand bell on the window seat in the oriel embrasure, Cressida, Lady Harding will come to attend me. I think you will remember her and you two will be happy to meet again, if only for a short time.''

Cressida rose at once to obey and moved away from the Queen and Philippa, who was aware that the Queen had deliberately arranged matters so that they might talk in private together.

Her guess was proven correct as the Queen drew her a little closer to her chair and bent to speak softly.

''It appears to me that you have some aversion to Sir Rhys Griffith that you judge him so harshly. Believe that he has only your welfare at heart. He has confessed to me that he loves you well and has begged for your hand in marriage.'' She bent even closer and said, a trifle laughingly, ''I see that you blush at the thought, child. Is Rhys Griffith so abhorrent to you that you would dismiss him out of hand? It would be a fair match.''

It was the first time the Queen had ever truly revealed herself to Philippa and the girl could not hold back a sudden gasp.

She said falteringly, ''I saw Sir Rhys in the anteroom as we entered and I think I showed him in just one revealing look that I thought the worst of him. He must think ill of me.''

''Do you love him, Philippa?''

There was only the slightest of hesitations before the answer came. ''Yes, your Grace, I believe that I do.''

''Then, child, go immediately and tell him so. At the very least, inform him that you are now aware that your conclusion was hasty and misjudged. Your mother will be occupied here with Lady Harding and myself for some moments. It will give you the opportunity to put things right.'' She reached down and gently impelled Philippa to her feet, then gave her a quick little push towards the door.

She turned and afforded the Queen a deep curtsy and exited backwards. She had half-hoped that she would find the anteroom deserted or, at least, that Sir Rhys would have left by now, but he was standing gazing out of the window at some activity below in the courtyard. Philippa stood for a moment with her back to the door and then came forward in a little rush. The susurration of her gown brushing the rushes upon the floor alerted him to her presence and he swung round at once to face her, a frown forming between his brows on recognition.

She said humbly, ''Sir Rhys, the Queen has informed me of your kind intent in having us conveyed here. It seems we are for ever in your debt.''

He stepped a little closer and she observed that his chest was rising and falling as if in a state of agitation.

He said thickly, ''But you, as usual, thought the worst of me.''

She attempted to move back a trifle, for the first time in their acquaintanceship aware of a feeling of fear in his presence, but he frustrated her intention by seizing her wrist and held it tightly. ''What is this, Lady Philippa, that everything I attempt to accomplish for your happiness ends in disaster? I could see by your glance of pure vitriolic hatred as you entered just now that you believed I had betrayed you both and, it seems, for the very worst of motives: gain. Then know, my lady, that I am very well aware of your father's presence in England. I knew from almost the first moment he stepped upon English soil and that Richard Allard was there to meet him and conduct him here, also that Allard has taken him to Sir Owen Lewis's house where he is at present. Do you not think I would have accomplished far more in the way of favour with the King by betraying him rather than his wife and daughter?''

She gave a great cry of horror and covered her face with her free hand.

''Yes,'' he continued ruthlessly, ''the safety of you all has been in my hands from the beginning. I have my own informants, you see, and my reasons for keeping myself informed. I love you, Lady Philippa, have done from the first moment I clapped eyes upon you and your so-obvious aversion to me has not changed my attitude towards you. I have wanted to take you to myself, to hold you safe. Can you imagine I would cause you unhappiness by bringing harm to those you love?''

She made a little helpless choking sound.

''But I am fast losing patience, my lady. I cannot hope that you will ever return my love and will always regard my actions with suspicion. We cannot live together like that, my lady, however I would wish it otherwise. You must go your own way and I pray the Virgin will find happiness in the arms of another more patient and less exacting lover. I cannot hope to find such happiness, but that is no concern of yours. You will be conveyed safely back to Gretton and I assure you I will not impose myself upon your presence there again. You can inform Lady Gretton that I will be at her service the moment you and your lady mother have left for Burgundy. Your father is in no danger from me. I can only hope, for your sake, that he will bring no disaster upon his own head by taking an unnecessary risk. I will bid you goodbye, my lady. Perhaps one day, in the distant future, you will be able to look back on these last days and recall that you met a man who deeply loved you and will continue to do so till the end of his days.''

Before she could utter a word in her own defence he had torn himself free and marched to the outer door, opened it and, turning once to give her a stiff bow of leave-taking, he strode out, slamming it to after him.

''No,'' she gave a little moan of protest, ''no, no, please come back. It is not as you believe. I do…''

It was useless and she knew it. He had gone and she was left with nothing but empty regret.

She slipped down to the rush-strewn floor, crying helplessly. She had rejected him this one time too many. She could see now that on each occasion when their wills had clashed it had been because he had needed to save her from some foolish impulsive action, which could bring her into danger. Even his antipathy towards Peter Fairley had been brought about by his desperate love for her. She knew now, with a terrible bleak sense of loss, that she loved him, and her very antagonistic reaction towards his nearness was because she feared for her own need to surrender. All her life she had lived with this constant fear for her family's safety and her own blind awareness that she must trust no one she was not completely sure of. Yet her father was sufficiently convinced of Rhys Griffith's worthiness that he was prepared to give the man his most precious daughter's hand in marriage. She had fought against the match because she could not trust herself.

The Queen had spoken of her own deep loneliness and urged her to confront the innermost feelings of her own heart. And he had given her no opportunity to reveal to him her longing to be truly his. This final betrayal of trust had wounded him to the heart and he had accepted his rejection at last and gone from her. Was he here in the castle still? She must find him, tell him in simple words of her love, convince him of her sincerity. He could not have left yet, not without a formal leave-taking and dismissal from the Queen. She stood up determinedly and dabbed at her streaming eyes, hoped her lids had not been reddened and that the guards she would surely find keeping watch in the corridor would not notice and be curious. She brushed that thought aside impatiently. That was of no importance. She needed to find Rhys quickly before her courage deserted her and she would return miserably to the manor house and leave England without ever being entirely sure whether she could have found the total happiness she sought in his arms.

She moved resolutely to the door and opened it hesitantly. Immediately the two guards saluted and lowered their halberds.

"Sir Rhys," she ventured hesitantly, "the knight who was here in the anteroom recently—where is he, have you any idea where he went when he left the Queen's apartments?"

The men eyed her cautiously and the taller of the two cleared his throat in an embarrassed fashion.

"Sir Rhys Griffith announced his intention of walking in the town for a while." The guard's scrutiny did not waver and Philippa was aware that the men had noted the temper which had consumed the knight and his need to put a space between himself and those beings who had caused it. The man continued. "He informed us he would return later to take his leave of her Grace after your departure, my lady."

So he intended to deliberately avoid her. Philippa bit down upon her lower lip.

"I see," she said in a small voice. "There is some

urgent matter on which I need to consult him. Perhaps I could find him. Would you inform my lady mother that I will return shortly? She knows that I am acquainted with the town and the Queen is aware of my intentions and gave me leave. Will one of you escort me to the gate and afford me means of leaving the castle?''

They exchanged embarrassed glances, unwilling to leave their posts, yet if the Queen had given leave the matter must indeed be one of some urgency. The taller man bowed and nodded to his companion. He stalked beside her in dignified silence as they left the keep, crossed the inner and outer baileys, and reached the main gate where she was passed through with the proviso that she would return shortly and require admittance once more.

Chapter Eight

Philippa found herself standing uncertainly outside the main gate house of the castle, the focus of several pairs of curious eyes. The day was already drawing to a close for those engaged in marketing and passers-by were moving towards the town gates. She was grateful for the fact that the sergeant had instructed her to wear a cloak, for, already, the evenings were beginning to become chillier once the sun had set. She drew her hood up and her cloak more tightly round her as it would serve to keep her from being observed too closely by onlookers.

She had become reasonably familiar with the pattern of streets in Ludlow and turned at once in the direction of the inn where Peter had taken her to meet Richard Allard, the Golden Fleece. Since it lay in the vicinity of the castle she judged that Sir Rhys Griffith would chose to drink there before returning to the castle, as he had promised, to take formal leave of her Grace the Queen.

She was aware that a noble woman walking without escort would attract undue notice, but she was dressed simply and her cloak was of dark brown fustian; she believed she would be taken for a merchant's wife going about her business. She hesitated for a moment at the door of the inn. It was unlikely that Rhys Griffith would greet her warmly and she had no wish to cause a scene. Perhaps it might be better if she enquired after Richard Allard. If he had returned to Ludlow he might be persuaded to enquire after the whereabouts of Rhys Griffith for her.

The tap room was crowded, as many of the market folk were drinking and taking refreshment there before commencing their homeward journeys. She glanced round quickly but could discern no sight of Rhys Griffith. More than likely he had bespoken the use of a private room since he had been in no mood to counter the jovial banter of the other customers.

One of the serving wenches came towards her, noting her hesitation.

"Can I be of service, mistress?"

"I was wondering if either Sir Rhys Griffith or Master Allard were here."

The girl shook her head. "I do know Sir Rhys well, mistress, he often gives us his custom, but he ain't been 'ere today. As for Master Allard, he left us some days ago and we don't be expecting 'im back."

Philippa thanked the girl and declined her offer of ale or food and hurriedly left the inn. Neither her mother nor Sir Rhys would thank her for drawing undue notice to herself and it was clear that she must seek Sir Rhys elsewhere. Outside she stood perplexed. Where would he have gone? Obviously there were several respectable inns and taverns in the town, but she doubted the wisdom of visiting each to enquire after him. It was possible he had acquaintances in the town whom he might have decided to visit and she had no knowledge of any of them.

She was very close to tears. She had been so sure she would find him at the Golden Fleece and that it would be easy to talk to him there or to request him to accompany her outside. She needed desperately to explain herself to him before she left Ludlow. Since he had declared his intention of remaining clear of Gretton until after she and her mother had left there was scant opportunity of seeing him again unless she could find him now. She could not, in all honour, seek him out at his own manor. That would be too humiliating. He could refuse outright to receive her and what could she tell her mother?

There was nothing for it but to return to the castle. Soon her mother would be looking anxiously for her when she had been dismissed from the Queen's presence. She must not be kept waiting.

She gave a little helpless shrug and turned reluctantly towards the castle gate. Almost immediately she was hailed by a familiar voice.

"Mistress Weston, is it not? I had not expected to see you again so soon in Ludlow, that is, after the funeral." The pleasant tones of Roger Maynard halted her in her walk and she turned at once, pleased to see a friendly face.

His expression was a trifle more grave as he added, "Are you alone?" He glanced round uncertainly and she thought he believed that she might well have been escorted by Sir Rhys Griffith; she knew well the two men had no liking for each other. He said gently, "You should not really be walking alone in the streets, Mistress Weston. You are a stranger here and do not know the dangers. This has been market day and markets attract pickpockets as honey attracts bees. While they can often be only a nuisance and inconvenience, occasionally they can attack vulnerable people. Will you allow me to escort you wherever you might be going? Isn't your servant with you today?''

She gave a little nervous laugh. ''Why, no, Master Maynard, Peter is not with me.'' She hesitated, then plunged on somewhat inaccurately, ''Sir Rhys Griffith was coming into town on business and I requested that he escort me. My mother and I will be leaving Gretton shortly and there are one or two items I wished to purchase. Unfortunately we became separated. I am sure I shall find him shortly.''

She was convinced that mention of the man he had most reason to dislike might well put Master Maynard off remaining with her. She could not allow him to know she was on her way to the castle. The visit of her mother and her on the Queen had been arranged in the utmost secrecy and must remain so. If, indeed, he had happened to see Sir Rhys, he might well be able to point her in the right direction.

He looked much better today. He was still limping slightly and leaning upon a cane, but it was clear that his broken leg was healing nicely and that soon he would be fit enough to ride. Rhys Griffith would be relieved to see the back of him.

''I am pleased to see that you are recovering well, Master Maynard. Does the leg pain you still?'' she enquired politely.

He gave her his little respectful bow. ''Only when I put too much weight upon it, but I am, as you see, fortunate, Mistress Weston, that there was no infection and the bone appears to be knitting well. I have you and your servant to thank for the prompt treatment I received.''

''And Sir Rhys Griffith,'' she reminded him.

He nodded. ''Indeed. Despite his wish for privacy and disinclination to allow trespass on his land, he has been very generous towards me. I have much to thank him for.'' He paused and smiled down at her. ''Actually I am now in a position to do him a service for which I am sure he will thank me profusely. He must be half out of his mind with concern about you, mistress, and I am able to reunite you. I happened to see him entering a house on the other side of town. Perhaps you know of it, that he has friends living there?''

She shook her head and said eagerly, ''No, I know nothing of his acquaintances. It is possible that he went there to request assistance in finding me. Can you direct me to the house, Master Maynard? I will be very grateful.''

His smile broadened. ''Why, certainly. I am charmed that I can be of service to both of you. Please, take my arm, mistress. The house is not far away and Sir Rhys will be delighted that he need not call out a hue and cry.'' The last words were spoken teasingly and she responded shyly.

Timidly she took his arm as he requested and gave one hurried glance, back towards the castle gate. She must not be too long in her search for Rhys Griffith but, surely, he, too, would not delay since the Queen would wish to conclude any business that she might wish to entrust to him.

She noticed that Roger Maynard was still walking somewhat slowly and wondered if, in fact, his leg was paining him more than he liked to admit. He talked to

her easily, pointing out one or two of the more interesting places of the town as they passed.

"You will be pleased to get back to London," she
said. "I imagine your business has been inconveniently
delayed."

He shrugged. "I have one or two people on whom I
need to call before returning to the capital, but that can
wait." He smiled down at her. "My master is an understanding man and will be prepared to give me all the
time I need."

"That must be a relief to you."

"It is well to know one is trusted."

"Certainly."

They had passed through the centre of the small market town, which was familiar to Philippa by now, and
the streets were less frequented. She noted that the
houses here were more down at heel and clustered together, many in a dilapidated condition. She paused for
a moment and glanced round uncertainly. It seemed
most unlikely that Sir Rhys would be acquainted with
the denizens of these types of properties, yet he was a
strange man and she wondered if, like many noblemen
of her father's company, he employed private spies to
keep ears and eyes out for any possible danger which
might lurk for those unwitting victims. In these uncertain times men feared their neighbours. The King's new
Court of the Star Chamber had been invented to track
down any men who entertained ideas or beliefs not acceptable to the new monarch and she knew men could
be punished by swingeing fines and even greater pen-
alties if they were summoned there and found guilty of
any hint of disloyalty. She doubted that Rhys Griffith
could ever come under such suspicion, but he was in
somewhat dangerous correspondence with the Queen—

she had seen that for herself—and he had always been suspicious of strangers on his demesne. It was, quite likely, that he might engage underlings to spy out any whiff of intrigue in the area.

Roger Maynard paused before a house, set back somewhat and apart from its neighbours. It appeared to be in better condition than others in the area and Philippa felt somewhat reassured. Her escort unlatched the gate in the rough-hewn fence and beckoned Philippa courteously to precede him up the overgrown path. She could glimpse no sign of occupation although it was already becoming dusk and she thought the inhabitants would soon need to light their candles and prickets.

Roger Maynard knocked peremptorily and after a few moments of delay the door was opened and a man appeared, holding a lighted candle. He glanced at Philippa uncertainly and she could see, even in the waning light, that he was dressed in homespun like a servant and yet there was a touch of military bearing about him, which suggested that he had been a soldier.

Roger Maynard spoke politely. "This lady wishes to see the master. She is in search of a friend she believes is visiting here."

The man gave a faint grunt in answer and stepped back so that the two of them might enter. Philippa was surprised to see that Roger Maynard should choose to go with her and had expected that, once having delivered her to the right house, he would take his leave or possibly wait outside, since his previous encounters with Rhys Griffith had been less than pleasant. Instead he followed her closely into the small gloomy hall and the heavy door closed with a sudden bang behind them.

The man, who had admitted them, led the way through into a backroom, probably the solar of the

house, though, at the moment, it was impossible for
Philippa to recognise it as such, since the shutters were
already closed over the casement and the room had not
yet been illuminated with either candles or oil lamps. It
was so dark that she stumbled against something near
the doorway and hurt her shin, so giving a little cry of
pain. She was now beginning to get alarmed. Why
should the servant show her into an unlit room, an action discourteous in the extreme? Before she could utter
a word of doubt she was unceremoniously shoved further into the room, the man with the candlestick advanced and Roger Maynard came up close behind her
and seized her arm. His grip was so fierce she let out a
second cry, then stifled it hurriedly as the door to this
room also was banged shut behind them.

She made no attempt to free herself, knowing, instinctively, that it would be useless.

Drawing herself to her full height she turned and
faced Maynard. ''I do not understand, sir. Where is Sir
Rhys Griffith?'' Her eyes roved the chamber hastily,
finding it to be almost unfurnished. There was a truckle
bed, set against the far wall, on which she discerned a
straw-filled pallet partially covered with a homespun
rough blanket. Beside it was a wooden bucket and near
the door she discovered the object over which she had
stumbled on entry into the chamber, a simple oaken
joint stool. Apart from these utilitarian and poorly fashioned articles the room was empty. The wall had been
lime-washed at some time in the past but that had
clearly been pealing for years and there were damp
patches near the shuttered window.

Roger Maynard stood leaning easily, his back against
the door, for he had now released her so quickly that

she stumbled again and almost fell. He made no attempt to prevent her from hurting herself.

"Well, Lady Philippa Telford," he addressed her sneeringly, "did you really expect to find Sir Rhys Griffith in such a hovel?"

She stared at the sound of her true name and her heart began to beat even faster than when she had felt the first twinges of alarm at sight of this room.

She had recovered herself now and faced him as haughtily as if she had been in the Queen's audience chamber.

"I do not know what this is all about, Master Maynard—"

"My name is Hilyard, in fact, a slight deception but, since your true identity was kept from me, I think it can be allowed." He smiled a trifle mockingly and folded his arms. "Ah, I see the name is familiar to you, as much so as yours is to me. John Hilyard was my cousin and, like me, in the service of his majesty." He paused then added, very deliberately, "He was killed in that service and his body thrown ignominiously behind a hedge. I think you were present on that occasion, Lady Philippa." He emphasised her title mockingly and she drew back a trifle, though still holding her dignified stance. She would not allow her fear of him to be shown.

Since she made no reply to his challenge, he regarded her thoughtfully. "I wonder that you were so very anxious to find Sir Rhys Griffith. In the past you have never displayed any liking for the man, the opposite, in fact."

Stung, she replied, "That is no business of yours, Master May—Hilyard," she corrected herself, "since it appears that he is not here."

He shrugged. "I have not the faintest notion of where

he might be, but your need of him served my purpose well, since I have been waiting patiently to find one of you ladies unescorted and able to be made my prisoner.''

Philippa knew that despite her resolve she had betrayed herself with a slight shiver of apprehension at his final word. She was aware that the man who had admitted them to the house was standing stolidly behind her, on guard, though she did not turn her head to look directly at him. So he was a man-at-arms.

''I am unable to discover any possible reason you might have to imprison me, Master Hilyard,'' she said curtly. ''Neither my mother nor I are proscribed under any act made by King or council, though I now understand you to be not a merchant but a spy of King Henry.''

''*You* may not be, Lady Philippa,'' he said suavely, ''but your father, the Earl of Wroxeter, most certainly is and will, undoubtedly, surrender himself to me once he receives my message that you are my prisoner.''

She shook her head vehemently. ''My father is in Burgundy, well away from any harm you might do him.''

Slowly he shook his own head, smiling. ''Now, Lady Philippa, you know that to be untrue. The Earl is in England and has indeed, visited you and his lady wife at Gretton only days ago. I saw him myself in Ludlow with another gentleman of your acquaintance, Master Allard. I am not entirely certain of his present whereabouts, but am convinced that my men will be able to ascertain that within a very short time. Indeed, you might well be prepared to supply me with that information and thereby shorten your own period of detention which…'' he gazed round deliberately ''…will not be entirely comfortable, as you can see for yourself. I have four men within this house whose duties will be to guard you continuously, never to let you out of sight. In fact, one will be with you inside this room at all times. They are veteran soldiers and they have instructions not to offer you insult or harm. That is, of course—'' he grinned meaningfully ''—unless you should give them cause to do so, in which case they have carte blanche from me to take whatever steps necessary to ensure that you remain my honoured guest; then, I think, you will find their presence discomforting.''

The very thought of such close confinement and the indignity it suggested to her personal privacy caused her to go dry mouthed with dread but she made no answer.

He grinned again, and she thought how his appearance had become so changed by her discovery of his perfidy and wondered that she could have ever considered him pleasant and affable. Her lip trembled as she recalled that Sir Rhys had ever been aware of a deep aversion towards the man and had warned her against placing any trust in him. Had he known that the fellow was a creature of the King, a paid spy? Probably he had not been certain, but had been cautious in his dealings with the fellow and revealed a desire to get him from the district without delay. She looked down at Hilyard's injured leg. Had he deliberately thrown himself from his horse that day, knowing she was riding close by? If so he had taken a grave risk, since that fractured bone could have lost him his life. It was more likely that he had expected to suffer a sprained ankle or some less serious injury. At all events he had thought the reward he might gain for her father's capture well worth the pain and trouble he had been caused.

And he was anxious for vengeance! She thought back wearily to that encounter on the road to the coast four years ago when John Hilyard had attempted to arrest her and return her to the King's custody—and paid for it with his life. Then, as his cousin's was now, his intention had been to obtain her father's surrender to the King. The Queen had feared that and been determined to send her into exile for that very reason even though she'd been reluctant to part with Philippa's company. So Roger Maynard, or whatever he chose to call himself, had a double reason for imprisoning her and capturing her father: a rich reward of preferment from the King and vengeance for his cousin's death. She bit down savagely upon her lower lip. He would have so tight a hold over these men who served him that the likelihood of any one of them relaxing his guard over her would be nigh on impossible.

She was trapped here. She had seen for herself that the house was set apart from others, had been well chosen for a prison, so no cries or pleas of hers would be heard by passers-by. Sir Rhys had abandoned all interest in her. Whatever desperate measures her mother and grandmother took to discover her whereabouts would be entirely frustrated and Sir Rhys had declared his intention of absenting himself from Gretton until she had departed the country, so they could expect no help from him in their search. She had foolishly placed herself in Hilyard's hands and could think of no way of obtaining a release from this terrible predicament. The one thing she had feared, from the moment they had stepped ashore in England, had come to pass. Her father must not be lured to his death. She would prefer her own demise to that, but she knew, instinctively, that he would come to her rescue—and she could do nothing to prevent him.

She turned away from her tormentor, her shoulders shaking in utter revulsion.

Hilyard said abruptly, "I just wish to impress upon you one fact, Lady Philippa. Each one of my men is aware that if he touches you, apart from the necessity to keep you safe, he will hang for it. The King would offer me no reward should the daughter of any one of England's nobility be violated. You will be kept close, but your virginity is safe."

She did not so much as turn her head at his attempt to reassure her. Her despair was too great. After some moments she heard the door open and then close again and knew that she was alone with her guard. Her legs were trembling so much now that she thought she might fall and she groped her way to the truckle bed and sank down upon it, her face hidden in her hands. She was determined that she would not burst into tears before her grim-faced jailer, who stood watching her dispassionately with his back against the door.

It was about an hour after Philippa had left Ludlow Castle that Sir Rhys Griffith returned to present himself and take formal leave of her Majesty the Queen. When he was ushered into her presence, he was startled to discover the Countess of Wroxeter still with her and both women appeared to be in a state of considerable alarm. Lady Hartley had admitted him and then taken her stance some distance from the Queen and her visitors.

The Queen addressed him without preamble. "You have seen Lady Philippa, Sir Rhys, since she left our presence?"

He hesitated and glanced awkwardly at the Countess. "I had a brief conversation with Lady Philippa before I left the castle, your Grace."

"The two of you quarrelled?" The Queen's question was blunt.

Again he hesitated. "No, your Grace, I would not say that we quarrelled, merely that matters came to a head between us and I made it clear to Lady Philippa that I no longer considered myself her ardent suitor and that I would withdraw from her company, as she appeared to desire that I should."

The Countess gave a little gasp of alarm and the Queen reached out and touched her arm lightly.

"Sir Rhys, we are closeted in private here. Nothing of what was said will be repeated. Will you tell us what took place between you two?"

Griffith was beginning to feel distinctly uncomfortable. In fact, he was becoming aware that something was gravely wrong. One glance at the Countess's distraught features made that clear to him.

"Before I answer that, your Grace, I must know, where is Lady Philippa? I would hate to reveal what went on between us without obtaining her permission to do so."

The Queen gave a heavy sigh and the Countess let out a distinct sob.

"That, Sir Rhys, is exactly what we hoped you would be able to tell us. Apparently Lady Philippa left the castle over an hour ago and has not returned. We have been waiting for her appearance so that she and her mother can be returned in secret to Gretton—but there is no sign of her. We are afraid that some harm might have come to her—unescorted—" The Queen broke off and appealed to Sir Rhys mutely with her eyes. "We had hoped that she might be with you, sir. Now we realise that is not so.''

Startled, Rhys Griffith almost forgot protocol in his angry expostulation. ''But, why, in the Virgin's name, was she not prevented from leaving?''

Mildly the Queen reminded him, ''Lady Philippa is not a prisoner, Sir Rhys. The guards at the gate had no orders to detain her.''

Cressida said tearfully, ''What we cannot understand is why she should wish to leave the castle. When the guard was summoned he informed us that she left in search of you. That is, she enquired if you had left and so we presume she went to find you, but,'' she added anxiously, ''why should she do that?''

He shook his head angrily, ''I cannot—I do not know.''

''When you informed her that your pursuit of her was at an end, did she appear to be relieved or sorry?'' the Queen pressed him.

He gave a little muffled sound of suppressed fury and shook his head again helplessly. ''I confess that I left her little or no time to answer me at all. I simply thought it was what she wished—to be left in peace.''

The Queen said, very softly, ''When she left me, Sir Rhys, I was under the impression she wished to inform you that she had misjudged your motives. She believed...'' she hesitated ''...that you have informed on her and her mother and wanted preferment as the price of that betrayal.''

''I was aware of that, I saw it in her expression when she arrived here. I told her that it was untrue and that if she thought so hardly of me I would remove herself permanently from her company—and then—I left—to drown my sorrow in some tavern,'' he added bitterly.

The Queen said gently, "This was all such a waste. I think—Philippa had a completely different solution in mind. She must have been deeply distressed and tried to find you to explain."

"Then, dear God in Heaven, *why* has she not returned?" he stormed wrathfully.

The women gazed at one another in utter bewilderment and he drew his dark brows together in a scowl.

"It is likely that she sought me at the Golden Fleece where she had previously gone with Fairley, but I chose another tavern." He paused and half-turned from them, his lower lip jutting out in thought. "Yet I cannot imagine why she has not returned. She knows Ludlow well enough and, at this time of day, there would be many unescorted women abroad, stall-holders, merchants' wives. She should have been safe enough. Pickpockets abound, of course, but they would not prevent her—" He broke off and rubbed his chin. "She might, of course, have met with…" He hesitated, glancing meaningfully at the Countess, then thought the urgency of the moment could displace natural caution. "We saw Richard Allard the last time we met in Ludlow and she might have gone with him, but I doubt she would have delayed returning, knowing that to keep you waiting would be discourteous in the extreme, your Grace."

The Queen sighed. "Then it is as we feared. Some harm has come to her and we should send out men to search."

Rhys Griffith nodded. "It would be best if you send with me the men who escorted the Countess and Lady Philippa here. They can be trusted to keep close mouths. In the meantime, could the Countess continue to remain here in privacy?"

The Queen glanced towards Lady Hartley, who nodded. "That can be arranged and I will send a messenger to Gretton to inform Lady Gretton of what has occurred here and that her daughter, at least, is safe here with me."

The Queen gestured to Lady Hartley, who went immediately to the door to summon the sergeant at-arms, as the Queen required. The man presented himself almost at once and the Queen nodded towards Sir Rhys, who put the man in the picture hurriedly.

"I need you and two of your most trusted men to accompany me into Ludlow to search for Lady Philippa. I want no word of this to leak out and the guards on the gate who allowed her out must be made to realise what the penalty would be should they gossip."

The sergeant saluted and bowed to the Queen. "May I take my leave, your Grace?"

"At once, sergeant, and report to me immediately you have news."

The sergeant exited, having informed Sir Rhys that he would meet him at the castle gate-house.

Sir Rhys went to the Countess and took both her hands within his own. "My lady, you know I would gladly die to save Philippa. Everything that can be done will be done. You have my word."

She brushed away a tear and forced a smile. "I know that, Sir Rhys. It is just that I cannot dispel from my mind the thought of Philippa lying injured or dead in a town alley."

He shook his head and said gruffly, "Unfortunately that thought is not far from my mind either, but it is also my dread that she might have been abducted with a more deadly purpose."

The Queen gave a little strangled sound and he

looked towards her apologetically. "Your Grace entertains the same fear?"

"Four years ago I feared she might be used as a pawn to entrap her father and for that reason sent her away from me. I should not have sent for you both, Cressida. There is the dread within me that I might well have caused this."

"Your Grace would never willingly endanger my child," Cressida said, horrified.

"Never, knowingly, but unwittingly..." The Queen left the rest of the sentence unsaid but her eyes appealed to Rhys Griffith.

He was frowning again in thought. "There is a man in Ludlow whom I have distrusted since I set eyes upon him. He represents himself as a wool merchant's apprentice, yet it is not the time for such men to be doing business and unlikely for one to be upon my demesne."

"You think he is a King's spy?"

"It may be so, your Grace. As you know, since the proclamation of Sir James Tyrell's confession there has been some disquiet amongst some of the former Yorkist gentlemen in the district."

"Men who are angered by the undoubted falsehood of its claims," she murmured bitterly.

"Aye, your Grace, and I suspected the man was sent to sound out the depth of feeling in this area and where *he* is—" he paused significantly "—there will be others, his trusted minions. I will send to enquire if he is still at the inn where I lodged him after he suffered a broken leg, and, if not..." he gave a gusty sigh "...well, then I shall believe the worst."

The Queen nodded sagely. "And it is well known how deeply the Earl of Wroxeter would be anxious to refute that confession and that he could well be in England to try to convince others that its claims are false.''

There was a short silence, then Sir Rhys bent his knee before the Queen and she offered him her hand.

''Go with our blessing and our prayers for your success in your mission to find our beloved Philippa, Sir Rhys.''

He gave a comforting glance in the Countess's direction and bowed himself out of the presence chamber.

An hour later he was back in the castle and admitted at once into the Queen's presence. He found both the Countess of Wroxeter and Lady Hartley closeted with the Queen.

He came immediately to the point. ''So far we have not found Lady Philippa, your Grace, but it is as I suspected, the man, Maynard, has left his lodging, apparently departed for London, so I am informed...'' He paused, then added deliberately, ''accompanied by two companions.''

''That may well be the truth,'' the Queen said doubtfully.

''Indeed, your Grace, but I beg to suggest that we should pray that what I feared earlier could be closer to the mark.''

''But if he has abducted her,'' Cressida put in fearfully, ''surely that is more to be feared.''

''No, my lady, if Maynard has abducted Lady Philippa he will see to it that she comes to no harm, at least until she has served her purpose.'' He gave a brief uneasy shrug. ''Otherwise we have cause to fear that she might have been attacked by some other who had no requirement to keep her alive.''

Cressida went white around the lips at his grim assessment and the Queen reached out and took her cold hand.

"Philippa is a resourceful young woman, as she was when a child," she said consolingly. "As Sir Rhys says, we must pray that she is held safe a prisoner somewhere." She looked coolly up at Sir Rhys. "What, sir, is your proposal now?"

"I have already instituted a thorough search of the town, which will continue through the night, if necessary, your Grace." He bit his nether lip and added harshly, "Meanwhile, I have my own sources of information. I intend to find this fellow Maynard. If he is on the road to London, as he gave out, then all my suspicions pertaining to his character can be set aside and we must continue to make the usual enquiries for Lady Philippa. I suggest that I escort Lady Wroxeter to Gretton personally, then set out to my own manor to commence my own enquiries."

Cressida rose to her feet, clearly agitated. "Should I not remain in Ludlow until we hear some news...?"

"No, my lady, your presence here could only compound our problem. If you should be recognised, then you would add a further dimension to the dangers which threaten the Earl. Your part must be to wait patiently at Gretton. Do not think that I underestimate your agonies while you are doing so."

Her lip trembled and she rose and turned to the Queen, bending her knee in a deep court curtsy. "Then if you will excuse me, your Grace."

The Queen rose and embraced her former friend. "My anxieties are as great as yours until I hear—" She broke off hurriedly. "The Virgin guard and aid you, Sir Rhys, in this mission."

He took the Countess's arm and, together, they bowed themselves out of the chamber.

Rhys rode beside the wagonette with the Queen's ser-geant-at-arms bringing up the rear of the small com-pany. Once at Gretton, Lady Wroxeter clung to his hand as he assisted her down. Already he saw that Lady Gret-ton was standing anxiously on the hall steps, with Peter Fairley beside her, and her steward hovering worriedly in the rear.

Rhys said quietly, "Send your man Fairley to me first thing in the morning. Try not to worry too much, though I know how almost impossible that is. I am convinced that Lady Philippa lives." He touched his breast briefly. "If she did not, I would feel it here."

Cressida gave a wan smile. "You love her."

"With every particle of my being. We will find her. The only thing which concerns me is the length of time that will take. I would not have her afraid for one sec-ond of time longer than necessary. I know you are afraid for your husband too. If God is good, he can be kept safe out of this."

"If he should learn…" she faltered.

"He would surrender himself immediately. I know it. If Philippa is discovered as quickly as I hope, he may never need to be informed."

She was slightly turned away from him when she said very softly, "Sir Rhys, if she has been harmed—" Her lip trembled and he was aware of her meaning.

"Trust me, Lady Wroxeter. I was prepared to let Philippa go because I believed she wanted that. Now, whatever may have occurred, if she lives she will be mine. I will allow nothing to come between us, not even her own desire."

Cressida gave a little shaky laugh. "She does not know how fortunate she is, sir."

"I assure you I shall make her aware of it and very quickly."

Again she gave a little half-strangled laugh and he reached out and tilted up her chin. "I believe Philippa is like her mother in more ways than one. She inherited your beauty, my lady, and your fortitude and spirit in adversity. I can only guess at what sufferings of mind and, not to say, the privations you have endured over the years since Redmoor and I sense your great and enduring love for your husband. I pray Philippa will come to love me as deeply as you do the Earl."

Her smile now was very wondrous. "I will pray fervently that it will come to pass, sir."

He bent and kissed her palms and straightened up as Peter Fairley strode towards them. He sensed the man's innate hostility and frowned.

"Lady Wroxeter will inform you of what has occurred," he said a trifle harshly. "I shall need your services tomorrow morning and hope that you will put aside all suspicion and work with me to bring Lady Philippa home soon."

Fairley bowed, but he did not relax his rigid stance as he took his lady's hand.

"I will present myself tomorrow early, sir," he replied curtly.

Rhys waited to see them safely within the manor house, then led the way to his own demesne.

After supper he was informed by one of the Queen's men who had been left to continue the search in Ludlow that no information regarding Philippa had come to light. The only comforting thought was that there had been no reported findings of any injured girl or of a body either.

Rhys went to bed at last seething with conflicting emotions. Though he was trained as a soldier to induce sleep when necessary, tonight he found it well nigh impossible. Despite his reassurances to the Queen and to Lady Wroxeter, he could be by no means sure that Philippa had not been set upon by some thief or outlaw, murdered and her body conveyed out of town and weighted down in some nearby stream. He tossed and turned upon his bed, picturing her frightened and threatened, hurt—and he almost choked upon his own fury. Who dared lay one finger upon the body of his love? Whoever had done so would pay with his life.

He had managed to fall into an uneasy doze just after dawn and was awakened by his cousin and squire, David, who was shaking him urgently.

"Sir, the man you sent to scour the London road has returned and is anxious to report to you."

"Send him in while I dress and order bread and meat to be brought here to me at once. I will not delay to break fast in the hall."

As the boy reached the door to obey him he called, peremptorily, "After you have eaten I want you to ride over to Sir Owen Lewis's manor and request speech with Master Richard Allard, whom, I am sure, is staying there. Tell him I wish to confer with him urgently here and, David, try not to alert Sir Owen's other guest to the knowledge that we have some crisis here. You understand me?"

"Yes, Rhys."

"Then off you go. Lose no time. Every second is urgent."

The Queen's man-at-arms looked dusty and wearied. Obviously he had ridden through the night without pause.

"There was no sighting of the man, Maynard, upon the London road, Sir Rhys. I made enquiries at every tavern upon the way, giving a description of the man before turning back, knowing how quickly you would want my news."

"You are convinced, then, that he did not set off for the capital as he had told the innkeeper of the Golden Fleece?"

"If he had done so, sir, surely someone would have noted him upon the road. He still carried a distinctive limp, or so I was informed."

"He did," Rhys said grimly. "Then it seems I was right. The fellow is still skulking somewhere in the town. Why? It seems more than likely that he encountered Lady Philippa soon after she left the castle and conveyed her to some safe house for his own purposes. No one else in the town would have had reason to detain her apart from common robbery and we appear to have ruled out that from our other enquiries."

"But—" The man was clearly reluctant to put into words the notion he might have entertained himself and Sir Rhys glanced at him sharply.

"You think she might have been seized upon by some brothel keeper?"

The man hesitated, then blurted out, "She is so very beautiful, sir."

"Aye, she is, but the town sheriff has been alerted to my need to discover her whereabouts and, since he knows all the houses of ill repute in the area, and has the authority to make searches, I doubt that that has been her fate. If it has, we shall know very shortly."

He waved the man away. "Get yourself to the kitchen and take some refreshment, then get what rest you can, you'll need it. I may summon you soon. One of my servants will find you a pallet."

The man saluted and made to leave, almost colliding with a young servant girl who came into the chamber bearing Sir Rhys's breakfast upon a tray.

He ate hastily and without tasting anything. He had only just finished when a tousle-haired boy thrust his head round the chamber door and informed him that Master Fairley had arrived from Gretton Manor and had asked to speak with him.

Rhys descended immediately to the hall and beckoned Peter Fairley into the room he used as a study. He wasted no time in empty preamble.

"Lady Wroxeter has informed you of the situation?"

Fairley nodded, his eyes wary and, testily, Rhys waved him to a chair.

"Sir down, man, and let us call a truce in hostilities for Lady Philippa's sake. We have much to do and little time at our disposal. I understand that you are the Earl of Wroxeter's squire and fought with him on Redmoor field, therefore you are an experienced warrior. I take it I can rely on your services and expertise?"

"Of course."

"Do you agree with my surmise that she may well be held somewhere as hostage? I am aware that the Earl is being sheltered at Sir Owen Lewis's manor."

Peter Fairley's eyebrows rose in shock. "You are, indeed, very well informed, Sir Rhys."

"I make it my business to know my neighbours and their loyalties. In this day and age it is as well to do so. It also seems likely that I am not alone in knowing the Earl's whereabouts. I warned you several times to be wary in your dealings with the man, Maynard, but you chose to disregard my hints and allowed Lady Philippa to continue to interest herself in his welfare. This behaviour was incautious in the extreme and likely to endanger her father.''

Fairley jolted to an upright stance upon the stool and leaned toward his host, his eyes stormy.

"You knew the man was a King's spy?"

Rhys shrugged. "I was simply not sure, but all strangers in the district are suspect, as I would have thought you would understand.''

"I thought the man was a merchant..."

"Aye, well, the harm is done and naught to be done on that score. He did not set out for London as he gave out and it is my opinion that he is the one man Lady Philippa would have trusted and the one man in Ludlow to lead her into a trap.''

Fairley scowled and moved his feet restively. "But we do not know where he is.''

"No, and that is our main problem. Under the circumstances we cannot knock on every door in Ludlow and demand to search. We have no warrant and such behaviour would bring us under official scrutiny and further endanger Lady Wroxeter and the Earl.''

Peter Fairley gave a snarl of anger. "If he harms one hair of her head—''

"You love her. I suspected as much.''

"Aye, I love her, have done since the moment of her birth, but I am almost twice her age and have no resources to keep her, even were her father to accept my suit. She regards me as a trusted elder brother. There it stands between us and will ever do so. I will give my life willingly to save hers and there you have it.'' He turned abruptly and faced Griffith. "I have my own understanding that she loves you—therefore, for her sake, I will do everything in my power to find her, rescue her and give her safely into your keeping.''

Rhys Griffith gave a long sigh and reached forward across the table to take the other's hand.

"Then we shall be truly comrades-in-arms in this and sworn to her service.''

Fairley sank down upon his chair again and gave a long, lugubrious sigh. "I pray to God we shall be able to do so, but at present we seem helpless to move." He looked up suddenly. "Richard Allard is in the district still and would help us, but I imagine you know that as you seem to be well informed of all our movements.''

"I have sent for him. No—" he held up one hand to silence Peter as he was about to spring to his feet in alarm "—I have warned my cousin, David, whom I sent to summon him, that he was not to alert either Sir Owen or his guest to the fact that we have a serious problem here. I am only too aware that should the Earl discover that his daughter is missing he will come to her aid immediately.''

"He will not thank us for keeping the truth from him.''

"Let that be. I consider it necessary and what Philippa would wish and I'm happy to suffer the consequences in good time." Rhys grimaced. "And, as I am anxious to remain in the Earl's good opinion, I have much to lose.''

They were interrupted by Sir Rhys's steward, who ushered in Richard Allard and, at a sign from his master, withdrew and left the three men together to confer.

Richard Allard listened gravely to Fairley's explanation and his face whitened. "Sweet Virgin, it is what we all most feared, yet we cannot be sure.''

"Since this man, Maynard, did not take the road to London, though he informed all and sundry that that was his intention, we imagine he must have had some other plan in mind. That, and the fact that we've had no other news of Lady Philippa, despite numerous searches.''

Richard nodded, stroking his chin. "Yet, if we are unaware of his hiding place, we can do nothing.''

"I think gentlemen—'' a quiet voice came from the doorway "—I can help you with the required information.''

They had all three been so intent on the matter in hand that they had not heard the door open and they spun round instantly to face the speaker. Rhys Griffith rose from his chair and scrutinised the newcomer curiously.

He was tall, though just a trifle stooped now, despite the arrogance of his bearing; a lean man, of soldierly bearing, still handsome, with a long face and deep-set eyes beneath half-closed lids, giving the false expression of lazy indifference. There were but faint touches of grey to the temples and Rhys judged him to be about fifty years of age. He could be in no doubt of his identity. Despite all their efforts to keep him in ignorance, Martyn Telford, Earl of Wroxeter, had come to his daughter's assistance.

Chapter Nine

Philippa had spent a sleepless night, lying still and tense upon her pallet in case she moved and alerted her guard. He was seated on a joint stool near the door. She had managed to rig up a blanket diagonally across one corner of the small foetid chamber to shield the bucket left for her toilet from view, assisted by the oldest of the guards, who had produced a hammer and two nails, genuinely affected by her modest distress at the lack of privacy afforded her. He had, he told her, two young daughters of his own and their mother would castigate him for his treatment of his prisoner if she were to hear of it. He had left, leaving his junior on guard, but warning the man sternly to leave the improvised curtain in place and to do nothing to embarrass the prisoner. Philippa could not help entertaining the fear that, should he discover the simple act of kindness, Hilyard would order the curtain to be torn down. In that one brief moment before he had left her, she had seen the vindictiveness of his true nature and her fears had begun to mount and she had thrust a hand hard against her mouth to prevent herself from dissolving into desperate tears, which would be heard by her guard.

Through the dark hours she had lain watchful, her only comfort were her prayers. There seemed no way out of her terrible predicament. Either her father would surrender himself into the hands of his enemies or she, herself, would eventually be taken to London and become the King's prisoner, more than likely accommodated within the dark recess of the Tower. Yet she knew that would not happen. It was not her greatest fear. Her father would come for her, she knew that, and he would lose his life. Though King Henry had pardoned most of the remaining Yorkist gentlemen who had survived the field at Redmoor near Bosworth, he would never forgive her father, who had been one of the late King's principal advisers. She had refused to reveal his whereabouts and would keep staunchly to her resolve. Hilyard would not dare to harm her; the Queen would protect her, Philippa was convinced of that, but in the worst moments of her dread she realised that the Queen would not know of her imprisonment. Even if she were conveyed to London and the Tower, it was likely that the Queen would not be informed, neither would her mother or grandmother. She shivered with cold beneath the thin covering, yet knew it was not really a cold night. Her fear was freezing her to the marrow.

She continued to pray soundlessly. Though her situation appeared desperate, surely the Virgin would aid her. Then, suddenly, she knew that her prayer for courage was answered. She knew, without a shadow of doubt, that Rhys Griffith would come and find her. Her doubts yesterday that he would abandon her, after his conviction that he could never win her trust, were groundless. Rhys Griffith loved her. He might say that he would let her go but, once informed that she was missing, he would come to her aid. Relief washed over her as a cleansing tide. She had but to wait for him. Somehow he would find her and come and now her one prayer was that he would do so in time to prevent her father from endangering himself. How he would manage to accomplish her rescue, she had no idea. Her faith in him was complete. He would do it.

She pictured him vividly as she remembered him so many times when he had come to her assistance, tall, unyielding, strong, yet compassionate beneath that air of domination she had told herself that she despised. She saw how he had stood up to the mob when Nan Freeman had been threatened, one man, alone, but with the innate authority to subdue the infuriated villagers. Her heart pounded as she recalled the moment when she had first realised his underlying compassion, the moment he had held her close in silent comfort after the death of her beloved grandfather. She had turned to him blindly then, knowing instinctively that he was the one being in the world who would understand her torment.

When Roger Hilyard came unceremoniously into her prison early the next morning she was suddenly aware of her disordered appearance. She had slept in her gown, afraid to undress with her guard ever watchful. It was crumpled and dusty at the hem from her walk through the streets with Hilyard yesterday and she had no comb. Her hair had come free from its pins during the night and she had caught it up, smoothed it with her fingers as best she could and braided it beneath her linen cap which she had hastily pinned into place after rising. She had no idea if the cap was straight, but she smoothed down the folds of her mourning gown and faced her jailer with as much defiant courage as she could summon up.

He made her a mocking bow after dismissing the guard with instructions to bring up my lady's breakfast in a half an hour or so after he had left.

"You see, Lady Philippa, I have your welfare in mind. We shall not let you starve."

"And if I choose to do so of my own free will?" she snapped.

He smiled affably. "I shall not allow you to do that either," he said mildly. "You realise how important you are for my purpose. If necessary I will have you fed by force, but that is unlikely to become necessary since your father will have given himself into my hands before then."

Deliberately she lowered her gaze that he might not see the flash of stark fear revealed in her eyes. "I do not see how that can be possible, Master Maynard—or is it Hilyard? I confess I cannot remember, since you are such an insignificant creature in my eyes. You do not know where my father is."

"No?" he questioned, his grey eyes dancing. "You think that I do not without your divulging it? Ah, Lady Philippa, you must think me a fool and without resources. I understand your father employed an efficient spy network in the service of the late murderer who called himself Richard of England. Well, my network is smaller, but just as hard working and efficient. I know of one man in the district who might agree to shelter an enemy of the king. Sir Owen Lewis was once squire to Sir Guy Jarvis, I am told. Is not your very good friend, Mistress Anne Allard, the daughter of Sir Guy? Now I know Master Allard was very recently here in Ludlow. Did I not see him in talk with you and Master

Fairley, your father's former squire? Oh, yes, I know that too. Fairley fought beside your father at Redmoor. Now why, I asked myself, should Master Richard Allard come to Ludlow? His father's manor and that of his wife's father lie far from here. He came for a purpose, I am quite sure. Now, could it have been to meet and help to protect the Earl of Wroxeter? Since Wroxeter's wife and daughter are here at Gretton it would seem likely that he would venture himself to be near them, especially at a time of deep sorrow for Lady Wroxeter.''

He knew instantly that his arrow had struck home for Philippa's eyes had widened, first in doubt, then in horrified discovery that he was right. She bit hard down upon her bottom lip to prevent it from trembling.

''You are guessing wildly, Master Hilyard,'' she said tonelessly.

''I am sufficiently confident that Lewis still harbours Yorkist loyalties,'' he said lightly. ''So much so that I have dispatched a messenger to his manor to alert his honoured guest to the knowledge that his daughter is a prisoner in my hands and issued instructions as to the wherewithal to find this house. I am reasonably sure that he will heed my summons. After all, I am sure he has sufficient affection for his only child to come to her aid when she is in peril.''

Philippa managed to keep control over her emotions, though she was very close to tears. She would not allow this creature to see her desperation.

She lifted her head and stared back at him defiantly. ''Sir Owen Lewis fought for the present King both at Redmoor and at Stoke. He is the King's man. My father would never seek his aid.''

He gave a little snort of amusement. ''We shall see, my lady. If I am, indeed, wrong in my assumptions, we can always try the homes of other gentlemen in the area whose loyalties have ever been suspect, but I do not believe that I am wrong. I expect my lord Earl to present himself here before the day's end or at the very latest in the morning.''

He made her another mocking bow and left, ordering the guard to keep a still tighter watch over his prisoner.

She sat upon the pallet bed, her heart racing. It seemed that Master Hilyard knew more about the loyalties of the gentlemen of the district than she could ever have suspected. And if he did, the King, more than likely, was aware of them also. Not only was her father in peril, but many other good men with him. She shivered again, and turned so that the guard would not glimpse her growing panic. During the night she had been so sure that Rhys Griffith would come, but would he now be in time? Another terrible thought struck her forcibly. If he did so, would he place himself in peril? Had his love for her put him in mortal danger?

Later, when another of the men-at-arms entered with a tray of food, consisting of a dish of gruel, coarse rye bread moistened with a smear of honey and a cup of watered sour wine, she forced herself to eat. She would need all her strength and courage to endure the long hours of waiting.

Rhys Griffith rose to greet his noble visitor and courteously offered him his chair.

''I am glad to welcome you to my home, my lord, but wish it were under happier circumstances.''

The Earl waved to his host to seat himself again and hooked a joint stool forward, nearer to the table and between his two companions, and sank down.

''I only hope that I have not put you under suspicion,'' he said, fumbling inside his doublet to find a folded piece of parchment, which he laid open upon the table. ''I am afraid I have upset your steward by my unexpected arrival and insistence upon being brought to you immediately, but I thought you should see this at once.'' He glanced round at the small, assembled company and grimaced. ''I take it this is a council of war.''

Rhys looked up irritably as his steward apologetically poked his head around the door.

''Sir, this man forced his way in and—''

''Yes, I know, man. All is well. When the sergeant returns send him up if we are still in conference. In the meantime, see that no one else is admitted and, Crawley, make sure none of the household servants gossip about what is happening here. Keep them well occupied within the manor house.''

''Yes, Sir Rhys.''

The head disappeared and the Earl gave a brief snort of a laugh. ''It seems that you impose discretion upon your household, Sir Rhys, which is just as well.'' He tapped the parchment with his forefinger. ''I received this message this morning soon after Richard, here, left, I imagine. He went without informing me of his destination, but Owen and I drew our own conclusions. I decided that, dangerous or not, for Philippa's sake you would need to see this.''

With a muttered word to excuse himself, Rhys snatched up the parchment and scanned the contents.

''We were right, then,'' he informed the others, who were leaning forward eagerly. ''The man, Maynard, is holding Lady Philippa hostage. He demands that the Earl surrender himself immediately or face the consequences. He does not state what they might be,'' he added grimly then, peering closer at the parchment, he murmured, "I see that he signs himself Hilyard, not Maynard, which is interesting."

Richard Allard uttered a soldier's oath. And the others glanced at him blankly.

"You know the man, Richard?" the Earl queried.

"No, I think not, but John Hilyard was King Henry's esquire of the body. He showed a particular interest in my wife, Anne, while she served the Queen at Westminster. It was Hilyard who followed us when we were escaping to the coast, escorting your daughter, my lord. In the skirmish Hilyard was killed."

"Ah." The Earl leaned back slightly upon his stool. "Then this fellow is most likely kin of his and is anxious for revenge as well as preferment." He was watching Rhys Griffith closely as he traced his finger across the crude map scrawled upon the parchment. "You know this house, Sir Rhys?"

"I know the district. It lies somewhat clear of the town and appears to be apart from other properties."

Richard Allard said curtly, "Then it lies open to attack without the likelihood of being observed by townsfolk."

"It is also likely to be well guarded from within," the Earl drawled, his heavy lids narrowed. "This is a King's man. He will have men at his beck and call, fighting men."

There was a brief silence, then Peter Fairley said heavily, "And Lady Philippa is at their mercy and could be killed while we are about it."

"Exactly," the Earl agreed.

Rhys made a little explosive sound and the Earl turned to him. "I know you have a deep regard for my daughter, sir, but you have much to lose if you venture yourself with us."

Rhys gave a harsh laugh and dismissive movement of his hand. "I will fight for her with the last breath in my body. Do you doubt that, my lord?"

"No, I merely point out the disadvantages of allying yourself with us."

"That is of no account. Now that we know where she is, our plan of action is clear. We must free her."

There were nods of agreement from the others. Peter said quietly, "How many men would you estimate are within the house, my lord?"

The Earl shook his head and turned to Rhys. "You would know the size of the property, sir."

"It is quite small but, because that is so, easy to defend. I would imagine Hilyard has, perhaps, five or six men, to have more at his command would have excited notice amongst the townsfolk. It seems obvious that he instructed his men to remain apart from him for the most part while he was engaged in spying out the situation. Had a troop of men arrived in the town we should have learned of it."

Peter asked, "Can we rely on the services of the Queen's men who have been searching the town, Sir Rhys?"

"I would be reluctant to do that, Master Fairley, as that could embarrass the Queen."

"That is not to be countenanced," the Earl said quietly. "No action of ours must place her Grace in danger."

"Agreed," Sir Rhys said. "I take it, gentlemen, that all of us here are prepared to risk ourselves in order to save Lady Philippa."

There was a murmur of assent.

"What we *can* do is allow some of the men the Queen placed at my disposal to spy out the house and its environs and report to me,'' Rhys proposed. ''I think a night attack will be advantageous.''

''Any attack will be dangerous for Philippa,'' the Earl said firmly. ''I propose, gentlemen, to do just what this message instructs me to do. I intend to present myself at the door and allow Master Hilyard the pleasure of arresting me.''

Rhys sprang to his feet in horror. ''I cannot allow you to do that, my lord.''

''And how, pray, would you prevent me?''

''By force if necessary. Philippa would never forgive any of us if anything were to happen to you.''

''Philippa is truly my daughter. She knows when to obey me and when to bow to the inevitable. Always she is conscious of that fact that I might be killed in the service of the Duchess Margaret. She fears it but, like my wife, Cressida, she has learned to live with it and face it bravely, but I am by no means sure that anything will happen to me.''

''But, my lord, you propose to walk into the trap unarmed.''

The Earl shrugged. ''It would seem to me that it is the only plan possible to allow us any chance of success.''

''How so?'' Richard Allard demanded harshly.

''While Hilyard's men are occupied in securing me, you would have a better opportunity of taking the other men by surprise and, once in, I shall be in a better position to reassure Philippa.'' The Earl gave a little crooked smile. ''Assuredly, at my request, Hilyard will allow me to see my daughter. It will give him an added sense of satisfaction to witness her distress, a fillip to his revenge for the death of his kinsman.''

''But he could dispatch you at once with the intention

of taking your head to the King at Westminster,'' Rhys grated, while Peter Fairley moved restlessly on his stool, his eyes dark with alarm.

''He will not do that. I tell you, Henry will wish to speak with me.'' The words were spoken lightly but Richard Allard winced at the thought behind them. The Earl would be subjected to interrogation in the dark dungeon within the Tower where he, himself, had suffered.

''Don't do this, Lord Martyn,'' he pleaded. ''Philippa would not wish it and many things could go wrong. I am the first to admit that we could be badly outnumbered and you taken and held, despite our best endeavours.''

''Then what would you suggest?'' The Earl queried blandly, opening both palms facing upwards upon the table top. ''Philippa lies in their hands and cannot be left to Hilyard's mercy, not even to his continued insults.''

Rhys's brows drew together in a black scowl of fury.

''The Earl is right,'' he grated. ''His surrender does offer us the best chance of success. We are like to be outnumbered and surprise is the only tactic which is open to us at this stage in the game.''

He paused as there came a tap upon the door and he called an imperative instruction to enter. The Queen's sergeant-at-arms stood on the threshold and saluted.

''I regret, Sir Rhys, that I have to report no success in our search. It appears to me that we have exhausted every possible place of concealment, except within one of the houses, of course, and we have no jurisdiction to demand entrance to any of those as yet.''

''We have discovered where Lady Philippa is held

and for what purpose. Our difficulty now is the best way of effecting her release,'' Rhys said.

''Then what can we do to help you, sir? Each one of us would gladly die in the service of her Grace the Queen, and Lady Philippa is her favourite.''

''As each one of us would,'' Sir Rhys assured him gravely. He prodded the parchment with one finger. ''I can give you instructions about where to find this house. I suggest that each of your men, who is willing, remove all livery and go with you to the street and discover as much as you can about the place's defences. We shall join you later, just before nightfall, I think.'' He turned to receive the affirmation of the others. ''We shall then enter the house and try to free the Lady Philippa. I think it best if you surround the property for us and try to ensure that none of the men of Hilyard's company escape to carry tales. I do not want any of us embroiled in any skirmish in the town. Information of that sort reaching the King would not only endanger you all but also injure the reputation of the Queen.''

The sergeant considered for a moment, then gave a brief nod of acknowledgement. ''But you four could easily be outnumbered and the lady hurt or killed in the attempt.''

''We are only too aware of that,'' Sir Rhys conceded.

The sergeant said huskily, ''I am willing to risk myself…''

''No, for the Queen's sake, better not.''

''But just four of you and hindered by the need to protect the lady…''

''There will be five of us, if you will grant me permission, Rhys,'' a youthful voice spoke from the doorway.

Rhys turned and smiled a little grimly as his young

cousin and squire entered the chamber. The boy was attired in martial clothing, a boiled leather jack and heavy riding boots, and was armed with sword and dagger.

Rhys nodded. ''I think you are ready to see action, boy,'' he said quietly, ''but remember to obey my instructions implicitly.''

''You have my word.'' The boy gave a broad smile. ''After all, it is likely that Lady Philippa will become the chatelaine of this house and my mistress and very soon, so I should have the honour of taking part in her rescue.''

''If God wills it,'' Rhys said heavily, and he looked towards the Earl for confirmation of his claim to Philippa's hand.

After the sergeant had taken his leave to instruct his men in their duties and the other three had set about their own preparations Rhys sat alone in his study with the Earl. He had already sent young David to Gretton with a letter informing the Countess that he intended to take steps very shortly to restore her daughter to her.

While he was penning it the Earl queried sharply, ''You have not mentioned my intended part in this rescue?''

''No, my lord.''

''Good. Let that remain a secret between us.'' The Earl paused, then said quietly, ''I know I do not have to ask you to care for Philippa if the worst should happen to me but...'' and he hesitated momentarily ''...but I do need to ask you...''

''To ensure the welfare of the Countess Wroxeter and Lady Gretton,'' Rhys finished and the other gave a little shrug of acknowledgement. Rhys continued. ''You know that I will do so, you have my word and, indeed, if later, after the Duchess of Burgundy can no longer offer her protection, I would wish Lady Wroxeter and Fairley to come to me here.''

The Earl gave a little contented sigh, then leaned forward towards his host, ''You realise all this could cause you trouble—if not place you in very real danger?''

''Yes, my lord, I am fully aware of that.'' Rhys then sealed the letter with his signet ring and handed it to David. ''See that you give it into the hand of no one but the Countess or, failing that, into the hand of Lady Gretton.''

The boy nodded and took his leave. The two men sat on in silence for a moment, then Rhys said softly, ''What hope do you have of success in this?''

Again the Earl gave a faint Gallic shrug. ''I think, like you, we have a fair chance. Our comrades are brave and true which I doubt can be said about Hilyard's men. They serve him for gain and their hearts will not be set on a fight, but we cannot escape the knowledge that they will be experienced warriors.''

''Yes.''

Again the two seemed lost in thought, then Rhys said abruptly, ''You said the King will be most anxious to question you personally. Information concerning the whereabouts and movements of other Yorkist gentlemen could be obtained by others, by lesser officials. You imply that Henry has his own reasons for ensuring he has you in his hands. Is it that he wishes to know the fate of the Princes?''

A slight smile curled the Earl's long lips. ''Ah, you, too, are not sure that Tryell's confession is genuine.''

''I never for one moment believed that it was.''

''Then you would wish to know about the Princes for yourself?''

"On the contrary, the fewer who are entrusted with that deadly secret the better. It is just that it is one more reason why you should not surrender yourself. Can we even the balance of risk by arming you with a poniard, at least, well hidden on your person? It would give you some means of defence.''

Regretfully the Earl shook his head. "I shall be immediately searched. If I am found to be armed and you and your companions fail to enter the house, Philippa could be further endangered. That risk I must take. My late master would understand my need. At all events it would be difficult for the King to take action against his most dreaded enemies now. It is merely that, if possible, I would wish him to remain in ignorance of the true situation.'' He gave a little bitter laugh. "It grants me a measure of satisfaction, that is all and,'' he added thoughtfully, "it is better for the Queen's peace of mind that the truth should not be made public.''

As evening approached the five comrades-in-arms, clad in dark, serviceable garments over brigandines and well armed, but for the Earl, mounted and rode from the manor. In Ludlow Rhys arranged for them to stable their mounts at an inn and they then proceeded on foot to the rendezvous agreed with the Queen's sergeant-at-arms.

A dark shadow emerged from the bushes that bordered the neglected garden of one of the properties and revealed itself to be the sergeant.

"Two men entered the house about an hour ago. They appeared to be carrying food supplies and an ample supply of wine bottles. I could not estimate the number inside, but two, beside Master Hilyard, would be guarding the prisoner, I imagine. There might be more.

The two we saw were ruffianly in appearance, but undoubtedly fighting men still in early middle age, both of them, and capable of putting up a fair fight and an unfair one too if pressed.''

Sir Rhys nodded. "What of windows and doors?''

''There seems to be one main door at the front, made of stout oak, not easy to broach but an axe should suffice.'' He produced one from beneath his cloak and handed it to Richard Allard. "It will take some time, but if the men are engaged in another part of the house it might be managed.'' He glanced back towards the house in question, from which they could see a glimmer of candle light from between closed shutters. "There is one window, heavily shuttered at the back and I would guess that that is the room where Lady Philippa is confined. There is a very small upstairs casement, also shuttered, but it would not be easy to climb to that, or, indeed, for a big man to enter it, especially as he would have to deal with the shutters, while suspended in an ungainly and difficult position and without adequate foothold. There are no sturdy creepers in evidence nor, I regret to say, a suitable tree near with overhanging branches. I have managed to deal with the bottom casement shutter with the point of my dagger. It had to be done very quietly. While there I detected no sound of voices within the chamber but there is a pricket burning and I believe it to be occupied.''

Rhys nodded grimly.

"It would seem that we have no alternative but to do as my lord Earl proposes, allow him to surrender himself while the rest of us hold ourselves in readiness to make an assault upon the front door and rear window.'' He addressed the sergeant-at-arms. "You have done well, man, and have my gratitude. Now I think your

men should retire to the cover of those bushes and
watch for what happens, particularly to deal with any
one of Hilyard's men who runs out to seek help.'' He
glanced around. ''The houses nearby are sufficiently
away from this property to avoid undue notice, which,
I imagine, is the reason why Hilyard chose it. That
should prove an advantage to us, too. Well...'' he
turned to the waiting, silent, little company ''...I take
it that we are all ready?''

There was a mutter of assent and the Earl put a hand
upon Rhys's shoulder. ''God guard us all and especially
you whom I trust to help Philippa whatever the consequences to the rest of us.''

Rhys nodded and answered gruffly, ''You can trust
each one of us to do his part, my lord, and I pray the
Virgin to bring you safely out of this.''

The Earl turned and briefly embraced his squire, Peter, who had been his trusted and loyal companion over
many years. ''I know I can trust you with the safekeep-
ing of your mistress, should you come out of this un-
scathed.''

Peter's voice was husky with emotional tears.
''Come, my lord, we have come through worst scrapes.
Did I not believe you dead on Redmoor field and yet
you survived? Our cause is righteous. We'll bring the
Lady Philippa safe home to Gretton, never fear.''

The Earl gripped his arm tightly, acknowledged the
rest with a nod and then strode off towards the house.
The sergeant saluted and withdrew to join his men and
Rhys signalled silently for the others to draw closer to
the house, ready for action after the Earl had entered
and they had given sufficient time for the occupants to
be busy with his capture.

He glanced briefly at the others. ''Master Allard, you

are too big a man to go easily and silently through that window and I would prefer that young David here remain close to me during the attack. I think, Master Fairley you will be the best man to broach the casement and, if you can, to get to Lady Philippa that way. The rest of you come with me to make an assault on that door.''

Peter made no objection, simply moved off to take up his position.

Rhys looked briefly up at the sky. It was a dark night, with only a fraction of the new moon peeping through the cloud. It was calm but cold and he could discern no sound of people moving in the vicinity. He hoped, if it were possible, to manage this rescue without causing any trouble within the town which could involve the Earl and bring him eventually to the notice of the authorities. He bared his teeth. By all the saints, he would save Philippa and dispatch Hilyard whatever the consequences to himself or any other man. He gave the signal to advance and felt David's heavy breathing at his back.

Philippa stirred uneasily on her pallet when she heard the sound of raised voices outside the door of her prison. Her guard, seated on his stool as usual, lifted his head and had turned to listen intently, too, but turned his watchful gaze to her again and made no move to stand or unlock the door. The noise continued, the scraping of booted feet upon the flagstones of the hallway, the mutter of voices, then the voices were muted. She bit down hard upon her bottom lip to prevent it trembling. She was aware that the two men Hilyard had sent out earlier for supplies had returned some time ago. All his men were within the house, yet she was sure that the outer door had been opened. She sat back against her pillow, her ears straining. Who had been admitted? She dared not even think that her worst fear might be realised.

Then, abruptly, there came a harsh command in Hilyard's voice, and the guard rose, moved his stool and unlatched the door. Philippa found her heart racing as it seemed an age before it finally opened and she saw Roger Hilyard standing on the threshold with his arm raised high, brandishing a lighted candle in its holder. She saw clearly in that instant of time that he was deliberately illuminating the face of the man who stood by his side. She gave a sharp cry of anguish and Hilyard smiled.

"You see, my lady, I was right. Honour determined my lord Earl's decision. He could not allow his only daughter to remain a hostage. He has come to surrender himself into my hands, his only request that he might see you and speak with you. Naturally," he mocked, "I could not be cruel enough to refuse that request, but for moments only." He addressed her guard. "Leave them together, man. He has been well searched and was found to be completely unarmed as I ordered."

Philippa sprang from the pallet and rushed to her father as he stepped into the chamber. He drew her close to his heart as Hilyard gave a final mocking laugh and he and the guard exited. Close to her ear the Earl murmured softly, "Give your heart peace, child, you are not abandoned. Rhys is outside with three good men. No, do not cry out again. Just be ready and do what I or Rhys command. Stand clear and allow us to do what must be done."

He felt her tremble against him and steadied her gently. "I need you to be very strong, my daughter. Do not faint on me, now.'' As she gave a little sob, muffled against his heart, he said aloud, "Do not upbraid me, Philippa. I could not leave you a prisoner, you know that.''

She stifled her weeping and said hoarsely and loudly enough, she hoped, for Hilyard to hear through the cracks of the ill-made door, "You should not have come. You have walked into a trap. He will not release me. You must be aware of that.''

He said, "I do not believe the man to be completely without honour. He gave his word...''

He held her tightly by one shoulder, as there came the sound of splintering wood and the hoarse cries of men taken by surprise. Almost immediately her guard unlatched the door and, with an oath, sprang at the pair in the centre of the room. He swung the Earl aside, tearing him apart from his daughter, and Philippa felt the bite of cold steel against her throat as the man's dagger grazed her skin. She knew her father would do nothing at this moment to endanger her and so would not make his move against her assailant. Her breath was coming in hard, dry pants but her eyes peered round desperately.

As if in answer to her unspoken prayer, a soft voice sounded from behind her as Peter wrenched aside the shutter and crashed through the horn window.

"Harm her and you are a dead man, my friend.''

For moments there was stalemate. The Earl glared at her attacker and Philippa felt, rather than heard, Peter come close up to her captor's back. She dared not struggle, as she could feel the harsh beat of the guard's ragged breaths and smell the rank body stink of his raw fear. Outside the room she could hear the noise of conflict, shouts, trampling of feet, thuds, as if an axe was being wielded, and the scrape of steel on steel. Nobody moved in the little prison chamber.

It seemed an eternity as the noise of battle went on, yells of pain as a weapon found its mark and soldiers' oaths flowed freely. Caught tight against her jailor, she could do nothing but pray. Sweet Virgin, Rhys was out there and probably Richard. Let them come through this safely. Through her own heedlessness she had brought them all into this peril and, if Hilyard's men were triumphant, in moments they would all be killed or carried off as prisoners.

Her father's eyes were fixed relentlessly upon her captor and Peter did not move. They were helpless to join the combat, since their one aim was to ensure her safety. She longed to call out to them to leave her to her fate and go to the help of the intruders, but her father's implacable gaze warned her to remain silent. Her captor was turning his head desperately as he could hear the battle, but not see one sign of how it was progressing. His breath was becoming even more ragged and Philippa felt a thin trickle of blood run down her throat and on to her breast as his dagger bit yet closer, though she felt no real pain.

Suddenly her captor's attention was drawn from her as a man's body fell against the door of the chamber and Roger Hilyard stumbled backwards through, then righted itself, his sword held protectively forward. Abruptly, taken by utter surprise, her captor released his hold and she fell forward, almost into her father's arms. At the same moment Peter gave a cry of triumph and thrust his dagger into her erstwhile captor's back, so that he gave one terrible scream and fell forwards almost at her father's feet. Held against the Earl, she watched with mounting horror as the wounded man's feet drummed against the floor in his death agony and his breath rasped in his throat, then he fell silent and his sprawled body stilled. Peter knelt and retrieved his and the man's weapon.

Philippa's father urged her gently backwards as he made a clear way for the two men who were fighting their way into the chamber while Peter also moved. He was watching the combatants carefully, alert for any sign that he might aid Rhys without hindering him. Roger Hilyard had recovered his balance and appeared now to be unhindered by his injured leg. He was expertly defending himself against the sword thrusts of his opponent and Rhys Griffith pushed him ever more relentlessly further into the chamber.

Horrified, Philippa watched as the two fought doggedly on. The other men in the room were silent and that emphasised the clang of weapons and the ragged breathing of the two fighting men. Philippa had thought that Roger Hilyard would be inexperienced in the use of sword and dagger, but that was not so. Evidently he had been well trained in the King's service and he parried and attacked with considerable skill. Also he was as light on his feet as a dancer. She had no idea if he had kept clear of the fighting until now and, if so, he would be much fresher for the fray than Rhys was. Had he deliberately feigned lameness when he had brought her here last night?

She saw that her father was watching the conflict with frowning interest and since he had come unarmed into the house he could not intervene. Peter evidently considered that as matters stood he would only make matters worse for Rhys by plunging into the fight and he, too, stood aside, lips pursed, his sword at the ready to jump in if necessary. Philippa could only stand still helplessly, in desperate fascination. Her lips moved in silent prayer.

Once or twice one or other of the combatants let out a cry and she stifled her own answering one with the back of her hand across her mouth in case her distress should draw Rhys's attention to her and so bring about his downfall.

Rhys was the bigger man, less agile, but stronger and tireless in the use of the heavy broad sword. Steadily he pushed his opponent back further into the room. Someone outside in the corridor groaned and, for a second, Roger Hilyard hesitated and Rhys thrust home at his sword arm calling forth a sharp cry of pain, but immediately Hilyard riposted, infuriated by the cut, and appeared unconcerned by the heavy flow of blood dyeing his doublet sleeve. Surely one or other of the two must tire and make a fatal mistake now, Philippa thought, and as if in answer to that thought, Rhys suddenly stumbled and fell to one knee. He appeared to have taken a cut across his right wrist and his weapon faltered momentarily and almost fell from his hand. Despite her determination not to hinder him by her fear, Philippa let out a scream of terror as Roger Hilyard came on eagerly and leaned forward for the kill. In that same moment Rhys, magically, it seemed, retrieved his weapon and his sword leaped forward as if by its own volition and Philippa glimpsed the lightning flash of the rushlight on the tempered steel. As an echo of her own cry, Roger Hilyard let out one shrill scream of agony and fell backwards across the shattered window casement. There was a strange, tinny sound of splintering horn, as his body was bent across the broken wood of the sill and, for a moment, Philippa thought it would topple further backwards into the darkened garden beyond, but it convulsed, as her former attacker's had done, and then lay horribly still. This time she detected no death rattle and she caught at her father's hand as Peter Fairley strode forward and bent over the stricken man.

He straightened and turned back to Rhys who was struggling to his feet, nursing the deep cut in his wrist from which crimson blood flowed onto his hand so that he cursed and let fall his blade.

"You got him squarely in the throat with that final thrust. A daring move and a desperate one, if I may say so. Are you badly hurt, Sir Rhys?"

Rhys was attempting to stem the blood welling up in his wrist with his free hand and the fingers of both his hands were stained and slippery. Now, at last, as if released from some malign spell, Philippa rushed into his arms, unmindful of the bloodied fingers, which reached up to stroke tenderly her disordered hair.

"There, there, my heart," Rhys murmured, bending to nuzzle the bright gold waves, "it is not so bad and you and your father are safe finally."

She pulled herself free, as he was unable to hold her, hampered by the wound as he was, and she bent and impatiently tore strips from the hem of her cambric petticoat to tie around the wound, pulling the bandage tight to staunch the heavy blood flow.

"Do not dare," she murmured through gritted teeth, "tell me that you have had to rescue me from yet another foolish scrape."

He gave a shaky laugh and pulled her protesting into his arms again. "I was not about to. Frankly I am too wearied to argue with you, only thankful to have you alive, that is enough for me." He leaned forward and peered intently into her eyes. "Did one of those devils so much as touch you? You are unharmed?"

She shook her head vehemently. "No, I have been frightened and humiliated but Hilyard threatened them with hanging if they so much as insulted me."

"As for me, Sir Rhys," the Earl said quietly, as he came to their side, "you have my eternal gratitude."

"What I want is your permission to wed this shrew of a daughter of yours," Rhys grinned, "and I hope and pray she will learn gentler ways with the sick and dying. Ouch," he said sharply as she pulled even tighter the improvised bandage.

"You are a very long way from dying, sir," she said tartly, then burst into sudden tears of relief from the unbearable tension, "though every moment I feared that you were, and when he had you on one knee like that— I thought—dear God—I thought it would be the end."

He cupped her chin in his two, still bloodied hands, but she gave no heed to the unsightly smears upon her skin. "My heart, I was beginning to glimpse the gates of Heaven or Hell myself," he chuckled darkly. "Thank the saints I was not to discover which, at this time, at least."

Richard Allard and Peter were counting up the dead. Young David had sustained a chest wound and was clearly pale and shaky, though the gash had been padded by one of the victorious men and he was protesting loudly that he was not feeling faint. Peter, Philippa now noticed, was disfigured by several gashes on face, throat, hands and arms, where he had burst through the broken horn casement.

Rhys said sharply, "Sit down, David, and keep still. We need to get you to a surgeon and soon, after we have cleaned up here."

The Earl was looking round at the carnage. Richard could be heard mounting to the upper room to make sure there were no further opponents in hiding and awaiting an opportunity to make yet a further assault. Though still somewhat trembly from shock, Philippa went and knelt by Roger Hilyard's sprawled body. His face, she was relieved to see, was not contorted and his wide blue eyes were open and gazing blankly upwards. His expression now appeared as she had first seen it, bereft of guile, like the simple youthful merchant's journeyman he had purported to be and, she sighed heavily at her loss of trust in humanity in general. Very gently she closed his eyes and Rhys joined her, looking down dispassionately at his fallen enemy.

"Do not pity him too much, my heart," he said soberly, "his only intention was to snare your father and many other good men of dubious loyalty within this county and his motive was gain. I doubt very much if he would have released you, even after he had given his sworn word to your father. You would have been too great a prize and you might well have ended up within the gloomy dungeons of the Tower, accused of treason for the simple act of trying to protect your own father."

She rose to her feet with a little sob and he enclosed her in his arms again, turning her so that she might cry into his shoulder, as she had done on that dreadful day when her beloved *grandpère* had died and he had comforted her.

There came a thundering noise from the stairs, which made them all turn and stare. Richard Allard erupted into the chamber, pushing before him a man he held roughly by one shoulder.

"I found this fellow hiding behind a chest upstairs."

The man was whimpering a plea for his life, promising complete surrender.

Rhys regarded him sternly. "You are one of Master Hilyard's men?"

"I was, my lord, but I was taking no part in the fighting. I…"

Rhys turned a contemptuous gaze upon the man, older by some years than his companions who had engaged in the fight.

"Take him outside and kill him," he ordered Richard Allard "and, for God's sake, do it quietly. We need to keep this business from the attention of prying neighbours."

The man fell to his knees, holding out two hands before him in supplication.

Philippa went slightly towards him and gave a little start of recognition.

"Please, Rhys," she begged, "spare him. He was the only member of this household who treated me with the slightest consideration. He did try to spare me humiliation. He told me he has children of his own, young girls and…"

Rhys shook his head angrily. "That may be so, Philippa, but he can do us irreparable harm. None of Hilyard's men must leave this place and talk of what has occurred here. Your father's life depends on this and possibly the lives of the rest of us, too, to say nothing of the lives of other good men he may harbour secret information about. I understand your pity but this is war, and we cannot afford to be merciful."

She appealed to her father. "If he swears that he will go far from here and say nothing…"

"It is a risk," he said quietly. "We have the right to play with our lives but not those of our friends."

The man had fallen forward on to his knees and was whimpering or praying softly, Philippa could not tell which.

She turned away, shocked. "I do not think I can bear this," she whispered, looking down at Hilyard's sprawled body and that of the other man who had held her by the throat, "so much bloodletting and all because I was incautious in placing my trust."

The Earl lifted both shoulders and let them fall. "I ask you to let the fellow go, Rhys," he said. "Philippa is right. There has been killing enough and this dispatching in cold blood sickens me."

Rhys looked from one to the other of his companions and they each hesitated for a moment and then nodded, averting their eyes from the proposed victim.

Rhys said harshly, "Very well, then. On our own heads be the consequences."

Richard had released his grip on the prisoner who had not moved from the spot but had lifted his head now to turn in mute appeal to Philippa. Rhys moved near to him and stirred him with his foot.

"All right, you heard my Lady Philippa. You can thank her for your life for what is left of it. You can go, but I ask your word that you will leave this district at once and delay any report to your masters in London for at least two weeks."

The man still did not climb to his feet, but gazed uneasily around the chamber at the impassive faces of his captors as if he could not even now believe his good fortune.

"I was simply engaged by Master Hilyard there to keep guard on his prisoner and do common tasks about the house while we were waiting for him to capture her. I'd no notion who'm it was to be, not even that it was to be a woman. I knows no one of importance in London, and I swear to you, my lords, that I'll be off back to my family the moment you let me and never stir.''

Rhys frowned slightly as if he were uncertain as to the truth of the fellow's tale, but he turned away at last, signalling to the man to stand up.

''Then take yourself off and remember that one word from you to anyone about what has happened here could threaten the life of your benefactress.'' He turned back abruptly and bared his teeth in a grimace. ''Do that, fellow, and you will have all of us to answer to and, make no mistake about it, one or other of us will hound you down and end it once and for all.''

The man was backing towards the chamber door. Not one of his captors moved a muscle, but he felt the steel-like gaze of them all. He knuckled his brow as a salute to Philippa, then turned and dashed out. They could hear his stumbling steps on the flagstones of the corridor.

Philippa said a trifle huskily, ''Thank you, all of you. I know I have been perhaps a little—unwise in asking this of you but—'' Tears sparked her eyelashes and she gave a little choking sound. ''I could not have borne to have him summarily taken and killed. If he had died in the conflict I could have accepted it—but—but—''

The Earl took her briefly into his arms and patted her shoulder as her body heaved with tearful distress.

''Sir Rhys, is there somewhere I could take Philippa, out of here?'' He looked round distastefully at the signs of carnage.

Rhys looked questioningly at Richard Allard who said, ''The kitchen would seem to be a more appropriate place, for the moment. There was less—disturbance in there.''

Following Richard's instructions, the Earl led his

daughter into the back part of the house and was relieved to see that there was an overturned joint stool
beside the neglected fireplace. He righted it and gently
set her down upon it, sensing by the violent shivering
of her body that she was very close to complete collapse.

Richard stood in the doorway, his expression sober.
"What do you think we should do about cleaning up,
my lord?" He gestured with a backward glance towards
the bodies sprawled in the sleeping chamber.

Rhys had come up behind them and was looking with
concern at Philippa.

The Earl said reassuringly, "She is very shocked, has
been through much. She is strong in body and will. She
will recover. Give her time." In answer to Richard's
question he addressed Rhys. "You should make the decisions, sir. You live in the district and will have to face
up to any consequences after the rest of us have gone."

Rhys inclined his chin. "I think we should leave
them all where they lie. To attempt to bury them would
take too long and shallow graves would soon be discovered." He gave a grim smile, "Stray dogs could root
around—I do not think I need elaborate." Again he
glanced towards Philippa who gave a great shudder and
turned away.

He continued. "The sergeant-at-arms said the men
had returned with wine bottles and supplies. I suggest
we leave food and overturned wine bottles about. The
investigating constable will assume the men have quarrelled over dice or some wanton and a fight broke out.
He will not know how many men were here or how
many others have fled." He gave a little dismissive
shrug. "I imagine he will see they have paupers' burials
and make few enquiries. Naturally we must search the

house and the bodies before we leave and make quite sure none of them, especially Hilyard, carried any official papers or warrants. If you will remain with your daughter, my lord, we will see to that. With your permission I will send Master Fairley to the inn for our horses and dismiss the Queen's men. The sooner they are dispersed the better and the sergeant will be able to reassure her that Lady Philippa and you, my lord, are safe and will be soon in hiding again.'' He frowned, considering. ''I would rather not have had the horses brought to the house, but I need to get young David to a surgeon in the town and neither he nor Lady Philippa are in any condition to walk. It is safe enough, I think. Most of the respectable townsfolk are tucked up in their beds and—'' he gave a little dismissive shrug again ''—we must risk them being noticed and remarked upon later.'' He dropped upon one knee before Philippa. ''Can you hold on here for just a little longer? I would spare you this but—''

She reached out and took his hand. ''Do what you must, sir, to protect all of us and I pray Master David will soon be well again. Is his wound grievous?''

''I think not, but it requires more attention that I can give. It is a chest wound, but I do not believe vital organs have been affected. There is no lung damage or he would be coughing frothy blood by now. We must get it stitched and cleansed against future infection.''

He gripped her hand tightly and rose. ''I will be back very shortly. David is resting quietly on a pallet we managed to find, for the present. His wound is well padded and there is not too great a blood loss. Give your gentle heart ease on his account.''

She watched him leave to give instructions to the

others and turned to her father with frightened eyes. "I pray no one will pay with his life for this night's work."

The Earl sank down beside her on the rush-strewn floor. "Philippa, I may not have another opportunity to speak with you again. When we leave here I must go into deep hiding. You understand?" She nodded, her bottom lip trembling.

"Tell your mother I love her deeply and will, God willing, see her again soon at Malines, if not before."

"She knows how you love us. She will be anxious to join you. Papa." Philippa's voice was very soft. "Take no more risks, for her sake and mine."

His hand squeezed hers. "Trust me." He looked at her intently. "I have given Rhys Griffith permission to wed you, but, the decision is up to you. I am convinced he will make you a good husband and I know he loves you with all his heart, but the choice must be yours. Can you love him in return?"

"Oh yes, Papa, I love him with all my heart, only…"

"Only?"

"I fear if he weds me I will endanger him. The King will be informed and will withdraw his favour. Rhys should not marry a traitor's daughter."

The Earl was silent for a moment, gazing down at the rushes. "That choice is his, Philippa. He wants you and it is for you to accept him or no. I will not press you in this, but…" He hesitated, then said, clearing his throat a trifle as if to stifle emotion, "To have you near Gretton would be a great relief to me. You will be able to comfort your grandmother and…" he paused and she leaned forward to stare into his face, striving to read his expression "…if—if anything should happen to me—I believe your mother would be able to come to you here, and I would trust Griffith with her care."

She said slowly, "I will consider very carefully what is best for Rhys. I love him too greatly to bring him to harm."

She looked up as Rhys entered again. "The horses are outside and we are ready to leave, my lord. Will you take up Philippa before you? I must carry David."

Philippa rose with her father and joined the others who were gathered in the corridor, Richard supporting the injured young squire.

It was almost pitch black outside and very cold as it often is just before dawn. Philippa turned once to stare behind her at the house which had held such terror for her and from which she had not expected either her father or herself to emerge free. The men were mounting up. Richard was assisting David to mount behind his cousin and Peter lifted Philippa up behind her father. There was no sign of any of the Queen's men. A dog barked somewhere, otherwise, except for the jingle of their horses' harness, the silence was profound and eerie. They set off for the town centre.

Peter waited with the Earl and Philippa in a little copse just outside the town while Richard Allard and Rhys conveyed David to a surgeon whom, Philippa was informed, lived near the Golden Fleece inn. David had made no sound during the short ride, but Philippa had glimpsed his pain-contorted young face just as they had left the house and she was very concerned for his recovery.

She was relieved to hear the clatter of hoofs approaching and Peter rode forward slightly to assure himself that the newcomers were, indeed, Sir Rhys and Richard.

Rhys rode up to the Earl and Philippa gave a little cry as she saw he was riding alone.

"Where is David? Is he—?"

"He needs special care. He will stay with the man for a day or two. I am assured he will recover." He smiled a little grimly. "This man is known to me. I have ridden beside him in combat on the Marches. He is skilled in the treatment of combat wounds and also extremely discreet. I can trust him rather than the town physician, who is a notable gossip." He turned to the Earl, his horse sidling a little as he drew level.

"I think you and Allard should leave us now, my lord, and I would advise you both not to return to Sir Owen Lewis's manor."

The Earl grinned mirthlessly. "We have already come to that conclusion, my friend. If Hilyard was able to discover my whereabouts, it is obviously unsafe for Owen to be burdened with my company any longer. Give your heart peace. We have other bolt-holds."

"If Master Allard can be at the Golden Fleece round about noon in two days' time, I can send a messenger there to let you know how young David progresses and how the ladies at Gretton fare." Rhys leaned forward a little in the saddle. "And now, my lord, if you will allow me, I will take your most precious burden from you and return her to Gretton. Master Fairley will accompany us."

The Earl dismounted and lifted Philippa down. She clung to him tearfully as he kissed her, then he lifted her up before Rhys who drew her tightly close against his body. She strove once to glance behind her at the two men, still lingering in the copse to see them go, and then she nestled close to Rhys's heart, moving a little fretfully as she rubbed against the protective metal pieces of his brigandine, and settling close again, nestling her head against the soft leather, as he rode slowly from the copse and took the road to Gretton.

Chapter Ten

Philippa sat in the herb garden, which appeared as bleak as her spirits. The earth was brown and barren, though one or two of the more hardy herbs were still struggling to throw out new leaves. An autumnal chill was in the air and she clutched her black frieze cloak yet closer and pulled up her hood against the biting wind. Her mother and grandmother were busied in the house with the brass image maker who had come from Bristol to discuss the design and wording of the memorial which was to cover her grandfather's tomb. Gwenny had accompanied her into the garden, but had sat shivering uncomfortably and was clearly so miserable that Philippa had dismissed her, giving her duties within the house, and, for the first time since she had arrived back at the manor, held close to Rhys's body, she had been left alone. She glanced at the gardener's boy, some distance away clearing remaining dead leaves and sweeping up the paths. Gwenny had considered the boy sufficient chaperon for her mistress, but he was far enough from her for Philippa to feel free of his watchful presence.

This was the third day since she had returned to Gretton and Rhys had not called. In spite of all his protestations of love, had he decided to abandon her, and give way to his doubts about allying himself with the daughter of the King's enemy after all?

When he had lifted her down into a waiting groom's arms after arriving at Gretton Manor, she had been reluctant, even then, to part from him. Shocked and frightened though she had been by the night's events, and relieved to be once more restored to her family, she had watched his departure with mounting despair. His arms had been so strong, so dependable around her, that she had wanted never to be parted from him again. Peter had supported her trembling form while Rhys had spoken briefly with her mother and then he had ridden away and she had been led inside and handed into Gwenny's care. Her grandmother had called for a bathtub to be carried up to her chamber and filled with pails of steaming hot water, despite the lateness of the hour, knowing Philippa's need to ritually cleanse her body and mind, for she had felt soiled by the sights she had witnessed, and sickened by the betrayal of the man she had believed to be sincere. She had trusted and helped Roger Hilyard, defended him against the suspicions Rhys had entertained towards him, and it hurt her now to know that he had so deliberately sought to use her. She had sat shivering in the hot, rose-scented water and her mother had come in and helped Gwenny to rub the soft homemade soap into her skin and then had wrapped her snuggly in the heavy white tufted towels which had been imported from the East. Gwenny had combed out the wet tangles of her hair, but even after they had dried her, and clothed her in her own bedgown and seated her by the hearth fire, hastily kindled within the chamber, she had still felt deadly cold.

Finally, the Countess had insisted that her daughter sleep with her in her own bed for what remained of the night and had gently and firmly dismissed Gwenny to her own truckle and, at last, Philippa had given way to a storm of weeping which had, in some part, relieved her of the terrible numbness which had taken her prisoner following the death of Roger Hilyard and his followers.

Her grandmother had come in, anxious to be told more fully the details of her abduction and the subsequent happenings in that house in Ludlow, but Philippa had found it impossible to describe the rescue and its horrible consequences. She had not been present before at the violent deaths of men after combat and it had been later, next day, before she had felt herself able to relate the full story and give tongue to her continued fears for her father and Richard Allard.

Her mother had tried to reassure her. "Your father has spent so much of his life in avoiding dangers such as this, that I am convinced that, by now, he has found a safe hiding place and will soon be off back to Burgundy where I shall join him as soon as possible, that is…" and she had hesitated, smoothing back Philippa's bright hair and looking deeply into her daughter's eyes, "…once I have assured myself that your welfare is in safe hands here or—" and again she had paused deliberately "—you are well enough and prepared to accompany me."

Philippa had given a little sob and shaken her head. "I know that Rhys Griffith cares for me, but he will sacrifice so much if he marries me."

"He knows that well enough."

"But suppose that he is entertaining second thoughts and who could blame him?"

She had said that then and the same thoughts were running round in her head as she sat in desolate mood, kicking idly at a flint edging stone near her seat.

She knew that he was there without even turning her head. She sat quite still for moments then did turn slowly, imploring him with her eyes to come close.

He was standing tall in the entrance arch, one hand holding lightly to the wooden trellis which, in summer, supported a climbing rose. He was dressed, as she last remembered him, in serviceable dark velvet doublet, his warm cloak thrown back from his shoulders, and he was smiling, yet she sensed a question which lurked behind that smile which made him hesitate before advancing towards her.

She stood up and held out one hand. Huskily she murmured, ''I thought that you had deserted me.''

Immediately he came to her and gathered her into his arms. She nestled against the muscular strength of him, smelling the familiar male, clean scents of soap and horseflesh, the faint tang of oil he used for protecting the metal of his weapons. He drew back for a second, gazing deep into her eyes, ''You have recovered? I was impatient, but thought it best to give you time. I know how the sight of those horrors in Ludlow distressed you. And, my darling, I thank the Virgin they did. Those reactions conveyed to me the knowledge of a sensitive, compassionate heart.

She nodded, suddenly shy in his presence without knowing quite why as he drew her down beside him on the wooden bench.

Head bent, her fingers toying with a fold of her black mourning kirtle, she asked, ''How is David? I thought, when you did not come to us, that his condition might have worsened and you felt the necessity of staying by him.''

"No, no. David is progressing well. Tomorrow he will ride home. The wound was deep and he lost a deal of blood but, fortunately, the sword did not penetrate his lung. My surgeon tells me he no longer fears infection so all should be well. I confess to feeling guilty for allowing him to accompany us, but there—'' he lifted his shoulders in a slight shrug ''—all boys must face a first taste of combat and a possible blooding. He is feeling remarkably pleased with himself for the part he played in the activities, as well he might.''

She gave a little shaky laugh as he captured her hands, then held both in one of his and with the other, tilted her chin so that she was forced to look full at him.

"I wanted to give you time to consider my proposal though, I tell you now, I have already bespoken the priest and made my arrangements for our nuptials which must be soon since your mother will leave soon for Malines.''

She tried to look away, but he continued to hold her chin fast. "Well?''

"I love you," she confessed, "I was seeking you to tell you that in Ludlow when—when it happened. I know you were angry with me for my lack of faith—''

"Philippa, my heart's love, that anger was soon spent. That accusing look at me cut me to the heart and yet I knew how it must be with you and that all your life you have suspected treachery and sensed hidden dangers directed at those you love. I came straight back to the castle to claim you, to compel you to trust me and—'' he drew a hard breath ''—when I discovered you had not returned I feared that I had lost you for ever.''

"I want to be your wife, Rhys, yet I fear for you. The King—"

"Tush, sweetheart, Henry cares little about what I do. I am no courtier to fawn upon him at Westminster. If strike at me he does, and I doubt he would even stoop to do so, so unimportant he considers me, then we must fly together to Burgundy as your mother did when your father was forced into exile."

"Then you would lose everything."

"Nothing I value as much as my possession of you."

She lifted shining eyes to him and he swept her possessively close, again raining passionate kisses upon her forehead, nose, lips and throat. She had never before tasted such ecstasy and she became dizzy and swayed in his arms so that he lifted her lightly off her feet and she clung yet closer to him, heart to heart, thigh to thigh, revelling in total surrender.

Triumphantly he murmured close to her ear. "To-morrow, then? David should be well enough to attend and he demands to be present and we must not delay, for your mother's sake."

She nodded, as he drew back, holding her at arm's length, devouring her loveliness with his eyes. "I dare not hold you so a moment longer, my heart, or I will not be able to wait," he murmured huskily. Then he said gently. "Give me your hand."

Wonderingly, she obeyed him and he placed his betrothal ring upon her finger. It was a simple signet ring bearing an unknown crest and she looked up at him questioningly.

He explained. "I would not have you wear my mother's ring, as is sometimes customary. It brought her nothing but unhappiness. This ring was given to me by the man I most admired, the man who trained me to arms. I have had a special one fashioned for you for your marital ring and with that will go all my love and pledges that you shall never live neglected nor shamed as my mother did. Will you trust me, my heart?''

''Oh, Rhys, my dear love, I do now and will ever do so.''

He bent and kissed her more gently this time upon the brow, then drew her back to the bench and seated her.

''I think it best if we hold the ceremony in the hall at my manor. It is fitting that it should be private since your family is still in mourning, but we cannot afford to wait in order to summon the county gentry to our nuptials. Will you mind that, my love?''

She shook her head vehemently. ''You know I would have the ceremony quiet and in private for many reasons.''

''Aye.'' He gave a faint sigh. ''I wish your father could be present to place your hand in mine, but that cannot be and we must accept that. I will send a wagonette for your party early tomorrow and arrange for the priest to attend at noon.''

She bowed her head in acceptance of the arrangements, knowing how secretive and hurried they must be.

He stood up and adjusted his cloak. ''My man met with Richard Allard at the Golden Fleece yesterday and learned that all is well with your father and I also ascertained that Sir Owen Lewis has not been bothered by over-officious King's men and he will be able to attend our wedding.''

Her lips curved into a smile. At least some of her father's friends would be present at this, the most momentous day of her life. Rhys bent and kissed her palm then bowed and took his leave. Afterwards she sat on for moments, her heart pounding wildly.

An hour before noon next day she stood within the master bedchamber of Rhys's manor house attended by her mother, grandmother, Gwenny and Rhys's trusted housekeeper. She had already taken the ritual bath and knew that her skin glowed with scented oils and that her hair fell, unrestrained by pins, combed lovingly by her grandmother. The servants and lesser women were dismissed at last as she stood with her mother and grandmother, looking anxiously down at her bridal gown. Both her loved ones had assured her that for this special day she must lay aside her mourning and the gown was simple and yet splendid, of white silk with an undergown of brocaded white and cloth of gold. Her mother touched that tenderly. ''This cloth was given to me by King Richard's Queen Anne. The bolt was a Christmas gift from the King and she wore a gown fashioned from it at the last Twelfth Night feast of her life.'' She put a trembling hand to her mouth, as she recalled that the present queen, then the Princess Elizabeth, had worn a similar gown, of the same material, a choice which had been ill judged and caused a scandal within court circles. ''Anne had a small piece over and made a present of it to me and I have kept it until now and sewed it only days ago into this undergown for you, knowing how proud your father would have been to see you wear it.''

Tears sparked momentarily in Philippa's eyes as she longed for his presence, but she brushed them impatiently aside. This was no time for such recriminations. Her hair she would wear uncovered as a virgin bride and Rhys had sent up a page with four white rosebuds, apologising for the fact that they were all that were left of the past summer's blooms in the pleasance. Gwenny had formed them into a simple wreath with strands of rosemary and her mother crowned her bright hair with it and stood back to admire her handiwork. She nodded, satisfied. "The silk gown was one of mine left behind when I travelled to Westminster to see your father for the first time and it fits you well and is becoming, if a little outmoded." She held up a small Italian glass mirror for Philippa to view herself and smiled as she saw a rosy blush suffuse her daughter's cheeks and knew she was well pleased with their efforts.

"Rhys cannot be anything but proud and delighted, as your grandfather would have been," her grandmother said.

They could hear the noise below of final touches being completed in the hall for the ceremony. Lady Gretton raised her eyebrow to enquire if Philippa was ready and, on receiving an answering nod, went to the door to inform the page outside that they were ready when summoned. Philippa placed a trembling hand in that of her mother and forced a smile. They had talked together well into the night and, though she was prepared, she could not but be a little afraid of what was facing her now, a fact, her mother assured her, that was natural to every virgin bride.

"I am convinced by what I have seen of him throughout this visit that you have nothing to fear," she had assured her daughter. "Rhys will be a considerate bridegroom, but a loving and lusty one."

Philippa turned sharply as her grandmother made a sudden exclamation. She was standing by the door with one hand pressed to her heart. Philippa hastened towards her and then went pale herself. A man was standing on the landing, waiting for the bride to emerge from the chamber. Dressed though he was in a servant's livery, Philippa could be in no doubt of his identity. She suppressed a little cry of joy.

He said softly, "My lady, Sir Rhys has sent me to escort you into his presence," and he held out one hand.

Philippa turned to direct one warning glance towards her mother and then she stepped outside and accepted the strong clasp of her father's hand. She dared not make any comment, as there were men at the stair foot looking upwards expectantly for the arrival of the bride. She stepped beside the Earl, her mother and grandmother close behind and, heart beating wildly with delight and anxious anticipation, went down to greet her groom who was waiting in the great hall before the priest who was standing, breviary in hand, beside the makeshift altar.

Though, later, she was to gaze round and marvel at the efficiency of Rhys's servants who had transformed the hall into a beautiful place for the ceremony—green garlands adorned the walls and the altar was covered with a fine white silk cloth and the brass candlesticks and Pyx shone brightly in the light from the fine thick wax candles—she was in such a daze of hopefulness and joy that the ceremony passed over her completely. As if from a distance she heard Rhys's strong, melodious voice with its faint Welsh lilt making his vows, and her own timid replies. The ring he placed upon her finger was heavy and cold and she remembered that he had had it specially fashioned for her so that no sad memories of the past should mar their union. She was aware that her father was standing within the crowd farther back in the hall and that her friends Richard Allard and Sir Owen Lewis came quickly afterwards to offer their congratulations and that her mother and grandmother both embraced her warmly, their glad smiles mingled with emotional tears.

She sat beside Rhys afterwards at the lord's table upon the dais, realising for the first time that she was now lady and mistress of her father's former lands and demesnes. Rhys's hand was clasping hers beneath the napery-covered trestle and his dark eyes were shining with his love for her. She peered hopefully for a glimpse of her father's tall form amongst the lesser folk who sat feasting at the boards below the dais, but could not see him. She knew he must take his leave quickly, for he had risked all to see her wed and she hoped he would have had time and opportunity to speak privately but briefly with her mother.

This was not a great feast, for the bride's family were acknowledged to be still in mourning and it had been hurriedly prepared, but the dishes and delicacies were of excellent quality and well served and she found herself partaking of the food with more appetite and pleasure than she had expected, for she had thought that she would be too excited and anxious to do so. Rhys pledged her in the traditional loving cup and she drank after him, placing her lips where his had been and smiling up at him in gratitude for all he had arranged for her to make this day a happy one.

She went with her mother to the master bedchamber later and, once the door was closed on the clamouring well wishers outside, they had embraced avidly.

"You saw him?" Philippa breathed excitedly. "He looked well and happy. Rhys must have arranged it. Oh, Mother, will he be safe, do you think?"

"Dressed so, I am sure he could not be recognised,

except by eyes so loving as ours,'' her mother assured her. ''I managed to speak with him briefly and I shall join him aboard ship at Milford on the fourth day from now. I regret I must leave you so soon, but I am sure I do so with confidence that Rhys Griffith will love and cherish you to the end of your days together.''

They were alone and no mention of the time to come was mentioned as her mother helped her to undress and then slipped a silken white shift over her daughter's head. There was no need. Philippa knew the duty she owed to her new lord and was ready to pay it in full. After her mother had kissed her fondly and left her, Philippa sat on a joint stool watching the firelight play upon the furniture of the room. Her mouth was strangely dry and her heart raced with expectation, but there was no fear in her. She longed for the moment when Rhys would escape the bawdy badinage directed at him below and come to her.

When at last she heard his familiar step upon the stair and the latch of the door was lifted, she turned to welcome him.

He stood upon the threshold, regarding her. She had risen and the light of the candles and the firelight played upon her lovely form. The thin silk of the night shift hid nothing of her youthful splendour and his eyes went to the mass of reddish-gold hair which cascaded in soft waves down her back well beyond her waist. His heart raced at the sight of her and the ache in his groin to possess her which had troubled him throughout the day worsened. His throat thickened so that he could find no words with which to greet her and he felt like a callow boy again. She was his at last. He had wanted her from the moment he had first met her at the Milford inn and now he could not believe that his ardent prayer had been granted, that he had managed to overcome her reluctance to wed the man she believed had stolen her father's lands from him. He swallowed awkwardly and turned to close and latch the heavy door behind him, which would shut out the world outside.

She did not move but stood and watched him as he steadily advanced towards her, then she gave a little shaky laugh. "I see you managed to escape. I thought—feared—that those friends of yours would insist on entering our chamber and assisting you to undress."

He made a dismissive gesture and gave a throaty chuckle. "My heart, even had I been forced to fight them off with sword and dagger, I would not have allowed that."

"I am relieved." She lifted a tentative hand to touch his shaven chin, then traced the lineaments of his nose and mouth as if anxious to re-acquaint herself with those loved features.

He bent to take her in his arms but, abruptly she pulled away a little and turned from him. Perplexed, he made to advance on her again, then thought better of it. He must not be too impatient now. She was his, at last, heart and soul, he was sure of it, but he must not frighten her with too great an ardour. She must be wooed gently.

He said quietly, "I made a vow to myself that I would make you my wife, if only to keep you safe, and then I would wait until you were ready, but I find I am quite unable to keep that vow."

Head turned from him, she murmured, "I would neither expect nor want you to."

Still she was hiding her face from him and he turned awkwardly to the bed and began to hastily divest himself of his fine clothing. His doublet of mulberry velvet with its expensive silver buttons was thrown on to the bed, his shirt of finest cambric followed and then his hose. He could hear nothing from her and his breathing quickened as he reached for a brocaded bedgown laid ready to hand, but he could not stem his impatience and swung round blindly to face her.

His lip parted in startled amazement for she had slipped the white silk shift from her shoulders and it lay at her feet, a shimmering mass, then she stepped clear and stood gazing at him proudly as the firelight flickered upon the ivory beauty of her form, the breasts firm and high but already ripening to the roundness of womanhood, the slender hips, the high white throat and the head held as high as any queen. With a little nervous movement she shook back her hair and lifted one hand as if to receive him, then dropped it back to her side as if she were unsure of her welcome. This was no faery child but a woman, full grown and ready for his love. He made an inarticulate sound deep in his throat and drew her into his arms so that she was crushed against the hard maleness of him, held tight against his shoulder while she gave a little sigh. He bent and lifted her chin with one finger and she held her head high again and smiled into his dark eyes.

"You are not afraid?"

She shook her head and he saw the movement in her slender throat as she swallowed and knew that though she faced him bravely, as any maiden would, she was pleading with him silently to be gentle with her.

He was, indeed, lifting her high and carrying her to the bed, pausing to gaze at her again and let his eyes take in the wondrous beauty of her before he lowered himself into the bed beside her.

She was shivering with fearful anticipation, but he

would not let her fear him for that would spoil their union, which he would not allow. He kissed her gently, teasingly upon the forehead, lips, throat and then his questing lips moved lower and lower until her body arched in an agony of impatience too and she made little throaty sounds to match his own. Then, and only then, he knew that she was ready and lowered himself fully upon her to take what was his.

His patience was rewarded for he felt her respond at once and he was able to carry her to the heights of ecstasy so that she almost swooned in the wonder of their final coming together. The pain had been momentary and almost a delight in itself and he laid her back until he felt her eager body ready for his again and they made love passionately, uncaring of any sound from beyond the chamber and the wide bed which held their two responsive bodies.

He cradled her at last, when both were spent, her head against his heart, one hand of his cupping her breast. Her lovely hair spilt, sweat dampened, across his body and his breath stirred the silken strands smelling sweetly of rosemary and lavender.

"I have waited for this hour all my life," he said hoarsely, "and now my one question, sweetheart: are you content?"

"Have I not proved it to you?" She started up, her expression anxious as if she feared she had failed him in some way she could not comprehend.

His lips claimed hers again demandingly. "Hush, do not ask such a thing. You are all I ever needed or craved for and ever will be. Can you forgive me now, for possessing that which should have been your inheritance?"

She gave a little half-strangled laugh. "It will be our child's inheritance. How could I fault that?"

And he kissed her again.

Later she murmured sleepily, "I have to thank you for the finest marriage gift, my father's presence."

"He wanted it so. I felt it was a risk, but only a slight one, when I had thought it through. We had few members of the county gentry here who would recognise him in any guise and those who might do so would wish him no harm."

She frowned slightly. "Yet he should not linger in England. Have you heard any news from Ludlow about—about the house and what the constable must have found there?"

"Aye, I received a report from him yesterday and it is as I thought. He surmised that friends had fallen out in drink, with tragic results. Have no fears, my darling, I arranged for a respectful burial of all those who died and the parish officials will rest content and ask no more difficult questions."

"But, eventually, Roger Hilyard's masters at court will miss him."

"True, they will suspect foul play but will be unable to prove anything against us. But you are right, it is necessary for your father and mother to leave England hastily now and arrangements are well on the way to see them safely to Milford."

He kissed her brow as he felt, rather than saw, her give a sigh of regret.

"I will take you to Burgundy when I feel it safe to do so," he reassured her.

She slept at last, safe in his arms, and woke to find him gone from her. Alarmed, she sat up and then rose and ran to the door. He had been so loving to her throughout the night that she could not believe he would have deserted her so soon.

Young David Griffith looked up from the foot of the stair, pale and still leaning upon a cane for support. She saw that he was glancing worriedly at his new mistress as she stood, in her bedgown, hair cascading below her waist.

"Sir Rhys?" she demanded.

"He is at breakfast and will soon prepare for a journey, my lady."

He was leaving her so soon. She said softly, "Ask him to come to me before he leaves and send Gwenny to me."

He made her a little bow and she turned back into the chamber and stood, uncertainly, looking around for suitable clothing.

Rhys came running up the stair and the moment he entered the chamber she threw herself tearfully into his arms.

"What have I done or failed to do that you should abandon me so soon?"

He bent to kiss the top of her head. "My heart's darling, I go only to escort your mother and to see her and your father safely to Milford and aboard ship. She wrote me a message to say that she thinks it necessary that she leave immediately. She has heard that King's officials will arrive in Ludlow to escort the Queen to Westminster and is anxious to be gone from here before they arrive."

"Can I not go with you?"

He hesitated, then nodded. "Yes, I think it would be acceptable for you to be escorting your mother on her journey. Her true identity is not known, but you are her daughter and now my wife. It should be safe enough, but it is a longish journey. After your recent troubles, do you think you can keep up the pace?''

''Of course I can.''

''Very well. Dress quickly. Gwenny can accompany us to see to your needs. Do not be alarmed. Your father will join us two days from now and travel in a servant's guise. All should be well.'' He rumpled her hair with a gentle hand. ''I confess I cannot bear to be parted from you so soon and will be heartened and delighted by your presence.''

And so it was that Philippa re-trod the journey she had taken when she had first met Rhys. Her joy at her reunion with her father made every problem along the way worth while. Though he could not ride by her side, Philippa was constantly aware of his loving presence and, when in groom's guise, he did approach to hold her leading rein or to lift her from the saddle, she felt her heart throb with mingled distress that they must part so soon and relief that he and her mother would soon be safe in Burgundy once more and together.

The nights she spent clasped in her husband's arms and gloried in his lovemaking. Though she was often weary and saddle sore for, as Rhys had warned, they were forced to keep a steady pace, lest they miss the sailing of the ship he had arranged for the Earl and Countess to board for the port of Damme, she never once complained or regretted her decision to accompany him.

The journey was accomplished without incident and when Philippa was tearfully embraced by her parents in parting, she knew that, in spite of her loss of their company, she had made the right decision. In exile in Burgundy she would have been a greater burden to them, since they had heard from the Burgundian shipmaster that the Dowager Duchess of Burgundy's health had worsened and Philippa was aware that her parents must eventually find themselves in a state of penury, should the Duchess's favour be lost to them. She also knew that they were heartened by their knowledge that their daughter was madly in love with her husband and that he would devote his life to ensuring her happiness. She took a regretful farewell of Peter, hoping he would find some woman he could soon find happiness with, as she had found hers.

The journey home they were able to make more leisurely and comfortably and it was with a sense of deep happiness and homecoming, even after so short a time of residence there, that she rode into the courtyard of her husband's manor.

Before she could be lifted down from her mount or Rhys dismount, she was struck by the same terrifying fear which had possessed her at Gretton when she had seen the King's officials arrive at her grandmother's house. The courtyard was alive with bustle and confusion and she recognised immediately the King's personal badge of the Tudor rose and portcullis upon the livery of the recent arrivals. Rhys rode alongside and reached across to take her gloved hand within his own.

"Can they know of my father's escape?" she breathed and he looked at her steadily.

"That can hardly be possible. Keep a good heart and behave naturally."

He dismounted as his head groom rushed breathlessly to his side. Clearly the man was greatly agitated.

"What is it?" Rhys enquired casually enough and the man gulped hard as he said, "Sir Rhys, you have a royal visitor. We do not know what to do. Mistress Cheswick is entertaining him within the hall and…''

Rhys lifted Philippa down and felt her body shake with terror against his own. Though the day was warmer today he could tell she was icy cold with dread.

''Come, my lady,'' he said encouragingly, ''as chatelaine of my manor you must greet our distinguished visitor.'' He half-supported her up the steps and into the screen's passage.

Philippa forced herself to stand upright and proceed without her husband's assistance. This sudden arrival of King's men could only herald disaster and she must meet it with a display of courage. Could her husband's part in her father's escape be known? If so, was an imminent arrest possible or had Rhys come under the King's extreme disfavour for his alliance with the Earl of Wroxeter's daughter? He was still holding her hand and, together, they entered the hall which, like the courtyard, seemed unaccountably crowded with strangers, some elegantly dressed, obviously courtiers, and others more soberly, clearly members of their distinguished visitor's household.

For a moment her eyes were too blurred to see the man who was seated near the hearth fire being waited upon by her husband's steward while Mistress Cheswick hovered nearby, anxiously harrying their pages and serving women about their duties.

A youthful clear voice greeted her jovially as their noble visitor rose courteously to greet his hostess. ''I regret that we appear to have come at an inconvenient time, Sir Rhys and my lady, but I am delighted to see you returned, as I was charged by my royal father and by my lady mother, to offer my congratulations to you both on your recent marriage in person and, of course, to wish you happiness.''

Philippa was momentarily too confused to curtsy deeply as she was in duty bound to do as she stared into the wide-spaced blue eyes of young Prince Henry. She had seen him often at the Queen's court at Westminster, but he had been scarcely more than eight years old then, and now he must be almost thirteen and a man grown. He was tall and would soon, she thought, be massively built and truly handsome like his famed grandsire, King Edward IV, who had been termed the Rose of Rouen because of his extreme beauty of form and face. He was dressed, as she herself was, in mourning black for the death of his elder brother, but jewels gleamed dully in his velvet cap and in the gold and enamelled chain around his neck. As he held out his hand for the now kneeling Sir Rhys to kiss, she saw the richness of rubies and emeralds in his heavy rings there too. His red-gold hair curled into the elegant collar of his velvet doublet.

He was laughing merrily. ''I see you find it hard to recognise me, Lady Griffith, but it is full four years since we last met and I have grown and filled out considerably since then. Please, do be seated. Do not stand on ceremony in my presence. I am sure you must be wearied after your long journey.'' He led her to a chair opposite, with the manners of an accomplished courtier, his bright blue eyes raking over her in admiration and she recalled how, even when he had been but a child, she had noticed what a practised eye he had then for the younger ladies of his mother's household. Now she felt uncomfortable in presenting herself before him in her travel-stained garments. He was now Prince of Wales, she remembered, and heir to his father's throne.

He was addressing Rhys. "I have come to Ludlow Castle to escort my mother back to Westminster and, as she is slightly indisposed, she charged me with the task of wishing you both well, as I explained. My father also, once he received the news of your betrothal, was glad to hear of your approaching nuptials and hope you will both prosper and be granted an heir."

Watching him in jovial talk with her husband, Philippa could not think that there might have been something more sinister in the last remark, but the prince turned to her, his face beaming.

"I have never forgotten, Lady Philippa, that you were present at the hunt at Sheen that day when I almost lost my life under a boar's tusks. Master Richard Allard came to my assistance then, although..." and he grinned in remembrance of his childhood impetuosity which had almost proved fatal "...we knew him by another name then. Since you were Mistress Anne Allard's friend, I am sure you have kept in touch and know that he is once more settled in England, pardoned after his part in meeting with the unfortunate Earl of Warwick."

Philippa murmured an almost incoherent reply. She felt she was living in a dream, or was this a nightmare? Could this courteous and elegant young man, who was the son of her father's greatest enemy, be really offering them congratulations upon their marriage and could he be truly sincere?

As if aware of her doubt, he turned to her and said charmingly, "I am sure that it is time for old enmities to be laid aside, Lady Griffith. It pleases us well that you have come into possession of your father's lands." He paused, then added, "It may also be possible, in time, for him to be able to return from exile. I am sure his presence here would present no threat to me or mine.''

He rose and picked up his riding gloves. ''I must return to Ludlow. My mother will be delighted that I have seen you both. I trust, Sir Rhys, that once you have had time to settle into matrimony—'' and here his teeth gleamed in a smile again ''—you will bring your lady wife to court. We shall all be delighted to receive you both.'' He bowed over Philippa's hand. ''And, Lady Philippa, I can assure you, all the court will worship at the feet of your beauty.''

She stood awkwardly, still numbed and confused by the suddenness of the encounter as he swept out with his retinue, Rhys at his side, to escort him, as a host should, to the courtyard and to oversee the efficiency of his household in the arrangements for the royal departure. The hall emptied abruptly and Philippa could hear the sounds of bustle from the courtyard again and she forced her limbs to move and go to the hall steps to see the company ride off. Henry turned in the saddle and doffed his hat to her and she leaned against the door post for support as, eventually, Rhys returned to her.

''Well, it seems that the King has decided to accept our marriage and all your fears for my future can be laid to rest.''

She looked deep into his eyes. ''Do you believe that my father could ever be given a pardon by the King and that we could be welcomed at Court?''

He thought for a moment, then bent and kissed her. ''I believe that what young Henry was suggesting was that that will be possible after his accession.''

She stared at him in amazement. ''He is still scarcely more than a child.''

Rhys chuckled. "But a very precocious one. I think England will see great changes when once the reins of government are in his hands, and, my darling, I will see to it that he will see you infrequently at court. He was right in his assumption that I intend to keep you to myself for a long time yet, and later, I shall be very cautious at bringing you too much into that young man's company. I saw his expression when he gazed at you."

"But, Rhys, I am all in my dirt and…"

He laughed heartily. "My treasure, you are the most beautiful woman in the kingdom and all mine. Later, just later, I may be prepared to share your loveliness with others but—not yet."

He lifted her into his arms and carried her into the hall again and then up to their chamber, slamming the heavy door to with a bang as he laid her upon the bed.

"Our return to our own chamber has been too abruptly interrupted," he said, as his lips closed on hers, and she gave a little sigh of relief and satisfaction. No one would dare to come up to the chamber and later— much later—they would summon refreshment. For the moment they were too engrossed in each other to even feel hungry.

* * * * *

Don't miss the next exciting volume in
MEDIEVAL LORDS & LADIES
COLLECTION,
Christmas Knights.
Available in October 2007 from M&B™.